**The yellowbacks... classics of popular fiction**

The yellowjackets or yellowbacks were a great series of bestselling adventure and crime thrillers that had its origins in the mid to late 19th century following on from the 'penny dreadfuls'. They virtually began the mass market revolution of the early 20th century with a clear standard format and imprint/series livery (what would today be called branding). Hodder & Stoughton published the yellowjackets in two main series with series run dates of: 1923-1939 and later 1949-1957.

As the tagline ('where thrillers really began') on the back cover implies, the imprint and series focused on thrillers that were the bestsellers of their time. This current reissue or retro revival if you will, brings back many of these masterpieces, now classics in their own way and extends it further by including key titles from that period that were either great crime or thriller or even general commercial fiction (including sub-genres of noir, horror, gothic, romance, westerns, etc.) influences of their time. There are some perennial favourites and many rarities either lost or not easily available being revived in the current series. Writers and characters ranged from adventure heroes like Bulldog Drummond, Allan Quatermain, Richard Hannay or the Saint through thriller grandmasters Edgar Wallace and E. Phillips Oppenheim, crime and mystery maestros like Patricia Wentworth, GK Chesterton, Agatha Christie and the Detection club, to western and swashbucklers like Zane Grey, Max Brand, Captain Blood and even romance or general fiction classics like Hermina Black, Denise Robins, Marie Corelli or Stella Morton. These were books that had storytelling at their heart and always entertained.

The yellowbacks had both hardback (with varying design elements) and paperback (which built the series look) versions with the latter still carrying the imprint 'yellowjacket'. The current reissues pay tribute to both and use an amalgam of elements from both editions while retaining the complete yellow (or 'mustard-plaster') livery with the author's name in blue beveled type with a 'simulated emboss' effect and a white outer 'outline', and the book title in black. These reissues retain the distinctive size of the original mass market paperback and follow the three main category variations—the thrillers (crime, westerns, mystery, adventure) had blue lettering for the author's name, while Romance and softer general fiction had red; and other categories like humour had green.

For more detail and a full list of titles visit https://www.hachetteindia.com/home/yellowbacks

# THE RICHARD CHANDOS OMNIBUS

# THE RICHARD CHANDOS OMNIBUS

**Dornford Yates** was Cecil William Mercer (7 August 1885 – 5 March 1960), an English writer and novelist whose novels and short stories, some humorous (the Berry books), some thrillers (the Chandos books), were best-sellers during the Interwar Period.

The pen name Dornford Yates, first in print in 1910, resulted from combining the maiden names of his grandmothers – the paternal Eliza Mary Dornford, and the maternal Harriet Yates. Mercer originally wrote short stories for the monthly magazines. His first known published work, Temporary Insanity, appeared in Punch in May 1910 – this is the first known occasion of his use of his pen name – and his second, Like A Tale That is Told appeared in the Red Magazine in July 1910. The first known 'Berry' story to be published, Babes in the Wood, appeared in Pearson's Magazine in September 1910. The Berry books are semi-autobiographical, humorous romances, often in short story form, and, in particular, feature Bertram "Berry" Pleydell and his family – his wife and cousin, Daphne, her brother, Boy Pleydell (the narrator), and their cousins Jonathan "Jonah" Mansel, and his sister, Jill. Collectively, they are 'Berry & Co'. Their stories capture the English upper classes of the Edwardian era, still self-assured, but affected by changing social attitudes and the decline of their fortunes.

The 'Chandos' books, starting with Blind Corner, in 1927, marked a change in style and content, being thrillers set mainly in Continental Europe (often in Carinthia, Austria), wherein the hero–narrator, Richard Chandos, and colleagues, including George Hanbury and Jonathan Mansel (who also featured in the 'Berry' books), tackle criminals, protect the innocent, woo beautiful ladies, and hunt for treasure. These were originally published by Hodder and Stoughton although later they were re-issued by Ward Lock.

Cecil William Mercer died in March 1960.

# THE RICHARD CHANDOS OMNIBUS

Dornford Yates

HODDER AND STOUGHTON
YELLOW JACKET

hachette

*The Richard Chandos Omnibus*
*Perishable Goods* first published in 1928 by Hodder & Stoughton; and
*An Eye for a Tooth* published in 1943 by Ward & Lock.

This Hodder Yellowback edition © Hachette India 2023
(Registered Name: Hachette Book Publishing India Pvt. Ltd.)
An Hachette UK Company www.hachetteindia.com

1



The texts in these editions in most cases have been reprinted as is, with minimal editorial changes and by and large no bowdlerizing for political correctness; though in some editions, a few words and phrases considered archaic, or those considered offensive now, along with archaic punctuation may have been modified in places to make the text more accessible to today's readers. The narratives, language, beliefs, social mores and/or cultural depictions, in these volumes are a reflection of their times and must be viewed as such. They may also contain certain cultural, racial and gender prejudices and stereotypes that may be outdated or clearly wrong then and wrong today; but their removal would be tantamount to claiming these prejudices never existed. The Publisher does not endorse or support those depictions or stereotypes; and these books have been made available for a discerning audience that will read it for entertainment value and a chronicle/record of popular fiction of past times.

Cover design by Priya Singh adapted from the original classic yellowjacket by Hodder & Stoughton.

Cover illustration: Hodder original.

Series note: Some of the books in the series (unless otherwise credited) may have cover or inside illustrations from the original yellowbacks or early editions, and while full restoration has been attempted, some images may be grainy or faded due to the condition of the original material. The end notes or bonus material or blurb details may have been sourced from the public domain or free use publications such as Wikipedia and attribution is hereby made also allowing similar free use reproduction from here. Sources requiring further specific attribution may write in and further detailing and/or corrections shall be made in subsequent printings/editions.

Reprint specifications may be subject to change including but not limited to finishes, paper, colour sections.

ISBN: 978-93-5731-212-7

Hachette Book Publishing India Pvt. Ltd.
4th & 5th Floors, Corporate Centre,
Plot No. 94, Sector 44, Gurugram - 122 003, India

Typeset in Electra LT STD 10/12.5 pt by Manipal Technologies Limited, Manipal

Printed and bound in India by Manipal Technologies Limited, Manipal

MIX
Paper from responsible sources
FSC™ C043100

# CONTENTS

# Perishable Goods

# CONTENTS

# I

## FIRST BLOOD

It was in October, 1926, that George Hanbury and I first set up house in Wiltshire; and, since for the next six months we hunted four days a week, yet would commit to no one the pleasant task of setting our home in order, I do not think we slept out of Maintenance – for from time immemorial that has been the name of the place – more than seven times. But two of the visits I paid stand out of my memory, and, as they bear upon the matters which I am to tell, I will set them down.

In the first week of December the wedding of one of my cousins took me to town.

Now neither Hanbury nor I would have dreamed of visiting London without calling on Jonathan Mansel, whose flat was in Cleveland Row; for we three had made our fortune together and together had proved the stuff of which friendship is made. That apart, Mansel was the very finest gentleman that ever I knew: his ways were quiet, and his address was simple; but there was a natural royalty about him such as, I think, few monarchs have been able to boast.

I started betimes and travelled to London by road, and the clock of St. James's Palace was striking nine as I turned out of Marlborough Gate into Cleveland Row. Except for my servant, Bell, I was alone.

Here let me say that it was Mansel who had taught me the virtue of being early abroad and, particularly, of taking a journey before the world was awake; "for," said he, "the dawn you may nearly always have to yourself, and, since it is the fairest of the hours, that a free man should lose it is more than lamentable."

I had no need to ring, for, when I had mounted the stairs, I found Mansel's hall-door open and his body-servant, Carson, watching two workmen who were busy about its lock. He took me directly to the study, where Mansel was standing before a cheerful fire.

"Ah, William," says he, "I'm glad to see you. How was it you didn't ring?" I told him.

"That's right," said he. "Those fellows are changing the lock. Yesterday this flat was entered – by some person or persons unknown."

"Thieves?" said I.

"Thieves," said Mansel.

At once I looked at the wall, where I knew there had hung a monstrance. This was golden and jewelled, and, though there was plate-glass about it, I could have forced the case in two minutes of time. But the monstrance was there.

"And they missed that?" said I, pointing.

"They didn't come for that," said Mansel.

For a moment we looked at each other: then I sat down in a chair and took out a cigarette.

"They came for my papers," said Mansel. "And got them." He pointed to his writing-table. "In the right-hand pedestal of that is a little safe. They cut it open and took my papers away. There were fifty sovereigns there and five hundred pounds in notes: but they didn't take them: so it looks as though they meant me to understand that they came for my papers alone."

"Were there papers of value?" said I.

Mansel frowned. Then he moved swiftly to a window and stood, looking down upon the street. So he stayed for some moments, because, I am sure, he would not trust his voice.

Presently –

"They were of interest," he said, "to no one but me."

I was concerned, for Mansel was plainly moved, and, though I knew no more than the man in the moon the nature of the stolen papers, I had never before seen him betray himself.

At length –

"What's to be done?" said I.

"Nothing," said Mansel, turning. "But, as you know, Chandos, I have a dangerous enemy, and, if he should study those papers, he might see a line of attack which would hit me hard."

"Us," I said quickly.

"Us," said Mansel, and smiled.

And there we left the business, for that was clearly his will: but, though we spoke of it no more, I could not get it out of my mind, for I knew as well as did Mansel that the theft was the work of 'Rose' Noble and that it was not to be thought of that he would fail to perceive the significance of his spoil.

'Rose' Noble was a sinister man, and, though he came but seldom into the light, was undoubtedly concerned in some of the greatest robberies of his time. He was never taken, and the police of more than one country feared his name, for he had a reputation so evil as to be almost fabulous and was commonly believed by those who knew him to be gifted with second sight. That he deserved this fame I can testify, for Mansel, Hanbury and I had made our fortune in his teeth: we had more than one brush with him and found him a monster of iniquity, bold, swift and strong, in whom there was no pity at all. I do not say that he had second sight; but his instinct was supernatural, and I do not think that any living being could deceive this terrible man.

Now, had we not made our fortune, 'Rose' Noble would have made his; and, since nine hundred thousand pounds is a huge sum of money to forego, I was not greatly surprised that he was, so to speak, returning to the charge: and, as it was Mansel that had captained our enterprise, it was, I suppose, natural that 'Rose' Noble should pitch upon him. How he would use the papers which he had stolen I could not think, but Mansel had said plainly that they could be turned to his hurt, and his demeanour had shown me that this hurt might be very sore.

On my return to Maintenance I told George Hanbury my news, to find that he shared my concern: but, since Mansel had promised to apprise us if trouble came, yet week after week went by and brought no message, we began to believe our apprehension baseless and the robbery nothing more signal than a flash in the pan.

It was early in the following April that Hanbury and I spent three fine days at White Ladies in the New Forest, that is to say, at Mansel's country home. This he shared with his cousins, whose name was Pleydell. It was not our first visit, but the Pleydells were absent when we had been there before, and, though the four Sargents in the gallery had told us what to expect, I do not think that either of us believed that all five members of one family could prove so charming.

Adèle Pleydell was the youngest and had married Captain Pleydell five years before: I learned later that she was American by birth. She and her husband seemed very young for their age. Major and Daphne Pleydell were clearly older and were by one consent treated as the heads of the house. Yet all were equal; and, when once Adèle Pleydell affirmed that she was an interloper and the only one of them whose ancestors had not known White Ladies, there was an amicable uproar, and Major Pleydell said gravely, "That I regard as one of the misfortunes of our House."

She was a tall, slim girl, very graceful and wonderfully and beautifully made. Her face was lovely; her thick, dark hair, lustrous; the light in her fine, brown eyes, a glorious thing. She was quiet, yet tireless and seemed to do all things well: she could drive a car and could ride with any man: yet she was always maidenly and looked as delicate a-cock-horse as when, in silk and satin, she sat to a piano and lifted her exquisite voice. She was naturally eager and responsive, and I shall always see her, as did Sargent – with her beautiful lips parted and her soft, brown eyes alight.

If the others were less attractive, that was no fault of theirs, for I think Adèle Pleydell would have diminished anyone. She was plainly their darling, yet did not seem to know this; and, since she was very quick-witted, this one simplicity made her the more worshipful.

Hanbury and I, as was natural, fell down at her feet, and I am proud to remember that she made us free of her friendship, before we had known her an hour.

So, indeed, did they all: and I do not think I ever paid a visit one half so agreeable.

Much was made of the adventure to which I have already referred, and, when Major Pleydell proposed that they should go fishing in Carinthia later that year and then explore the very scenes of our endeavour, the idea was heartily received.

"And you'll come and stay with us," said Daphne Pleydell, addressing Hanbury and me. "If they will let us the farm we rented before, we shall have plenty of room, and Jonah's a poor showman when it comes to talking of himself."

That this was so I proved the very next day, for I rode with Adèle in the morning at six o'clock and found she knew next to nothing of what Mansel had done. Be sure I enlightened her, if only for Justice's sake.

When I had finished, she set her chin in the air.

"Tell me," she said. "Is 'Rose' Noble the man to take this lying down? I mean, nine hundred thousand is a bag of money to lose."

I suppose I hesitated, for her head was round in an instant, and her steady, brown eyes were on mine.

"Didn't you know," I said, "that Mansel was lately robbed?"

She let out a cry of excitement and checked her horse.

"I never knew," she said. And presently, "Go on."

I shook my head.

"It's not my secret," I said. "As it is, I've said too much."

With that, I would have gone forward, but she leaned down and caught my rein.

"Tell me," she pleaded, "tell me. I swear I'll not breathe a word."

In the end I yielded, and, before we were back at White Ladies, she knew as much as I.

When I said I was concerned, she laughed.

"I snuff a romance," she cried. "Jonah, the celibate, has had some passionate affair, and he's frightened to death that 'Rose' Noble will bring it out. But he never will. You can't blackmail a man for playing the game: and Jonathan Mansel's never done anything else."

"That I believe," said I. "But why was he troubled?"

The lady shrugged her shoulders.

"A celibate sees a scandal in every bow. The memory of the most harmless flirtation is a millstone round Jonah's neck."

Her interpretation relieved me, for I was sure she was wise; but, though I was greatly tempted to share it with George, I did not care to admit that I, and not Mansel, had told Adèle of the theft. So I held my peace.

The next day we left for Wiltshire promising soon to return. Yet we did not, though our homes were but fifty miles apart; for with the coming of summer there was much to be done at Maintenance, and, though the hunting was over, we had our hands full.

The Pleydells and Jonathan Mansel left for Carinthia in July.

Mansel was soon to come back, for he had business at home; and then, on the first of September, he and George Hanbury and I were to go out together by road.

And so it fell out – though not as we had expected: for, though Mansel came leisurely to England, he took the road back to Carinthia, like a man possessed. And Hanbury and I with him.

On the thirtieth day of August we dined in Cleveland Row, to settle the hour of departure and other things.

Our plans were simple and soon laid.

We were to meet at Folkestone and cross by the morning boat; and, since it seemed idle to take two cars, yet send three servants by train, we arranged to keep two with us and to send the third to Salzburg in charge of our heavier stuff. As luck would have it, all three had done this journey before – for Rowley, Hanbury's old servant, had lately re-entered his service – and, since they were all efficient, any one of the three could be trusted to shift for himself: but, as Carson and Bell were accustomed to handling a car, but Rowley was not, the latter was chosen to take our baggage by train.

Not until the cloth had been drawn did Mansel tell us that he had some unfortunate news.

"Boy Pleydell," he said, "Adèle's husband, has broken his leg. I heard this morning. Years ago, not twenty-five miles from the scene of his accident, he broke a couple of ribs; so it looks as though Carinthia was bad for his health. However, there's nothing to be done. He's under a Salzburg surgeon, and I'm taking out thirty novels to help him to pass the time."

Here the door was opened, and Carson came in with a note. This was addressed to Mansel and marked 'Immediate.'

"Who brought this?" said Mansel, taking it up.

"The porter found it on the steps, sir, one minute ago."

Mansel asked us to excuse him and broke the seal.

After a little he gave me the letter to read.

*The stolen goods will be returned on the receipt by the Manager of the—Bank, Zurich, of your cheque for five hundred thousand pounds. This sum you can raise, if you please. No time should be wasted for the goods are perishable.*

*August 30th.*

The body of the letter was written in a clerkly hand, but the date had been rudely added, I suppose, that day.

I passed the letter to George and turned to Mansel.

"'Perishable'?" said I. "'Perishable?' What does he mean?"

"I can't think," said Mansel slowly, knitting his brows. "And why has he waited nine months?"

"It must be 'Rose' Noble," said Hanbury, looking up from the sheet: "for nobody else would know you could raise such a sum. Otherwise, I should say that the writer was out of his mind. I mean, half a million for some papers..."

"I agree," said Mansel. "It's fantastic. I value them certainly: but I wouldn't give more than a hundred to get them back. If as much. I can't understand it," he continued, taking the letter again; "for 'Rose' Noble must know what they're worth rather better than I."

For a while we sat silent, for there was nothing to say: but I could not help wondering what was the nature of the papers which 'Rose' Noble held and reflecting that, until we knew that, neither George nor I could make any useful remark.

Mansel was speaking in a quiet, even tone.

"The papers are the letters of a girl – occasional letters and notes – in all, I suppose ten or twelve. Their matter is so casual and ordinary that I feared that 'Rose' Noble would wonder why I had kept them safe. They were in order of date, with her photograph. I feared he would think that she meant something to me. I mean, *that was the only explanation* of my keeping so carefully such artless documents."

There was a long silence, and all that Adèle had said came to my mind with a rush. And I could have laughed for relief, but that I knew that 'Rose' Noble was no fool.

At length –

"I still see no daylight," said Hanbury. "He offers you those letters back. When you ignore his offer, what will he do?"

Mansel shrugged his shoulders.

"He may send them to her husband," he said. "I would very much rather he didn't, but that's as far as I go."

Again I took the letter and read it through.

" 'The goods are perishable,' " I said. "That's a curious way of saying 'I'm going to send them to him.' "

"I agree," said Hanbury. "And it's not at all like 'Rose' Noble. He always made himself clear."

"Painfully clear," said I, and could have bitten out my tongue.

But Mansel gave no sign of having heard what I said.

Then a bell was rung, and, sitting in breathless silence, we heard a servant pass to the flat's front door.

The next moment Carson entered, bearing a telegram.

Mansel ripped open the envelope, glanced at the sheet and clapped his hands to his face.

The three of us stared at him.

Presently –

"Tell the man to wait," he said quietly. "He shall have an answer in five minutes' time."

Carson withdrew.

Mansel rose to his feet and handed the telegram to me:

*Return Adèle disappeared shall I call in police Pleydell.*

"Good God," I cried, rising.

Hanbury snatched the form from my hand.

"You were quite right, Chandos," said Mansel. " 'Rose' Noble has a way of making himself painfully clear."

I could only stare, and Mansel gave a short laugh.

"Let me do the same," he said. "*The letters he took had been written to me by Adèle.*"

"Oh, my God," said Hanbury.

"And, when he says 'stolen goods,' he's not referring to the letters, but to something more – more valuable, *something which 'disappeared' a few hours ago.*"

Not until then did the scales fall from my eyes: but though I would have spoken, I could not utter a word.

I watched Mansel pick up the letter and read it through.

"'Perishable goods,'" he said quietly, speaking as though he were alone. "Yes. I suppose you might call *Adèle in 'Rose' Noble's hands* – 'perishable goods.'"

There was champagne on ice on a sideboard, and Mansel opened a bottle and poured the wine.

When we had drunk, he sat down and wrote his reply:
*Pleydell Poganec St. Martin Carinthia*

*On no account*

*Mansel.*

And when this had been dispatched, he picked up 'Rose' Noble's letter and lighted a cigarette.

His agitation cannot have been over, but all sign of it was gone; and from this time on until the end, he was, as always, the coolest and most patient of us all. Few men, I think could have maintained such mastery of themselves; but Mansel's self-control was absolute, and, though it was now to be proved as surely no man's has ever been proved before, it never failed and seldom enough gave any sign of strain. Indeed, I often think that the flash of feeling he showed, when the telegram was brought in, was because when he read it, he knew that his secret was ours. Had 'Rose' Noble's letter followed instead of preceding the telegram, he never would have told us the nature of the papers which had lain in his safe, and I am sure that neither George Hanbury nor I would ever have suspected the truth. Yet I am glad we knew it and I think that, now it was done, Mansel was glad also; for, be a man never so reserved, there is a pitch of trouble which he is thankful to share.

After a little, Mansel folded the letter and held it up.

"I am not going to act," said he, "upon the suggestion here made, because, for one thing, such a sum is ruinous, and, for another, I do not trust 'Rose' Noble."

I got to my feet.

"We're all three in this," I said. "That's abundantly clear. If he'd drawn blank in this flat he'd have started on George or on me. But, whichever of us he'd attacked, his price would have been the same."

"That's beyond doubt," said Hanbury. "He's out to recover the fortune: and, not knowing how much it came to, he's put it as high as he dares."

"Exactly," said I. "Very well. My share was two hundred thousand: in two days' time you shall have three fourths of that back."

"Same here," said Hanbury.

"I know that," said Mansel. "Thank you. But it would break her heart. Sooner or later she would most surely find out, and then – well, you can't lay anyone under a debt like that. It's not to be thought of. And, since, as I say, I do not trust 'Rose' Noble, I think it will be convenient to count this document out."

With that, he put the letter towards a candle's flame, but after a moment, withdrew it and put it away in his case.

"So all that we know," he continued, "is that Adèle has disappeared: and, since my cousin, her husband, is out of action and we three know Carinthia as the palm of our hand, we are naturally going to seek her with all our might. Of course we *suspect* abduction: I think anyone would. *But that is all.* Have I made myself clear?"

"Yes," said I.

"Good," said Mansel. "And now please don't talk for a minute. I want to think."

I was glad to sit still, with my head in my hands, for the turn of events had shocked me, and I felt as though I were dreaming some disagreeable dream.

The disclosure of Mansel's secret, the unconscionable daring of 'Rose' Noble, the horror of the plight of Adèle had dealt me three swingeing blows; but what had hit me still harder was the sudden appreciation that, thanks to our talk in the forest, *Adèle herself must now know that she was the very lady that Mansel loved.*

What Mansel would have said, had he known this, I dared not think: but I was quite certain that, when he found it out, as he most surely would, he would be most particular never to see her again.

This was no conjecture, for I knew the man.

Full measure he gave in all things, though it were to his own beggary; and that he would palter where a girl's heart was concerned was unimaginable.

Adèle was his cousin's wife, at once his liege lady and his familiar friend: that much I had seen with my eyes: there never was, I believe, so gentle a relation. That the one valued this was patent: it was, I suppose, the light of the other's life. And now it was soon to founder, sunk by Mansel's own hand, rather than let come into the shallows of embarrassment.

The thought that my tongue would be to blame for this most bitter upshot haunted me for days, although, as I shall show, I need have had no concern. Indeed, throughout our venture Mansel bore himself with such exalted gallantry that I have often thought since that, though he could not have known of the speech I had had with Adèle, yet he knew in his heart that she would know why she had been taken and that he was carrying her colours for the first and last time.

My mind being so exercised, I do not find it surprising that I cannot clearly remember all that was said that evening, but I know that Mansel determined to sail the next night, but not before then, because he must have a day in which to prepare for the battle to which we were now to go.

Rowley was to leave with our baggage by an earlier train and Hanbury was to change the arrangements for shipping the cars.

Mansel's Rolls-Royce was furnished with secret lockers and trays, but ours had no such fittings, and, since we must now carry arms, he gave me a note to his coachbuilder and bade me seek him the next morning at eight o'clock. While he and his men were at work, fitting a hidden coffer, Carson and I together were to test and prepare the two cars, so that, with luck, if need be, they could run for a month on end without attention.

Bell was to cross to France by a morning boat, there to buy food and petrol against our coming and to promise ten thousand francs to the officials concerned if we were clear of the Customs in half an hour.

From the port we should drive to Salzburg as hard and as straight as we could and thence direct to St. Martin, for that was the name of the village which served the Pleydells' farm.

That Adèle was in Austria seemed certain, for without her passport and against her will she could hardly be taken out: moreover the countryside lent itself to violence, for much of it was most solitary, and the lives of its inhabitants were too strait for them to intrude upon matters with which they had no concern. I suppose there were constables of sorts, though I never saw one, except, of course, in the towns: and they would have shrugged their shoulders upon any business less homely than a breach of the local peace. For this, indeed, we were thankful, for official notice of the matter was the last thing we desired: this for more than one reason, but most of all because, so far from aiding, it would have put our enterprise in deadly peril.

I have no doubt at all that, had the police been called in, Adèle would have paid with her life for their assistance. The fight was between us and 'Rose' Noble, and the bare threat of an ally to whom, if he lost, 'Rose' Noble would have to answer, would have been instantly silenced in the most dreadful and effective of ways. Another man might have balked at so detestable a crime, but 'Rose' Noble was ruthless and would, I think, have slain ten pawns, had they stood in the way of his safety or revenge. I verily believe it was this terrible quality, if, indeed it can be so called, to which he owed his immunity, for, while 'dead men tell no tales,' it has but to be known that a man keeps that for his motto and those who have to do with him will tell none either.

It was midnight before we parted, and three o'clock of the morning before I fell asleep: but six hours later the coachbuilder was urging his men, and Carson and I were at work. Except that we drove to St. James's and back again, we laboured incessantly till four, but, when I reported to Hansel at five o'clock, the cars were as ready for the road as the wit of man could make them and both were at hand in his garage by Stable Yard. There they were packed and loaded by Carson alone, and at half past six they were standing in Cleveland Row.

Rowley and Bell were gone, so we were but four to travel as far as Dieppe: yet in a way we were five, for Tester, Mansel's Sealyham, went with us, and, if he was but a dog, he was ever better company than many a man.

He was fine to look at, very strong and healthy, intelligent beyond belief. Given an order that he could appreciate, he would obey it to the death. He knew no fear, was very quick and cheerful, would countenance no one but those his master had commended and worshipped Mansel himself with the most lively devotion that I have ever seen.

At a quarter to seven we passed out of Cleveland Row.

We made no secret of our going, simply because it was a movement we could not hide: "all the same," said Mansel, "it doesn't very much matter if they do send 'Rose' Noble a wire. He never expected that I should pay out of hand: but he means me to find it hopeless and then to put on the screw."

We dined at Newhaven and saw the cars taken on board: then we turned into our cabins to take what rest we could, for, though Mansel had not said so, we all four knew very well that, until we were come to Carinthia, we should none of us sleep again.

The steward roused me by order half an hour before we were due, and I came on deck to find a clean morning and two or three lights marking the coast of France.

Mansel had told me to breakfast before I left the boat, so after a turn or two, I went below, there to find him and Hanbury making a wretched meal.

Whilst I was waiting to join them, he gave me a map.

"We must keep together," he said: "but, as we can't see ahead, this is in case we part. Don't use it at all until then. I've marked the route in blue pencil, so that you can't go wrong. I'd better take the lead. I shall go pretty fast, but please try to keep me in sight. If I lose you, I shall slow up, but I don't want to have to do that. If you want to attract my attention, use your horn. I'll take Carson to start with; but later we might make a change, and you or Hanbury drive for a while with me."

"First stop, Carinthia," said George.

"If you please," said Mansel. "I hope we shall be at St. Martin in twenty-four hours. We must water and feed, of course, and fill up the cars: but I wired to my cousin that we should be there by dawn, and I rather fancy, poor fellow, he'll watch the clock."

We had already decided that, though we might rest at Poganec after our run, we should leave our baggage at Villach, at an inn which we knew; for not only was this town more central, but to have to 'report progress,' as we should if we stayed with the Pleydells, whenever we came or went would be intolerable. This may seem a harsh decision, as they were so deeply concerned, but we should be dealing, we knew, with life and death, and that we should be hampered by any sort of obligation was not to be thought of. We did not expect, however, to have much use for a base, but to be constantly moving in search or pursuit of Adèle: and this was why Mansel had been insistent that the cars should demand no attention, yet withstand incessant use.

As the boat entered the harbour, we came on deck and presently made out Bell, who was standing with three officials on the edge of the quay. So soon as he saw us, he pointed us out to his companions, one of whom boarded the steamer before she was fairly at rest. I met him with our papers, and, since they were what he had come for, he took them without a word.

This was well enough, but the cars had to be unshipped, and, since the boat-train was waiting, the ordinary registered baggage must, as always, be taken off first. That this would be a long business seemed very probable, for there was but one crane manned, and, as luck would have it, there were many passengers.

As the man who had taken our papers regained the quay, the main gangways were run inboard, and I saw for the first time that Bell had a watch in his hand. A little way off was a lad in charge of a basket and a small stack of petrol cans.

"Full marks to Bell," said Mansel. "They're going to take the cars first."

And so indeed they did – such is the power of money.

Mansel's Rolls was ashore before any of us, and, at a sign from Bell, the lad with the basket began to fill her tank. As the second car was landed, the man who had taken our papers came running out of some office with the documents stamped and signed, and, after a glance at our number-plates, handed me back the wallet and raised his hat. Then our baggage was hastily chalked, and, as Mansel started his engine, Bell put away his watch.

"We're free to proceed, sir," he said, touching his hat. "By your leave I'll pay them the money and find you outside."

"Well done indeed," said Mansel. "How long have we been?"

"Just under a quarter of an hour, sir. I promised them five thousand if they did it in half an hour, and I said I'd double the money if they did it in half the time."

With that, he disappeared, and Hanbury started our engine, as Mansel, with Carson and Tester, drove off the quay.

The lad charged to fill our tank was a clumsy workman, so I told him to stand aside and did it myself: and George descended and helped me by taking the caps from the cans.

"You drive first," he said. "It won't be light for some time, and your eyes are keener than mine."

"Very well," said I.

The landing of the registered baggage was now in full swing, and the quay was alive with porters, bustling to and fro in the lamplight and making less progress than noise: and, since the baggage itself was being swung over our heads, I was glad to screw its cap to the tank and to take my seat in the car.

Hanbury picked up the basket and followed me in.

The eastern sky was pale, but it was yet very dark.

Now as we were moving slowly towards the street, I became aware of some paper upon which I seemed to have sat down. So soon as I had a hand free, I plucked this from under my legs, to find it a dirty envelope, bearing no superscription, but sealed.

"What's that?" said George, peering.

"It must have fallen from the baggage," I said. "The nets passed over the car. See what it is. If it's a bill of lading, we'd better give it back."

As Hanbury ripped open the envelope, Bell stepped out of the shadows on to the running board.

"Captain Mansel's fifty yards on, sir; on the right of the street."

"Very good," said I, turning across the lines.

"It's not a bill of lading," said George sharply.

"What then?" said I, setting a foot on the brake.

By way of answer, he held it to the light of the lamp which illumined the instrument board.

It was a half-sheet of notepaper on which were printed four words:

*The goods are perishable.*

# II

## WE TAKE THE FIELD

To show Mansel a memento so ugly went against the grain: yet we dared not suppress it, so I drove to where he sat waiting, and Hanbury gave the paper into his hand.

He glanced at it, turned it about and then put it away.

"Where did you find it?" he said.

I told him on the seat of the car.

At once he turned to Bell and asked him to try to recall every person that he had seen in the last two hours: "for," said he, "one of those men was a spy, and, though we can do nothing now, it might be very convenient if you would know him again."

Then he asked if I was ready and let in his clutch...

The day was coming, but, so long as the night lasted, we had the road to ourselves. Taking advantage of this, Mansel went like the wind, and, since all I could see was his tail-light and this poor pointer vanished with each dip and bend of the road, it was more by luck than by cunning that I managed to cling to his heels. Indeed, the first hour of our journey imposed a continuous strain, for he drove as though the way was familiar, but I did not know it at all, and, what with fear of leaving the road if I drove too fast, and of losing my guiding light if I slackened speed, I wished for the day with a fervour which I think would have opened the eyes of St. Paul himself.

Yet, in a way, this trial stood me in stead, for, when at last it was light and I could see the landscape and Mansel's Rolls scudding before me like a gull, to follow behind seemed child's play and, though he went faster than ever, I was able without any trouble to maintain the pace which he set.

The sun rose about six into a cloudless sky, and, since rain had lately fallen, the country was fresh to look on and smelled very sweet. Mansel raised next to no dust, for this had been laid by the rain and was not yet dry, and, as the chill of the dawn changed to the cool of the day, our passage became every moment more agreeable. There was, however, a look of heat in the heaven which there was no mistaking.

Our road was no longer so free as it had been by night, but I was surprised to encounter so little traffic, and, indeed, the clocks had struck seven before the pace at which we were travelling had to be sensibly reduced.

At a quarter to eight we met our first definite check in the shape of a level crossing, the gates of which were closed.

To make the best of the business, we halted for a quarter of an hour, and, while Tester was given his freedom, we ate and drank of the food which Bell had brought.

Mansel was plainly pleased with the pace at which we had come, but insisted that now was the time for Hanbury to take my place: then he turned to Bell and asked if he had recalled the people he had seen at Dieppe.

"I've done my best, sir," said Bell: "but I fear there's not very many I'd know again."

"That remains to be seen," said Mansel. "But please try to bear them in mind, and picture to yourself the time you spent on the quay. I expect you walked up and down. Try to remember if anyone was doing the same."

"Very good, sir," said Bell obediently.

Five minutes later I was sitting with Mansel, and we were again under way.

We had now come to roads that we had travelled before, but, though the features of the way seemed faintly familiar, I could not have taken it safely without the aid of the map nor have threaded a single town without direction. Mansel, however, drove with the utmost confidence, never hesitating where the road forked or peering at any signpost, but whipping through town after town as though it were the place of his birth.

When I remarked upon this, he said it was nothing at all and that I knew the way to Salzburg as well as did he, but that he was using his knowledge, while I was not.

"And that," said he, "is why I'm badgering Bell. Bell is observant, and I'll lay a hundred to one that he observed the fellow that left that note. I don't think I did, for when he saw me coming, he probably made himself scarce. And you were behind the car. But Bell and he were both waiting for the boat to come in. Well, there's the making of a clue. It's slight enough in all conscience, but – well, I don't know where Adèle is, and Austria's quite a big place." After a little, he continued thoughtfully. "Memory's a store-room, that's all: the store-room of things you observe. If you're observant, so much the richer your store. But you must be a good storeman – able to produce the requisite, when the moment comes. Some time ago I observed the way to Salzburg: and now I'm producing it. Bell undoubtedly observed the man who carried that note: let's hope he'll be able to produce him – when the moment comes."

We said no more at the time, and, being, I suppose, more tired than I had suspected, I fell asleep.

When I awoke, it was noon, and the day was immensely hot.

Mansel was driving in the same effortless way, looking very well content with his lot and seeming to be perfectly fresh.

When he saw that I was awake, he told me that we should make Strasbourg in two hours' time. We had stopped for fuel whilst I slept, but that was all.

Sure enough, we came to Strasbourg at two o'clock, and at half-past two we were lunching on German soil.

Then I changed places with George, who was white as a miller with dust, for the sun had done its work, and, since there was next to no wind, the cars would have had to travel a mile apart if the second was to escape the clouds which its fellow raised.

The afternoon was made dreadful by the heat and glare of the sun, which oppressed us mercilessly and made the air so sultry that our pace brought us no relief: I never found shade so grateful in all my life, nor yet so scarce, and how Mansel, who had had no respite, bore the burden of that day so lightly I never shall understand.

Twice we were checked by the gates of level crossings and once we stopped for fuel, but these delays were too brief to be refreshing, and I, for one, was thankful when we came to rest at sundown by the side of a little stream. Into this we were happy to plunge our heads and shoulders, and, whilst Mansel and I ate and drank, George and the servants cleaned the windscreens and sponged down and sluiced the cars – by no means a fruitless exercise, for we were sick of the dust, and the sight of the glistening coachwork did us all good.

Night came upon us soon after eight o'clock, but a fine moon was westering, and two and a half hours later we entered Austria.

At Salzburg we drove straight to the station, where Rowley lay, stretched on our luggage, fast asleep. It took but a moment to rouse him and lift the trunks into the cars, and I do not think this digression cost us five minutes of time.

So soon as we were clear of the city, a halt was made, and Mansel called the servants to listen to what he would say.

"You all know what has happened," he said. "Mrs Pleydell has disappeared. Everything points to abduction – by no ordinary gang. As one of the family, I should in any event have done what I could: but, with Captain Pleydell out of action, it's up to me to take charge. Very well. Here's my first order. Discuss this business with no one. We're certainly going to friends, but we're going to enemies too, *and the latter are already in touch.* I've had two letters already warning me not to proceed.

"We're going to drop Rowley at Villach, where he will go to bed. Tomorrow he will take four bedrooms and unpack all our things. And he may as well order supper, for we shall surely sleep there tomorrow night.

"The rest of us go to Poganec, and, whilst we are there, Carson and Bell will stay with and sleep in the cars."

Then he told Carson to drive and called for Tester, and a moment later we were moving again.

All of us knew the way now, so there was no thought of leading or being led, and though I remember little – for Hanbury was driving and I slept most of the way – I know that we stopped at Villach, to find the inn shut, that the landlord looked out of the window, with an old-fashioned cap on his head and that, when he saw who it was, he began to cry to his household that at last his luck had turned, for the best guests he ever had had were come again.

We were gone, however, before he had opened the door, leaving Rowley in the midst of the luggage, with his hand to his hat.

We were now in most handsome country, very mountainous and closely wooded, with streams and pastures lying in every dale: the air was most soft and rich, and plainly suited the engines, for the cars sailed over the hills like giants refreshed.

We swept through St. Martin, to hear the church clock strike one, and ten minutes later sighted a long low house, lying in the lap of a meadow, with rising woods behind.

This was Poganec: and I well remember remarking how fantastic a picture it made, for the moonlight was all about it and all its windows were open and lights burning in every room.

It was, I suppose, ten minutes before Mansel came to a window upon the first floor.

"Will you two come up?" he said.

The front door was open, and Hanbury and I passed in.

Major Pleydell met us at the top of the stairs and brought us into a room at the back of the house.

Daphne Pleydell rose to greet us, and her brother propped with pillows, called to us from the bed. Beside him sat Mansel.

As I went to take his hand –

"Jonah can drive, can't he?" he said with a smile.

Before I could answer – for I had some sort of condolence upon my tongue – he began to speak of the cars, reciting their qualities with judgment and remembering runs he had taken against the clock and, so, making smooth an encounter which I had been dreading more than I care to admit.

"I've often followed Jonah," he concluded, "but I've never had to chase him when he had his whip out and, to be perfectly honest, I hope I never shall." He laughed lightly. "And now sit down, you two – anywhere except on my leg – and Berry will bring you some beer. I think you've earned it."

I tried to reply, but the words stuck in my throat.

I could not cope with such bravery. The man was jesting: his eyes were steady and his speech was firm, but the thick, dark hair I remembered was white as snow.

As Major Pleydell came forward, with a glass in his hand –

"And now to business," he said.

"Today is Thursday. At seven on Monday morning Adèle went out for a ride. She rode in the direction of Sava, a village ten miles away. Her mare came in on her own at a quarter past eight. Everyone turned out at once, but found nothing. The mare was clean and unhurt. Inquiries were made at all farms in the direction of Sava. They proved fruitless. Nobody saw Adèle on Monday morning. The day was hot, and she was wearing breeches and boots, a white silk shirt and gloves. She had no hat on.

"Early on Tuesday morning Fitch found one of her gloves. It was lying by the side of the road almost exactly eleven miles from here, but not in the direction of Sava.

"Well, there you are. I'm afraid I've no more to say."

There was a little silence, and presently Mansel spoke.

"You've had no demand for money?"

His cousin looked away.

"None," he said quietly. "I've got the money ready: it's all I've been able to do." He stretched out a trembling hand. "There's five thousand pounds worth of notes in that chest of drawers. They've only to come and ask. But they – they don't do that."

There was something so dark about the way he said this as took us all three by surprise: and this, I suppose, he was expecting, for he let out the ghost of a laugh.

"I know," he said. "I didn't get it at first. You know, I made quite certain that they were out for money. *It never occurred to me that Adèle had been taken for herself.*"

Mansel started to his feet.

"I don't believe it," he cried.

"I know," said the other calmly. "Neither did I. But you'll come round in the end and face the facts – when the days go by and you don't find her, but no demand is made; when the weeks go by and I'm crawling round with a stick and people are forgetting what she looked like—"

"Oh, Boy, Boy," wailed Daphne.

"—but no demand is made; when—"

"Never," cried Mansel. "Never."

"Then, why don't they ask?" said the other, with the sweat running down his face.

"They will," said Mansel.

The other shook his head.

"What about the police?" he said suddenly. "Why don't you want them called in?"

"Because I want my hands free. If battle and murder will help, I'm out to do both: but I can't do either, if I've got to apply for a warrant before I can force a door. We're six men armed: we know how, to work together; and we're not afraid of lying out in the rain. Call in the police and you put us out of court."

"That's right," said his cousin, nodding. "The police wouldn't do any good." He lay back and closed his eyes. "But, as they're not out for money, neither will you."

"I know they're out for money," said Mansel.

"Face the facts," said his cousin. "Seventy hours since they took her, and no demand. Face the facts, Jonah: and, when you've had a good look at them, come back and try to tell me not to turn my face to the wall."

There was a dreadful silence, broken only by Daphne's sobs.

At last her brother called her and asked for some drug.

While she was pleading with him, we others stole out of the room.

I was confounded by this perversity of Fortune and I dared not look at Mansel, for here, at the outset of our venture, he was faced with a choice of two evils, neither of which, it seemed, he could possibly accept.

To conceal the truth from his cousin was to withhold water from a dying man: yet how could he ever allow that he, *and not her husband*, had been offered the lady back? Explain it as he would, the fact must arouse misgivings in the steadiest mind: to a man in his cousin's condition, it would be plain poison.

Major Pleydell was speaking.

"If they don't make a demand, he'll lose his mind. He hasn't slept since she went. His hair was grey on Tuesday, and yesterday it was white. If they'd only hold her to ransom, he wouldn't care. If they asked a million, he wouldn't care a damn. We might not be able to pay it, but he'd know she was safe and sound. But when the hours go by and there's no demand—"

"Where have you looked?" said Mansel.

The other stared at him.

"Looked?" he said.

"D'you mean to say," cried Mansel, "that you've been waiting for it to come by post? Why, man alive, that's the last agency they'll use! *Haven't you even looked in the box in the gate?*"

The front door was open and we pelted out of the hall.

Mansel cried to Hanbury and me to bring some tools and a torch and, in spite of his limp – for he was lame of a wound he had had in the War – ran well ahead of his cousin down the drive.

It was seldom that he took some action which I could not understand: but now I was bewildered, for I knew as well as did he that the box in the gate would be as bare as my hand. Still there was no time to think, and, Hanbury being gone with the tools, I plucked a torch out of a pocket and ran in his wake.

The box was a doll's-house business, cut out of the gatepost itself, with a slit for letters before and a little iron door behind. No doubt it was meant to be used in days gone by, for a man on horseback could reach the slit from the road, but the door had not been undone for many a year, although there was nothing to show this upon the other side.

I held the torch, while Mansel played with the chisel and presently forced the lock.

As he wrenched the little door open, Major Pleydell thrust in his hand.

When he drew out a folded paper, I could hardly believe my eyes.

*The stolen goods will be returned on the receipt by the Manager of the—Bank, Zurich, of your cheque for five hundred thousand pounds. This sum you can raise, if you please. No time should be wasted, for the goods are perishable.*

*August 30th.*

Before my wits were in order, Major Pleydell was well up the drive, shouting for Daphne and crying aloud his news.

"It's come!" he bellowed. "It's come!" "It's been here since Monday. The demand..."

As we walked after him—

"Learn of me," said Mansel. "*Never burn anything.*"

When we came to the house, he called a footman to serve us with food and drink and himself went up to the chamber where Captain Pleydell lay.

Ten minutes later he returned, to say that the latter was asleep.

A brief council was held the next morning at a quarter to twelve, and the moment I entered the bedroom I saw with half an eye that the patient was a new man. He spoke with eagerness, and the grey look was out of his face. His sister sat beside him, with shining eyes.

There was no argument, and everything went our way.

All were agreed that the sum demanded was fantastic and that the letter be ignored: and, when Mansel said that we should leave after lunch and should not return, Daphne began to protest, but the sick man inclined his head.

"I thought that was coming," he said. "You were ever a dark horse, Jonah, and dark horses train alone. But tell me where I can find you and send me word when you can."

"That I will do without fail."

It was then decided that the Pleydells should take no action, whatever befell, without communicating with us, that they should accept no message as coming from us unless one of us had brought it, but should detain the messenger; and that we should recognize no one as coming from them but Major Pleydell or one of the servants we knew.

And, so far as I can remember, that was all.

Mansel had already ridden most of the way to Sava and had driven with Major Pleydell to the spot where the glove had been found: he had also seen and talked with all the servants employed about the farm; "and, since," he said, rising, "I believe them all to be honest, though painfully unobservant, this is where we come in."

Then he asked that Adèle's dressing-case should be sent for and packed with such things as she would be glad to have. This we were to take with us wherever we went.

Daphne left to arrange this, and we bade Captain Pleydell "Goodbye."

For a moment he held my hand.

"Adèle's very lucky," he said, "to have such good friends."

"Oh," said I, "the boot's on the other leg."

"Sleep well," said Hanbury.

Two minutes later the engines of the cars were running, and Hanbury and I were about to take our seats, when Mansel called us into a parlour and shut the door.

"It is inconceivable," he said, "that Adèle was taken by chance. Her movements had been watched for some time. Let me go further. They watched her ride out on Monday and met her six miles away.

"Now no one was seen near Poganec, with or without a car: it follows that their observation post was distant, yet close to a road, so that once they had seen her ride out and the way she went, they could instantly move to meet her – six miles away. Very well. Now turn to the window and lift up your eyes."

We did so, to see the breadth of a valley, as fresh and green as you please, and, beyond, a press of high hills, rising up very sudden and wooded cap-à-pie. These lay, I afterwards found, four miles away. High up in their midst rose a fountain that fell by leaps and rushes down to the valley below, a considerable head of water, for the trees could not hide it, and, from where we stood, I could see its unbroken length.

"Can you see the bridge?" said Mansel. "A fifth of the way down the fall."

"Yes," said Hanbury, and after a moment or two I made it out.

"Good," said Mansel. "Now their observation post was somewhere about that bridge. A post in the woods would be useless, for the trees would get in the way; but that torrent commands Poganec; and a man sitting there with a glass could see anyone come and go. Then, again, that bridge serves a road to Sava – the only road thereabouts."

I took a step to the window, but Mansel stopped me at once.

"I hope and believe," he said, "that they're watching Poganec now. I mean, our movements must interest them no end. So don't give them food for thought by looking straight into their eyes.

"And now come and look at this map.

"Here's Poganec, and there's the bridge – due South. We're all going there at once. But Chandos and I are going to come up from the West, while Hanbury, Carson and Bell will drive from St. Martin to Sava and come from the East. We may find; we may draw blank; we may meet our friends by the way." He turned to Hanbury. "Your way will be much the longer, so, if, when you come to the bridge, Chandos and I are not there, drive on round to St. Martin and thence to Villach. If you find anyone suspicious, detain him, but not by force: if he won't be detained, follow him: drop Bell at the first cross roads, to put us wise: but, whatever you do, don't lose him, for he'll show us the way to Adèle."

With that he put up the map, and two minutes later the cars were clear of the drive and were making towards St. Martin at a leisurely speed. Not until we parted were we to let them go.

"There's a road on the left," said Mansel, "somewhere just here."

With his words the turning appeared, and, as we swung round, Hanbury flashed past our tail-lamp in a pother of dust.

Our road ran into the valley and lay in full view of the bridge, and, since anyone who was watching must now suspect our move, we went like lightning till we came to the foot of the hills and a pretty, white-walled hamlet where four roads met.

A woman, busy at a runnel, gave us goodday.

"I'm looking for some friends," said Mansel. "Have you seen any car go by?"

"I only came in from the fields, sir, a quarter of an hour ago. But no car has passed since then."

Mansel thanked her and immediately turned to the left.

Almost at once the road rose into the woods, doubling upon itself, like any serpent, and so beset with foliage as to afford no view of anything beyond a ribbon of sky.

For a while there was no sound at all, except the brush of our tires: but, after a little, we could hear the roar of water some distance away. This grew gradually louder, until it quite stopped our ears, so that we knew less than ever what each bend of the road might bring forth.

It was, I suppose, an ideal site for an ambush, for with every turn you entered an inner bailey of the wood, and, though upon such a score we had nothing to fear, I remember thinking that, where two men were at variance, the odds were on him who came first to such a place. Be that as it may, our ears being stopped, there was nothing to be done but watch: and this I know I did with a quick pulse, for the scene was set for a surprise as I have never known it.

It was soon evident that we were approaching the bridge, for the noise of the fall was thunderous and the pleasant smell of wet earth was unmistakable. Indeed, an instant later we saw the bridge not sixty paces away, and at half that distance a car in the midst of the road, with a man bent double beside it, trying to pull off a wheel.

He was so much engaged that we had stopped alongside before he knew we were there, and, when on a sudden he was aware of our presence, he gaped at us and the Rolls as at an apparition.

Now this was not the way of a spy; and, indeed, it was easy to see that the fellow had nothing to do with those we sought. His cloth apart – for he wore a clergyman's habit – one look at his face was enough. The man was a genial simpleton, in whom there was no guile. And I think Mansel would have gone by, for his hand went out to the brake, if the other's delight to see us had been less manifest.

"You're English," he cried, twittering.

"Yes," said Mansel. "And we were to meet a man here. By that bridge. But we're late for our appointment, and I'm afraid he may have gone."

"No one was there," said the other, "ten minutes ago. And I've been there more than an hour. But he might have come since."

With that, before we could stop him, he started to run to the bridge. We overtook him halfway, for, fool though he looked, it seemed prudent to be there first: but he only sought to step on to our running-board and, fouling the tool-chest, fell heavily into the road.

And there you have Hannibal Rouse, clerk in holy orders. He was, I think, the embodiment of that imaginary curate who has for years been the target of an unkind age. The man was futile. He was most garrulous, seldom said anything worth saying and laughed at everything he said: he was prodigal of energy, seldom did anything worth doing and bungled everything he did. I have never known anyone whose company was so distracting; and the patience with which Mansel endured it was more than human. Yet out of the fool came wisdom, and, but for this pelting idiot, I do not believe we should ever have traced Adèle.

I helped the man to his feet, and, since, in view of his report, there was nothing to be gained by proceeding, Mansel berthed the Rolls by the bridge and walked with us back to his car.

Rouse may be fairly judged by the fact that he was seeking to change a wheel without first raising his car by means of a jack: and, when, perceiving that the wheel was sound, we asked him why he wished to change it, he insisted that its tire was punctured and seemed dumbfounded to find it as tight as a drum. It presently emerged that another of his tires was flat and that he had confused the two. He was not at all abashed by these errors, but attributed them boldly to his being "no engineer."

He then told us that he was touring and cared not where he went, but proposed to stay at Villach and prove the country round. This was ill news enough; but when, after staring upon Mansel, he presently addressed him by name and then, in an ecstasy of triumph, went on to remember White Ladies and how he had attended some fête there before the War, I know that I groaned in spirit and wished the man at the devil. But Mansel was perfectly civil, though something cold.

We had changed his wheel, in spite of his assistance, and were upon the point of leaving, when Hanbury arrived. This necessarily delayed our going and gave Rouse time to remember that he had a camera with him with which he must photograph us all. We protested that we could not wait, but, while we were still protesting, the thing was done. I confess that it did not delay us, for he took his picture as we re-entered the cars, laughing the while like a maniac and promising to show us a proof.

"The man's a scourge," said I, as we sped back the way we had come. "He'll make Villach untenable."

Mansel shrugged his shoulders.

"I think we must suffer him," he said. "He may be of use."

"'Of use?'" said I.

"Of use," said Mansel.

With that, he drove very fast to where Adèle's glove had been found, and set us all to seeking some mark of a tire; "for here," he said, "I am certain that she changed from one car to another and, while she did so, contrived to drop her glove, for they would have watched her too closely to let her throw it out as she went."

In proof of this, he showed us where oil had been dripping on the edge of the grass by the road, as is sometimes the way of a car which is standing still.

"The relay was waiting," said he, "half on and half off the grass, close up to the hedge. The other ran up alongside, and the transfer was made. And now we'll all work in a line, searching the ground as they do on a dairy farm."

We did so for more than an hour, but found nothing.

Then we took to the cars and drove very slowly west, now travelling together, now parting and presently meeting again, until by evening we had come to a great hog's back, some fifty miles from the spot where the glove had lain. There we rested and watched the sun go down, and then Mansel led us to Villach as fast as he could.

There, more to my disgust than surprise, we found that Rouse was to lodge in the very same inn. Indeed, he announced his presence by springing out like a child from behind the parlour door, so that even Mansel was short with him, while I could have taken the fool and wrung his neck.

I will not dwell upon his follies, the tale of which was enough to make the angels weep, but merely record that for the next three days he continually invited violence, taking the most curious interest in all we did, pressing his company upon us whenever we were at hand and openly trying to follow us when we went forth.

This we did every morning at break of day, as best we could to search the country towards the west, for, to that quarter, we made sure, Adèle had been carried off. Mansel, who alone could speak German, visited the villages in turn, stopping at wayside inns and engaging in conversation men and women whose business kept them in sight of the roads. George or Carson or I went always with him. The others repaired to the hog's back, from which four men with glasses could command a very great view: if ever a car was sighted it was carefully watched, and two would leave in pursuit, so soon as the line it was taking could be fairly presumed. But questionings and scrutinies alike bore us no fruit, for Mansel learned nothing of value, and the occupants of the cars, which were few, gave us no cause to doubt their honesty. Indeed, at the end of three days, we seemed to be no nearer Adèle than when we left Cleveland Row. In that time, however, we received a savage monition that, though we had no idea where 'Rose' Noble was, he had his hand upon us and could, so to speak, twist our tail whenever he pleased.

# III

## IN TOUCH

When we came in at nightfall, at the end of our second patrol, Rouse was still abroad in his car. For this relief we were thankful, for the evening before he had sat with us during our supper and, hungry though we were, had gone far to spoil the meal. Our respite, however, was short, for we had scarcely sat down before we heard him arrive, and a moment later he thrust his head into the room.

"Guess who I've seen," he said archly.

No one vouchsafed any answer; but Tester spoke for us all, by leaving his cushion and passing beneath the bed.

"Mr Wilberforce," said Rouse triumphantly.

The name meant nothing to me, and a glance at Mansel and Hanbury showed that their case was the same.

At length –

"Who's Wilberforce?" said Mansel wearily.

Rouse's grin faded, and his eyes grew round with surprise. Then he came into the room.

"He – he said he knew you," he stammered. "He said he knew you quite well. I met him by the side of the road. He asked me the way to Salzburg, and then we got talking and, when I said you were at Villach, he asked how you were."

"What was he like?" said Hanbury.

Rouse described some man I had never seen.

"When was this?" said Mansel.

Rouse said about six o'clock.

"I think you must know him," he added. "He said that he lived near Bournemouth and he asked all about you and how you were getting on. I said you were out a great deal and – There now, I've left them in the car."

As he turned to the door –

"Left what in the car?" said I.

"The flowers, of course, stupid," said Rouse. I could have choked, but Mansel and Hanbury began to shake with laughter. "I tell you he gave me some flowers. Carson will you be so good? The box in the car."

With a resigned look, Carson left the room.

"The man's mad," murmured Hanbury.

"No, he isn't," said Rouse excitedly. "He said you were a great gardener."

"He said I was?" said Mansel.

"Oh, yes," said Rouse. "I've no doubt about it at all. We were talking of horticulture and he said—"

"You must have got the name wrong," said Mansel. "I know nothing of gardening."

"You must mean fishing," said Hanbury.

"No, it must have been gardening," said Rouse. "Why else should he give me the flowers?"

Here Carson appeared in the doorway, with a shallow, white cardboard box, fastened with string.

"There you are," said Rouse, handing the box to Mansel, as though there were no more to be said. "He asked me to give them to you."

"I'm sure you're mistaken," said Mansel, taking a knife. "I'm certainly fond of flowers, but—"

"He cut those himself," said Rouse, "and he said he could think of no one who would value them more than you. James Wilberforce, his name was, and, when I asked—"

"My God!" said Mansel, and Hanbury and I cried out.

The box was full of beautiful, soft, brown hair.

In an instant the room was in an uproar.

As I leapt to my feet, my head struck the electric light and put it out; but I saw George throw himself forward, as Rouse recoiled against the wall. There was a lamp by the bed, and I sought like a madman for the switch, while Tester was barking and George and Rouse were shouting and Mansel was calling George to order in a steady, metallic voice.

As the light went up—

"It's beyond a joke," said Rouse, painfully getting to his feet. "You might have hurt me very much. Supposing—"

"How did you come by that box?" said Mansel.

"I tell you," said Rouse, "he told me to give it to you. I understood they were flowers and that you—"

"You say he was going to Salzburg?"

"I think so," said Rouse, wincing. "He—"

"Please describe him again."

Rouse gave the particulars, staring.

"And now describe his car."

When he had done so, Mansel stepped to the door.

"I'm sorry for what's happened," he said. "The fault was not yours. And now please go. We've plans to make and rather a lot to discuss."

Without a word, Rouse turned and limped from the room.

For a little, none of us spoke.

Then—

"Do you believe him?" said Hanbury.

"Why not?" said Mansel. "If the enemy knows we're here, you can bet he hasn't missed Rouse. And there you are. I said Rouse might be of use, and I was right. He's just been of use to 'Rose' Noble. Perhaps tomorrow he'll be of use to us."

My room and Mansel's shared a small balcony, and that night Tester waked me by putting his nose on my arm. I was up in an instant, for the dog was plainly uneasy and I feared that something was wrong. As I passed barefoot to the window, I saw that the light was burning in Mansel's room...

Mansel was on his knees by the side of the bed, with one arm across his eyes, like a weeping child, and the other hand full of the curls which lay in a little heap in the midst of the counterpane.

For a long time he never moved, but at last he lifted his head and, when the dog came running, he picked him up in his arms.

I stole back to bed.

The next day was Sunday.

Mansel started for Salzburg at seven o'clock, taking Carson with him, and the rest of us left for the hog's back within the hour.

I ran into Rouse on the doorstep, as I was leaving the inn.

"I must beg your pardon," he said, "for the way I spoke last night. It was very wrong of me. And I feel you were most justly provoked." He laughed inanely. "I was very disappointed myself. But I do hope Captain Mansel won't take it up with Mr Wilberforce. After all, we're all liable to make mistakes, and I'm sure he had no intention of playing a joke."

At first I could make no reply.

At length –

"That's all right," I said. "I'm afraid we were rather – rather hasty. Supper's a bad time, you know."

With that, I rushed off, before he could clasp my hand.

When I told Hanbury –

"The man's half-witted," he said. "And I'm ashamed of myself for bringing him down. I don't wonder 'Rose' Noble hangs his hat on him. I think we should soon find Adèle, if *he* had a comic idiot round his neck."

"Yet Mansel has hopes of him," said I.

"As a hat-stand," said George. "That's all."

Not until ten that night did Mansel return to the inn.

We had come in at sundown, and Rouse had badgered us nearly out of our lives, for, remembering our offences of the night before, we felt constrained to be civil, and the fact that the day was Sunday seemed to entitle his cloth to consideration. Before retiring, he asked if he might read us the Gospel. We could hardly refuse, but I fear it did us no good and only enlarged the sympathy we felt for his flock.

Very soon after, we heard the sigh of the Rolls, and a moment later Mansel entered the room.

"Gone to bed?" he said, looking round.

"Ten minutes ago," said I, "by the grace of God."

"Then you're friends again," said Mansel.

I told him how Rouse had spoken on the steps of the inn and what we had suffered since sundown at the hands of the fool.

"Good," said he. "Any news?"

"Devil a bit," said I. "And you?"

"Salzburg's no earthly," says he. "Indeed, I was so sure of that that I've been at Poganec all day." We opened our eyes. "But don't tell Hannibal R."

"He never dreamed you'd gone to Salzburg. If he had – "

"Oh, yes, he did," said Mansel, sitting down in a chair. "But he knew I should waste my time. I tell you, he's pretty hot stuff, is Hannibal R. And you must admit he's put up a wonderful show. Talk about sheep's clothing."

Hanbury was looking at me in a helpless way, and I fancy he found slight comfort in my expression, for he soon returned to Mansel, and I did the same.

"Last night," said Mansel, "you asked me if I believed him. The true answer was 'No'; and the whole truth, 'I never did.'

"And now listen."

"The moment I saw him, I felt sure that he was our man. He was where I had expected to find him, and he couldn't escape, because he had a flat tire. Yet in the first five minutes he played the fool so beautifully that *against my better judgment* I found my suspicions failing and I had to fight with myself to keep them alive. And then he made a mistake. It was a very slight one, and I don't think he thought I saw. He did a thing that no clergyman that wears a round collar would ever do. He put up two hands, as though to straighten a tie."

He paused there, to pour himself some ale: and, when he had drunk, he lighted a cigarette.

"Well," he continued, "the obvious thing to do was to play his game – satisfy him that we didn't suspect him at all. And that's why I didn't tell you. Your undisguised contempt for him has been simply invaluable. I should think he's been revelling in it – I know I have. By the way, I'm telling you now, because you won't see him again – at least, not upon the same terms.

"Now, first, what was his job? His job was to keep in touch. 'Rose' Noble holds a fine hand, but he knows us too well to sleep sound when we're out of his ken. So Rouse was to keep in touch – an extremely difficult job. We were six to one, you see, and ready to find a spy under every hat. So what does he do but step in *under our guard*? It was done in the War, you know: but only a born artist can bring it off. And Rouse is an old master.

"And now for his value to us. It may become imperative that a spy should return to his chief. Very well. If Rouse thought we suspected him, he'd never return, until he had shaken us off. Never. But, *now that he knows we don't*, he'll go when he thinks he'd better and never take the trouble to look behind. *And I think he'll think he'd better before very long, for he'll have some news for 'Rose' Noble which will not wait.*

"And now, if you please, we shall all go to bed at once, for I've no idea when or where we shall sleep again."

I had slept very ill for three hours when I heard a car making like fury towards the inn. At once I sat up, for, in view of what Mansel had said, I fully expected that it was bound for our door; but it swept up the street, like a squall, and presently turning some corner, passed out of earshot.

A moment later, however, I heard it coming again.

Again it went by the inn, but stopped, with its brakes screaming, a score of paces away. Then the reverse gear was engaged, and the car shot back with a snarl, to come to rest under our windows, before the inn.

The next instant someone was pounding upon the front door.

As I rushed to the window –

"What is it, Berry?" said Mansel, from the balcony.

Major Pleydell stepped back on the pavement and threw up his head.

"*Jonah*," he cried, "*she's sent word. She's got a message through.*"

"I'll come down," said Mansel.

But George and I were before him and had the front door open, while he was still on the stairs.

For a moment the cousins spoke together: then Mansel turned to us.

"The man's at Poganec," he said. "We must go there at once."

For all our haste, Mansel was ready before us, and I heard him call Carson and tell him to follow with Rowley and that Bell was to pack our light luggage and load the second Rolls.

Two minutes later we left in Major Pleydell's car: Mansel was driving, while the chauffeur sat by his side.

We did not go to Poganec, but, instead, twenty miles to Crayern – the first station after Villach, if you are travelling east.

Arrived there, Mansel descended, and, wondering what was to happen, we followed him out of the car.

To our surprise, he bade Major Pleydell "Goodbye."

"And thanks very much," he said. "You did it most awfully well."

"I wish it had been true," said his cousin.

"So do I," said Mansel. "So long."

"Goodnight, you two," said the other. George and I cried "Goodnight."

Then the car slipped into the darkness and Mansel turned to us.

"You must forgive me," he said. "I'll never blind you again. And now let's walk to the station, and talk as we go along.

"Rouse's room's above mine. I'm sure the car must have waked him, and I'm sure he heard what was said. *She's got a message through*. And that's the 'news for 'Rose' Noble which will not wait.'

"Very well. What will Rouse do? He'll clear out at once. Well, that's all right, but I don't think his car will start. He'll try to locate the trouble, and so will Bell – they're probably sweating blood now – but they'll only waste their time. And so Brother Rouse will have to take to the train. I think it more than likely that Bell will drive him to the station, for an Innsbruck train leaves Villach at a quarter to three. The same train leaves Crayern at a quarter past two, that is to say, in exactly ten minutes' time. So, if we're quick and that's the station ahead, we four shall travel together as far as Rouse wants to go.

"Now it's all very well to make plans for somebody else. I think Rouse will start right away and I think he will take this train. But Rowley will be on the platform to see if he does. If he doesn't, look out for a flash from Rowley's torch. If, as the train moves out, we see a flash, we leave the train at the next station: and there we shall find Carson waiting to bring us home. If we don't get out, he'll follow the train along, calling at every station until he finds one of us waiting to pick him up.

"Well, there you are. I've set my trap and I've tried to look ahead. I'd have given a very great deal to have your counsel, but I dared not tell you that Rouse was 'Rose' Noble's man."

"Thank God you didn't," said Hanbury. "I couldn't have played the hand to save my life."

"I covet his nerve," said I.

"You may well do that," said Mansel. "Look at that – those flowers. Of course it made you suspect him, but he had you back in your place by eight the next day."

By now we had come to the station, and ten minutes later we had our tickets for Innsbruck and were aboard the train.

As luck would have it, there was a sleeping car; and, as this was nearly empty, we were able to buy a compartment which held three beds. Comfort apart, this would save us no end of trouble, for now we could lock ourselves in and put out the light. To insure against interference, we told the attendant to make our beds at once and on no account to disturb us till Innsbruck was reached.

He was a talkative fellow and proud of what English he had, and I was soon in a fever lest we should come to Villach before the beds were made: indeed, as the minutes went by, I could hardly sit still, but at last he had set all to his liking and wished us goodnight.

Two minutes later the train began to slow down.

"Draw the blinds," said Mansel, "because of the station lamps."

When we had done so, he took his stand by the window and Hanbury put out the light.

As the train drew into the station, we stood as still as death, and to this day I remember every sound.

From the resonance of all noise, I judged the station empty, except for those on duty and a handful of freight. There was no haste or clamour, and, if passengers came or went, they gave no sign. After a little, a gong clanged five or six times, and a moment later somebody slammed a door. Then the guard, I suppose, wound a horn, the engine whistled in answer and the train began to move.

As Mansel was lifting the blind—

"I must be alone," said Rouse.

I think we all started.

"Orright, orright," said the attendant.

The voices came from the corridor outside our door.

Mansel stood like a statue, with the blind half raised in his hand.

"Well, get a move on," said Rouse. "I'm pretty tired. *What time do we get to Lass?*"

Then the two passed on down the passage, and we could hear no more.

It was safe enough now to move and to switch on the light: yet we did neither, but continued to stand breathless, each of us busy with his thoughts.

For those of Hanbury and Mansel I cannot answer, but I know that I was thinking neither of what was before us nor of the secret which Mansel had so brilliantly won. I was thinking how the tone of a man's voice may show the colour of his heart: for the voice was Rouse's voice, but the tone was that of a harsh and evil man.

At length Mansel let the blind go and asked me to switch on the light.

A short study of the map suggested that we should reach Lass not later than six o'clock. The place lay fifty miles from Innsbruck and was either a fair-sized village or a very small town. The country about was highly mountainous.

It was then arranged that each should watch for one hour, while the others slept. I was to take the first watch, and Mansel the last; "although," said he, "I think that may be a short one, for, before we get to Lass we must settle one or two things. Still, I shall begin to get pensive at five o'clock, and so, if you two don't mind, I'll sleep till then."

Then the light was put out, and he and George lay down, whilst I sat still by the window, to watch the landscape go by, very fair and peaceful and, under the rule of the moonlight, like an enchanted land.

When Mansel waked us, I found to my surprise that it was half past six, but it seemed that at some small station we had waited nearly an hour, because of some disorder a few miles ahead.

"Which is all to the good," said Mansel, "for now, when we get to Lass, there will be more people about and we ought to be able to follow without being seen."

Then he arranged that, until Rouse was off the platform, we should not leave the train, and that, once outside the station, we should immediately disperse: we were then to ignore one another and each in his own way contrive to keep Rouse in view. I was not to follow for more than a quarter of a mile, but was then to return to the station and wait for Carson to come.

Rough as were these proposals, I believe they would have wholly succeeded, had not Fortune served us a very ill turn: for Rouse left the train as casually as though he travelled to Lass every day of his life and made his way out of the station without, so far as I saw, once looking behind.

He paused outside for a moment, to light a cigarette, and then started down the short road which served the station alone. The road was planted with lime trees six paces apart, and, as he walked down the middle, we had but to keep to the path to be out of his view. Mansel and I took the left path, and Hanbury the right.

All of a sudden, Mansel who was leading, stopped dead.

I instantly looked at Rouse, still sauntering carelessly on, with his head in the air, *as yet completely unconscious of the two Rolls stealing towards him, perhaps fifty paces away.*

In a flash I knew what had happened.

The delay on the line had put a spoke in our wheel, and Carson, with Bell behind him, had caught up the train.

Even as I looked, my gentleman saw the two cars.

For an instant he faltered. Then he glanced over his shoulder and walked straight on.

As they approached, he spread out ridiculous arms, and, when Carson stopped, he stepped abreast of the car and engaged him in talk, laughing and stamping and stooping and slapping his thighs, as though he found the encounter a matter of infinite jest, and completely ignoring the approach of a small motor bus. This had met our train, in the hope, I suppose, of custom for some hotel, and, the hope proving vain, was at last going empty away.

Of the little road the Rolls took more than its share, and, since Rouse with his antics occupied all that was left, the bus could not have gone by without running him down. This it very nearly did, for its driver did not seem to believe that the man would not budge: but, in spite of all manner of warnings, Rouse held his ground to the last, so that the driver was forced to clap on his brakes and actually lock his wheels to let the other get clear. Some argument followed, and this seemed natural enough; but, before it was over, Rouse took his seat by the driver and under the eyes of us all was rapidly driven away.

Maybe we were fools, but the thing was cleverly done.

The cars were facing the station and were far too long to be at all quickly turned: the town lay five hundred yards distant, and no other car was in sight.

Too late Rowley leapt from his seat and flung up the road, in a vain endeavour to mount the bus from behind: too late Carson spurted for the station, to turn in the yard: only, as the bus disappeared, a figure flashed out of the lime trees and into its dust. This was Hanbury: and, since Rouse could not have known that he was behind, I think we all had some hope that he might be able by his speed to pull the unfortunate business out of the fire.

I do not mean to submit that we had cause for complaint. If Adèle was not lying at Lass, she was in the neighbourhood: our quest, from being desperate, had become full of promise; and we had passed, so to speak, at one stride into the running. Yet, but for the train's delay, we might well have been led clean up to the prison gates and, taking 'Rose' Noble unawares, have had his prisoner out *before he knew we were there*. And there was the rub. To have lost Rouse was tiresome: to have shown him that we were at Lass, and that in full force, was nothing less than a disaster. There is an old saying that a miss is as good as a mile; but, unless we could overtake Rouse *without his knowledge*, we were like to lose half the ground we had been at such pains to win.

Such thoughts and the like slid into and out of my mind, as the cars went about in the yard and, waiting a favourable moment, I boarded the second and took my seat by Bell.

Only pausing to take up Rowley, we tore after Mansel and Carson, now well under way.

Had the town lain further away, we must have come up with the bus, but the road this had taken was crooked and after a quarter of a mile ran into the streets. These were as narrow and faithless as any I know, for almost at once Carson was in a blind alley, and, though I saw his mistake in time to save Bell, the way we took brought us into a miniature market and left us there to get out as best we could.

At once I jumped out of the car and, calling to Bell to follow, began to run back. A passage presenting itself, I took this at once, in the hope of striking that quarter which we had failed to find, but, though it led into a street, I had to turn right or left, whereas, to my way of thinking, I needed to hold straight on. I ran to the right and turned up the first street I saw, but this curled round in a hoop, and, as soon as I had the chance, I turned again.

It follows that within five minutes I knew neither where I was nor how I had come, and, since I could speak no German, I had no means of obtaining any direction. Bell I must have outrun, for he was not to be seen.

Now why I called Bell to follow, instead of Rowley, I never can tell: it was against all reason, for Bell could handle the Rolls, but Rowley could not, and we had left the car so blocking the jaws of the market that nothing could come or go. It was, indeed, so unnatural a mistake to have made that I have often wondered whether Providence itself did not put his name into my mouth, for, had I called Rowley instead, we should have lost a chance which would not have come again.

I had walked for another five minutes, without result, and was standing at a corner, where a very ancient fountain was playing behind a grill, wondering which way to take and thinking how childish it was to be lost in a town the size of St. James's Park, when a soft, green fig fell suddenly down at my feet. I at once looked up and around, to see Hanbury's face at a window and Bell's behind.

As our eyes met, George beckoned to me to come up, but, before I could give any sign, they had disappeared.

The window at which I had seen them was that of a handsome oriel, serving a fine, old house, which must once, I think, have lodged persons of high degree, for a coat of arms had been cut above the doorway and each of the oriel's corbels was charged with some device. The floor below was now used as a bookseller's shop, and little but the doorway remained to show what it had been.

I immediately crossed the street and entered the shop, when an old man at once came forward and, using very fair English, inquired of what service he could be. Before I could answer, Bell came from behind a bookcase and said that I was a friend, whereupon I was ushered upstairs without a word.

A moment later we entered a handsome room, more than half of which was loaded with books, while the hither or oriel end was curtained off and made an agreeable parlour, full of light.

George was sitting on a table, gazing out of the window from which he had beckoned me up: this was commanding a close, at the corner of which played the fountain by which I had stood.

"Bill," said George, "where's Mansel?"

"God knows," said I. "Where's Rouse?"

"Down in that close," said George. "He went into one of those houses, but I've no idea which."

"How on earth did you do it?" said I, clapping him on the back.

"I don't know," said George. "I couldn't stand up when I got here, but just fell down in the shop. The old fellow was quite upset. By the grape of God he speaks English, and, when I could breathe, I pointed to *Alison's Europe* and asked him how much it was. He said 'Two pounds – English money.' So I said I'd give him five if he'd let me sit up in this window as long as I pleased. He threw the figs in, but don't touch them – they're the only munitions I've got. And not everyone stands by that fountain: I had to throw three at Bell. And now what's to be done? I know how to hurry, but I look to you for the brains."

Standing well back from the window, I stared at the close.

How many houses there were I could not tell, for they were irregularly built and several were overhung: but the close was shallow – a bare fifty paces in depth, with a heavily timbered mansion blocking the farther end. The place was plainly most aged and would have been a feature of any city I know, but Lass was so old and curious and had been so little touched that the close was no more than in keeping with the rest of the town.

"I think one thing is certain," said I, "that Adèle is not in this town: it's much too busy for 'Rose' Noble. Rouse has gone to ground in some house of call – some lodging or other they've taken down in that close. And, unless there's a back way out,

I don't think he'll leave before dark. If I am right and the house is a meeting-place, there's no reason why he should, for he can send word to 'Rose' Noble by someone we've never seen."

"That's encouraging," said Hanbury. "Not that it seems a very popular walk: only five people have used it since I've been here. But it's early yet and – well, there's a man coming now. He doesn't look very likely, but then they never do."

"I don't see what we can do," said I, "until we know which is the house. You can't run after a man just because he comes out of that close. It's suspicious, of course, but we're only six, all told, and, until we've got more to go on—"

"Sir," said Bell, "that's the man. *He was on the quay at Dieppe.*"

# IV

## THE CASTLE OF GATH

There was no time to make any plan.

The man was walking fast, and, as I have shown, Lass was no better than a maze.

With one consent, the three of us rushed to the door, and, while Hanbury was speaking the bookseller, Bell and I stepped directly into the street.

Mercifully a cart was standing not six feet away, and as we darted behind it, I saw that we had before us the very deuce of a task. The man was, of course, on his guard and knew us by sight: the hour was early, and, though the shops were open – because, I suppose, it was Market day – there were not twenty people in view: yet, had the street been crowded, our dress was fatally distinctive and had only to be seen to betray us and our design.

In a flash I had my coat off and had flung it into the cart. I pitched my hat after it, rolled my sleeves to the elbow and, seizing a sack of refuse, which was standing open-mouthed on the kerb, swung this on to my shoulder and started, bent double, down the street. I know the disguise was feeble, but I dared wait no more; and that was as well, for, before I had taken five steps, the man glanced over his shoulder and turned to the left.

We had now a stroke of good fortune, without which I cannot believe that we should have got very far, for it gave us a breathing-space and let me fall back a little and Hanbury and Bell come up.

I had hardly come to the corner, when I saw the fellow enter a tobacconist's shop.

At once I turned to see Hanbury close behind. He was wearing a black overcoat, green with age, and the bookseller's hat, which came down over his ears. In his hands was a newspaper, open as though to be read.

"Watch the tobacconist's," I said, and dashed between two houses to tear off my collar and tie.

As I returned a man passed, wheeling a bicycle. His form seemed familiar, and, when I looked at him again, I saw that it was Bell. He had no coat, hat or collar; his trousers were clipped at the ankle and seemed to be falling down; his face and hands were filthy beyond compare. He glanced down the street on his left, and, there, I suppose, seeing Hanbury, picked up his cue and turned.

As I came again to the corner, our man came out of his shop. For a moment he looked about, him, but seeing, I imagine, nothing at all suspicious, presently turned on his heel and went his way.

He was a tall, loose-limbed fellow, with a pasty face: he walked as though he liked the look of himself and wore his hat cocked on one side: and, since I presently learned that he was called 'Casemate,' from now on I will speak of him by name.

I was slouching along behind him, still shouldering my sack, very conscious of my respectability and full of admiration for Bell, when I saw a crowd gathered ahead, where the street bellied into a place in front of a church. This seemed to interest Casemate, for all his haste, for I saw him peering to see what the matter might be; but, when he was nearer, he suddenly turned away and passed by on the opposite pavement, with his eyes on the ground.

I was wondering at his behaviour, when the crowd began to move and then fall away Then I saw a familiar bonnet and Mansel, with Rowley beside him, driving a Rolls. Behind came Carson.

Now such a meeting was more than I could have hoped for, for I had been racking my brain for some way in which to find Mansel and tell him what was afoot. Yet, though we were so happily met, I dared make no sign, for Casemate had his chin on his shoulder, and I could not have caught Mansel's eye without catching his.

Going as slowly as I dared, with the tail of my eye I watched the car draw abreast; but the crowd was about her wings, and Mansel never looked up. I could have stamped for vexation, for Hanbury was shuffling upon the far side of the street, and Bell was already by. Then Carson cried out a warning and I heard a clatter and crash. Bell had wheeled his bicycle into the second car.

As he picked himself up, I heard Mansel asking for news.

"It's all right, sir," said Carson: "a cyclist – " Bell gave him a malignant look – "a cyclist walked into the car. And, excuse me, sir, but you're rather down on the right. *I think you must have broken a spring.*"

That was as much as I heard and all that I wanted to know, for, if, when upon the road, one of us wished to say something which was not for everyone's ears, he had but to state that the car before or behind him had broken a spring; such a statement would naturally call for investigation, and, while this was being conducted, the communication could be easily made.

Now all this was well enough, but, when I returned to Casemate, I saw that he had stopped and was standing under an archway, with his eyes on the two cars and a hand to his mouth.

For a moment my brain faltered. I dared not dally, and the last thing I wanted to do was to overtake the man. He had but to dwell upon my clothes to find them strange, and to walk with his eyes upon my back would be the way of a fool. Then I saw a garage before me and, without so much as blinking, I plodded in.

An engine was running, and two mechanics were busy about its head. As I came in, one lighted a cigarette and pitched the match still flaming, on to the floor. There must have been petrol there, for flames leapt up. As the fellow stood staring, I shot my sack of refuse on to the fire, and a moment later the three of us stamped it out.

Both seemed very grateful and clapped me upon the back. This goodwill was just what I wanted, and after an age of dumbshow, the taller of the two took off his dirty overalls and helped me to put them on. I gave him far more than they were worth and I think this satisfied them that I was in fear of the police: and, when I plunged my hands into a tray of old oil, wiped them upon my sleeves and smeared these across my face, I am sure they no longer doubted that a warrant was out for my arrest. Still, with my sack of refuse, I had done them a very good turn, and, though they looked none too easy, they shook me by the hand when I went and gave me a cigarette.

At first I could not see Casemate. Then I saw him striding along fifty yards off. He was just passing Bell, who was pumping up one of his tires, and Hanbury was shuffling along twenty paces behind. Mansel and the two cars were gone.

I was now much easier in my mind and followed with confidence, for my greasy suit had given me a new lease of life, and the thought that Mansel was soon to be in the background did my heart good.

Casemate went down to a river and over an arched, stone bridge. This was in the midst of the town, and here for the first time I was able to see about me and to mark the lie of the land.

Lass lay in a trough of the mountains, the wooded slopes of which pressed close upon every side: the approaches to the town were hidden, and even the railway line was not to be seen. I have known villages so bound, but never another town, and the dignity of spires and gables so landlocked was very pleasing. Yet, as I have said, I was sure that Adèle was not here, and, when Casemate soon took a way which ran out of the town, to curl out of sight between two beetling woods, I was not at all surprised.

That here, however, we three must make ourselves scarce was obvious enough, for, if the streets had been idle, except for a labouring waggon the road to come was bare. And, while I was thinking how we should bring this about, the thing was done.

Bell mounted his bicycle, slowly overtook Casemate and passed out of sight: Hanbury turned up a passage which seemed to lead to the woods: and I was left. As plainly as though they had spoken, they meant me to bring up the rear.

The manoeuvre was sound and perfectly carried out: I was filled with admiration for Hanbury and Bell: but the burden of Casemate's suspicion was now thrown full upon me, and I was by no means certain that I could carry the weight. I had no cover: mechanics are seldom seen tramping a country road: no man or beast seemed to be going our way.

I continued to walk on slowly, watching Casemate approach the bend and racking my brain. As he turned, he hung on his heel, and after a long look behind him, passed out of view.

My fears now came to a head, and I dared not go on. I was sure the fellow was waiting for me to come up. Yet I dared not stop without reason, nor, without reason, disappear. Then I saw a café beside me, with a table outside its door...

As they brought me wine and cigarettes, I saw Casemate's head appear round the bend of the road.

How long he watched me I do not know, for I dared not look again at the bend until I had drunk my wine: but, when at last I threw it a careless glance, he was out of sight.

At once I left the café and took to the road.

Ten minutes went by before I saw Casemate again, for the way was a natural pass and humoured every whim of the mountains, rising and falling and twisting as these decreed. Indeed, I was afraid I had lost him and was on the point of breaking into a run, when I rounded a corner to see him ten paces away. I drew back at once out of sight, but the encounter shocked me, for it showed how unfitted I was for such an exercise.

But worse was to come.

I had gone, I suppose, a mile in fear and trembling, and the road had begun to rise in a steady climb, when I peered round a bend, to see Casemate *retracing his steps*.

Now I had just covered a fairly long, straight reach of road, and, before I could have retreated, he would have had me in view. This was plainly the reason why he had gone about, for, if he was being followed, here was the very place to discover his man.

Frantically I looked round for cover, but there was none at all. On one hand an open meadow fell down abruptly to the level the road had left: on the other a high bank of earth rose into a crumbling cornice that overhung the way. Only an oak leaned out of the earthy wall and was thrusting a branch like a roof-tree over the road.

I am a tall man, but heavy, and to this day I cannot tell how I managed to leap so high: but, if I am heavy, I was desperate, and, as I have found before, desperation is a remarkable goad.

Be that as it may, in an instant I had hold of the bough and a moment later was astride it, looking down upon the ground. I then fell forward and cautiously raised my feet, till I was lying along it and, though there was little foliage, pretty well hid. The branch was massive and rigid as any rock.

Casemate rounded the corner and passed below where I hung. Finding the road deserted, he stopped in his tracks and, after a long look, turned on his heel and began to walk back up the hill, whistling some air as he went. He paused for a moment beneath me, to take out a cigarette, and, as he did so, we both heard the sound of the horn of an oncoming car.

Now this meant nothing to me, for the horn was that of some car which was going to Lass, but Casemate stiffened like a pointer and stood with his ears pricked and a match in one of his hands and its box in the other. Indeed, so concerned was his demeanour, that I expected him every instant to take to his heels, though why he should fear some car which could hardly be one of ours I could not think.

The horn was not sounded again, but soon we heard a car coming at a high enough speed.

Casemate immediately whipped to the side of the road, and, taking his stand by the bend, peered anxiously round. The next moment he was out in the fairway, spreading and waving his arms as a signal to stop.

I heard the brakes clapped on, but the car was round the corner before it had come to rest.

Casemate came running back, and somebody put out a head.

"What is it?" said 'Rose' Noble.

I was so much dumbfounded that I nearly fell down from the bough, and then I saw that the luck I had found so unkind a moment ago was playing clean into our hands.

"Somebody's talking," said Casemate. "She's got word through to mother, and Big Willie's at Lass."

There was a moment's silence.

Then—

"How d'you know?" said 'Rose' Noble.

"Jute," said Casemate. "Last night they came for Big Willie and told him that she had made touch. Jute heard them say so.

Big Willie was off like a cracker, and, when he was good and gone, Jute slipped up to the station and took the train."

"*And led him to Lass,*" said 'Rose' Noble. "Go on."

"B – but—"

"Go *on.*"

"He's there," said Casemate doggedly. "I've seen him. Stuck up in the streets, with a Punch-and-Judy crowd round both of his cars."

"Where's Jute?"

"Lying low in the lodge."

"Thought he'd done enough harm, I suppose?"

"He didn't bring him," said Casemate. "Big Willie's—"

"Of course he brought him," roared 'Rose' Noble, bursting out of the car. "You snake-faced idiot, what do you take me for? 'Got word through to mother.' This isn't Marlborough Street." He slammed the door with a fury that shook the car. "By—," he added, using a dreadful oath, "wait till I get at Jute. I told him they'd try to bounce him and I made him swear never to move when Big Willie was out of sight. *Never.* Why did he come by train?"

"Car wouldn't start," said Casemate.

"And *that* never showed him?" raged 'Rose' Noble.

Casemate essayed no answer, but only stared upon the ground, plainly resenting a trouncing which Jute had won, yet sullenly conscious that, by adopting Jute's reading, he had put himself out of court.

'Rose' Noble ripped off his hat and mopped his face.

"Who was with Big Willie?" he demanded.

"Two of the servants," said Casemate.

For a moment 'Rose' Noble stood still, with his head in the air. Then he lowered his eyes and looked at Casemate.

I suppose there was that in his gaze which shocked the other, for he shrank back against the wall, protesting the truth of his words.

"Quite right," purred 'Rose' Noble, "quite right. You only saw two of the servants. *I passed the third on the road five minutes ago.*"

A moment later the car was being turned round.

I think this short colloquy must show how fine and swift a brain our principal enemy had. No matter how clogged, he had the truth free in an instant, and, though, when he passed him, he had not recognized Bell – and for that he can hardly be blamed, for he had seen him but once – the moment he learned that one servant was not with Mansel, he knew why the dirty cyclist was taking his subordinate's road. That he made no mention at all of Hanbury or me, was, I confess, a considerable blow to my pride, but I fear he credited us with little cunning, but only a blunt pugnacity when it came to a fight.

Now whether this stung into action my mother wit I cannot say, but I know that, as he and Casemate entered the car, I saw at my feet a chance which never would come again.

The car was closed, and its canopy was fixed: the road was narrow, and, in his endeavours to turn, the driver was bringing his charge directly below where I hung. For me to alight on its roof was the easiest thing in the world, and, once I was there, lying flat, although there was no luggage-rail, I could grip the canopy's edge above the driver, for a shield, which is called a 'sun-visor,' was there to conceal my hands.

In a flash I was sitting sideways upon the bough, and, as the car came back for the last time, I stepped gingerly on to its roof, trusting to my rubber-soled shoes to make no noise. I was flat in an instant, or the branch would have knocked me down, and a moment later I had fast hold of the rim which was to keep me steady and save me from sliding off.

As the car thrust forward—

"Bunch," said 'Rose' Noble to the driver, "if you see that cyclist, run him down."

"You bet," said Bunch, and put the car at the hill with the rush of a bull.

I was not much alarmed for Bell's safety, for I was quite certain that he had observed 'Rose' Noble and, if he was yet upon the road, had only to hear the car coming to disappear. Indeed, I had my work cut out to think for myself, for the road was none too even and I was mortally afraid of losing my place.

Bunch was a good driver and swooped at his corners in a spectacular way, but, whenever he swung the car round, I had to fight like a madman to stay where I was, and if the fowls of the air have a sense of humour my progress must have afforded them infinite mirth. Except for one sharp descent, our road continued to rise or to keep the height it had won; and so far as I can remember we met no other vehicle. Two or three peasants passed, and the sight of them staring at me sent my heart to my mouth; but no one of those in the car seemed to notice their gaze, or, if they did, to find it curious.

At last we came to cross roads, where we turned to the right, and very soon after, we left the road for a drive which led into a wood so artlessly and was so shrouded with moss and the litter the trees had made that a man might have passed it by, as promising nothing at all. Yet in less than two minutes of time the wood was behind us, and we were heading for a castle which seemed to me to command all the kingdoms of the earth.

We were now upon the spur of a mountain, and, I judged, some three thousand feet up. The drive ran straight down the spur, the sides of which were plainly precipitous, for, after a little, the turf which flanked the drive fell suddenly out of sight. The whole of the end of the spur was masked by the castle's facade, and it was easy to see that the building had been set on the spur as the nail upon a man's finger, that is to say, moated on three of its sides by God knows what depths and accessible only on the fourth.

The walls were high and massive, rose into battlements and looked as good as new; and the place had an air of being old rather than ancient and more of an aerie than a keep. It was clearly inhabited, for there were blinds in its windows and smoke was rising from some chimney I could not see. Indeed, I could see nothing beyond the great facade, except a crocketed spire which stood up on the left. A stout, round tower rose at each end of the wall: these were corniced and had red, conical roofs: in the midst of the wall was a gateway, the great doors of which were shut.

I was now trembling with excitement, for the castle, of course, was the goal to which we had been trying to come, but what carried me away was the knowledge that I was about to be landed within its walls. Once I was in, and my presence unsuspected, who could tell what might not come about?

A yard or so from the gateway Bunch brought the car to rest. As he did so, his passengers alighted and passed at once to a wicket, cut out of the left-hand door. Then a bell clanged, and almost at once I heard steps. There was a grill in the wicket, and somebody drew its shutter to look between its bars. Whoever it was must have seen me, had not 'Rose' Noble's head been in the way.

"All right?" I heard him say.

"O.K.," said the other, and opened the little door. 'Rose' Noble and Casemate passed in.

Now, as soon as the car had stopped, I had moved as far as I could to the right of the canopy, so as to make the most of what cover I had: whether I moved again was depending on where the man stood who admitted the car. With one of the great doors set wide the car could pass in, and, if, as I fully expected, the left-hand door was opened, the porter was sure to hold it and I should be out of his sight.

Now so much fell out very well. Only one door was opened, and that was the left: I saw the hands of the porter pulling it back: *but the door had been made in two halves, and, while the lower swung open, the upper stayed fast.*

The car was about to pass in – *with three inches of headroom to spare*, and, if I stayed on her roof, I should be swept off or crushed – probably crushed.

Had I not been on the edge, I must have been badly hurt, for Bunch thrust forward, as though he knew I was there.

I got to my knees and jumped as best I could.

Happily I lit upon turf, but this sloped down from the drive, and I tumbled, like a clown in the sawdust, before I could bring myself up. As I did so, I heard the door shut and the bolts shot home.

To report to Mansel was plainly the first thing to do: and, since anyone at a window could have shot me down, I got to my feet and started to run for the wood. Except that I was shaken, I felt none the worse for my fall; and here I think I was lucky, for I had leapt blindly and had not taken off clean.

Halfway to the wood I rested behind a tree and looked about me.

The prospect was magnificent indeed: all around were mountains and forests, rising and falling as far as the eye could see, and, the sky being very blue and the sunshine brilliant, the castle looked fabulous, and a man that came suddenly upon it might well have been forgiven for rubbing his eyes.

How 'Rose' Noble had come to be so installed I could not think, but, had he spent his life searching, he could not have found a prison one half so suitable. The place was solitary and most secure: no cries could be heard, nor any signals seen: the one approach was hidden, and such as found it could not conceal their coming, for there were not six trees on the spur and the wood lay two hundred yards from the castle wall.

This reflection made me take to my heels, for, if I could withdraw unseen, that would be a point in our favour, and we had none to spare. Indeed, when I thought of those walls my spirits sank, and remembering how near I had come to passing in, I could have struck myself. What was worse, I was sure that, had he been placed as I, Mansel would somehow have done it and not have let slip a chance which surely was gone for good.

So I came to the wood, and, after watching for some time for any sort of sign that I had been seen, made my way down the drive as fast as I could.

Twenty minutes later I reached the cross roads.

There to my great surprise, Rowley rose out of a ditch and said that Mansel was waiting a stone's throw away. Then he told me which way to take, and a moment later I saw the two cars below me and Mansel and George poring over a paper book, whilst Carson was feeding Tester and Bell was washing his face in a little rill.

They seemed very glad to see me and most eager to hear my news.

I told my tale.

When I had finished, Mansel put a hand on my arm.

"William," he said, "she will thank you. I haven't got the words. But please don't count it bad luck that you were shut out. If you had gone in, you'd have made a fatal mistake. Alone, unarmed and with no idea of the building, you wouldn't have stood an earthly: and, what would have been far worse, *we shouldn't have known where you were.*"

"But – "

"There is no 'but' here," said Mansel. "You've played and you've won your game: but, if you'd gone on, you'd have thrown the rubber away. Do please remember that battles have gone wrong, wars have been lost and the history of the world has been changed, because valour has outrun discretion and *men have lost touch.*"

It was easy enough to see the force of his words, and I have often thought since that the ways of Providence are strange indeed, for, if Casemate had not turned back, I should not have hung in the oak, and, if the castle door had not been cut asunder, I am sure that I should not have lived to tell this tale.

Then Mansel told me that Bell had seen 'Rose' Noble go by and had followed him down; that George and Bell had both seen me on the roof of the car and, while George had pushed on to the cross roads, Bell had raced back to meet Mansel and bring up the cars.

"And now," said he, "to breakfast. I picked up some food at Lass. And you'll be glad of a wash. And as soon as ever we've done, I want you to show us around."

Whilst we were eating, we decided that Mansel and George and I should go out on foot, that one servant should watch the cross roads and the others stay with the cars until we returned. If one of the enemy passed he was not to be stopped or followed, but only marked, "for," said Mansel, "Mr Chandos has done the trick, and we don't want to start a new hare till we know where we are. Of course, if 'Rose' Noble comes by, you will shoot him at sight: but, unless I'm much mistaken, he won't come out any more."

With that, he told Carson and Bell to serve out a pistol apiece, and, when this was done, he and George and I set out for the wood.

As we went I asked what was the book which I had found them reading when I came in.

George pulled it out of his pocket and held it up.

"Souvenir," he said. "When I gave the bookseller his money and borrowed his plumes, he pressed this into my hand. He had a speech ready, I fear, but, beyond that he was the author, I have no idea what he said. Whilst I was waiting at the cross roads I looked to see what it was. It's a guide in English to Lass and the neighbourhood. The grammar's unequal, but, if I could write half as good a guide in German, I should be more than pleased. And it's got a good plan of Lass and a couple of maps."

We said no more at that time, for we were approaching the wood.

This we afterwards found was nearly a mile across, by some half a mile in depth. The drive which led to the spur went to the heart of the thicket and there turned sharp to the left: from there it ran slightly up hill to the edge of the wood and then directly down to the castle gate. It follows that, from anyone walking, the spur and the castle were hidden till he came to the edge of the wood, but then burst upon him in an instant, as though some curtain had suddenly been let fall.

Before we breasted the rise, for caution's sake we had stepped in among the trees, and, when I had parted the branches and Mansel and George had come up, I heard the one catch his breath, while the other stood staring like a zany upon the remarkable scene.

Presently we moved to a knoll and lay down behind its swell.

The spur was empty, and the castle walls bare as I had left them: only the smoke I had noticed gave any sign of life.

"Where's that guide?" said Mansel suddenly. "See if it mentions this place."

Hanbury had the book in an instant and was studying one of its maps.

"Gath," he said, after a moment. "This should be the Castle of Gath. And now for the text."

Hastily he scanned the pages.

Then he bent the book open and gave it into Mansel's hand.

And, since I cannot better the bookseller's description of the place, I will set it down word for word.

## THE CASTLES OF GATH

*Few peoples know of this castles, because great care was taken from at first that it must be most private and for a long time it was not mark on the state maps.*

*Gath was builted in the end of the fifteenth century by the great King Maximilian, Holy Roman Emperor, 'The Last of the Knights,' as he is named by his proud loving subjects, so as to be a tranquil castles where he can retire to rest sometimes from the cares of reign. It was always kept in readiness to receive him and a small suite.*

*The visitor who will go the seven miles according to the plan of the page 7 will be handsomely rewarded, for the site is unique and the building is posed on the brink of a mountain and seems to be a veritable 'castles in the air.' It is easy to believe that the great King was happy to stay here during his short respites and in the company of a few trusteds retainers to find peace and refreshment, not to be said inspirations for future glory.*

*But if one has found it so fine to see from afar, it will be a pity not to visit the interior. This may be done on Wednesdays and Saturdays between two and four o'clock by permission of the present owner. Count— of—.*

*The visiting of the apartments is made under the custody of a caretakers who fulfils intelligence with curtesy.*

*We now enter by a deep archway into a fine courtyard, with a waterbason in its midst. A spring rises in the bason and flows in a cascade through the courtyard and under a smaller archway. Let us follow it. Lo, we are in a pretty terrace, where flowers blow, and running all of the length of the South of the Castles, not counting the round tower at each end. Here we seem to be standing on the edge of some earth, for the green cliff falls down directly and the cascade curves over it like a bow. This is the water supplies of the Castles.*

*We now retrace our steps to the courtyard and ascend the Grand Staircase on the West. The first room is an antichamber, as the furniture suggests, for everything has been left in the State Apartments as when the great King died.*

*The following was the reception room of the King. The tapestries are notable.*

*From this we go into a gallery of stone. Here, no doubt, were guards when the King was there, for the gallery is at the corner of the courtyard and the King's apartments are about to begin. This gallery leads into the south-west tower, which is not shown and has been modernized, and another staircase goes down from it to the terrace where the flowers blow.*

*Now we come to the south front and the King's apartments. These are untoucheds.*

*The first is another antichamber.*

*Then we enter the royal dining-room. The tapestries are very fine. The visitor will observe that the room is not large because the King has not entertained a guest here.*

*We now pass into the King's Bedchamber. This is very stately. The crimson hangings of the magnificent bed and the superb furniture and tapestries, the richery of the polished woodcarvings all reflects the departed majesty of 'The Last of the Knights.'*

*The King's Closet comes next.*

*From this we enter the Queen's Bedchamber, which is like the King's, but, of course, less magnificence. The hangings are purple.*

*Then comes another day-chamber for the uses of the Queen, and we then enter an antichamber before passing into a stony gallery similar in all respects to the first.*

*The south-east tower is not shown.*

*Now we come to the oratory. There is a door and stairs going down from the oratory into the chapel. There are many shrines in the mountains, but not like this. It is still here always, in the midst of the storm. The glass in the panes is unquestionable and the finery of the woodcarving is beyond praise.*

*That is all that is shown.*

*The other part of the Castles have been modernized.*

*It is regretful that, since above written, the owner of Gath has lately died and there is a lawsuit for the possession of the Castles. Because of which the interior is not now shown.*

This admirable description we read all three together, Mansel holding the book and waiting, until we had finished, to turn a page.

When it was done, he looked up into the sky.

Presently he sighed.

"One has much to be thankful for," he said. And then, "Let's hope they let her walk on 'the pretty terrace, where flowers blow.'"

Hanbury and I said nothing, for, indeed, there was nothing to be said.

Presently Mansel spoke again.

"One thing stands out – any chance of a snap division, which we may have thought we had, can be written right off. If they thought we were still at Villach, it would be different: when your enemy's that far away, you're apt to be careless about keeping the door he can't enter and watching the wall he can't scale. But to rush a position like this when it's properly manned is quite impossible. Very well. There's only one thing to do, and that is to go on play-acting.

"If Chandos was not seen on the spur – and I think it unlikely that he was – 'Rose' Noble has a right to infer that when we came to the cross roads we didn't know which way to go. Well, he hasn't much use for inferences, and so I propose to prove to his satisfaction that this inference is a fact. We're going to forget about Gath, and we're going to scour the country for miles around. We shall take up our quarters at Lass, come to the cross roads at dawn and spend the whole of the day visiting villages and farms and combing the countryside. While we are doing this we shall take care to study Gath *from every side*.

That'll be easy enough. And tomorrow, to round the picture, we shall discover the castle and drive up and ring the bell. I don't imagine 'Rose' Noble will answer the door, but I'm sure that he'll be within earshot and I'd like him to hear what I say.

"And, if all goes well, two or three days later we'll call again. But this time we'll come by night, and I think we'll let the bell go."

For a little we lay there silent, digesting his words.

Then –

"At the moment," said I, "they've lost us. Doesn't it seem a pity to let them find us again?"

"Yes," said Mansel, "it does. But no man can have it both ways. So long as he's out of touch, 'Rose' Noble won't close an eye: and so long as his eyes are open, we shall never get into Gath. So far as I can see, one sentry is more than enough to watch those walls. Very well. Would you omit that precaution, when the last time you'd seen the enemy he was two miles away?"

Hanbury fingered his chin.

"How did 'Rose' Noble get there?" he said. "I mean, it's a private house."

Mansel shrugged his shoulders.

"I imagine he's bought the caretakers. It's often been done in London – in the good old days. And there it was dangerous: but here there's next to no risk. No neighbours to raise their eyebrows: seven miles from the nearest town: ownership in dispute, and no visitors allowed. Once he had found the place, it was too easy."

"I agree," said Hanbury. "And the greatest of these is 'ownership in dispute.' Supposing the disputants heard that the Castle of Gath was taking in paying guests."

"What then?" said Mansel.

"Well, wouldn't they take some action?"

"Of course they would," said Mansel. "But what action would they take?"

"I don't know," said Hanbury. "But— "

"Neither do I," said Mansel, "and there's the rub. If they'd let me take the action, well and good. But they'd never do that. If I pitched it in pretty strong, they'd probably come along with a couple of local police and a lawyer's clerk... And don't forget – whatever action was taken, 'Rose' Noble would know whom to thank. He'd know that I was behind it, and I'm frankly afraid to think what his answer would be. You see, 'the goods are perishable.' Because of that, *we must never let him see that the game is up. It's got to be up, before he sees that it's up... before he has time to hit back...*"

Half an hour later we were at the cross roads.

It was now eleven o'clock, and within a quarter of an hour our plans were laid.

For five miles about we were to prove the country, making no attempt at concealment and courting the observation of anyone watching from Gath: in this way, whilst appearing to search, we should gain such a knowledge of the district as might any moment be of the greatest use. In the course of our movements we were to visit two points from each of which it seemed likely that a man could look full upon Gath: these particular visits were, of course, to be surreptitiously made, and we hoped that they would help us to discover whether an endeavour to climb to the castle by the cliffs could possibly succeed.

Mansel and I would take one car, and Hanbury and Bell the other: each patrol was to go its own way, returning to the cross roads at sundown, en route for Lass.

Carson and Rowley, meanwhile, were to lie close in a wood and take their rest, "for tonight," said Mansel, "you two must drive to Poganec and take Captain Pleydell our news."

"How much shall you tell him?" said I, as we took to the car.

"Only where he can find me and that we know where she is."

Yet when the time came to send it, the note was longer than that.

It was half past three when Mansel and I began to ascend a mountain which we thought must command the castle and be commanded in turn. Its sides and peak were wooded, so we had little to fear. The Rolls we had left with Tester by the side of the way, and each of us carried a binocular of a considerable power.

At last we came to the summit, and almost at once we saw Gath, not directly opposed, but lying a little to the left, so that we could observe the whole of its south and east sides.

I could dwell upon its emplacement, but I should waste my words, for I have not the pen to hail a miracle, and that is what we saw.

Enough that the face of the cliff was 'produced' in the castle walls, and that Gath was the crown upon a crag that no man could ever scale.

So much the naked eye showed us.

It was the binoculars that showed us Adèle.

She was standing on the little terrace, with her hands on the balustrade. Whether she was watched I cannot say, but she was alone. Below her was the leaping cascade, and, behind, an archway, framing a door that was shut. She was standing very still; her head was up, and her eyes lifted to the peak upon which we stood.

Mansel tore off his wrist-watch, ripped its case open and thrust the watch into my hand.

"Flash it in the sun," he said, clapping the glasses to his eyes. "If she sees it, she'll understand."

The silver was bright as a mirror, and, while Mansel watched her, I twitched the case to and fro.

At last –

"She's seen it," he said. "Now flash it six times, and cover it up with your hand between each flash."

I did so.

"Now flash it once more," said Mansel. "And then cover up."

I did as he said.

After what seemed a long time –

"Flash it again," said he.

I did so: and, after a little, he told me to pocket the watch.

At last he put down his glasses and wiped the sweat from his face.

"She saw the signals," he said. "She raised her hand. When you had acknowledged her gesture, she turned away. She's – very wise."

"Has she gone?"

He nodded.

"She went up the staircase into the left-hand tower. And, after a moment, she showed some white at that window, halfway up. When you acknowledged that, she took it away. She's very wise – Adèle."

That was a true saying: only the quickest wit and the steadiest brain would ever have done so well. I think her heart must have leapt, but she took no needless risk. One wave of her hand, and then – straight to her quarters to show us where she was lodged. And that was all. She had no more to tell us, and the game was a dangerous one. The sooner it was done, the better for all concerned.

And here for the first time I saw how well and truly she and Mansel were matched. They were made of the same fine substance, a little higher than their fellows, and could speak a common language which others did not know. And, as Mansel and I lay there, on the edge of the great gulf fixed between us and Gath, I remember wondering whether, could she have done so, Adèle would have kept such letters as she had received from him.

At sundown we joined the others at the cross roads, and within the hour we sat down to supper at Lass.

When they had eaten, Carson and Rowley left for Poganec, taking a note with them.

This was brief, for Mansel was a man of few words.

*September 6th,*
*10 p.m.*

*I know where Adèle is confined and saw her today from a distance. She seemed to be well. I am glad to say that I managed to attract her attention, and she now knows that help is at hand. I have reason to think that she is comfortably lodged. If need be, I can be found at the Three Kings Hotel, Lass. Please destroy this note and communicate its contents to no one but Daphne and Berry alone.*

# V

# MANSEL TAKES OFF THE GLOVES

At ten o'clock the next morning Mansel, Carson and I visited the Castle of Gath.

From first to last this visit had been closely rehearsed, so that even a spy in the wood would not, I think, have suspected that we were play-acting.

Indeed, the play began some miles away, for we first seemed to notice the drive, as we were returning to the cross roads after a thirty-mile run. After due hesitation we determined to see whither it led...

At the sight of the Castle we stopped, as anyone would have done, and were plainly uncertain whether or no to proceed: but, after a little discussion, I drove the car down the spur and drew up before the gateway in a perfectly natural way. Then Carson opened a door, and Mansel got out.

When he had rung, he stood waiting, with a hand on the great stone jamb, while Carson, with his hands behind him stood leaning against a wing, and I pulled out tobacco and started to fill a pipe.

I shall never forget those moments or how hard it was to keep cool. Eyes were upon us, watching each breath we drew: it was likely that we were covered and certain that we were at the mercy of those we were seeking to dupe. What was about to happen, no one could tell. For once 'Rose' Noble was dealing, and, whatever the cards he dealt us, with those we should have to play.

The day was very fine, and a gentle breeze was blowing across the spur: except for the whisper of the engine, there was no sound: and I remember thinking how gay the greenwood looked in the brave sunshine and how black the clean-cut shadow which the battlements threw upon the turf.

After a little, Mansel rang again.

For an age we waited: then I heard a step on the pavement and the click of a lock. Then two bolts were drawn, the wicket swung open, and a woman put out her head.

"Goodday," said Mansel, using German. "What's the name of this place?"

"The Castle of Gath, sir."

"Who lives here?"

"No one, sir. My husband and I are the caretakers."

"D'you know if it's for sale?"

The woman shook her head.

"It's not for sale, sir."

"Which is the castle hereabouts which is for sale?"

"I have no idea, sir."

"Well, there's one somewhere," said Mansel, "not very far from here. It belongs to an English lady, who's out of her mind. She drives about in a car without any hat, and she has male nurses with her wherever she goes. Surely you've heard her spoken of?"

"No, sir," said the woman, evenly.

"A big, closed car, painted grey. Sometimes the nurses use it when she is ill."

The woman shook her head.

"You surprise me," said Mansel. "It's common talk down in Lass."

The woman shrugged her shoulders.

"In Lass, perhaps, but we are so isolated here."

"I wonder if your husband could help me."

"I fear he is out, sir. But I do not think he would know."

"Which way has he gone?" said Mansel.

The woman mentioned a hamlet four miles away.

"Perhaps I shall meet him," said Mansel. "But ask him about this grey car when he comes in."

"I will, sir."

"And the castle, or house, somewhere round about here. And, if he thinks he can help me, send him to The Three Kings at Lass."

"I will, sir."

Mansel gave her money and returned to the car.

"Nothing doing," he said shortly. "I was afraid it was useless. Too much off the beaten track."

As he spoke, the wicket was shut, and the bolts were shot.

"Let's have a look at the map," said Mansel.

I gave him the sheet.

As I did so, the sharp clack of wood striking wood came from the door. We all looked round – naturally enough. *Someone had drawn the shutter which masked the grill.* No doubt they would have done so in silence; but the shutter, I suppose, resisted, and then gave way with a rush.

Mansel laughed.

"Seeing us off the premises," he said. He returned to the map. "There's the village she spoke of: we might as well go that way." He began to fold up the map and turned to the door. "By the way," he said, using German, "was your husband on foot?"

As he spoke, he stepped to the grill, pocketing the map as he went.

No answer was given.

With his hand in his pocket, Mansel peered through the bars.

"I say," he said. "My good lady..."

No one replied.

"Come on," said I. "She's scared."

Mansel took his hand from his pocket and turned away.

"That's the worst of these people," he said. "No sense, no observation and an inherent fear that you're trying to do them down."

With that, he got into the car.

Carson followed, and I drove slowly away. Not until we were five miles off did Mansel open his mouth.

"'Rose' Noble was there all the time. On the woman's left. He was standing with his back to the doors, with his arms folded and a pistol in his right hand. I could see him in the glass of a lantern that hangs from the archway roof: its sides were tilted, and it couldn't have been better placed.

"It was he that drew the shutter and stood looking out: that's an assumption, of course; but I'm sure it's correct. I went back in the hope that he'd stay there – to, laugh in my face. But he very properly didn't. He resisted a great temptation and thereby saved his life. He wouldn't have expected a bullet, and I don't think I could have missed. When he saw me coming, he stooped. If he'd moved, I should have heard him: so he stood where he was and stooped. And that was why the woman never came back: he was in the way, and she couldn't get to the grill."

Then he turned to Carson and asked him how much he had seen.

"The walls are forty feet high, sir – that is, from the gaps to the ground."

"'Embrasures' they're called," said Mansel. "Yes?"

"I'm sure they're not more, sir: they may be a foot or so less. The first windows are fourteen feet up, but they're very heavily barred: so are the ones above. There's no downpipe at all and no ledges that you could hold."

"Then we must have a ladder?"

"Three, sir. Each twelve feet long. The first hooks on to the bars of a window fourteen feet up: the second on to the bars of a window above: and the third to the top of the wall."

"Very good," said Mansel. "Are the windows above each other?"

"No, sir. Clear by about a foot. But you go up the left of the first and the right of the one above. There's a gap – embrasure directly between the two."

"I see," said Mansel. "Wrought-iron, one-pole ladders, made by a village smith: ends and rungs covered with rubber tubing, so that they make no noise."

"I hadn't thought of that, sir."

"You would have," said Mansel. "Once they're in place, it'll be like going upstairs."

"A rough night would help, sir."

"We must hope for one," said Mansel, "in two days' time. And now, Chandos, let me drive. We must find a forge: and it's got to be forty miles off."

The tale we told the smith is of no consequence: the ladders were simple to make, and Mansel's directions were clear: we were to find the work done by the evening of the following day.

Then Mansel found a rope factory and purchased a quantity of rope, after which we drove to some town, whose name I forget, where we bought what else we had need of to aid our assault. All this gear we presently hid in a dell – a pretty, private place, high up in the fold of a mountain, some ten miles by road from Gath. There we could work upon it during the next two days, and thence take it direct to the Castle when the moment came.

Of foul weather we had not much hope, for the sky was clean, and Mansel's barometer set fair: "however," said he, "I'm not going to wait any more. At two on Friday morning we're going over the top: even if we don't get Adèle, we shall see the inside of that rat-trap, and that'll be devilish useful next time we come."

How much we were nowadays watched I do not know. A spy can go out, but he is plainly useless unless he can later come in; and, in view of the Casemate business – to say nothing of that of Jute – I fancy 'Rose' Noble was shy of sending his subordinates further than the edge of the wood. Had he but known, he might have spared his concern: the last thing we wished was to be led to the Castle, and Mansel had given orders that, if we saw anyone watching, we were, if we possibly could, to turn a blind eye.

Now not to look for a spy is easy enough: yet, because, perhaps, we did not want him, Fate must needs deliver one into our hands.

This was the way of it.

Both cars left Lass the next morning at eight o'clock. We were bound for the dell, where there was work to be done. Hitherto, on reaching the cross roads, the cars had gone different ways: but today both took the road out of which ran the drive which served Gath, so that, if someone was watching, he should be able for once to account for us all. Mansel was leading, and I was sitting with Hanbury, who was driving the second car.

No doubt our ways were known; but, be that as it may, when Mansel had swept past the drive, a man rose out of the bushes, stepped to the edge of the road and stood watching the car out of sight.

To ignore him was out of the question: we were less than a hundred yards off. If he ran, we were bound to give chase; and we were three to one. We might contrive to lose him, but you cannot run through a wood without declaring your line, and, unless he had a fair start, such a failure would be instantly suspected, if not by the spy, by 'Rose' Noble, the moment he made his report.

"Take him aboard," said George. "It's the only way."

That this was so became increasingly clear, for we made no manner of sound, and the man was absorbed in his view of Mansel's car. Indeed, I had no time to think and barely enough to act. The man had no time to do either.

As we passed, I took him by the neck, and Bell leaned out behind me and dragged his legs into the car.

Not until then did I see that it was Jute.

He did not attempt to struggle; but I held him as I had seized him, till Bell had strapped together his ankles and wrists. Then we took a pistol from his pocket and put him on the floor of the car. And so we had meant to leave him, but such was his criticism of our conduct that after a little we gagged him with a handful of cotton waste.

"Understand this," said Mansel. "It's entirely your fault that you're here. Chandos would have ignored you, but you didn't give him a chance. You served your turn very well, but I finished with you at Lass. A man of your parts should have known that and have taken the greatest care to keep out of my way."

Jute made no answer, and presently Mansel went on.

"I have no time for a prisoner, for prisoners must be watered and fed. So I'm going to do one of two things. Which I do will depend upon you. Either I return you to 'Rose' Noble, or else I hang you by the neck."

"Murder?" said Jute, and laughed.

"Murder," said Mansel, beginning to fill a pipe.

I glanced round the dell.

The spot was peaceful: a gurgling brook, a little lawn and the shade of spreading trees made it seem fit for a shepherd's piping-match. Jute and all of us looked curiously out of place.

Perhaps, because of this, I had a strange feeling that I should presently awake and find that I had been dreaming, and to this day, recalling the happenings of that sunshiny morning, I seem to be remembering some vision rather than a downright business of life and death.

Mansel was speaking.

"Now, if I return you to 'Rose' Noble, I shall take you up to the Castle and watch you go in. That is, if it's dark. If it's during the day, I shall watch from the wood. You see, I don't want to be seen."

Jute's face was a study.

"Now, in view of what 'Rose' Noble said when you reported, after you had 'led me to Lass' " – I saw Jute start – "I imagine your next meeting will be even less cordial – *unless you return precisely when you are expected, and say nothing of having met me*. I mean, he might easily argue that you had 'led me to' Gath."

His eyes upon Mansel's face, Jute was plainly thinking extremely hard.

Mansel continued slowly, pressing his tobacco home.

"I can't return you today, because I've too much to do. In fact – "

"See here," said Jute. "You can make it tomorrow night. Do that, and I haven't seen you since you went by in the car."

"Don't try to bluff," said Mansel. "It's only wasting my time. You haven't a card. You had quite a good one about five seconds ago: but I've just drawn that. You see, I wanted to know whether 'Rose' Noble would worry if you didn't come in tonight."

I watched the blood come into the other's face.

Mansel continued in the same even tone.

"I tell you this to show you that it's no good playing with me. Bear that in mind. And now to business."

I cannot describe the coldness with which Mansel spoke: there was no insolence in his speech, only an iron contempt, which must, I think, have entered into the other's soul.

"I'm going to ask you some questions, and I'll allow you one lie: if you tell two lies, I shall hang you from a branch of that oak."

"And you talk about bluff," sneered Jute.

"It's not bluff," said Mansel. "I've got the gloves right off. Two lies, and you're for the high jump, as sure as I'm sitting still. And now we'll begin. Assume you're on the ramparts above the gateway. How would you go from there to where Mrs Pleydell lies?"

Jute gave a short laugh.

"I thought," he said, "you'd finished with me at Lass."

"So I had," said Mansel, bringing a match to his pipe.

"Looks like it, doesn't it?"

"I don't care what it looks like," said Mansel. "But I think you may as well know that I'm pressed for time: and, if you elect to be hanged, I shall have less still, because it'll take two hours to dig you a grave."

"Rake it out," said Jute sharply. "I know your shape. You can wear a gun on your back side, but it'll never fit. You're out of your depth, Mansel: and, if you take my advice, you'll kick for the shore. Your job's to pay and be damned. We've got your girl, and—"

"Carson," said Mansel, "get a rope on that bough. Timber hitch on the wood, slip knot the other end."

For a moment the servants spoke together. Then Bell was on Rowley's shoulders and up in the tree, and Carson was down in a gully, with a knife in his hand. The next minute he reappeared, with a coil of rope on his arm...

I knew that Mansel was bluffing, for he was not a hard man. He would have killed 'Rose' Noble, for he was the head of the corner, and, with his death, the conspiracy would have gone. He would have killed anyone whose death would materially help him to reach Adèle. But a spy that, when taken, refused to open his mouth, was as safe in Mansel's hands as a priest on his altar steps. I knew he would never hang Jute, though God knows he had just cause. Mansel was bluffing: and I was greatly afraid that the fellow would call his bluff.

Mansel returned to Jute.

"As I said, I'll give you one lie. A refusal counts as a lie. Assume you're on the ramparts above the gateway. How would you go from there to where Mrs Pleydell lies?"

After a long silence –

"Which way am I facing?" said Jute sullenly.

"You are facing the wood."

Jute shut his eyes.

"I turn to the right," he said, "and go as far as the tower. Then I turn again and walk along by the wall. At the end of that I come to another tower. There's a door there."

"In the tower?"

"Yes."

"Go on."

"You go through that and down steps till you come to a hall. Cross this to the door in front. That leads you into a room out of which runs a flight of stairs."

"Yes."

"Go down them, and they'll bring you into her room."

"Or the chapel?" said Mansel quietly.

Jute started violently. Then he glared at Mansel, with a working face.

"That's one lie," said Mansel.

Jute let himself go.

Out of a foam of imprecation odd sentences thrust, like timbers plunging in a flood.

"I'll see you, you one-legged—... Put it over, you movie king... When next I meet you, I'll cut my name on your back... We've got the goods, and, by—, we'll make you sweat... 'Cut flowers' won't be in it... I'll make you covet the day you played me up."

Mansel put his pipe in his pocket and rose to his feet.

"You refuse to answer?"

A beastly light slid into Jute's bloodshot eyes.

"My answer's here," he said, glancing down at his coat. "You were to have had it tonight, but, if you're not too 'pressed for time,' perhaps you'll look at it now."

To this day I cannot tell what possessed the man.

I suppose he could not forgive Mansel for beating him at his own game: the thought that all the antics of Hannibal Rouse had been gravely accepted at exactly their proper worth, the memory of the trap into which he had so readily rushed and the bitter reception which he had met at Gath had, I think, inspired a hatred which knew no law. And now to be again confounded, outwitted and scornfully reduced had sent the blood to his head.

"What do you mean?" said Mansel.

"Try my inside pocket," said Jute.

At a nod from Mansel I stepped to the fellow's side and took a bulging envelope out of his coat.

"That's my answer," said Jute, "to all your back-chat today. And, between you and me, Big Willie, I guess it's pretty complete."

Mansel ripped open the paper and took out a white silk blouse...

I thought he would never move.

After a long time, very slowly he lifted his head.

"Call the servants," he said, "and put the gag in his mouth."

He spoke so low that I scarcely heard what he said: but, with his words, I knew that Jute's hour was come.

For a moment the glade seemed misty, and my knees loose. Then my head cleared.

I saw Jute's eyes follow Hanbury, as he stepped to the oak: then his gaze flashed to me, as I picked up the cotton waste. When I approached, he recoiled.

Sharply he looked at Mansel, and caught his breath.

"You – you'd never dare," he said hoarsely.

At last we had the gag in his mouth...

"This man," said Mansel, "is engaged in one of the vilest crimes. In his lust for money he is not content to play even that filthy game according to its filthy rules." He held up the blouse. "*He is trying to win by taking Mrs Pleydell's clothes from her back and advertising that outrage to make me throw in my hand.* I do not think that a man who does that is fit to live."

His eyes bulging out of his head, Jute fell upon his knees.

Mansel turned to Hanbury and me.

"You will return to the cars and wait there until I send."

We did as he said.

Two hours later, Rowley brought us back to the dell.

Mansel was sitting smoking, with a distant look in his eyes: as he worked, jacketing a crow-bar, Carson was whistling to himself: Bell was wiping a spade with a handful of grass.

The contented mien of the servants, if nothing else, showed that the world was the cleaner.

By half past one the next morning all of us, except Bell, were standing upon the roof of the Castle of Gath.

The night was starlit, but the moon had set.

Each of us carried a knife as well as a pistol and wore a coil of rope, like a sash. Bell was at the foot of the ladders, with a signal-cord in his hand, and Tester was back in the wood, guarding the cars.

The castle was built four-square, as college buildings, about a great courtyard. Its roof was flat and paved and so made a spacious rampart, which the battlements fenced upon one hand and a massive balustrade upon the other.

Indeed, standing there in the starlight, we seemed to be upon some ectype of the walls of Babylon, upon which, if I rightly remember, six chariots could be driven abreast.Peering between the balusters, I could see the ripple of the water of which the bookseller had written and could hear it fall out of the basin on its way to the terrace and the cliff.

Now the basin was our first objective: and, since a rope provides the most silent path, we let one fall to the courtyard, and Carson and I went down.

We gained the basin and passed to the channel it fed. This was ten inches deep, and its floor was as smooth as glass. I followed the channel along till I came to the arch. This was shut by a gate, beneath which the water flowed. The gate was of iron and exactly fitted the arch: a man might have lain in the channel and crawled underneath, but, no doubt to foil such cunning, the channel was barred with a grating, through which the water fussed. I tested the bars and found them firm as rock.

I made my way back to Carson, and together we sought the rope down which we had come. Upon this Carson pulled twice, when a hundredweight of fine rope was lowered into our arms. We carried this to the grating and laid it down. To its end were attached three floats weighted with lead. With these in my hand, I thrust my arm under the grating as far as I could. Then I released them, and Carson paid out the rope. Now if there was another grating, this would arrest the floats: but, if there was not, the floats would leap with the water and carry the rope down the cliff. With a hand on the sliding rope, I waited for the check. But none came: only a sudden pull told us that the floats had leapt. There were eight hundred feet of cord, and, when we had paid them all out, we returned for more. Six hundred feet more we lowered, and that was as much as we had. The end we made fast to the grating below *the water line*. Then we went back to the rope down which we had come, and at a signal the others pulled us up.

Whatever the night might bring forth, we had taken at least one trick; for, though this time we might fail to release Adèle, we had now a way up to the terrace which the enemy would not dream of and a desperate man might take.

We were now beneath the shadow of the tower to the right of the gateway as you came from the wood: the south-west tower, from which Adèle had signalled, lay the length of the castle away.

So far as we knew, there were two ways into that tower from the open air – one by the roof and another by the steps from the terrace upon which we had seen Adèle. The windows which lighted the tower were not to be reached, and the conical roof of the tower gave us no hope. And, since the way by the roof was plainly the first to try, we began to steal over the pavement, one by one.

Mansel went first: the rest of us followed, at one-minute intervals. Only Rowley stood fast, with a signal cord in each hand.

I had gone most of the way, when I felt a hand on my arm.

At once I stopped, and Hanbury, who was before me, spoke in my ear.

"There's an alarm-cord, knee-high, two paces from where you stand. Tell Carson and then come on."

He left me to wait for Carson and disappeared.

I was desperately afraid of fouling the cord, so I went on my stomach until the danger was past. I afterwards found that the others had done the same.

Mansel and Hanbury were waiting, when I came to the tower. And, as we had expected, there was a door...

The door was of wood, very massive and studded with iron. It was shut and locked, or bolted, upon the other side. Whether we could have forced it, I do not know: but Jack Sheppard himself could not have had it open without making noise enough to awaken the dead.

And there, of course, was our principal handicap.

The door of Adèle's apartment was sure to be locked; but that we were ready to force, no matter what noise we made: until, however, we were standing without her door, we dared make no manner of sound, for, the instant the alarm was raised, 'Rose' Noble was certain to fly to his prisoner's side and, if he was there before us, to put her life in the balance against our further advance.

There was nothing to be done but to try the terrace steps.

In silence we passed to the battlements, and from there looked down upon the terrace and the sliding ribbon of water that cut it in two. It was quieter here than in the courtyard, where the four walls gave back sound; the steady rustle of the cascade was only just to be heard.

In a moment a rope was dangling, and Mansel and George went down.

That the steps would offer an entrance we had great hope, for the bookseller's guide had said nothing of any door, but only that the steps led out of the 'gallery of stone.'

Carson and I stood like statues, he holding the signal cord and I with the rope in my hand.

Two gentle pulls from below told us to take the strain, and a moment later Hanbury was by our side.

He put his lips to my ear.

"There's a door at the top of the steps – locked. Mansel's reconnoitring the terrace and then coming up."

I confess that my spirits sank.

To enter by some window seemed now the only way: and we had already decided that, if we were put to such a shift, we must essay some window that looked upon the terrace below. What windows looked into the courtyard we neither knew nor cared, for anyone at work in the courtyard would be working in a four-walled trap and could be observed and commanded from any side.

Now the windows that looked upon the terrace were those of the royal rooms. *They were not barred*, because, I suppose, with guards upon the roof and in the galleries, no one could have come upon the King.

Again, *that the royal apartments would be occupied was most unlikely*. The caretakers might have been bribed, but they would certainly stipulate that the state rooms were not to be used. The last thing we wanted to do was to force an entrance into an occupied room.

Finally, *the windows of the royal apartments had the world to themselves*, for the towers which flanked the terrace were presenting two empty walls. Of no other side of the castle could the same thing be said.

Now which of the seven windows might be the best to essay we could not tell, but reason suggested that the one which was nearest Adèle should be the first to be tried. This we supposed to be serving the antechamber which admitted directly into the 'gallery of stone.'

It was our belief that if we could reach the gallery we should have the control we sought, for, so far as we could determine, no one could enter the tower without passing through the gallery, unless he came down from the roof by the door which we had found shut. This belief we found to be just: the gallery was the key to the tower, and whoever held the gallery held Adèle. But one thing we did not suspect, namely, that there was a way into the gallery of which the bookseller's guide said nothing at all.

A quarter of an hour went by before Mansel gave us the signal to hoist him up.

As he alighted, I perceived that he was drenched to the skin.

At once he drew us together and spoke very low.

"At the head of each flight of steps there's a massive door: both doors are fast. The door at the mouth of the archway is shut and locked. I managed to pass beneath it, by lying down in the channel and working my way along. In the side of the archway I found a flight of steps – a very steep spiral staircase, that comes to a sudden end. I'm certain it serves a trap-door. If the bookseller's guide is sound, that trap-door should be in the King's Closet. That would be natural enough.

"We can't go that way tonight, because the trap-door is fast. At least, I imagine it is, because I can't move the slab I found at the top of the stairs: but, if we can enter the Closet by some other way tonight, we can unbar the trap-door, and then, when we come by the terrace, we shall have our way in. Don't think I've no hope of tonight, because I have: but, *if we fail this time, we shall certainly fail the next – unless we can turn this failure into a stepping-stone.*"

With that he told Carson to let him have his shoes, because they were dry, and then to stand fast where he was, with the signal cord in his hand. George and I were to follow the way he went.

We moved as before, one by one, and, when again I found him, he was standing above the archway through which the water flowed.

I knew that below us was a window of three long lights.

An instant later Mansel was descending the wall.

This time we used two ropes, one fastened about him and the other down which he slid. When he jerked the one about him, we were to make this fast: and, if he should pull it five times, George was to go for Carson and they were to let me down.

Wet to the skin, clinging like a fly to the wall, with only one hand to help him, without a glimmer of light, Mansel worked upon that window for half an hour. I was kneeling directly above him, but I never heard a sound. Indeed, I could not believe that he was at work, but supposed that he had seen someone within the room and was content to watch them from where he hung. Yet all the time he was drawing the wrought-iron latch – a feat which, had he not done it, I would have put beyond the power of man.

At last the ropes trembled and then swung slack in my hands. An instant later he signalled that he was within the room.

When I came down, he swung me in like a baby and asked for my torch.

The room was stately and full of the smell of age. The floor was of polished oak: the walls were panelled head high and tapestried above. The furniture was rich and massive, but very stiff, and had been ranged in order against the walls. A heavy carpet, much smaller than the room, lay in the midst of the floor, but all the furniture stood clear upon the oak. The two doors were conspicuous, for their frames rose above the panelling and each of them was fitted with a box lock of polished steel.

With one consent we turned to the door upon our left.

Very slowly, with infinite care, Mansel drew the spring latch. At once the door yielded, and Mansel set it wide. Not until he had wedged it with a morsel of rubber did we pass on.

So we entered the King's Bedchamber.

Not even the unjust light of the torch could deny the majesty of that room.

I have never beheld a chamber so fit to lodge a king, and all the standards of greatness which the fairy-tales I read as a child had set in my heart were in a twinkling supplanted by what I saw.

The ceiling was of black oak, picked out with gold. The walls were panelled head-high: between the panels stood pilasters, picked out with gold. The carving of the panels and pilasters was very deep. Above the panelling hung tapestries, very rich in colour, presenting hunting scenes. The bedstead was four-posted: each of the posts was carved into the life-size semblance of a man-at-arms: coverlet, canopy and curtains were of what seemed to be a crimson faced cloth, very fine to look at and clearly of a great weight: all the stuffs and hangings with which the furniture was done were of the same dignity. The floor was of polished oak.

We stole across to the door in the farther wall.

This admitted us to the royal dining-room.

This chamber resembled the Closet and was of much the same size. A handsome table stood in the midst of the floor.

We wasted no time but passed on.

A moment later we stood in the antechamber.

This was small, but notable. The walls were not panelled, but covered with tapestry. Two massive, high-backed chairs were all the furniture.

The door we now found before us was not at all like those through which we had come. It admitted of course to the gallery which led to the tower: and it was like a church door, that is to say, iron-studded, and Gothic in shape. A wrought-iron lock of great size was fixed upon the inside, and above this a simple latch which had only to be lifted to be freed.

If hope could but open gates, I think this door would have crumbled before our eyes: but hope cannot open gates, and – the door was fast.

Mansel stood very still.

At length he gave a short sigh and touched me upon the arm. A moment later we were moving the way we had come.

When we were again in the Closet, he put his mouth to my ear.

"Take a message to Hanbury. He and Carson will bring every tool we have to the south-west tower: then they will let fall a rope to the window of the antechamber, moving it to and fro until we take hold: when we do that they will come and take up the ropes which are hanging outside this room."

When I returned, Mansel was down on his knees by a hole in the floor. On the carpet, now drawn to one side, lay a square of polished wood. The recess which he had disclosed was floored by a grey, stone slab: this had a ring in its midst and was rudely locked into place by a pair of hasps and staples, the pins of which Mansel had withdrawn.

Gently I lifted the slab, to disclose the winding stair which led to the archway below.

"Can you hold it?" breathed Mansel.

I nodded.

At once he replaced the square of polished wood: then he laid the carpet, face downward, between my legs.

I lowered the slab.

Using the carpet as a sledge, we drew the slab into the Bedchamber and up to the King's bed. There we transferred it to my coat, and, lifting the crimson valence, thrust it beneath the bedstead and out of sight.

To restore the carpet to its place, close the window and take the wedge from the door took but a moment of time.

Then Mansel gave me a cloth and bade me polish the woodwork where we had stepped, especially about the casement which we had used.

When I had done so, he overlooked all with the torch.

Then we stole out of the room and closed the door.

Five minutes later we stood again in the antechamber and when we had opened a casement and found the rope, there was nothing to show, much less to suggest that we had seen the inside of any other room.

"And now the tools," said Mansel, "and then Hanbury. Carson to stay where he is. We shall make the devil's own noise, and he is to shoot at sight." I climbed up and gave the message as fast as I could.

The time was now half past three: the stars were no more to be seen, and rain had begun to fall. This to our liking, for now any footprints we had made above or below would be wiped out: but the wet was against our foothold, and, as I came back, I slipped on the window-sill.

We had received the tools and were awaiting Hanbury, when some door within the castle was sharply closed.

It was some door behind us – not very far away.

Called upon to say which, I would have named the door of the Closet. The clash of a heavy, spring lock was unmistakable.

Mansel put out the light, and we stood as still as death, straining our ears for footsteps and hearing none.

A rustle without the window told us that Hanbury had begun to descend the rope.

We could not stop him, for we had no signal-cord, and together we stood to the window to take him in without sound.

As we did so, came the creak of a floor-board, faint yet distinct. I would have said that it came from the Dining-room.

It was now as dark as pitch. I could not even see Mansel, two feet from where I stood.

Something swayed at the window...

Then we had George in our arms and Mansel was unfastening the rope which was holding him up.

Again I heard a board creak – somewhere at hand.

With the greatest care we lowered George to his feet. As we did so, the daïs upon which we were standing tilted suddenly forward, and, with nothing to save us, the three of us crashed to the ground. As we fell, the massive step resumed its proper position with a deafening clap.

There had been nothing to show that the step was not fixed, and, indeed, it was so solid that I do not think it would have moved under ordinary use: but the weight of three men happening to fall upon its edge had, I suppose, been too much for its counterpoise.

For a moment we lay as we had fallen, straining our ears: then Mansel got to his feet and lighted the torch.

"You two all right?" he said.

We told him 'yes.'

"Then quick," says he, "for, by thunder, we've rung the bell."

With that, he set Hanbury to watch the Dining-room door and hold the torch, while I took the stoutest chisel and laid its edge where the lock met the wood of the door.

"You strike," said Mansel, taking it out of my hand.

I picked up and swung a hammer with all my might...

I cannot attempt to tell the noise we made.

Perhaps our reluctance to make any noise at all and the infinite care we had taken to smother all sound magnified for us this sudden breach of silence: certainly the hour, the emptiness of the apartments and the style and proportions of the building made so many sounding-boards. Be that as it may, had the castle been full of troops and these been suddenly summoned by trumpet and tuck of drum I do not think the uproar could have won to our ears.

It took us, I suppose, two minutes to reduce that lock.

As Mansel wrenched it away, an iron fillet, into which its tongues were protruding, came also. This fillet was a false jamb, that ran the whole length of the door and was laid upon stone. Now that it was displaced, we could see that the door was bolted, top and bottom, upon the opposite side. The bolts were shot into the stone, but, the fillet gone, we could reach them and, with the slightest manipulation, could draw them clear of their sockets and open the door.

I put up a hand, but Mansel caught my arm. *Someone was pounding upon the other side of the door.*

Together we stared at the oak.

Then came Adèle's clear voice.

"Is that you Jonah?"

"Yes, dear," said Mansel. "One moment, and—"

"*No, no,*" cried Adèle. "*Stop. Stay where you are. 'Rose' Noble's here by my side. And he says if you open that door you'll lose your match.*"

# VI

## THE LOVE OF A LADY

Never, I suppose were hopes lifted so high one moment and dashed so low the next.

Indeed, I was so much confounded by the sudden overthrow of our fortune that I stood staring at the door, as a clown at a strange fish, and when I turned to Hanbury, who had come across to our side, he was wearing the blank expression of a player of chess who, having but two moves to make to win his match, suddenly perceives that his opponent has but one.

And this shows how fine was the stuff of which Mansel was made, for, though our dismay was nothing to the bitterness which must have been his, beyond raising his eyebrows he gave no manner of sign that he was put out, and, what was far more, he had a plan in an instant to save the game.

Before he could answer Adèle, we heard the clatter of footsteps and, then, 'Rose' Noble's deep voice speaking Casemate and Bunch by name.

Under cover of this distraction, Mansel caught us each by an arm.

"Time to be gone," he whispered. "We've shot our bolt. Leave everything and clear out. *I'm going to stay.* Food and dry clothes to me by the waterfall cord. And paper and pencil. So long."

Before we could speak, he had returned to the door.

"My dear Adèle," he said, "I'm delighted to hear your voice."

"Same here," said Adèle, cheerfully.

'Rose' Noble laughed.

"'Journeys end in lovers meeting,'" he said.

"How's Boy?" said Adèle.

"None too bad," said Mansel. "A bit hot and bothered you know, till we'd run you to earth: but that was natural. His leg's just splendid."

"How much does he know?" said 'Rose' Noble.

That was as much as I heard, for Hanbury was at the window, and I had something to say before he was gone.

"I stay with Mansel," I said. "Give me your pistol and torch."

"I can't leave you here," said George.

"Quick," said I. "We'll argue another time."

With that, I put my hands in his pockets and helped myself. There was a bunch of wedges we had not used. These I took, and his torch. He gave me his pistol unwillingly enough. Then he shook his head and went up the rope.

High words were flying as I swung myself into the rain. 'Rose' Noble was clearly angry, and I heard Adèle's scornful laugh...

As soon as my feet touched the terrace, I made my way to the water and scrambled under the door. I had a vile wet passage, but I managed to save both pistols and Hanbury's torch. The archway was dank and draughty, so I lost no time in finding the little staircase that served the trap-door and, when I had found it, in climbing as high as I could. Here I was out of the wind and might have been snug; but my clothes were wringing wet and that made the stone seem cold.

I was quite sure that this was the spot at which Mansel proposed to be hid – for that, of course, was his plan. He intended 'Rose' Noble to think that he had withdrawn, and, presently taking the monster off his guard, to strike again.

And here I may say that I found his plan very good. To release Adèle might be beyond our power, but our luck would be out indeed, if we could not kill 'Rose' Noble before two days were gone by, and his death, as I have said, would break the enemy's back.

What Mansel would say, when he found me, I could not tell. He did not like disobedience: but for one man to stay alone in such an enemy's camp seemed to me out of reason, and I hoped very much that he would share my view.

I had not long to wait.

A sudden quickening of the rustle the water made told me that Mansel was passing beneath the door, and an instant later I heard his foot on the stair.

"Mansel," I breathed. "Chandos speaking."

"Ah, William," said he: and that was all.

He sat down on the step below mine and put his head in his hands.

After a little he spoke.

"I didn't dare stay. 'Rose' Noble was bound to exploit a chance like that. You see, without an audience there's no point in doing her harm: but with me, so to speak, looking on... He struck her, Chandos. And, because she wouldn't cry out, he struck her again... And so it seemed best to go... Oh, my God," he cried suddenly, "there are times when I'd take your offer and buy her out."

"It's always open," I said.

"I know," he said, "I know."

For a long time we sat in silence. Then he gave a short sigh.

"Drink some of this," he whispered, and put a flask into my hand.

It was brandy and did us both good, for our state of mind and of body was wretched enough.

Presently he spoke again.

"No," he said. "No. What's the good of buying a broken heart? We've got to beat 'Rose' Noble: there's no other way. But it's a dreadful business to have to go so slow."

That was a true saying.

Indeed, the next sixteen hours were the worst I have ever spent. I can never remember them without a shudder, and to our restless senses they seemed more like sixteen days. Without cause we dared not emerge: no cause presented itself. The rain fell down without ceasing, and, though we took it in turns to watch from the archway, no one appeared in the courtyard, or, so far as I know, visited the terrace upon the opposite side. Command the terrace we could not, unless we lay down in the channel below the door: and that was dangerous, for the noise which the water made embarrassed the ear, and we might well have been noticed before we had time to withdraw. There was, however, the keyhole of the great door itself, and, whilst we were listening there, I do not think one could have passed without our hearing his steps.

We saw the dawn come in and the day draw to its close: we heard the drip of the rain and the sigh of the wind: and that was all.

One thing only we decided, for you cannot make bricks without straw, and we had no data with which to make any plan. We determined that, when night had fallen and we dared pull up the rope, we would enter the King's Closet and eat and rest in such comfort as that room could give. The risk of discovery was small, and, if we could not take shelter which would allow us to sleep, we should, we knew, be unfitted to strike when the moment came. I do not mean that when the day was over we had no resistance left, for we were both very strong and had suffered adversity far more exacting than this; but we knew that to rob 'Rose' Noble the eye must be clear, the hand unearthly swift and all the senses at the very top of their pitch or, as the saying is, a man might as well go home.

At last the daylight faded, and the rain ceased.

When it was quite dark, we laid hold of the rope in the channel and took the strain. To our delight it was loaded, so, bidding me stay where I was and haul it in, Mansel crawled under the door and made for the balustrade beneath which the waterfall leapt.

At last I felt a check, and, very soon after, a package done up in oiled silk was thrust under the door.

Two minutes later we were in the King's Closet, with good, oak boards beneath us and wedges under the doors.

As well as changes of clothing, Hanbury had sent us a blanket sewn into the shape of a bag: this was just what we needed and, with the square of carpet, promised a goodnight's rest.

But first there was work to be done.

There was food enough for five, and, what was better still, a bottle of excellent brandy by way of drink.

We changed and made our meal by the shaded light of a torch, for to do such things in the dark without making a sound required more time and care than we were prepared to expend: and, when we had done, Mansel wrote out the first message which we were to send to George:

*George.*

*Send up Adèle's dressing-case.*

(*a*) *Is there any reason why we should not descend by this rope at any time?*

(*b*) *Where is the cover nearest to the foot of the cliff and what shape does it take?*

I wished to go out this time, but Mansel would not consent. Whilst, therefore, I let down the message, he changed again into his dripping clothes, and, as soon as I took the strain, he returned to the balustrade...

Hanbury's answer was clear.

(*a*) *No reason at all. We have lengthened the rope, so that it reaches the ground. By day the last forty feet will be concealed in a bush. No one could ever climb up without help from above.*

(*b*) *Beechwoods two furlongs north-east. Unless you direct otherwise, one car will be always concealed within sound of the drive, and one at the foot of this cliff from nightfall till dawn.*

As soon as he had changed, Mansel wrote out his reply.

*Good. Visit the beechwoods twice daily at ten and three. Don't wait any longer tonight. Send Carson and another to Poganec with the enclosed note instead.*

The note was addressed to Captain Pleydell and was very short.

*I have spoken with Adèle. She is very cheerful and seems to be in excellent health.*

These dispatches I sent alone, and, when they were gone, we finally closed the trap-door and getting into our blanket, lay down on the carpet to sleep.

Whether Mansel rested I know not, but I slept like the dead. The Closet was full of pale light when I awoke, and Mansel was at the window, with his eyes on the east.

It was ten o'clock in the morning, the weather was very fine, and I had my ear to the keyhole of the archway door, when I heard a footstep upon the terrace beyond.

As I turned to summon Mansel, I felt his hand on my arm.

"Casemate is with her," he said.

The next instant he was down in the channel and was peering under the door.

Slowly Adèle and her warder passed into and out of my view. Her hair had been rudely shorn to the shape of her head, and about her shoulders she wore a rag of a shawl.

Then I heard Casemate's voice.

"— this sunshine," he said. "Don't you want a hat on your curls?"

"No," said Adèle.

"Well, I guess I do," said Casemate. "You carry on, an' move. You're not here to wave to Charlie: you're here for exercise. An' 'Rose' is red-hot this morning, so I shouldn't tread on his toes."

With that, he left her.

"Pull up the rope," said Mansel; and, before I could think, he was gone.

I was taken so much by surprise that, though I did his bidding, I could hardly believe that our attempt at rescue was fairly begun. Casemate was seeking his hat: that, before he returned, we should be able to let down Adèle to safety seemed to me a chance in a thousand, while, if we were caught in the act, her life would be in great peril and our present enterprise wrecked. I found it unlike Mansel to take such a risk and was wondering whether for once his zeal had outrun his discretion, when Adèle's face appeared in the channel almost between my legs.

In a flash I had her under the arms, and had drawn her clear of the door and lifted her up. Mansel followed at once, and, whilst I worked like a madman to pull up the rope, he spoke to Adèle.

"If we can do it in time, we shall let you down the face of the cliff. The moment you're down, unfasten the rope and run for your life to the beechwoods that lie north-east." He pointed the direction with his arm. "Over there. George or Carson will be there with one of the Rolls. Tell them to drive you—"

He stopped short there, and, after listening intently, caught my wrist.

"Let go the rope," he breathed...

For a moment I could hear nothing. Then came 'Rose' Noble's voice.

"Hat be damned. I said 'See that she moves.' By—, that's clean enough talking. D'you think—"

And there, I suppose, he saw that Adèle was gone...

For a moment there was dead silence. Then came a rush of steps to the balustrade.

Adèle and Mansel and I stood still as death, while the rope fled steadily back the way it had come. That 'Rose' Noble must now observe it seemed almost certain: *whether he would see that it was moving we could not tell.*

A sudden roar from the terrace made my heart stand still.

"By—, she's gone," screeched 'Rose' Noble. "Look at that— cord."

"She's never had time," cried Casemate. "I only—"

"*Time?*" howled 'Rose' Noble. "*Time?* It's only your white-livered sort that wants time to break out of hell. Bunch! Punter!" he yelled. "Turn out the—car. Go and help them, you—. And if we don't take her at the foot of this blasted rock I'll twist your block off your body with my bare hands."

Before the threat was issued, Casemate was gone. I could hear him shouting for Bunch like a man possessed.

The rope was now back in the channel and lying as snug and as taut as though it had never been touched.

Mansel was speaking low.

"Sit down on the step, dear, and let me pull off your boots."

Adèle obeyed him at once. She was, of course, drenched to the skin.

"Now go up these stairs: they'll bring you into a room. Your dressing-case is there. Change your clothes as quickly as ever you can. The instant you're through, come back."

Here came voices from the courtyard, and almost at once I saw figures about the car. This was in the midst of the archway that ushered the castle gate and directly opposed to that beneath which we stood. The car was standing, as we were, in deep shadow, but the courtyard was full of light. It follows that I could not distinguish whose the figures might be but, after a little, I heard 'Rose' Noble's voice. I suppose the car was unready, for her engine would not start for all the frenzy with which someone was swinging the shaft. Another – Casemate, I think – was clumsily dashing spirit into the tank...

At last with a stammer and then with a sudden roar the engine came to life: and that put an end to my observation, for the noise was deafening and a dense smoke from the exhaust screened any movement that was made.

Suddenly the gate was opened, and the car shot out.

Mansel's hand touched my shoulder.

"Can you see who's shutting the gate?"

"I think it's the woman," said I. "Yes, I can see her skirt."

"Good," said Mansel. "And now I think we'll follow. But I hope the others won't try to get in their way. Could you tell at all how many got into the car?"

I shook my head.

"'Rose' Noble?"

"I assume so," said I. "I certainly heard his voice. Besides, you heard what he said."

"I don't count what he says," said Mansel. "If he saw that the rope was moving, I've played my cards wrong."

"What else could you have done?"

"Followed Casemate and met him," said Mansel.

"But you couldn't have known—"

Mansel smiled.

"You never do – at cards," he said.

Adèle's voice came from the stairway.

"I'm ready, Jonah," she said.

A moment later we were in the King's Closet.

With the utmost caution Mansel opened the door: then he signed to Adèle to follow. I caught up her dressing-case and brought up the rear.

The King's Bedchamber was empty.

Like thieves in the night, we stole across its floor and into the Dining-room.

A moment later we entered the antechamber.

The door was as we had left it; but the hammers and chisels were gone, and the window was shut.

With a little manipulation I had the upper bolt free and wheedled it clear of the jamb. The lower, however, resisted, and Mansel, who was down on his knees, was able neither to turn it nor thrust it back.

At length he rose to his feet.

"Are the ropes there, Chandos?"

I stepped to the window, but the ropes were gone.

When I told him, he frowned.

Then he wedged the door, so that it could not be opened from the opposite side, and rose to his feet.

"Come," he said, turning. "We must try the other end of the suite."

So we came back to the Closet and, passing through the Queen's rooms, entered the other antechamber which the bookseller's guide had shown us that we might expect.

There was now before us a door like that we had left, which gave, no doubt, into the other 'gallery of stone.'

And this door also was fast.

I confess that here the sweat ran over my face.

To be within hail of freedom, to have the prison to ourselves, to have come so far, only to be prevented, as rabbits left in a hutch, was almost more than I could bear.

Mansel took a wedge from his pocket and thrust it under the door. Then he led us back to the Closet and down the winding stair.

"Wait here," he said. "It's no good our all getting wet. I'm going through the door at the head of the terrace steps. That should be open, all right. And then, if I can, I'll draw that blasted bolt."

With that, he was gone.

I clapped my ear to the keyhole, and Adèle's hand stole into mine. I remember thinking that she was seeking comfort, but now I know that she would have comforted me. I was trembling so much that I could not keep my head steady against the wood.

Then I heard the sound which I dreaded, and trembled no more.

*I heard Mansel go by with a rush, to try the opposite door.*

He was back in an instant.

As I helped him out of the channel –

"I should have kept a chisel," he said. "But, chisel or no, we must try that bolt again."

Adèle laid a hand on his arm.

"You'll die of cold, dear," she said. "Have you dry things?"

"We mustn't wait, my lady. I—"

"I won't stir from here," said Adèle, "until you've changed."

Mansel smiled and was gone.

There were dry clothes in the Closet, for Hanbury had had the foresight to send us two changes apiece.

Adèle had me by the coat.

"Oh, why did you stay?" she breathed. "If 'Rose' Noble gets him, he'll break him by eighths of an inch. I never knew what hate was, till I heard that terrible man. And he's got it in for Jonah from bottom to top. I'm nothing – a lever at most... one of the levers of the rack. It's only the money that can save him. Remember that. Dying men can't sign cheques. But if ever the cheque is signed... How much is he asking?"

"Five hundred thousand," said I.

I felt her fingers tighten upon my coat.

"He'd take a hundred thousand – *with Jonah thrown in*. I've heard him say so – not once, but fifty times. I tell you—"

"Chandos," said Mansel from the stairway, "pull in that rope. Cut a length of a hundred yards. If we can't shift that bolt..."

What else he said I never knew, for the moment I handled the cord, *I knew that it had been severed a few feet away.*

I think I must have exclaimed, for Mansel called sharply to know what the matter might be.

"It's cut already," said I, and, with that, I pulled in what was left and proved my words.

With his back to Adèle, Mansel looked me full in the eyes.

"I was right – just now," he said quietly. "I ought to have led out Clubs." Then he turned to Adèle. "Come, my lady," he said, "and we'll have another whack at that door."

"Tell me, Jonah," said Adèle.

"My dear," said Mansel, "'Rose' Noble's a careful man. He locks the door before the horse is stolen, but he takes the precaution of locking it afterwards, too. Never mind. We'll get out somehow."

When we entered the Closet, he picked up the bottle of brandy and poured some into a glass.

"The stirrup cup," he said, smiling, and gave the glass to Adèle.

Then he and I drank quickly.

A moment later we were crossing the Bedchamber's floor.

As we entered the Dining-room –

"That'll do," said 'Rose' Noble.

There was nothing to be said or done.

The fellow was sitting in a chair at the head of the table, with his elbows upon the board and a pistol in either hand.

Never before or since have I felt so far out of my depth.

A moment before, we had had the suite to ourselves: the entrance doors had been wedged and as good as barred: no sound of any sort had come to our vigilant ears. Yet our movements had been closely observed, our intentions had been accurately gauged, and our enemy had been able to snare us with the effortless ease of a nurse outwitting a child.

"Keep your hands up," said 'Rose' Noble, "and come and sit down – you two twopenny squirts to right and left, and the goods facing me. Move."

Slowly we did as he said.

"Now put your palms on the table." Again we obeyed.

"And if anyone wants to die, they've only to move a hand."

Desperately I tried to marshal my wits, for if ever a clear head was needed to save the game, it was needed now; but my brain was ever wayward, and I remember thinking how strange a picture we made and how much astonished King Maximilian would have been, could he have viewed such a company gracing his private board.

Before me Mansel sat easily, leaning back in his chair. His hair was wet and rumpled, and he wore no collar or tie. His light, tweed coat, turned up about his neck, became him admirably and a quiet smile was lighting his handsome face. On my left Adèle sat upright: her colour was high and, because of her short, crisp hair, she looked like some old picture of a beautiful boy. She was wearing a fawn-coloured dress, and white silk was edging her delicate wrists and throat. Laid upon the smooth, dark oak, her lovely hands were unforgettable. And on my right, deep in the King's great chair, sat 'Rose' Noble. One pistol lay before him: the other was in his right hand. His great bulk was loose as ever, and his huge face grey and flabby as when I had seen him first. He stayed so still that he might have been some gross idol, carved out of stone. Their lids, as usual, were almost hiding his eyes, and a faint smile was hanging upon the cruellest mouth that I have ever seen.

For a long time he held his peace, but at length he gave a smooth laugh.

"'Stone walls do not a prison make,'" he said softly. "An' I guess you three could heckle the guy that wrote that."

"My favourite maxim," said Mansel pleasantly. He looked across the table at me. "William," he said, "we must do better next time. There's a door behind our host – in the panelling. There's probably one in each room. They open into a passage which—"

"Quite so," drawled 'Rose' Noble. "Quite so. I call it 'The Listening Post.'" His eyelids flickered, and the blood came into my face. "And now, perhaps, you'll let the geography stew and listen to me. I wasn't at Oxford College, but I guess the notes I've sent you were plain enough."

"As plain as my replies," said Mansel.

"I didn't hear them," said 'Rose' Noble. "But, now we're so snug, maybe you'll say them again."

"The first thing," said Mansel at once, "is to clear the air. This lady may be your prisoner, but I am not. One doesn't imprison one's broker if one happens to want some funds. I mean, that's elementary."

"Maybe it is," said 'Rose' Noble. "One don't spoil his right hand either. But I've known a guy that kicked when he had two lights, as mild as his mother's milk when he had but one."

"I daresay you have," said Mansel. "It takes some people that way."

'Rose' Noble moistened his lips.

"I'm not out to break you," he said. "It's the goods that'll get the rough."

"Are getting the rough," said Mansel. "And there again I advise you to watch your step. 'Perishable goods' have a market: but 'damaged goods' make a very different price."

"They're not damaged – yet," said 'Rose' Noble. "And I'm still waiting for a bid."

Mansel raised his eyebrows.

"A few months ago," he said quietly, "you stole some papers of mine. Give me them back, and I'll pay you a hundred pounds and hold my tongue."

I was aghast at his boldness and fully expected a truly dreadful outburst by way of reply. But none came: and after a little silence I breathed again.

'Rose' Noble lifted his lids and looked at Adèle.

I cannot describe the awfulness of his gaze. Hatred, malice and all uncharitableness burned in those terrible orbs. Themselves monstrous, their message was like unto them, and before its beastly menace my blood ran cold.

"You hear?" he said grimly. "You're pretty enough to fool round, but, when it's a question of paying, your gentleman-friend gets off."

Adèle flushed under his tongue.

"It's never been a question of paying," she said.

"Big words," said 'Rose' Noble. "But they won't pull you out of this mess. Your health and your name's on the counter: and if you fancy either, you'd better trouble Big Willie to open his purse."

"My name?" said Adèle, frowning.

"Your name," said 'Rose' Noble softly. "You see, I'm not selling to your husband. I'm selling to the man next door."

Adèle's colour came and went. She looked round swiftly.

Then—

"You mean—"

"That I have not asked your husband to buy you back. That I have ignored his existence from first to last. That he's all sure and grateful that Big Willie's hoeing his row. *That Big Willie daren't undeceive him... daren't so much as breathe my name – for fear of its putting ideas into his innocent head.*"

The brutal accuracy of this saying was to me like a buffet which makes the head sing again: and my brain seemed suddenly pygmy beside that of this terrible man.

Adèle had gone very pale.

"You mistake us," she said coldly. "Our understanding—"

"So I guess," said 'Rose' Noble, as though she had not opened her mouth, "your pretty name is as much for sale as your health. Of course, if it isn't bought in, your husband can have it back. But it's not every fool, by—, that'll pick up a rotten rose."

"I agree," said Mansel. "In fact, all you say would be very much to the point, if I hadn't told Captain Pleydell that I was in love with his wife."

Very slowly the blood flowed into Adèle's sweet face. She did not look at Mansel, and her eyes which were resting on 'Rose' Noble, never moved. But, after a little, I saw that their focus had changed and that, though she was looking before her, she did not see, because she was lost in thought.

'Rose' Noble gave a thick laugh.

"I see," he said smoothly. "And, of course, he couldn't kick you – because of his leg. Well, well... And if you think that chokes me, you're nursing the dirty end. I guess I've a sleeve full of trumps – but if you don't want to see them you know the way."

"I'm afraid you'll have to play them," said Mansel. "You see, we don't mind paying, but it wouldn't amuse the lady to know she'd been bought."

"That's right," said Adèle.

'Rose' Noble sat back in his chair.

"You mean she don't care to be mortgaged outside your arms?"

"I didn't say that," said Mansel.

"I'll take it as read. I don't move around on your dunghills, but I guess a woman's a woman whether she's warming her maid or selling fish. This man can bend her fingers, and that one can go to hell. 'With love from little Willie' don't happen to suit her book. Maybe it don't suit yours. And so I'll help you out." He leaned suddenly forward. "Be here in this room yourself a week from today, with two hundred and fifty thousand in Bank of England notes, and I'll let the three of you go."

"Nothing doing," said Adèle swiftly.

"I am not prepared," said Mansel, "to continue to talk this over while Mrs Pleydell sits there."

'Rose' Noble's eyes narrowed.

"If you don't like the rules," he drawled, "you – well needn't play. I've picked my words so far, but run me up and I'm not going to cramp my tongue. If you're bunched round my table, God didn't put you there. You horned right into this parlour, and, if you don't like the eats, I guess you can swallow them whole."

"I repeat my request," said Mansel. "I decline to—"

"I don't fancy that verb," snapped 'Rose' Noble, using a savage oath. "You may feel ugly, but I've the right end of the gun. And now try and get me, you—. I'm running this—party from the soup to the pineapple's bush. If you wanted a Bible reading, you've come the wrong day of the week. We're talking business this morning. It mayn't smell as sweet as lipsalve, but, if I find your linen dirty, I reckon you made it foul."

"I repeat my request," said Mansel steadily.

'Rose' Noble sucked in his breath. Then he opened his blazing eyes.

"Then finish," he said, "you—. You say you've told her husband you want his wife. I'll give you some more to tell him, next time you meet. So far she's lived alone in her private suite. Bedroom and bathroom adjoining, as tight as you please. Now we'll cut out the bathroom, sonny, and she'll share—"

"I decline to—"

With a roar 'Rose' Noble flung forward, and Mansel's bare hands shot out. The left struck aside the pistol, as 'Rose' Noble fired: the right hit the beast on his mouth and knocked him into his chair. But for this, he must have gone down before the weight of the blow, but the chair was massive and, though it rocked for a moment, it held him up.

The sudden support saved him.

As I snatched at the second pistol, he swept it off the board, but the movement disordered his aim, and his second bullet went wide.

"Into the bedroom," yelled Mansel, hurling an oaken footstool, with all his might.

As I hustled Adèle through the doorway, I heard a screech of pain and a third report. Then Mansel whipped into the room and I slammed the door.

"Quick! Wedge the doors," breathed Mansel.

Now that we suspected their presence, the doors in the panelling were easy to find, and, since they opened inwards, before thirty seconds had passed the Closet and Bedchamber had been secured.

As I drove the last wedge, Mansel leaned his back to the wall and covered his eyes.

"That chair," he said brokenly. "That chair. It's enough to break a man's heart. I'd no time to hit him square, but I never so much as dreamed that that damned chair wouldn't go. If it had..."

Adèle put her arms round his neck, drew down his head to hers and kissed his lips.

"My darling," she said quietly, "no man could have done so well."

"By God, that's true," I cried.

"Oh, Adèle," said Mansel simply, "I do love you so much."

Then his arms went about her, and she hid her face in his coat.

Sitting on the floor of the Closet, I summed up our circumstances as best I could.

For the moment, Adèle was safe. What remained of the food which we had drawn up the cliff would last us with care for two days. We had three pistols, each holding seven rounds, and we had the run of two rooms and a way down into the archway – for what it was worth. That we could hold this position I had no doubt: indeed, it seemed most unlikely that 'Rose' Noble would make an attack, for, unless we three could break out or Hanbury and the servants could break in, we must in three or four days fall into his hands.

For us to break out would be extremely hard: we had long ago perceived that the two 'galleries of stone' were the keys to the royal suite, and that these were joined by a passage meant that we were surrounded by a guard-room which two men could hold against twenty, the inside of which we had not so much as seen.

With Hanbury and the servants we were no longer in touch. Our line of communication had been cut, and, even though George should decide to attempt our relief, I could not see that four men could bring this about. Six had been none too many two nights ago, and for four to repeat an assault which had only succeeded because it was a surprise seemed to me a hopeless adventure.

I found it hard not to believe that Fortune had taken her stand on the enemy's side. Had we known of the doors in the panelling, not once but five times over should we have won our match: without that precious knowledge, two nights ago we had all but rescued Adèle: if 'Rose' Noble had not met Casemate in search of his hat, Adèle by now might well have been thirty miles off: but for the weight of the chair, 'Rose' Noble must have been dead ten minutes ago. This last was a bitter thought. Looking back, I perceived how Mansel had made the brute angry in order to make him move and had actually lured the master into the way of a fool, how he had ignored gross insult and let Adèle suffer in silence to gain his end, and how only the fear of depriving Adèle of his service had made him break off a battle which he might well have won.

Then I fell to considering Mansel and Adèle and their love – for now I was sure that she loved him as he did her – and what ever would be the outcome of an affair at once so passionate and so much out of joint.

God knows I did not blame them: I was rather exulting to see two such great hearts at one. It was the future that troubled me, the reckoning that would have to be paid.

And whilst I was in the midst of this reflection, the two came into the Closet, with shining eyes.

I got to my feet, and Adèle gave me her hand.

I kissed it naturally.

"William," she said, "I think I have the finest lover in the world."

"You have, indeed," said I, gravely.

"William the Faithful," said Mansel and laughed like a boy. He stepped to the trap. "And now," said he, "I'm going to spy out the land. Don't talk too loud, you two, and stay in the doorway, please, so that you can watch both rooms."

"Very good," said I, and went to my post at once.

When Mansel was gone, Adèle came to my side.

"Sit down, William," she said. "I want you to know how I feel."

We sat down on the floor, like two children, and Adèle leaned her head against the wall and slid her slight arm through mine.

"I'm in love with Jonah," she said. "I think I've loved him for years, but I never knew. And then, when I first saw 'Rose' Noble and Jute pulled me off the mare, I remembered our talk in the forest and I knew what they wanted me for. They meant to hurt Jonah through me. That meant that Jonah loved me: and then, all of a sudden, I knew that I loved him. I was terribly worried at first, because it seemed so awful to be in love with anyone other than Boy. And then I came to see that, so long as nobody knew, no harm would be done. And I made up my mind that no one should ever know – not even Jonah himself... Well, you saw me break down. You saw me kiss him and put my arms round his neck. I suppose I shouldn't have done it, but I'm so thankful I did. I want you to know that, William. And Jonah's so happy, too. We've had it all out and we both of us feel the same. You see, we're locked up here, in a sort of No Man's Land that lies between life and death. If we die – well, that's the end. If we live, then we go back. But we can't tell which it will be, and, so long as we're in that land, we're going to love each other with all our heart."

"But, oh, Adèle," said I, "what about going back?"

A very soft light came into her wonderful eyes.

"You can't take away memory," she said. "That we shall have for ever, like a star that's always in the sky. I'm not seeking to justify myself. I know I'm another man's wife. But I don't care, William. Nature and Fortune have driven us into this Eden, and I don't think we should be human if we didn't help each other to pick the flowers."

"I don't think you would," said I heartily.

And that is the point of view I hold today. I daresay it cannot be defended. I can only say that Jonathan Mansel and Adèle were two of a kind that I never saw before and have never seen since. They were wise: 'they were lovely and pleasant in their lives': they were nonpareil: and, looking back, I find it most natural that, suddenly faced with life in the midst of death, two natures so alike and so peerless should have comforted each other.

Adèle looked at me swiftly.

"Do you mean that you understand? I don't think you can do that?"

"I can understand enough," said I, "to be very glad you're so happy."

"Thank you, William," she said. "And please don't feel left out. Jonah was only saying a moment ago that you were the only living being he didn't mind seeing our love."

"History repeats itself," said I, indicating the rooms. "The equerry doesn't feel left by his king and his queen."

"Oh, he's a courtier," cried Adèle, clapping her hands.

"Don't slander my lieutenant," said Mansel, putting his head through the floor.

"And here's a piece of good news." He sank his voice to a murmur. "The car is still out."

"Which means?" breathed Adèle.

"I hope and believe it means that it's gone for good, that George and the servants have got it and all or some of its crew. When 'Rose' Noble sent them out, he knew very well that there was nothing to see: he knew we were in the archway and he sent them packing to mislead us and draw us out: I admit he pulled that off, but, unless and until they return, I believe he's alone."

I suppose that I showed my excitement, for he continued at once.

"But please remember 'Rose' Noble's a host in himself. He may be single-handed, but he's worth ten ordinary men. And so we must watch and wait. If only we'd known of that passage two nights ago – "

"Then," said Adèle, "you'd never have known that I loved you. And now, please, I'm hungry. Will one of you give me some food?"

Mansel smiled.

"Feminine influence, William, is a terrible thing. With this girl-child round our necks, we shall forget we're at war."

"Forget it," said I, rising, "for half an hour. While you two lunch, I'll watch the castle gate."

"Very well," said Mansel, hoisting himself to the floor. "But keep in the shadow and report the first sign of life. If Hanbury's sunk the pinnace, I don't think what's left of her crew will come aboard before dark. At least, they'll be fools if they try. But we can't hang our lives on guess-work and so we must watch. And, by the time I've eaten, I may have some plan."

But he had not: neither had I.

Through all that afternoon we three might have been alone in the Castle of Gath. If others spoke or moved, we neither saw nor heard them, and, when the light faded, we were still without any grounds on which to base any belief.

Of the ways of the castle Adèle knew far less than we, for she had been brought in blindfold and had never, before we seized her, been beyond the 'gallery of stone': but, had she been able to tell us that a tunnel led out of the chapel to Salzburg itself, the knowledge would not have helped us, for we dared not use the passage, in case it was held.

What remained of the waterfall cord was some sixty feet long, and this we had all ready to help our escape. Could we, therefore, have gained the roof, we could doubtless have reached the spur; but we had no means of ascent, and, though I essayed both chimneys, these were built of hewn stone and only a very small child could have made its way up their shafts.

But for Adèle, Mansel and I would have sallied and might well, I think, have escaped. If the passage was under fire, at least it must be lighted by windows which overlooked the courtyard, and we would have chanced a lot in order to reach the gate. To such a risk, however, we dared not expose Adèle. Here I think we were wise. Unless he could starve us to surrender, 'Rose' Noble's hope of ransom was gone by the board: once we sallied, therefore, the fellow had nothing to gain by sparing our lives – but much to lose, for he knew very well that we would shoot him at sight. Add to this that we had lately enraged him as never before, and you will see that to run such a gauntlet, with Adèle, so to speak, in our arms, was out of the question.

At last we decided to write a message to George and making it into a parcel, to cast it over the cliff.

So far as my memory serves me, this was how the note ran:

*George.*

*The rope has been cut. We are fast in the Closet and the Bedchamber and we have got Adèle. There is a passage connecting the two stone galleries and looking upon the courtyard. You will attack tomorrow – Friday, half an hour after dark. As before, gain the roof: go directly to the door in the south-west tower: guard that: then let fall three ropes to the windows of the King's*

*Closet: the moment these are in place,* demonstrate. *You will demonstrate by letting down a ladder to one of the windows of the passage and accidentally breaking the glass. Carefully rehearse the demonstration, which must last one minute. Whilst it is going on, you will take up Adèle by one of the ropes: rush her along the roof, lower her down to the spur and run with her for the wood: Chandos and I will follow. Not counting the caretakers, 'Rose' Noble is, I think, alone – except for those who escaped when you stopped the car. Work out the whole attack with the greatest care: it must not fail.*

We wrapped the note in oiled silk and then in a wet coat of mine, to serve as ballast: this we made into a parcel, and at ten o'clock that night I hurled it over the cliff.

Neither Mansel nor I had expected to sleep at all, for the castle gate had to be watched as well as the doors of the chambers in which we lay; but Adèle insisted on taking her turn with us, so each of us slept for two hours and watched for four.

Adèle, was the first to rest, and I was the last; and I remember how I stole up the stairway at two o'clock, to find the rooms full of moonlight, Adèle in the midst of the doorway with her fair head against the jamb, and Mansel sleeping like a child, with her arms about him and his head in her lap. And, when he was gone to the archway and I would have lain alone, she would not have it so, but made me lie down as he had and pillow my head upon her.

The castle gate was not opened during the night: and this made us certain that those that had left with the car were in Hanbury's hands.

We, therefore, decided to watch no more from the archway, but only to use it as and when we required. To this end we stopped the keyholes of the door and the gate and wedged a cage-grate in the channel beneath the door, to prevent an entry by stealth while our backs were turned.

And here let me say that before it was light we had all three bathed in the channel and made as fair a toilet as our means would allow. Mansel and I could do no more than shave and make ourselves clean, but Adèle must change her frock for one of a powder blue, and, when we sat down to breakfast, she was as point-device in appearance as though she had just left her bedroom in London Town.

The day passed quietly enough, and, except that one of us was always in the Bedchamber, listening for any sound, we kept no particular watch.

Adèle and Mansel were happy as the day was long. I have never seen two beings so plainly glad of each other, so easy and natural in their love. There was nothing common or unclean in all their tenderness, and, so far from embarrassing my senses, my acquaintance with such devotion lifted up my heart.

One thing only troubled us, and that was the absolute silence which reigned without our doors.

That 'Rose' Noble should make no sound was natural enough: yet the continuous absence of any sign of life came to insist that we had the castle to ourselves and to tempt us against all reason out of our lair. This temptation we certainly resisted, but with every hour the suggestion that we were alone increased in strength, until, when the evening came, we were all three unsettled and did not know what to think. In a way this did not matter, for, if, indeed, 'Rose' Noble were out of the way, our release by Hanbury must be a simple affair: yet the bare idea of such fortune seemed something sinister, like the counsel of a prophet whose eyes are not straight in his head.

"The truth is," said Mansel, "we ought to have played his game. We shouldn't have made a sound for twenty-four hours. Then he'd 've begun to wonder if we were gone: and at last he'd 've tried to find out and shown his hand. As it is, the positions are reversed, and he's fairly got us guessing – which is just what he wants."

This was uncommon sense, but, even whilst I agreed, I found myself supposing that 'Rose' Noble was dead or gone and finding the supposition curiously untoward.

For this strange uncertainty of outlook I have never been able to account: I am not given to imagining vain things, or to letting my fancy fly in the face of fact: yet, though I was not uneasy, my mind would not come to rest, but continually dwelled upon the silence and the prosperous tale which it told.

At last the day was over, and dusk came in.

When it was dark, we opened the Closet windows and shut the trap-door. Then Mansel set me at a window, with Adèle by my side, and himself to watch the Bedchamber until the moment should come.

The night was most black and still, and I stood leaning out into the thunderous air, straining my ears for the rustle of a rope coming down...

But none came: and, after a long time, I began to feel sick at heart.

I did not move, for the night was before us, and while it was dark we could hope: but Hanbury was always punctual – and now he was late...

I do not know how long I stood there, but suddenly my heart bounded as I heard a movement above.

An instant later I had a rope in my hands...

As I put my weight upon it, another rope brushed my arms, and almost at once, a third.

By my silent direction, Adèle gave one flash with her torch and, in a twinkling, Mansel was by our side.

Himself he tested the ropes: then he bound one about her and lifted her on to the sill.

Adèle put her arms round his neck and pressed her face against his.

So we stayed, waiting...

Then came a clatter from the passage and the shiver of broken glass.

"My beautiful darling," said Mansel, and swung her out of the window and into the night.

For a second he watched her rising: then he drew back.

"You next, William," he said; "as quick as you can."

At once I leaned out to grope for the other two ropes.

As I did so, a second clatter came from beyond our doors.

"Quick," breathed Mansel. "That demonstration's too thin."

Desperately I flung out both arms, sweeping the air – *and found nothing*.

"They're gone," I cried, drawing back. "They were – "

Mansel was at the next window, leaning out and craning his neck.

As I did the same, a very faint exclamation came down from above.

And then a thick laugh.

"Isn't that nice?" said 'Rose' Noble.

# VII

# WE PRACTISE TO DECEIVE

Try as I will, I cannot distinctly remember what then took place, and I think that I acted blindly, as a man in a trance.

I know that we were both in the passage, the main doors of which were fast shut, that our rope was dangling from a window and that Mansel was about to go down, when the beam of a torch illumined his head and shoulders, and a bullet sang past his ear.

I know that the light and the shot both came from directly above, so that, placed as we were, we could not so much as reply.

I know that we were both on the terrace and that Mansel was casting the rope in the vain hope of catching a merlon in the noose he had made.

I know that we were both in the antechamber, that the great door was as we had left it and that, whilst I fought like a madman to shift the bolt, Mansel was kneeling beside me with his head in his hands...

At last I felt a touch on my shoulder, and Mansel got to his feet. I followed him into the Dining-room slowly enough. My head was strangely heavy, and I felt shaken and spent. Had he bade me lie down and sleep, I should have done his bidding without a word. The shock of what we had done had left me listless.

Mansel sat down in a chair, and I sat down in another and waited for him to speak.

To be honest, I hoped he would stay silent, for I could think of no comment upon our case which would not be bitter as death and wholly vain: but, when he began to speak, he did so with such composure as fairly shamed me out of a humour so recreant and so mean.

"Something, of course," he said quietly, "has happened to George. I can tell you the time when it happened – ten o'clock yesterday night. He was awaiting a message at the foot of the cliff. No doubt he was being watched. And, when the packet fell down, the enemy laid him out and picked it up. When I say 'George,' I mean 'George and the servants,' of course. They're not four any more – four effectives: they may not even be three...

"Point number two – *'Rose' Noble is not alone*. He may have been yesterday morning, but he's certainly not alone now. I suppose he took them in by a rope some time last night. Anyway, he's smarter than I am, and Punter or Casemate has certainly bested George.

"Point number three – *we must get out of this suite*. I should never have split our force: and now, by hook or by crook, I've got to join it again. If Carson or George is alive, they'll attack tonight, and we've got to open the gate and let them in. What's a thousand times worse, if we're still at his mercy tomorrow, 'Rose' Noble will put on the screw...

"Point number four – *the 'hands-up' phase is over*. From now on seeing is shooting, and shooting to kill. 'Rose' Noble's still hoping to break me, for the sake of doing a deal: but he knows it's a chance in a million and he's not going to risk his life by sparing mine."

And there, I remember, he happened to cast down his eyes.

We were not without light, for he had the torch in his hand, but this he was holding downward, so that its beam made a circle upon the floor.

For a moment he did not move. Then he was out of his chair and down on his knees...

Clean around the table there was a crack in the floor.

It was a very fine cleft and was choked with dust and the wax with which the floor had been rubbed; but these gave way at once to the point of a knife, and then we could see that the floor had been sawn asunder with the finest of saws.

I could scarcely believe that here was another trap-door, for, for one thing only, the cleft was surrounding the table with a fair two inches to spare, and a trap-door some eight feet by five seemed out of reason: yet, for some purpose or other, the floor had been cut, and, what seemed to me still more strange, except by the dust and the wax, the cleft had never been stopped.

Mansel was speaking in my ear.

"The table sinks through the floor. I saw it once before in some castle. The idea was to gain privacy. No servants in the room; but the table descended and rose between each course." He touched the smooth oak beneath the table. "This piece of the floor is really no more than a lift: and, if we can find out its trick..."

I sought to move the table, but it was fixed to the floor.

"That's right," breathed Mansel. "The other I saw was fixed. I remember they said it was raised by a system of pulleys and weights. The weights weighed far more than the table, so it couldn't descend on its own or so much as budge, but had to be hauled down by a windlass between each course."

"It's as firm as a rock," said I, stooping. "You don't think it's locked into place."

Mansel shrugged his shoulders.

"We must try to find out," he said. "If we can weight it enough..."

Then I saw that, with four counterweights, each, let us say, of the weight of the table and lift, these two would seem as much fixed as though they had beneath them a girder to hold them in place – *until there was laid upon them a burden three times their own weight*; but that if we could manage to load them to this extent the table would sink through the floor and open a way of escape.

In silence we lifted the chairs and set them upon the board: they were immensely heavy, but the table stood fast. Ten more chairs we added, bringing them one by one from the other rooms and using our rope to lash the perilous pile. But, though we added our weight, the mass never budged.

And here we were brought to a standstill, for, though there were yet more chairs, we had used all the rope we had and we could not think how to get them on to the top of the structure their fellows made.

Suddenly I thought of the slab which Mansel and I had hidden beneath the King's bed...

We had dragged this into the chamber, and I was under the table, with my feet braced against the great stretcher, hauling the stone into place, and sitting, as it happened, directly upon the cleft, when I felt a definite movement beneath my seat.

At once I told Mansel, and, after a short consultation, we lay down upon opposite sides and, taking hold of the stretcher, began to pass by inches on to the lift.

As I drew myself on, I felt this beginning to move, and all at once we were sinking into some cold, dark place.

We must have come down with a crash, but the chairs we had piled on the table were overlapping the lift, and, when these were prevented by the floor, the lift, thus relieved of their weight, immediately stopped.

The torch now showed us a cellar, with a door in its eastern wall. About us was the massive cage in which the lift ran, and at each of its corners were a pulley and a rope and a great counterweight of stone. A little to one side stood the windlass, as Mansel had said.

And now, once again, as they say, we had the wolf by the ears.

The floor was but eight feet away, but, if one of us was to descend, the lift would instantly rise and, taking the other up, lock him once more into the Dining-room; while, if both descended at once, the lift would shoot back into place with a shock which would shake the castle and send the twelve chairs crashing to wake the dead.

But, after a little reflection, Mansel found out a way.

On the under side of the lift, right in its middle, was a hook: to this was attached the great rope which the windlass controlled. If we could reach this rope, the trick was ours.

Mansel took my left wrist in his hands and lowered me clear of the lift. At once I swung to and fro until I could reach and lay hold of the great iron hook. With my left hand I then laid hold of the edge of the lift, and Mansel climbed round my body and seized the rope. Then we came down the rope together, on to the ground.

We let the lift rise by inches, until it was back in its place, and then, with one accord, we turned to the door.

This was unfastened and brought us directly into what seemed a great hall.

For a moment I thought we were out, for I heard the gurgle of water as plain as could be, but then I perceived that the air was the air of a crypt, dank and something musty and very still.

After listening carefully, we ventured to light the torch.

The place was a kitchen, but had not been used as such for a number of years. There was the huge fireplace, with the chains for the spits hanging down, and a grate like a hay-rack to serve a dozen joints. Five great, shuttered windows were looking upon the courtyard, and a doorway, whose step was muddy, was in the same wall.

And on the hearth lay George Hanbury, with his wrists and his ankles bound and a gag in his mouth.

That George had been left there to live, if he could, but, if he could not, to die we had not much doubt. He had lain there, gagged and bound, for twenty-four hours: his bonds had never been loosened, he had been given no water, much less any food: he had not so much as been visited. And such as will so use a prisoner are scarcely like to be troubled to find him dead.

Happily George was strong, and his condition of health as fine as ours, and, when we had set him free and had chafed his limbs, he was able to rise and to walk as straight as he pleased. It was clear, however, that he must have food and drink, and, since there remained in the Closet some brandy and bread and meat, we made our way back to the cellar without delay.

By using the windlass, we had the lift down at once, but, when I would have gone up, Mansel put me aside.

"I'm going," he said. "And please give me full five minutes before you bring me down. Now that one's got to go back, he may as well cover our tracks: the pile of chairs doesn't matter, but that slab would make anyone think."

With that, he mounted the lift, and I hoisted him up.

And while he was gone, George Hanbury told me his tale.

"When the car came out of the castle, I was down by the beechwoods at the foot of the cliff. Rowley was with me, but Carson and Bell and Tester were on guard, within sound of the drive.

"Carson heard the car coming, and the moment it passed he gave chase. I don't know whether they had expected this, but they did the best they could think of to shake him off. Of course they failed. They didn't bother much about the foot of the cliff: they certainly went that way, for I saw them go by, but they passed at sixty and never so much as slowed up. The sight of them worried me, but I didn't see what I could do but stay where I was. Of course Carson could have caught them, but, as Bell and he were alone, he thought he couldn't do better than cling to their heels. For half an hour they had the devil's own luck – never a check. Then comes a hairpin bend, and two hundred yards further on a flock of sheep...

"When Carson rounded the corner, Bunch was fifty yards off and *turning his car*. Sheep or no, it was an excellent move. The car has a shortish wheel-base, but a Rolls takes some getting round. Then Carson did well. He stopped, went into reverse and started to back to a turning he'd marked at the top of the hill. Before he could get there, Bunch was coming like hell. There was Punter beside him, and Casemate was back in the car. As they went by, Punter fired full at Carson and hit the brim of his hat...

"This annoyed Carson and Bell, and I must say I'm not surprised. And, as soon as the Rolls was round, they put her along. By this time Bunch had stolen a bit of a start, but they gradually overhauled him, and, choosing a smooth bit of going, Bell took a shot at their tank. He didn't hit it that time, but he laid it open the next...

"It was now a matter of time and nothing else. Bunch might do another three miles, but he couldn't do more, so Carson fell back a little, to keep, as he judged, out of range. Considering they'd fired again and made a hole in the screen, I think he was wise.

"They were now not more than six miles from the foot of the cliff, and heading that way. The road was full of bends, so half the time the cars were out of each other's sight. You can guess what happened. Three miles on Carson rounded a bend to see the car, doors open, by the side of the road. Of course, he put down his foot and went by a blue streak. Two shots were fired, but they didn't do any harm.

"Then Carson drove back to the spur, and he hadn't been there ten minutes when I came in. I was as pleased as Punch when I heard his report. I assumed they'd gone out to get food: and now their car was done in, and they were cut off. We fairly picketed that spur. A ferret couldn't have passed the line we held...

"Bell and I visited the beechwoods at three. I hated leaving the spur, but it didn't seem prudent for one to go out alone. We saw no one, and, when we got back, Carson had nothing to report.

"At last it began to grow dark, and I had to face two fresh facts. The first was this. According to plan, one of the cars must now leave for the foot of the cliff *and stay there perhaps till dawn*. That was awkward enough, but the second was worse. It was a yard of pearls to a bootlace that Punter and Casemate and Bunch would try to get home that night.

"After a lot of reflection, I decided to go alone to the foot of the cliff. I went. I meant to take Tester, but at the last I forgot. I found the rope gone and imagined you'd pulled it up. At ten o'clock something fell down about ten yards from where I stood. As I bent over it, somebody laid me out...

"Well, there you are."

"The next thing I knew I was lying in the back of the Rolls, which was doing forty over a wicked road. Then I was taken out and hauled through a ground-floor window into the Castle of Gath."

"Of course it was easy. When the servants heard the Rolls coming, they thought it was me. They probably thought it odd that I should drive on up to Gath, but, before they'd scented the trouble, the fat was burnt."

As I bent again to the windlass, my mind was full.

Not only was 'Rose' Noble's foresight a fearsome thing, but the fellow was very well served. Punter and Bunch and Casemate had done uncommonly well. But what struck me most of all was that, though their car had been ruined and the Rolls was at their gate, the temptation to take her inside had been withstood. That for this resolution we had 'Rose' Noble to thank, I have no doubt: the others would scarce have renounced so handsome a prize. Yet, had we seen the Rolls in the archway, the sight would have told us that George was out of the running, and Adèle would not have been delivered into the enemy's hand. This was the pink of strategy – the casting away of a sceptre to win a crown: and I must confess a sudden, craven fear that we should never outwit a man so firm of purpose and so unearthly wise.

The gurgle of water in the kitchen came from a little well. This had been sunk in the floor and was fed by a pipe which clearly ran out of the channel we knew so well. A similar pipe was conducting the overflow. By this simple device, the cooks had always fresh water ready to hand, and, what is more to the point, poor George was able to drink and to bathe his aching jaws. Then we plied him with brandy and made him eat what there was, for, though he made light of his bondage, a man cannot suffer as he had and feel as sound the same night.

While he was eating and drinking, we laid our plans.

That the servants were close at hand we had no doubt. Indeed, it seemed certain that they would any moment attack. If they did so before we could reach them, they would assuredly fail, for, for one thing only, they would enter by way of the roof, which the enemy was holding against our escape from the suite. They would thus walk clean into a trap, of which we, below, could not warn them, because we could not climb up. We, therefore, determined to make at once for the gate and, opening this if we could, to bring them in. If we could contrive to do this without being seen or heard, we should for the first time have the advantage of the enemy, for, whilst they were sure that they had but two men to deal with, and those under lock and key, in fact there would be six men free and within their camp.

The kitchen-door was unlocked and yielded without any fuss.

As we looked into the courtyard, hardly daring to breathe, the beam of a torch swept the wall beneath which we stood. It was little more than a flash and came, as before, from above; but it showed that the passage windows were still being watched. We had expected no less, but, although the beam was directed upon the wall, it lighted quite twenty feet of the courtyard itself, and, unless we could cross this belt between the flashes, we could not fail to be seen.

"No good waiting," breathed Mansel. "We must go across one by one. The first twenty feet on foot and as hard as we can: then, down on your face and crawl the rest of the way. If we go lightly, the water will cover our noise. Chandos first. Wait for me in the porch: I may be a little time coming, because I must shut this door. And now stand by."

Whilst he was speaking, the flashes came and went, but at intervals so irregular that no observation could help us, and we had nothing to do but to take our chance.

At last Mansel gave the word, and I made my dash.

As I fell on my face, a flicker lit up the courtyard...

Ten minutes later we were all three in the porch.

The wicket-gate was locked, and its key was gone. We, therefore, made ready to open the great gate itself, using the greatest care to make no sound. And here, to our vexation, we met with another check. Though we could feel the great bolts, we could not make out how to draw them, for each was engaged with some catch which we could not release. It was dreadful to stand there fumbling, because of some simple holdfast never devised to embarrass a porter's hand, but intended to prevent the bolts turning under battery of the gate. Yet show a light we dared not: and, as the minutes went by and the catch still mocked our fingers for want of sight, I began to feel that Fortune was not so much frowning upon us as laughing at us in her sleeve.

Then Mansel gave a short sigh and drew his bolt, and a moment later his fingers were playing with mine.

As the door yielded, he put his mouth to my ear.

"You go and find them," he said. "Hanbury and I stay here. If you don't strike them at once, try using the torch. But—"

And there, somewhere behind us, a shot rang out.

As we swung round –

"I saw the flash," said Hanbury. "Up *on the roof.*"

I ran full tilt into Rowley, who was standing at the foot of the ladders, with a cord in his hand.

"Oh, thank God, sir," says he. "We thought you were gone."

I shook him by the shoulder and pointed up to the roof.

"Recall them!" I cried. "Recall them! How can you get them back?"

He was tugging at the cord, like a madman, when another two shots rang out.

I could not stand there idle, but began to go up the wall.

I was on the second ladder, when someone above me looked down.

"Is that you, Bell?"

"Yes, sir."

"Get Carson and come down to the gate."

"Very good, sir."

I slid and fell back to the ground, to run to the gate.

Mansel was standing, waiting, cool as a man in a garden, regarding his flowers.

"Carson must stay out," he said. "I daren't have everyone in. He and Tester must feed us and keep the cars. Send him for food and drink, as soon as he's down. And two fifty-foot lengths of rope. The others come in."

Whilst he was speaking, another four shots were fired, and I ran back to Rowley with my heart in my mouth.

Him I sent to the gate and took his place. I think he was glad to go, for the firing was growing hotter, and to stand at the foot of the ladder in the knowledge that those you were awaiting might very well never come down pulled at a man's nerves.

Such concern will seem out of reason. When six men set out in a body to play with fire, it hardly becomes them to tremble lest someone be burned. But our outlook was not so simple. We feared no more for Carson than Carson feared for himself: but we all of us feared very much for the matter in hand. Our school was not that of 'Rose' Noble. If one of us was wounded, we could not let him lie: he would have to be saved and attended at any cost: how high that cost would be no one could tell, but, placed as we were, we all knew that such a distraction might ruin our enterprise.

It seemed an age before Bell began to descend...

"Are you hit?" said I.

"Oh, no, sir," said he. "Nor's Carson. But, of course, we had to go slow."

I sent him to Mansel at once.

Then a shot was fired right above me, and Carson came down with a run.

"Come," said I, and led him away up the spur...

It was well that I did so, for a light leaped out of the darkness, and a bullet went over our heads. To round the picture, I turned and fired back at the torch. No doubt the bullet went wide, but the light was put out.

Then I stopped and gave Carson his orders and told him that we were all safe, and he promised to be at the gate in a quarter of an hour. Then I stole back to the castle, and Mansel took me in.

Two doorways led out of the archway, one upon either hand. These Mansel set us to watch till Carson should come: "but I don't think," said he, "they'll disturb us: they've got their hands full. They've the roof to watch, and the passage, and it won't be light for three hours."

Here he was right, for Carson came and went, but nobody else; and, though lights flashed on the roof and the passage windows were closely and continually watched, no one came down to the archway or entered the great courtyard.

Carson went heavily away, for, though his part was most dangerous – because, except for Tester, he was alone – and though he would be the sole link between us and the world we knew, he had the true heart of a fighter and could hardly bear to leave us at such a pinch.

Early next morning he was to drive into Lass and there to take in supplies which should last us a week. He was then to bestow the two cars as best he could, somewhere beyond the wood and by the cross roads. He was not to move during the day, but by night he was to come to the spur and there wait till one of us met him or else it was dawn.

Then Mansel shut the gate and shot the great bolts and set his face again to the business of reaching Adèle, or, to be more precise, of thrusting between her and 'Rose' Noble, *before the latter knew we were there*.

One thing was plain. Before the night was over, we must either have accomplished our purpose or have gained some room or corner where we could lie hid. Now the only shelter we knew was that of the cellar beneath the dining-room's floor, but, since our goal was, as ever, the south-west tower, we decided to make for the latter and to trust to striking another and more convenient lair.

Now, though we knew next to nothing of the way from the porch to Adèle, we had one valuable clue.

When Casemate had been hounded by 'Rose' Noble to 'turn out the car,' he had certainly reached the porch as quickly as ever he could. Now his shortest path, as we knew from the bookseller's guide, was down the Grand Staircase and across the courtyard. *But Casemate had not crossed the courtyard.* It was, therefore, perfectly plain that that way was shut.

We, therefore, turned to the door in the western wall of the porch, for Casemate had come out of that, and that could, therefore, lead us back to the 'gallery of stone.'

I could set down our passage in detail, for I remember most clearly every step that we took. The hopes and fears which attended us, the sudden shocks of thankfulness and dismay, the waves of suspense, and relief – all these are engraved upon my memory as letters cut upon a stone. But I think that such a recital would be out of place, for only those that were there could find it moving, and I have not the mind or the skill to trick it out.

And so I will only say that by galleries, stairs and chambers we made our way in the darkness towards the south-west tower. Again and again boards creaked beneath our weight, and sometimes, do what we would, a hinge would whine: we made mistakes in our going and were forced to retrace the steps we had been at such pains to take; and we went at a true snail's pace and as blind men go, for we dared not use our torches in case their light should betray us and ruin our game.

At break of day we stood in a little lobby that looked out upon the mountains and seemed at that misty moment to command the world.

The place had the look of a guard-room, and so, I am sure, it had served, for a wicket gave directly on to a winding stair, which if a man ascended he came to the roof, but, if he went down, *he came to the 'gallery of stone.'* It was, indeed, the stairway of the south-west tower.

So we broke and entered into that jealous keep which for six long days had mocked us and all our works.

The need for caution was now paramount.

We stood at the enemy's elbow, and he did not know we were there. We had our hand almost upon him; but he had his hand on Adèle. He was unready, but we did not know the ground. If we could strike before he could, the game was ours: but if we were to be behindhand, we had better be sitting at Lass with our hands in our lap.

We afterwards found that there were in the tower three apartments, consisting of two rooms each. These were a bedroom and bathroom, very well done. The window from which Adèle had signalled was that of the middle apartment, the door of which, as she had told us, gave into the 'gallery of stone.'

For a long time we crouched like animals, straining our ears; but we could hear no sound. Then Mansel breathed his orders, and we began to move...

George stood fast in the lobby, ready to shoot at sight: Bell and Rowley stole three steps up the stair and stayed with their backs to the wall and their knives in their hands: and Mansel, with me behind him, began to go down...

It was dark in the gallery, for all its five doors were shut, but a pale smear of light was betraying the threshold of the door which led to the terrace steps. That gave us our bearings at once, but, if there was someone there, we could not see him, and the silence all about us was that of death.

Then came a sigh of the wind, and something moved.

It was a door on our right – the door of the prisoner's room.

Very slowly we watched it open, letting the daylight out. I could see Mansel just before me, covering the gap with his pistol and steady as any rock. I could see beyond him and into the very room. The floor was bare and polished, and the walls were panelled with oak.

Then, very slowly, the door began to close.

In a flash Mansel had stopped it, and we were within the room.

This was empty.

A window had been left open, and that had occasioned the draught. The bathroom was empty, too. Adèle was gone.

Two minutes later we had proved the truth to the hilt.

*The three apartments were vacant, and the door to the roof was shut. 'Rose' Noble, prisoner and all had withdrawn to the opposite tower.*

It was a bitter business.

That our labour was lost was nothing: but the waste of time shocked us, and the thought that, so far from progressing, *we were now twice as far from Adèle as we had been at the time when we stood in the porch* was plain torment.

That we never had any doubt where 'Rose' Noble and his prisoner were gone, I attribute to Mansel alone. Only a brilliant perception can rip the skin off an assumption and bare a fact. Everything certainly argued withdrawal to the south-east tower: but that was not nearly enough. We had to *know*. And Mansel knew.

I have said we were now twice the distance that we had been from Adèle. And so it seemed, for we dared not use the roof during the day and, as we had reason to know, the way by the Royal Apartments was straitly barred. Yet the thought of returning to the porch and thence beginning again to grope our way was hardly to be endured, because the clock was against us and we feared to let go so much time. Cross the porch in daylight we could not, because of the man on the roof. We must, therefore, wait until nightfall to make the move – some sixteen hours of inaction, when time was so very dear. The harder we stared upon this prospect, the more ugly and hazardous it grew: the more the daylight broadened, the more perilous seemed delay. Any moment 'Rose' Noble might discover that Mansel and I had escaped: any moment the kitchen might be entered, and Hanbury's release become known: any moment one of the gang might stumble into our arms, and, though we could stop his mouth, his failure to reappear would tell its tale. And if none of these things happened and we lay close until night, would our passage be so successful as the passage that we had made? *Was there a way within doors to the south-east tower?* And what of the caretakers? That we had not found them last night suggested most strongly that their rooms lay the other side: and if we encountered the woman, she was most sure to give tongue...

For an hour we stayed in the gallery, keeping such watch as we could and, for my part, feverishly considering what we should do.

At length Mansel bade us all listen and, with the plainest reluctance, unfolded the following plan.

"Mr Chandos and I must re-enter the Royal suite. That we can do from this end without any fuss. Mr Hanbury with Bell and Rowley will go to the top of this tower. Ten minutes after we have entered, Mr Chandos will give a great cry. The sentinel watching the courtyard will rush to the opposite wall, to see me piled up on the terrace, with a length of rope in my hand. I shall plainly have fallen down while attempting to scale the wall. Mr Chandos will be kneeling beside me, trying to lift me up. The sentry will rush to his tower to raise the alarm. He will surely leave the door open – the door from the roof. *Mr Hanbury and Bell and Rowley will immediately cross the roof and follow him in.*

"Now I think that 'Rose' Noble will go to the terrace at once: and the others with him. You see, if I were to die, Mrs Pleydell, comparatively speaking, would hardly pay for her keep. So I think they'll all get down to me as fast as they can. Very well. While they are gone, Mr Hanbury, Rowley and Bell will find Mrs Pleydell, release her and carry her off. Let her down to the spur with Rowley and see that she runs for the wood. Carson to drive her to Poganec there and then. *Not until she's down on the spur* will Mr Hanbury and Bell return to the tower – with the object of killing 'Rose' Noble before he kills them."

He paused there for a moment, biting his lip.

"I don't like it," he added slowly, "but I don't know what else to do. It washes me out of the battle and Mr Chandos, too: but a part must be played which no one but we two can play. 'Rose' Noble has got to be drawn from his prisoner's side. And nothing that I can think of will do that, except my health. Any ordinary demonstration would make him stick tighter than ever to Mrs Pleydell's arm. But tell him I'm down and out, and, though he won't believe you, *he'll go to see*. And on that point, one word more.

"Instead of rushing to the terrace, 'Rose' Noble might rush to the roof. He's a very shrewd man. If he does, you've got him, you three. Don't wait. Just let him have it – both barrels and one for luck. Once he's over, you won't see the others for dust."

As he spoke, some door was opened, and down the winding stairway came Punter's voice.

"An', when you're through, you might take a look at the Willie. I don't suppose he'd bite you if you took out his bit."

"Rose said – " began Casemate.

"I know," said Punter. "That's Rose. But I don't fancy dead men. You can shove the corpse in the ground, but a yard full of sextons can't bury the – shout. One or two dead's enough, and before this worry's over you'll see all that. No. Let the – waste if you like, but keep 'im alive."

At Punter's first word we had begun to withdraw, for it had been arranged that, at the first show of movement, we should immediately enter the room which Adèle had used. At a sign from Mansel, however, I let the others retire and began to follow him gently up the stair. This was, of course, of stone, so we made no sound.

It was a desperate move, but I knew where Mansel was going and I knew he was right to go.

*Casemate was bound for the kitchen: so Casemate had to be stopped*. And, if he reached the guard-room before us, the game was up. You cannot pursue in silence over a wooden floor.

Mercifully the voices continued, but I never knew what they said. My ears were strained to catch nothing but a step on the stair.

But none came. Only the voices grew clearer the higher we went.

We glided into the guard-room, after the way of a snake. Then we turned right and left and stood, one on each side of the doorway, with our backs flat against the wall. The wicket opened outwards, so we were very well placed.

"I don't care," Casemate was saying, "I don't like the – job. I don't mind dirty weather, but I like to know where I am."

"If you must know," said Punter, "you're up on the velvet top. Mansel put up a bluff, and its bottom's fell out. Rose has got 'im as tight as a – "

"Never knew when he hadn't," said Casemate. "First, he'd never find us: and then he'd never get in. Now you say 'That's all right, but he'll never get out.' An' what about Jute? Where's Jute?"

"Jute knows 'is garden," said Punter. "If Jute don't come in, it's because there's some rhubarb wants watchin' the other side."

"If you ask me," said Casemate, "Jute's – *well pulled out*."

"Oh, put it away," said Punter. "Why, Jute – "

" – well pulled out," repeated Casemate. "He's had a look at his seaweed and he's got in out of the rain. An' I don't blame 'im. 'Half a million,' says Rose, 'for the pickin' up.' '*Pickin' up.*' " He sucked in his breath. "I wonder what he'd call 'reachin' down.' An' when I said 'Who's this Mansel?', he says 'He's a one-legged Willie, with a college way of talking and a mouth full of rubber teeth.' "

"Now, look 'ere," said Punter earnestly. "I don't deny that Mansel's not big small stuff. He ran round Jute, an' he climbs like a – ape. But that's where 'e gets off. He's not up to Rose's weight."

"He never was," said Casemate. "But he – near got him down: an' he's not dead yet."

"Now look at it this way," said Punter, plainly doing his best to hearten his doubting friend. "A man don't cough up half a million because you tickle 'is chin. He's got to be broke in pieces, an' then some more. Well, he's not going to hand you the funny 'ammer, you know. He's goin' to bite an' scratch – till you've got him stuck. Well, he's had his bite an' his scratch, an' now he's – well stuck. I'll tell you this. So long as Mansel was out, I never slep' sound. I've seen 'im before, an' I like to know 'is game. But now I'll put my feet up, because the – 's stuck. – well stuck, like a bug pinned up on a board. An' you watch 'im come unbuttoned this afternoon. Wait till he hears the goods beginning to talk."

"It doesn't hurt," said Casemate. "I had my arm done once."

"I guess Rose didn't do it," said Punter. "And now slip after them eats. There's a pot o' strawberry back o' the cans of pears."

Casemate made no answer, but began to descend...

I think I shall always hear his steps on the stair.

To my fancy his tread seemed wary, as though the man were suspicious, apprehensive of ill to come. He certainly stood at the wicket for a quarter of a minute or more, as though he had remarked and was listening to the vigorous slam of my heart two paces away.

Then he pulled open the door and came into the room.

I did not see Mansel strike him, for the former had been a great boxer and was startlingly quick with his hands. But I heard the dull smack of the blow, and I saw Casemate spin on his heel and then fall away from me backwards, without a cry. I heard his head meet the stone, and his body fell down with a thud, but the sounds were dead sounds and could not, I think, have been heard at the head of the stair.

My eyes were still upon Casemate, when Mansel touched me and turned.

I pointed to the form on the floor.

"Safe for an hour," breathed Mansel. "The others will tie him up."

We whipped down into the gallery, and, whilst I summoned the others, Mansel undid the bolts of the passage door.

I must here confess that I quailed at the sight of that suite. For me it reeked of misfortune, of frantic endeavour doomed before it was begun: and to go back to such a cockpit of broken hopes was clean against my stomach. Yet, as Mansel had said, there was nothing else to be done; and, in view of the Casemate business, we had not a moment to lose.

I signed to Rowley to give me his coil of rope.

As he laid it about my shoulders,

"Shut the door, but don't bolt it," breathed Mansel. "And stand by to move in five – not ten minutes' time."

Hanbury nodded. I observed that he looked very pale.

Then Mansel stole into the passage, and I in his wake.

Before we had gained the Closet, the door had been shut.

The windows of the Closet were still open, as was the trap-door, and the room was full of sweet air and the murmur of the water below.

Mansel sat down on the floor, and swung his legs into the trap. Then he looked up and smiled.

"William," he said, keeping his eyes upon mine, "we're going to bring this right off. I know you're frightened to death of letting me down: but you won't – if you do as I say.

"I want you to stand at that window, and I'll tell you what you will see. Never mind whether you're dreaming or whether your sight is blurred. *This is what you will see* – and, consequently, what you will do.

"You'll see me come out of the archway on to the terrace below. You'll see me cast the rope and you'll watch it rise. At the second attempt you'll see it catch on something – you can't tell what. You'll see me test it and watch me begin to climb. I shall go up... up... up... Leaning well out of the window, you'll watch me with your heart in your mouth. When I'm six feet from the top, *to your indescribable horror* the rope will begin to slip. Instinctively you'll try to warn me – let out a hell of a cry. As you do so, the rope will go, and I shall come down. You'll see me asprawl on the terrace, lying appallingly still and you'll naturally rush to reach me as quick as you can. I shall be plainly disabled – for all you know, dead. Well, that means the game's over, and you'll naturally shout for help. When it comes, they may possibly seize you, but you'll only do your best to get back to my side. You see, I shall still be breathing, but the fall will have broken my back.

"And now let me have the rope.

"When you see my arm go back, you'll know that I'm going to sling it. Watch it rise and fall, and mark how I gather it up for the second cast."

As he spoke, he was making a slip-knot, but his eyes never left my face.

Then he smiled again and disappeared.

I made my way to the window, like a man in a dream...

I cannot swear to what happened in the next two minutes of time. That is the plain truth. Time and again I have called up the burden of those moments, started to set it down and then laid aside my pen. I remember it perfectly: but I cannot say 'This I imagined, and that I saw,' for the line between fact and fancy is a line that I cannot trace. Indeed I shall always believe that Mansel had influenced my will, for I did what I did dazedly and was conscious all the time of the smile upon Mansel's face and the light in his eyes.

I remember leaning out of the window and finding the air most heavy and the sunshine curiously dull: I remember how the sill of the casement punished my back and how the sweat was running upon my hands and face: I remember shrieking incoherence and feeling suddenly sick and staggering down to the archway, trembling in every limb...

And then I was all dripping wet and down on my knees, and Mansel lay huddled before me with one leg beneath the other and a loose look about his neck.

I got my arm under his shoulders and raised him up, but his head rolled over sideways and, though I tried to prop it, it would not stay.

I cried out at that, but maybe I had shouted before, for I saw 'Rose' Noble coming, with Punter and Bunch. They seemed to come down in a wave – down the steps from a door in the wall.

As they reached the terrace, a slim figure flashed in their wake. I watched it outstrip the three men... thrust them aside...

*Then Adèle was down beside me and sitting back on her heels, with agony in her eyes and Mansel's head in her lap.*

# VIII

## OUT OF SIGHT, OUT OF MIND

The shutting of a door roused me, and I sat up to find myself alone.

The mountain-tops before me were alight with sunshine, and in the huge void which lay between them and the terrace a great bird was sailing and wheeling, as an aeroplane at play.

For a moment I watched it lazily. Then I remembered with a shock the plan we had laid and how perfectly it had worked and how, in the moment of triumph, Adèle had brought it to nought.

In a flash I was on my feet, and trying to think what to do.

I had been left in a faint, not so much as bound. My pistol had been taken, but not my knife. It was clear that I was regarded as safe under lock and key.

At this my heart leaped up, for, of course, I could leave by the suite whenever I pleased: the only question was how to turn to account this unsuspected freedom.

In view of the turn events had taken, Mansel was sure to continue his pretence of a broken back: finding their purpose frustrated, George and the servants were probably lying concealed in the south-east tower: I was at liberty, and the enemy was clean off his guard. If we had shot at a pigeon, we had killed something more than a crow. We had made notable progress, and, before the day was over...

And there I remembered Casemate, and my dreams began to settle, as a house that is built upon sand.

*Casemate's failure to return would ruin everything.*

Quite apart from the finding of him senseless, which might any moment take place, the instant 'Rose' Noble learned that Casemate was not up to time, his ever-smouldering suspicion would burst into flame. He would see in a twinkling that here was our handiwork, and, with Mansel under his hand, would turn the tables upon us before we could think.

With a hammering heart, I ran to the channel and fought my way under the door. If I could do nothing else, at least I could get hold of Casemate and carry him out of sight. And, in any event, I was plainly better at large than cooped, like a dog, on the terrace, at the mercy of any whim that came into the enemy's head.

A moment later I was standing in the 'gallery of stone.'...

Casemate lay as we had left him, flat on his back.

To my surprise, he was neither gagged nor bound: then I remembered that we had never told George to tie him up. And I had no cord...

I carried him out of the guard room and along a passage by which we had come from the porch. There I found a bedroom that had not been used. I was preparing to thrust him under the bed and was wondering what fool had coined the saying 'Out of sight, out of mind,' and whether, had he known 'Rose' Noble, the adage would not have been revised, when another proverb came thrusting into my mind.

A *living dog,* saith The Preacher, is *better than a dead lion.*

And that made me think of the fable of the ass in the lion's skin.

And out of the two came wisdom, if you can call it such.

Richard William Chandos, alive and in Casemate's clothes, would be infinitely better than Casemate as good as dead. *Casemate could not return: but Chandos in Casemate's clothes could be seen in the porch...*

And here another idea leaped into my mind.

Casemate had been uneasy – had said so in so many words. "I don't like the – job." Punter had done his utmost to lay his fears, but the other would not be comforted, rebutting each effort of Punter's with some unpleasant truth. More, Casemate clearly believed that Jute had seen breakers ahead and had left the ship. 'And I don't blame him.' Was it incredible, then, that Casemate should follow Jute's lead? Open the castle gate, which he had to pass, slip out and up to the wood and so wash his hands of a business which he very plainly wished he never had touched? Even if he were not seen going, *the open gate would account for his failure to reappear*.

In less than three minutes Casemate was under the bed, and I was clad in his suit. This was none too clean and something tight; but I liked it better than his hat, which fitted me very well.

Now, though in this time much had happened, it was barely a quarter of an hour since Casemate had parted from Punter at the head of the stair. I had, therefore, a very good hope of suggesting that Casemate had flitted before he was due to return: but our hopes had so often foundered that, for all my haste, I stole, like a thief, from the bedroom, and went with my chin on my shoulder until the passage gave way to a flight of stairs.

So I came to the porch.

The courtyard was empty, and so, to my relief, was the roof. For a moment I found this strange: then I remembered that, when I had come to my senses, the rope which had lain on the terrace was no longer there, and, since without rope I could not descend from a window, it was plainly needless to post a sentinel.

At once I whipped to the gate and drew the great bolts. Then I set aside the shutter which masked the grill and, after a glance behind me, pulled the great leaf open and stepped outside.

I can never remember that moment without emotion.

The sparkle of the wet, green turf and the brilliant foliage beyond, the gay singing of the birds and the sweet smell of the earth filled me with a sudden amazement, as though I had clean forgotten that such things were. Yet, only three days before, I had drunk my fill of them. Which shows, I think, that the burden of those three days was even more exacting than we had guessed.

When I looked back through the grill, there was still no one to be seen; so, quick as a flash, I slipped back into the porch and, leaving the great door ajar, entered the doorway which stood in the eastern wall.

I was a little uneasy about the gate, for, to serve my purpose, it should stay so much open as to attract the eye; but this was the very thing which Casemate, deserter, would have done his best to avoid. Still, he could have done no more than draw it to, and, even while I stood thinking, the fresh north-westerly breeze took the matter out of my hands. At its instance the massive leaf began very slowly to move and had very soon swung so far that none that looked into the courtyard could ever have missed its tale.

Now all this was well enough: when his fellows began to wonder where Casemate could be, an excellent answer was staring them in the face: but a sudden fear came upon me lest Casemate himself should suddenly come to his senses and, rising as it were from the dead, offer a still better answer to his inquisitive friends. Mansel had said that he would be 'safe' for an hour; but it might very well be that more than an hour would elapse before we could afford to ignore the chance of his coming to life. And here, for the first time – fear, I suppose, breeding fear – I began to grow uneasy about the condition of things in the south-east tower.

I glanced at my watch.

Fifteen minutes had passed since I had sat up on the terrace to find myself alone. Yet there had been no action of any sort. I had seen no movement and I had heard no sound. We were four fit men to three, while the enemy thought they were three to one dying man. The odds were full in our favour. Yet, though time was precious, no blow had been struck.

As I stood, biting my fingers, the answer came into my mind. There was but one explanation – the old familiar stile was still barring our way. *Neither Mansel nor George nor the servants had been able to come between 'Rose' Noble and Adèle.* Close as they were to this bourne, the other's devilish instinct was holding them up: and, until this relaxed or the monster flew in its face, they dared not move.

Now that, I confess, was guesswork, but this was clear. Could they have done it, Mansel or George or both would have struck fifteen minutes ago. They had not, because they could not: and, if they could not then, God alone knew how long they would have to wait.

And that brought me back to Casemate. 'Safe for an hour.' Why, two, three, six hours might not be enough...

Now, though I could gag the man, I had no cord: and without cord I could not bind him as such a man should be bound. I, therefore, opened the door in the eastern wall of the archway in some hope of finding the store-room to which Casemate had been dispatched.

The door led into a chamber which was clearly the porter's lodge.

On either side of the window, which was some way above the ground, were steps leading up to two stalls, cut out of the wall, from which the porters could comfortably watch the spur. Facing the window was a door, with a key in its lock. I guessed at once that this led to the caretakers' room, or, at least, to the room in which they were now confined, for I had no doubt that they had been shut in their quarters, and these were sure to be within sound of the gate. A third door stood open, revealing a passage and staircase, both of stone...

Five rooms I entered, but, though I rummaged desperately, I could not light on so much as a foot of cord, or, for the matter of that, of any substitute. Not daring to wait any longer, I decided to make my way back, and, ripping the tick from a mattress, to tear this into strips and bind Casemate with those.

I, therefore, hastened back to the porch, but, before I crossed to the doorway in the opposite wall, I naturally put out my head to see that the coast was clear.

The roof was empty, but, standing in the courtyard, some ten or twelve paces away, was an elderly man. His back was towards me, but the cut of his clothes was not English, and, when he moved his head, I could see the shanks of spectacles resting above his ears. He was plainly hot, for he had his hat in his hand and was mopping his face, but he looked about him placidly and with evident relish, as a man who has made an effort and is content with his reward.

Then he turned suddenly about, and I knew him at once.

It was the bookseller of Lass.

To tell the truth, I was not greatly surprised.

The guide the old fellow had written showed very plainly his veneration for Gath: when he kept holiday, therefore, that he should visit the spur was natural enough: and though to walk seven miles to look at a castle wall may be the way of a zealot, I imagine his tastes were simple and his pleasures were few.

And so he had come to the spur to look upon Gath.

Finding the gate open, he had naturally seized the chance to make his way in and once more enjoy a prospect from which he had been lately debarred.

But, if I was not surprised, I was considerably moved.

Such was the emplacement of the castle, so thick was the wood that masked the spur and so lonely was the country round about that we had all come to ignore the chance of an outsider's entry upon the scene. This was now, however, an accomplished fact. A respectable citizen of Lass, an intelligent man, well acquainted with Gath and with its ownership, was actually within the walls and must already have found the open gate and the absence of any custodian matters for serious remark. More. His eyes had only to light upon George Hanbury, Bell or myself, when his suspicions would be instantly quickened by that most lively curiosity which our use of his apartment at Lass and our strange and precipitate departure must have aroused.

And here it seemed that Fortune was at last inclining towards our part, for, while the bookseller's presence could do us no harm, the last thing 'Rose' Noble desired was a witness of what was afoot.

Now all this swept through my mind in a tenth of the time it has taken to set it down, but right on the heels of this valueless speculation came a fair, clean-cut idea, upon which, for once, I had the good sense to act without any hesitation or weighing of odds.

The bookseller had not seen me, but I stepped out into his view. He looked very much surprised, but, before he could speak, I beckoned to him to follow and, crossing to the opposite doorway, led the way to a corner below some stairs.

"Look at me well," I whispered. "Have you ever seen me before?"

He replied directly that I was one of the strangers that had made some use of the parlour above his shop.

"That's right," said I. "And now, before I tell you how and why I come to be here, answer me this. Would you like to help a lady who goes in danger of death?"

"I would indeed," said the bookseller stoutly enough.

"Then listen," said I.

As shortly as ever I could, I told him a few of the facts. He heard me solemnly, with his big, blue eyes on my face.

"So you see," I said, in the end, "it's a business of life and death. You're not safe here. No one is: but a stranger, least of all. I'd be very glad of your help, but I'm bound to tell you that the only help you can give will involve you in a terrible risk."

"Thank you," said the bookseller politely. "Please tell me what I may do."

His calm firmness of purpose took me by storm: of pure gratitude I could have gone on my knees.

"In the first place," said I, "you're a doctor – remember that. A doctor out for the day. Hanbury met you in the road at the end of the drive. You can describe him, can't you? The man who bought *Alison's Europe* and borrowed your coat and hat. Very well. He asked you if you knew of a doctor, and when he heard you were one he begged you to come here at once. He said that you'd find the gate open and told you how to get to the south-east tower. There, he said, was a man very grievously hurt.

"Now that is the tale you will tell, when you get to the room: but, before you get so far, I think the fat man you find there will have rushed upstairs to the roof. The 'open gate' will fetch him, if nothing else. If he stays where he is, please pretend to examine the man who is lying hurt: take off his coat and shirt and feel his spine: then announce that his back is broken, but that, if he lies flat and still, he may possibly live. Then ask the fat man if he will kindly see if your son has arrived: say that *he was to follow you here as soon as he'd changed his tire.* That'll move the fat man all right. You see we've got to get him out of the tower."

"Sir," said the bookseller gravely, "it shall be done."

"It's a dangerous game," said I. "If he thinks that you're lying, the fat man will shoot you dead."

The old fellow smiled.

"I am old," he said simply. "And lonely. Since my wife was dead, I do not much value my life. But you and your lady are young... And, besides, I do not think he will think I am lying – this fat man of yours."

"He's pretty shrewd," said I.

"Let us go, please," said the bookseller, settling his hat on his head...

We had almost reached the guard-room and I had stopped to listen for any sound, when I heard the scamper of feet upon the roof.

The murder was out, and Punter or Bunch was running to shut the gate.

Mercifully the door of the bedroom in which I had hidden Casemate was less than ten paces away, so I opened it quickly and thrust the bookseller in. As I closed it behind me, I heard a flurry of footsteps and the clack of the guard-room wicket flung back against the wall.

Now, as I have said, the guard-room's floor was of stone; but the floor of the passage which followed was of oak boards that had been polished and highly waxed: and, since whoever was coming was running as fast as he could, I was not surprised that so soon as he left the guard-room and trod the oak, he slipped and lost his footing and took the deuce of a fall.

For a moment there was dead silence. Then I heard Punter's voice.

If he omitted any blasphemies, I cannot think what they were: he stayed quite still, vomiting a stream of imprecation and only interrupting his recital to groan with pain.

In the midst I heard other steps coming, and almost at once Bunch spoke.

"What's up?" said he. "Took a toss?"

"Oh, no," said Punter shakily. "Just 'avin' a lil lay down. 'Toss,' you gentle – ? I wish I'd got the – that shined these boards."

"It's comin' after the stones," said Bunch sententiously. "That's wot it is. You nips off of the stones on to – "

"My God," screeched Punter, "don't I know what you does? Ain't I jus' done it, you – ?"

"All right, all right," said Bunch soothingly. "But you ain't broke nothing, an' wot about shuttin' the gate?"

" – the gate," said Punter. "*An'* Casemate – the dirty swine. I knew the – was windy, but I never dreamed he was down to doin' a bunk."

"That's Jute," said Bunch. "'E would 'ave it Jute 'ad beat it, an' 'e thought the devil o' Jute."

"God knows why," said Punter bitterly. "It's Jute tore everything up. If 'e 'adn't let Mansel bounce 'im, we'd 've been in Paris by now – 'avin' our breakfast in bed, with our cheque books under our arms. 'Alf a million o' money, an' nothin' said. An' now you can 'ave my bit for a double Scotch."

"'E ain't dead yet," said Bunch.

"He's broke his back," said Punter. "Rose knows it better than us."

"Then, why's 'e waitin'?" said Bunch. "Sittin' there like a – policeman by the side o' the bed?"

"You can search me," said Punter. "I don' think 'e knows 'imself. But it's no good sayin' nothin' – 'e's just black ice. I thought the goods was dead when she slipped 'er cuff."

There was a gloomy silence.

Then –

"Come on," said Bunch. "Best shut that – gate."

The other got to his feet, and the two passed on.

I could hardly believe my ears when I heard the two of them making towards the porch. Here was a stroke of luck for which I had never hoped. And then I saw with a shock how wretched a plotter I was, for, with Punter and Bunch to waylay him, the 'doctor' would never have won to the room in which Mansel lay.

The bookseller was speaking.

"I have understood nothing," he said: "only 'Rose' is your lady's name."

"All slang," said I. "Thieves' talk. Never mind," and, with that, I opened the door.

Swiftly we passed through the guard-room and climbed the winding stair which led to the roof.

This was empty, and, now that I could see all around, seemed like the pleasance of some god-philosopher, whence he could watch and contemplate the world. The place did not seem like a roof, but like a gigantic terrace, hung in the air. Even the chimney-stacks could not disturb this illusion, for they had no chimney-pots and might have been great pedestals ready for statuary which had not yet been done. Indeed, the extraordinary prospect troubled my head, and I felt suddenly dizzy and the palms of my hands grew wet.

The sun was high now, and the shadow of the south-east tower lay sharp upon the flags. The stacks, too, threw their shadows and the battlements made a pattern along the side.

As I was peering, I heard the hollow clap of the castle gate...

A moment later we were standing by the door of the south-east tower.

"I'm afraid I can't tell you," I breathed, "which room they'll be in: but I think you'll find it leads out of the 'gallery of stone.'"

The bookseller nodded, and I put out my hand.

This seemed to please him, for he took it in both of his. Then he put his mouth to my ear.

"I go," he whispered, "to betray the violator of Gath."

Then he adjusted his spectacles, nodded, smiled and disappeared.

Now, if I had had a pistol, I should have stayed by the door, to kill 'Rose' Noble as he stepped on to the roof. But my pistol had been taken, and Casemate had carried no arms. I certainly had my knife, but I dared not trust my handling of such a weapon to make an end of such a man. I have often thought since that here I made a mistake and that I should have stabbed the monster as he came out of the door, but up to that day I had never done any worse violence than knock a man down with my fist, and I was frankly afraid of making a mess of the business and thereby wrecking the ship which I was trying to steer.

I, therefore, whipped to the nearest chimney-stack and crouched, with this between me and the south-east tower. This stack was to be my shield. As 'Rose' Noble came by, I would move, keeping it always directly between him and me, and, when he was by, I would dash for the south-east tower. Once within, I had but to shut the door and shoot the bolts to bring us over the bar which had balked us so long. The rest would be child's play. If five men armed could not break out at their pleasure... It occurred to me suddenly that, if there was no way by the chapel, Mansel would bring out Adèle through the Dining-room floor.

Looking back, I find it curious that I should have had no doubt that 'Rose' Noble would come up to the roof. That nine men out of ten would have done so is nothing at all. 'Rose' Noble was the tenth man in all that he did. I cannot pay him a higher compliment. Yet I never had any doubt that, once my decoy was in action, our enemy would fall into the pit which I had digged. I was as certain of this as if I had seen it written among the orders of Fate. This by the grace of God, for upon that certainty was founded the whole of my simple plan and, had I stopped to consider how bold was my postulate, I am sure that my judgment would have faltered and that I should have abandoned my design as out of reason.

'Rose' Noble came up quietly, without any haste. Had I not been expecting to hear them, I should not have heard his steps. I had thought that he would come running and crying for Punter or Bunch. But he did not. Rather he seemed to be prowling, like some suspicious beast.

For a moment he paused on the opposite side of my stack, for all the world as though he had heard me move. Then he went on his way to the south-west tower.

I let him take ten paces. Then I rounded the stack and made my dash for the door.

And here, I think, my heart stood suddenly still.

*The door was shut: and when I lifted the latch, I found it was barred.*

For an instant I stared at it blankly. Then the truth rose up in a blinding flash.

*Knowing nothing of me, Mansel had followed 'Rose' Noble up the stair and had played my hand before I could play it myself.*

The game was won – over: Adèle was saved: 'Rosae' Noble had been 'caught bending': *and so had I.*

A slight noise made me look round.

'Rose' Noble was standing, glaring, six paces away.

His face was working and his hand in his jacket-pocket was twitching with wrath. I think that he would have spoken, for twice he opened his mouth; but his fury must have choked him, for, though he gaped upon me, the words seemed stuck in his throat.

He was never a pleasant sight, but, so transfigured, he made as dreadful a picture as ever I saw, and I must confess that, as I looked upon him, my blood ran cold.

I was sure he was going to kill me, if only to serve his rage, for he knew as well as did I who it was that had shut the door and that Mansel, while he lay at his mercy, had bluffed him into discarding a winning hand. Indeed, had he guessed that George and the servants were actually in the tower, he would I believe, have shot me down like a dog: but, as the moments went by, yet he did not fire, I began to believe that he had still some hope of saving the game, and, since I was plainly his prisoner, had decided to hold me alive to his future use.

In a word, I was pretty desperate: but the thought of the part I had played in bringing him down did my heart good, and, what is more, it served to steady my nerves and to set my brain working to see if I could not hold out until help should come.

I folded my arms, leaned against the wall of the tower and waited for 'Rose' Noble to speak.

At length –

"How did you get here?" he said.

"Thanks to Hanbury," said I. "He opened the passage door."

In a flash he had me by the collar and a pistol was hurting my ribs.

"March," he said thickly.

Together we crossed the roof and entered the opposite tower. Then we went down the stair to the 'gallery of stone.' He held me to the wall with the pistol, while he bolted the passage door. An instant later we were back on the roof.

"How did you come by those clothes?"

"Mine were wet," said I. "And, as Casemate didn't need them – "

"Why didn't he need them?"

"Because Hanbury had laid him out."

The man's eyes burned in his head. They seemed to be striving to bore their way into my brain. Though he suspected it deeply, he could find no fault in my tale.

After a little he stepped to the balustrade.

"Bunch! Punter!" he roared.

For a moment he stood still, waiting: then he leaned over the stone.

"Come here," he cried.

Again he waited, like a great beast about to spring.

"Look in that – kitchen and see if it's all O.K."

There was a moment's silence: then I heard a scared voice.

"'E's gone!" cried Punter.

'Rose' Noble drew himself up and turned to me.

"Where's Hanbury now?"

"I don't know," said I. "He went to get the servants, but he hasn't come back."

"Why not?" said 'Rose' Noble.

"I don't know," said I. "I was waiting to let them in, when the doctor appeared. So I left the gate open and came straight up to the roof."

"I shouldn't lie," said 'Rose' Noble.

Before I could answer, Punter appeared on the roof.

"'Rose,'" he said, "Casemate's – "

There he saw me and stopped dead, with his mouth and his eyes wide open and a hand half way to his head.

Grimly 'Rose' Noble surveyed him.

"Well, what of Casemate?" he said.

Dazedly Punter regarded him. Then he pointed to me.

"'E's done 'im in," he said stupidly. "Look at 'is – soot."

The wretched man was plainly thinking aloud, but 'Rose' Noble was not in the mood to receive such gifts. He did not actually strike him, but he took him by the shoulders and shook him, till he wore the colour of death and I really thought that his brains must be loose in his head. Then he flung him away against the wall of the tower and, using a frightful oath, demanded the truth.

At first Punter could not speak. Then he put a hand to his temples and moistened his lips.

"I thought he'd beat it," he faltered. "When I saw the – gate open – "

"When was this?"

"Why, jus' now," said Punter. "I'd only that moment shut it, when you called down."

'Rose' Noble was plainly uncertain what to think.

My tale was unlikely enough, but the facts bore it out. That I should have quitted the porch before George and the servants were safely within the castle seemed to him a mistake which not even a child would have made. Yet, if they were truly within, a child would have had the good sense to shut the gate. Of these two incredible conclusions he did not know which to choose, and, as I watched his teeth at work on his lower lip, I was elated to think that I had contrived to embarrass so subtle a brain.

My triumph was short-lived.

"I guess Hanbury's only two hands – and those were fast. How did you make the kitchen out of that flat?"

The thrust was so unexpected that I could only stare.

"Speak up, you young fool," said 'Rose' Noble. "I saw the way he was tied."

I swallowed desperately. Lest Mansel should mean to use it, I dared not reveal the fact that the table sank through the floor.

"Out of the window," I said, "when the servants attacked. I went into the kitchen for shelter and found him there."

"Why didn't Mansel go with you?"

"He hadn't time," said I. "The light was back on the windows before he could follow me down."

"You knew the servants were there. Why didn't you go to the porch and let them in?"

"I tried to," said I. "But I didn't dare show a light and I couldn't undo the bolts."

"But you did in the end," said 'Rose' Noble, rubbing his nose. "That's why that attack was a washout. You whistled 'em down from the roof and handed them in. Are you sure you got out by the window?"

A sudden belief that the man was playing with me sent the blood to my head. In a trice I had lost my temper and found my tongue.

"Have it your own way," said I. "It won't be for long. I may have played the hand badly, but I've made the odd trick. You're the wrong side of the door, and we can afford to wait. That doctor comes out of Lass, and, if he's not back by sundown, I fancy his friends and relations will wonder why."

Now, if this was all Greek to Punter, it was so much gall to his chief. Servants within or without, so long as Mansel sat still, he could not act, and, unless he acted quickly, the chance would pass. The stranger within the gates had set the sand-glass up, and the grains which had lain so long idle had now begun to run. And nothing on earth could stop them. Happen what might, before many hours were over tongues would be wagging and eyes would be turning to Gath. Before any steps were taken, if 'Rose' Noble valued his freedom, he would be wise to be gone.

But, if I had stung him, the monster gave no sign.

"Yes," he said slowly, "I guess I shall have it my way."

The words were softly spoken, but his tone was so dark and so sinister that I found them more disturbing than any explosion of wrath. Indeed, his whole demeanour seemed to have changed: the red heat of passion was gone, and, in its stead, a coldness which was not human possessed this terrible man. And, if that did not show me, the next ten minutes declared why men endured his service and went in fear of his name.

He never once used an oath or two words where one would serve, and, if a sign could take the place of an order, he made a sign. He never hesitated or gave any sort of reason for the commands he gave; himself he did nothing and seemed to be oblivious of what was done, yet, when Bunch was about to gag me, he had knocked me down before I knew myself that my hand had instinctively moved towards my knife. No Pharaoh could have been more imperious, no beast so vigilant, nothing but a statue could have stood so still and cold. What was far more, the man compelled belief. That I had duped him was forgotten: if he said 'Shut that door,' I knew that to leave it open would have been a fatal mistake: he gave the impression of providing for what was coming to pass: from his orders alone you could foretell the future, till looking ahead seemed as simple as looking back. Little wonder that Bunch and Punter hung on his lips...

Casemate was found and heartily soused with water in a hope of bringing him to, but Mansel had struck too well, and after a little they left him to fare as best he could. I was gagged and my wrists were tightly bound. Food and wine were packed in a battered bag and, without passing through the porch, we left by a lower window and gained the spur.

This was of course, the window by which Hanbury had been brought in. The middle bar could be lifted, so that a man could pass. The contrivance was simple, but none from without could have reached the plate, like a damper, which locked the bar into place.

With never a look behind him, 'Rose' Noble passed up the spur and into the drive. Once out of sight of the castle, he turned to the right and, plunging into the thicket, swung back towards the castle, till he came to a little hollow, sunk in the midst of bushes and overspread with the branches of the surrounding trees.

We were now on the fringe of the wood, and I could see the castle between the leaves: the drive was ten paces away and the spur but three, but, while we commanded both, a man must have stumbled upon us before he knew we were there.

'Rose' Noble pushed back his hat and lit a cigar.

Then –

"Watch," he said shortly and flung himself down on the turf.

Without a word, Bunch wriggled into the foliage, until he could see the spur, while Punter opened the bag and began to eat. Of me they took no notice, and, since it seemed idle to stand, I sat myself down. This miserably enough, for my bodily state was wretched and my heart was heavy as lead. If ever a man 'meant business,' 'Rose' Noble was he, and there was death in the hollow for whoever came up to the drive. Carson was doomed: the cars were as good as gone: and I was the wretched decoy to draw Mansel out of the castle and into the snare. I could see it all coming as clearly as though it were past and could do no more to prevent it than one of those careless butterflies that we had passed on the spur.

Presently I laid down my head and stared at the sky.

At least the place was lovely, and the day as fine and smooth as a day could be. The fluting of birds and the steady hum of insects soothed the ear: and the wet grass was cool and fragrant against my cheek.

My head was aching, and I was parched with thirst: the gag was most hard on my jaws, and my wrists were already sore: but I was very tired, and, since Nature is a governess not easily put about, the murmur of the insects grew more and more slumberous, and, after a little space, I fell asleep.

"I reckon he's sweating," said 'Rose' Noble.

I was wide awake in an instant. With the tail of my eye I could see that, except that Bunch was eating and Punter had taken his place, nothing had changed.

"Sweating blood," said 'Rose' Noble. "One Willie up on the drop, and, unless he gets a move on, the other walks into our arms as soon as it's dark."

"Complete with car," said Bunch, licking his lips.

'Rose' Noble shrugged his shoulders.

"Maybe," he said. "But I guess they'll give us the cars before we're through."

Punter looked down from his post on the lip of the dell.

"He can lay to meeting 'is Gawd, if he comes out."

"That's why he's sweating," said 'Rose' Noble. "This – garden's all right from the castle wall, but it's just a shade too wild for a good close-up."

"Suicide 'All," said Bunch. "But 'e won't 'ave a dart by daylight. 'E knows – "

"Yes, he will," said 'Rose' Noble. "He'll never wait ten hours, while his Willies are getting wet. He'll bring two o' the servants with him, an' they'll come right up in a line."

Punter looked round.

"Didn't we ought to spread, Rose?"

The other shook his head.

"Stop one, an' you stop the lot. Say we lay out a servant – well, what'll Big Willie do? Fall on his – stomach an' pray to God. He's only the wood to shoot at, an' he's three down instead of two. An' that's when we move. By the time he's got his soul straight, I guess I'll be ready to flip a fly off his nose."

"You don' wan' to kill 'im," said Bunch. "If you – "

"'Kill him?'" breathed 'Rose' Noble. "'Kill him?'" I could hear him suck in his breath. "No, I'm not going to kill him. And if I were you, I wouldn't so much as loose off, if you see his face – *in case you killed him*, for, if you did, by – , I'd feed your tripe to a mongrel before your eyes."

A prudent silence succeeded this horrid threat, which was not so much spoken as snarled and suggested a return of the temper with which the monster was ridden a while before. For my part, I would have welcomed that cold, black mood, for now his manner argued a confidence so rich and ripe and lazy as made me twice as hopeless as I had been before.

"I'm going to sell him," said 'Rose' Noble. "Hang him up on a wall of that court – expose him for sale... with a bucket on either foot – the way they made 'Poky' remember the name of his 'bank.' If he won't buy himself in, I guess the Willies'll think when they see the weights. An' before we reach the reserve, I guess the goods will ask him to change his mind."

"But see here, Rose," said Punter. "They won't 'ave the cash to pay with, an' 'ow can we wait? That blasted chemist – "

"Who wants to wait?" said 'Rose' Noble. "I'll take their – word. Oh, I guess they've got false bottoms, the same as anyone else. I wouldn't trust Mansel a foot – if none of his like could hear. But let one of 'em pass his word *in front of his – kind*, an' he hasn't the spunk to break it for fear they'll think he's a swab. That's what they mean when they talk of *Noblesse Oblige*; if you want plain English, *Don' let 'em see your dirt.*"

The venom with which he uttered this ugly argument declared the deadly hatred he bore us all, and I could not help wondering what was the fellow's history, for he had a commanding presence and was by no means common, as Punter and Bunch, while his speech was constantly betraying a considerable education which for some unaccountable reason he seemed to despise.

Punter took a deep breath.

"This time tomorrow," he said, "we'll be on the – road."

"Out of the country, you mean, and pushing for France."

Bunch looked up from his victuals.

"Wot price the Customs?" he said. "I'll shift the – Rolls, but there's photos stuck on to 'er papers, an' I don' wan' to be asked why I'm drivin' a stolen car."

'Rose' Noble yawned.

"I guess we'll give one of the Willies a lift to France. They'll have to go back to London to raise the wind. An' he'll put us through the Customs – if we remember to ask him while Mansel's up on the wall."

Punter spoke over his shoulder.

"What 'Poky' was that you mentioned? There was a 'Poky' Barrett I saw in a Boston bar. But he, was a little old screw, with a jerky leg."

'Rose' Noble laughed.

"'Poky' Barrett," he said, "is forty-two."

"Go on," said Punter, incredulously.

"Forty-two," said 'Rose' Noble. "But he had... an illness... not quite seven years ago..."

Somehow I got to my knees and tried to speak.

The three watched me curiously.

I threw myself down and rubbed my head on the ground in a wild endeavour to tear the gag from my mouth. I heard Punter laugh and say something about a dog. The attempt exhausted me and was utterly vain. When I got again to my knees, my face was streaming with sweat.

'Rose' Noble looked at me and lifted his lids.

"An illness," he said softly. "Some people might say 'an attack.' It changed him... unbelievably... And the jerky leg came on about the same time. You see, when he wouldn't answer, *somebody happened to touch his sciatic nerve.*"

With a bursting head, I flung myself back on the turf...

I can never describe the agony of that hour.

I knew that Mansel would come, and I knew he would come before dark. He would never wait for ten hours before starting to my relief: and Carson had to be saved from walking clean into a trap. He had not rope enough to go by the cliff – the spur was his only way. And so he would come... by daylight... up to the wood... If he came, he was doomed. He could be seen approaching for two hundred yards or more, and no cunning would ever avail him against an ambuscade. There was no scope for cunning. The wood was dense, while, except for four or five trees, the spur was bare. I had no hope for him, and, if I had, 'Rose' Noble's air would have killed it, for he, the soul of prudence, was awaiting his enemy's coming with his hands, so to speak, in his pockets and his sword in the rack.

Of what was to follow his wounding, I tried not to think.

Whoever was with him would be taken, alive or dead: and Carson would walk into the shambles soon after the sun had set. With me for spokesman, those that were left in the castle would be apprised of the truth, and no doubt, at dawn the next day Adèle and Hanbury and I would be pleading with prayers and fortunes for the life of a broken man. And so the play would finish – in a welter of blood and tears. Redress was not to be thought of: the chances of vengeance would not be worth taking up. Then The Law would step in, pick over the ghastly business, madden us all with its ritual, ask unanswerable questions and believe what it chose. A hideous publicity would follow: the names of Adèle and Mansel would be in everyone's mouth: reporters would cluster round Poganec: char-à-bancs would be run to The Castle of Gath...

In this affliction of spirit I again and again forgot my bodily distress. This was as well, for the gag choked me and had broken the sides of my mouth, my wrists seemed to be on fire, the pain in my head was raging, and I might have been covered with blankets, so fast was I streaming with sweat. At times I made sure I was sickening for some disease, but I think that it was the tightness as well of my clothing as my bonds which joined with the heat of the day, not only made me so hot, but caused my blood to rebel against such usage.

Bunch drained his bottle of wine and lay down to sleep. Before he did so, he took a scarf from his pocket and bound my feet, and so put out the spark of hope I had cherished that, when the moment came, I could hurl myself into the bushes and betray his danger to Mansel by means of the noise I made.

'Rose' Noble was speaking.

"I guess you'll remember today. It'll spoil the greenwood for you for the rest of your life. When you see the sun on the leaves and you hear the birds piping around, I guess you'll remember today, and, when you remember, I reckon you'll wish it was raining and that the boughs were bare.

"May be it'll learn you something that they don't teach at Oxford or the schools for pretty, young boys. *Stick to your— last. Live an' let live.* If somebody pulls your nose, go to the police. Keep your—tadpoles, an' watch 'em turn into frogs, but leave the deep-sea fishing to them that know...

"When Mansel climbed into that strongbox, he cut his throat. *He gave me this wood for the taking*—just the kind of dam-fool error a squirt like Mansel would make. The poor trash couldn't see that, if ever it got to a dog-fight, *the – that had this thicket was bound to win*."

If the fellow's words enraged me, I think that they angered him.

He knew as well as did I that we could not have taken the castle and held the wood as well and that Mansel had had to stake all upon freeing Adèle: he knew that Mansel had taken trick after trick, though the game was not of his choosing and every card was marked – *that Mansel could still win the odd... and the game and the rubber and all... if he would but sit still in the castle and let Carson and me take our chance.* He had sought to belittle the man who in fourteen days had achieved what 'Rose' Noble himself had believed three impossible feats, first of all finding a needle out of a bottle of hay, then seizing a very bastille and, finally, plucking his lady out of the lion's mouth. He had sought to diminish Mansel, and he had failed, because the facts were against him and he had no sort of material with which to build his case. This poverty made him wroth, and, could he have called back his words, I think he would. But since he could not, he started to curse and swear, reviling Mansel in filthy and blasphemous terms and working himself into a very passion, because, I fancy, he knew that with every execration he was, so to speak, but further exposing his sores.

Throughout this exhibition, Bunch was pretending slumber, and Punter never moved, whilst I, of course, lay as I was, for, now that my feet were bound, I could not stir.

At last the storm blew itself out, and, after a decent silence, 'Rose' Noble turned to the future and left the past.

"I guess Jute'll bite his thumbs, when he finds we're gone."

Bunch propped himself on an elbow and let out an oath.

"Serve 'im – well right," he spouted, "the dirty goat. Sits down in that crooked village an' leaves us to get the wet. I know 'is – idea of keepin' the background warm. Oysters an' girls an' movies an' a skinful every night."

"He had his orders," said 'Rose' Noble, "an' he's broken 'em twice. If he'd done as I told him, we shouldn't have had this fuss. But maybe it's as well. It don't amuse me to suckle an insubordinate – that's let me down."

This definite intimation that no claim by Jute would be paid was greeted by Punter and Bunch with the highest glee, partly, no doubt, because each was expecting to profit by such a rule, but mainly, I think, because they detested Jute and the thought of his losing his share did their hearts good. Indeed, had they known the truth – that Jute was no longer alive to lodge his claim, they could not have been better pleased. They crowed and giggled like children, abused the dead man with a relish which must have made him turn in his grave, and showed an impatience for action which all their approaching welfare had failed to inspire.

Punter shook his fist at the castle and cried aloud.

"Come out, you one-legged—, and take your gruel."

"Easy now," said 'Rose' Noble. "He knows that he's for the high jump, and I guess you'd straighten your tie before buying that hop."

"Rose," says Bunch, all of a twitter, "are you sure we'd better not spread? You know. Just in case—"

'Rose' Noble sat up.

"If and when I say so, but not before. What the hell's the use of spreading before they show up? Or even then?"

"None whatever," said Mansel.

Then a shot was fired just behind me, and 'Rose' Noble fell back, staring, with the blood running into his eyes.

Himself, Mansel unbound me and took the gag from my mouth, while Carson and Bell, who were with him, stood covering Punter and Bunch – in a way, a needless precaution, for the two seemed stupefied and gazed about them slowly, as though they had just been translated into another world. And so, I suppose, in a sense, they had been, for 'Rose' Noble was stone dead, shot through the brain.

When he saw the state of my mouth, Mansel drew in his breath. Then his hands went under my arms, and he lifted me up.

There was a rill in the wood – we had heard the fuss of its water, whenever we used the drive. This we sought in silence, for I was past speaking, and Mansel held his tongue. Indeed, he had his hands full, for though I could walk, I had lost my sense of balance and but for his arms, must have fallen a score of times.

The water revived me, but, when I would have spoken, Mansel stopped me at once.

"All in good time," said he. "Those swine must be disposed of, and the cord's way back with the cars. You will stay here and rest, and I'll come back and find you as soon as ever I can."

With that, he was gone, and I turned again to the water and drank my fill...

After a little, I lay back and gazed at the sky.

To tell the truth, I was thankful to be alone.

I had been just as much shaken as Punter and Bunch, and the world seemed out of focus to my labouring brain.

One moment the enemy was rampant, and the next 'Rose' Noble was dead: before he had left the castle, Mansel had appeared in the wood: the inevitable had not happened, the impossible come to pass.

More than once an absurd fear seized me that it was all a dream, and, indeed, I was still uneasy when I heard a comfortable sound – the sigh of one of the Rolls.

Ten minutes later Tester was licking my face...

"It's very simple," said Mansel, filling a pipe. "The whole of the credit is yours. You cut the Gordian knot: and when, because of my failure, our case was ten times worse than it had been before, you pulled the whole show round and did the trick."

To this I demurred, but he brushed my protests aside.

"Listen," he said. "They carried me in and laid me down on a bed in the middle room of the tower. They took my pistol and knife, locked them up in a cupboard and took the key. *Then they locked every door, except the door to the roof and that of the room in which I lay.* Well, that washed out George and the servants, for they were in the oratory, very properly biding their time. Then they handcuffed Adèle to my bed-post, and, when she slipped out of the cuff, they clipped her ankle instead. Then 'Rose' Noble sat down and watched me – from a chair at the foot of the bed. Adèle told me afterwards that he never took his hand from his pocket or his eyes from my face... If you can conceive a tighter place than that, I'd like to hear what it is.

"Well, the 'doctor' appeared, and, before he'd said thirty words, 'Rose' Noble was out of the room. When I rose to follow, Adèle almost bent it again. She started up, forgetting her ankle was fast to the leg of the bed. I just managed to catch her in time...

"I shut the door to the roof and started to look for the keys. I found them at last, high up in a niche in the wall. Then I unlocked the doors. I had no idea where George and the servants were, and, as luck would have it, I tried the oratory last. Not until then did I go back to the 'doctor' and ask about you. To my horror, I learned he had left you up on the roof...

"Of course I realized I had shut the door in your face, and, when I rushed back to listen, I could hear 'Rose' Noble speaking and you reply. I took Bell's pistol, posted George and Rowley as best I could and cautiously opened the door, *to find that the roof was empty and the opposite door was shut.* This made me think very hard. Although he knew we had rope, 'Rose' Noble was giving us the roof: but the gifts of a man like that are always dangerous, and I instantly wondered if he meant to take to the wood.

"A moment's reflection convinced me that this was so."

"In the first place, to use his own words, 'if ever it got to a dog-fight, the fellow that had this thicket was bound to win': in the second, the dog-fight was coming – there was any amount to suggest that the servants were in: the castle would soon be unhealthy, because of the doctor's friends; and, then, the cars for the taking and Carson as well: finally, he knew I should seek you, and the very best place in which to hold you prisoner was, therefore, the wood.

"There was not a moment to lose. We couldn't go down the cliff, for we hadn't sufficient rope, and our only chance was to reach the wood by the spur not only before 'Rose' Noble, *but before he was in a position to see us go.*

"I left George and Rowley with Adèle, who was now as safe as a house, and Bell and I slid down from the roof to the spur. The 'doctor,' a gallant old fellow, drew up the rope behind us and then slipped back to the tower. Believe me, I ran for this wood, with my heart in my mouth...

"When we made the drive, I sent Bell off for Carson and lay in wait. Almost at once you appeared. I watched you come out of the window and start for the wood, but, when I felt for my pistol, *it wasn't there...*

"I'd given it back to Bell, before I went down the rope, and in the rush I'd forgotten to ask for it back.

"Well, there was nothing to be done. I retired, marked you to cover and then went off to pick up Carson and Bell. I'm afraid the delay cost you dear, for I had to be careful to meet them a long way back and, of course, we had to come up without snapping a twig. But I think, perhaps, after all, it was better so, for the sprint had unsteadied my hand, and, if I had missed or anything else had slipped, you were a pretty good hostage and I was but one to three.

"The rest you know." He rose to his feet and stretched luxuriously. "And now, if you feel like moving, we'll get into one of the cars and go back to Adèle. Carson and Bell are digging a certain grave, and I think we'll leave them to it – and him to them. To tell you the truth, I don't want to see him again. The sight of him rouses feelings that one shouldn't have against the dead. In his way, he was a great man, and, if he'd had the help I've had, he'd have wiped me off the map. He hadn't a servant worth having – they let him down right and left: he practically stood alone: and, even so, it took six of us all we knew to bring him down."

It is not for me to review that valediction: I heard it in silence, and in silence I leave it now. The quarrel was not mine, but Mansel's, and I will not pick over the blossoms he chose to lay upon the grave.

Without a word, we made our way to the cars, and, taking the first, drove slowly out of the drive and down to the castle gate.

Then Mansel climbed in by the window that had the loose bar, and two minutes later he swung the great leaf open and I drove in.

When I was in the courtyard, I stopped and sounded the horn. Before its echoes had died, a casement of the oratory was opened, and Hanbury put out his head.

"All over," said Mansel simply. "Open the doors."

He was on his way to the guard-room, before I was out of the car, with Tester scrambling before him, agog to prove the promise of so unusual a field.

I followed leisurely, still thinking on the death of 'Rose' Noble and of all that had passed, and trying to believe that the clock in the dashboard of the Rolls was telling the truth when it said that the hour was no more than half-past nine.

So I came to the guard-room and down the winding stair.

The passage door was open, and Mansel was standing in the passage, fronting Adèle. His back was towards me, but I saw that his head was bowed and he had her hand to his lips. The back of her other hand was across her eyes.

*And between them and me crouched Casemate framed in the passage doorway, pistol in hand.*

I let out a cry that might have been heard in Lass, but, as I did so, he fired, and I saw Mansel stagger a little and then sink down on his knees.

Before Casemate could turn, I had knocked him flat on his face and was kneeling upon his back. Then I took my knife and drove it into his spine.

But the mischief was done.

Mansel was still alive, but the bullet had entered his stomach, and there was death in his face.

# IX

## FULL MEASURE

I shall never forgive myself for forgetting that Casemate was still at large. I had thought of him twice since my rescue – once as I lay by the brook, awaiting Mansel's return, and again whilst Mansel was gone to open the castle gate: and each time, before he was back, I had let some other matter thrust Casemate out of my mind.

I have no excuse to offer. It was a monstrous negligence, for which I can never account, though sometimes I strive to believe that 'Rose' Noble's familiar possessed me to let Mansel down.

We bore him into the lovely bedchamber and laid him upon the King's bed.

When we would have taken his coat, he shook his head.

"He's got me all right," he whispered: "so let me be."

I tried to say I was sorry, with the tears running down my face.

But he only smiled.

"Rot," he said gently. "Luck of the battle – that's all."

Upon the great bed sat Adèle, steady-eyed as ever, but very pale. She might have been Eve, as Milton has pictured her, sitting upon the green bank, looking into the pool. Her left arm propped her, and she was sitting sideways, after the way of a child: one ring of the broken handcuffs was still about her slim leg. Her hand was in Mansel's, and their two hands lay in her lap: her beautiful head was bowed, and her eyes never left the eyes of the man she loved.

On his other side lay Tester, close up against his lord. Mansel's left hand was upon him; but, though, I think, he would have licked it, the poor scrap never moved, but lay as still as an image, with his chin on his little paws and his eyes upon Mansel's face.

If the others came and went, I did not notice them; and, after a little, I found the windows open and the doors of the chamber shut.

"Punter and Bunch," said Mansel. "Search them for money and take every penny they've got. Go to Innsbruck and buy them two tickets for London. Give them these and drop them outside the town. Someone must watch them in and see that they go. And the caretakers must be dealt with. Perhaps the 'doctor' will help. It shouldn't be very hard to stop their mouths. But try and mop everything up before you go."

I could only nod: and, when he had seen me do this, he closed his eyes.

If he suffered, he never showed it. Indeed, he seemed well content. And, when Adèle stooped to kiss him, a light that was not of this world came into his eyes.

Once I made to rise and leave them, but, interpreting my movement, Mansel lifted his hand and bade me stay.

So we three waited together, as we had waited together the day before, but this time under a shadow which would not pass...

My eyes stole round the room.

The chamber was full of light, and a broad sash of sunshine was lying athwart the wall. The black oak, the gold and the crimson feasted the eye. The tapestries beckoned into the glades they pictured, and the four men-at-arms about the bed insisted upon the presence they had been set to keep. All

I can say is that the presence was there. For once Fate had not bungled, but had laid a king upon a king's bed to die.

Then I thought of Maximilian and of the exquisite surname which he had won, and at last I saw the writing which had been all the time upon the wall.

Destiny will be served. For more than four hundred years that room had been swept and garnished, had stood ever ready and waiting for 'The Last of the Knights.' Jonathan Mansel, Gentleman, had come into his own.

My eyes returned to the bed – to read as dreadful a message as ever I saw.

We had drawn the coverlet, before we had laid him down, exposing a silken quilt that had, I think, once been white, but was now yellow with age. Upon this there was now a great blood-stain, very slowly spreading about his hips.

The terrible sight shocked me, and I covered my eyes.

Adèle was speaking.

"Can we do nothing, my darling? No single thing?"

Very gently he shook his head.

"If we were in London," he murmured, "they might have a shot: but I'm very comfortable, and it's a great relief to know that we're out of the wood."

A dry sob shook Adèle.

"Another wood's coming, Jonah: it's very near: I must go into that alone – and there aren't any leaves on the trees."

Mansel smiled very tenderly.

"The spring's in your heart, my darling. The trees will break at your coming, and the wood will become your bower."

Adèle shook her lovely head.

"Ah, Jonah, I've no heart left. If we could have gone in together, I wouldn't have cared: but it's... so dreadful, Jonah... to face it alone."

"Hush, my darling. William will see you through. Think only how rich you made me, that I'm going laden with a treasure which no Customs can take away. Remembering that, my lady, how can you mourn? See what a tide I'm taking. It's never been half so high in all my life. I'm going out on the very full of the flood, and the ebb that might have hurt me will never run."

"It's our tide you're taking, Jonah – our wonderful, shining tide. And I've got to stand on the shore and see it go down. I could have borne it with you. It never would have fallen, so long as you were beside me – to share our lovely secret and teach me to play the game."

For the first time a troubled look came into his face.

"It's better like this, my sweet. We might have slipped and fallen, or—"

"Never," sobbed Adèle. "You know it. Not if Boy were to live for fifty years. You love me, and that's enough. Your arms have been about me, and I've kissed your blessed lips, and I'd have lived on that memory—"

"Live on it still, my queen. Do me that matchless honour. Lift up the heart I touched, because I touched it, the eyes I kissed, because a man knelt and looked up and saw himself in them."

"Oh, Jonah, if love could do it, it should be done. But it's strength alone that can help me, and all my strength is in you. You don't know your strength, my darling. You carry so lightly what no other man could lift. We've always leaned on you, Jonah: the first thing I learned of Boy was to lean upon you. When they took me that day by Sava, I knew you'd come. I wasn't afraid, because I knew you'd find me and pull me out. I wasn't afraid of 'Rose' Noble – I told him so. I told him he hadn't an earthly and that, if he took me to Hell, you'd follow me down and break him and carry me back. And I wasn't afraid to love you and take your love – to play with the fire of Heaven, for I knew I could count on your strength to bring us through. But now... you're going, my darling... and I must fend for myself. And I'm lost and beggared and beaten, and – oh, Jonah, I'm terribly afraid."

Mansel put up a hand and touched her hair.

"I found my strength in your nature, in the light of your steady, brown eyes and the flash of your smile: in your beautiful voice and your laughter and the play of your little hands: in the lisp of your footfalls and, at last, in the brush of your lips... You gave me my strength, my darling: and the spirit that lighted my life can light its own. Two days ago in this room you made me a king – of your own sweet will, though Death had his ear to the keyhole, and Terror his eyes on the latch. That's not the way of fear."

"But you were with me, Jonah. I tell you, with you to lean on, I knew no fear."

"A fiction, my beauty, a fiction. You mustn't bow down to an image that you set up. It wasn't I that set the stars in your eyes or gave that fine, proud curve to your beautiful mouth. Adèle was a great lady, before ever she heard my name. So lift up your head, in the old familiar way. Look Fate in the eyes, my darling, and he'll always give you the wall."

Adèle seemed to brace herself. Then she took his hand and kissed it and held it against her heart.

"I'll try," she said quietly. "If Tester will let me, I'll do what I can to help him; and, as soon as we've got our bearings, Tester and I will try."

I saw the dog's ears lift, but he never stirred.

"Poor little chap," said Mansel. "I'm afraid it'll hit him hard."

Then he spoke to the scrap and told him that he must look after Adèle and that soon he was to be her dog, "for you see, old fellow," he murmured, "I've got to go away. And it's not like the other times, for this time... I shan't come back."

A tremor ran through the dog's frame, and he gave a little whimper that wrung my heart. As plainly as if he had spoken, he was acknowledging the sentence which the man that he worshipped had passed. Devotion so piteous and so absolute would have drawn tears from any stone, and I was not surprised when beneath this turn of the roller Adèle broke down.

She slipped from the bed to the floor, buried her face in her hands and shook like a leaf.

"I can't face it," she said wildly. "Three days ago I could have done it, but now it's too late. Two days ago the face of my world was changed. We changed it together, Jonah, you and I. But, when we changed it, we set a yoke on our necks... I wouldn't go back for fifty million worlds – our yoke's my pride and glory, the loveliest jewel that ever a woman wore. They were going to tattoo me, Jonah – to write your name on my back. I wish to God they'd done it: but it wouldn't have been the same as the yoke we put on together two days ago. And now I've got to carry... our yoke... alone... Between us, its weight was nothing. It had no weight. Day and night I'd have worn it, and life would have been the lighter because it was there. But alone, Jonah... *alone*. How can I lift up my head, with a millstone about my neck? How can I lift up my heart, when my fellow is gone?"

Great beads of sweat were standing on Mansel's brow: but his voice, though low, was steady as it had ever been.

"'The one shall be taken,'" he said, "'and the other left.' That is the private touchstone of the great Alchemist himself. Only the greatest hearts come to be put to such a shining proof, and those that pass it, my lady, emerge so tempered that no blow can ever dent them and they can turn the edge of any sorrow."

Adèle dragged herself up and knelt to the bed: as she leaned over blindly, Mansel put his arm round her neck...

And then, for a while, there was silence, and the whisper of the water, taking its leap from the terrace, was all the sound we heard.

Tester lifted his head and looked at the wall.

At first I could hear nothing: then came a step in the passage, and, an instant later, Hanbury opened the door.

As he looked at the bed—

"Ah, George," said Mansel, and smiled.

Hanbury glanced behind him, and a tall, fresh-faced man came into the room.

"This is Dr Buchinger," said George. "He is an Innsbruck surgeon, who happened to be at Lass."

The other bowed to Adèle: then he stepped to the bed.

I was just in time to catch Tester, who would have flown at his throat, but the surgeon ignored the flurry and, frowning a little at the blood-stain upon the quilt, stooped to set his fingers on Mansel's wrist.

There was a breathless silence.

Then he took a case from his pocket and straightened his back.

"I must give an injection," he said. "Please see if the room is ready and bring a shutter or something on which you may carry him in."

"You see," said George, "it was like this. I knew it was a chance in a million, but there was the car waiting, and the bookseller ready to help. I would have gone to Innsbruck, for I hadn't much hope of Lass. 'Can there any good thing come out of Nazareth?' But my father's a doctor, you know, and I knew we were up against time – haemorrhage. You don't die of the wound: you die of the loss of blood. I tell you, I had next to no hope...

"All the way I kept wondering how I could smother the rumours my action was going to start. Call in a doctor, and you always open the sluice. When I thought of the flood behind, my foot went out to the brake. It amounted to this – I was putting all our shirts on the rankest outsider that ever was saddled up. Then I thought of the shock his death would be to Adèle and the awful look in your face as we carried him in...

"By the time we ran into Lass, I had a half-baked plan."

"We drove to the local surgeon's. His door was open and, by the grace of God, he was just showing Buchinger out. Then I made a most happy mistake. I took Buchinger for the local, and the local for Buchinger's man. Before the bookseller could stop me, I'd asked if he could speak English, and, when he said 'yes,' I dragged him into the house and started in. There was no time for finesse: my only card was the money, so I jolly well bunged it in. I said if he'd do the case, we'd pay him a thousand pounds – *and another four thousand pounds three months from today, provided we'd reason to think that he'd held his tongue.* Then I took out the wallet that Mansel keeps in the car and laid the notes on the table before his eyes. He seemed rather staggered and looked at me very hard. Then the bookseller put in his oar. 'I will give you my word,' he said, 'that there is nothing to fear. This gentleman is saving a lady's name.' That seemed to reassure Buchinger, but still he wouldn't say 'yes.'

" 'Dr Rachel must help me,' he said, and looked at the wallah that I had thought was his man."

"Then I saw my mistake and that he must be another *and bigger* pot."

" 'By all means,' said I, and added two hundred and fifty to what there was on the board."

"The two of them looked at the notes."

"Then Rachel made a noise like a siphon and picked his up..."

"Well, he has a kind of clinic attached to his house. All the stuff for an operation was ready to hand. Without Buchinger, he'd have been hopeless – forgotten from A to Z. But Buchinger knows his job. He called for paper and pencil and made out a list. When he'd done, he checked it over: then he gave it to Rachel and told him to 'get those things into the car.' Five minutes later we picked him up at a chemist's two streets away."

"You've saved his life," said I.

"That remains to be seen," said George. "But, if I have, it's pure fluke. *Buchinger was leaving the house to catch his train. He was actually on the doorstep.* And Rachel could no more have done it than you or I. Clever enough, no doubt: but take him out of his groove, and he loses his mind."

This estimate, if not exact, was unpleasantly near the truth. As Rachel was bidden, he did – with an excellent grace: but the poor man's composure was gone, and his efforts to bring it to heel were as obvious as they were vain. This made us all fear for his discretion; but the bookseller presently insisted that the sight of familiar surroundings would send this disorder away and that, once he was back in his province, we could count upon his prudence as upon that of a sage.

This comforted us, for there was much to be done, and our cup of anxiety was full.

When the operation was over, Buchinger told us plainly that, so far from his life being saved, Mansel might die any minute during the next three days.

"When he thought he was dying," he said, "he was perfectly right. He was dying – and dying fast. He is now no longer dying: Dr Rachel and I have stopped that. But he is standing still – on the very edge of death. And there we must try to keep him, for, nothing that I can do can draw him back. If he should live for three days, he will himself draw back: and then a medical student could make him well. But if, before then, he slips – that is the end.

"I shall, of course, stay here. As luck will have it, my holiday does not end for another six days. But Dr Rachel must go. You will fetch him again this evening, when he will bring my things and some drugs that I want. And, if you will keep your secret, I think I should drive into Lass by some indirect way. Of course, you should have a nurse – two nurses. But women would talk. Only, I fear for the health of that beautiful girl..."

We drew what cheer we could from these solemn words and, since Adèle was with Mansel, turned with relief to the business of setting our house in order as best we might.

'Rose' Noble lay still unburied, for Carson and Bell had left him and rushed to the castle directly they heard the shot, and, finding the truth so dreadful, had rightly stayed within call. And, since another grave had now to be dug, we put these two matters in train before anything else.

The surgeons had not seen Casemate for, while George was gone for a doctor, the servants had taken the body into the Dining-room. For this I was thankful, for to help a man out of a trespass is one thing, but to stand accessory to homicide is, as they say, a different pair of shoes.

And here I may say that, if Rachel was too much bemused, Buchinger was far too wary to ask any questions at all: he must have suspected that Mansel's was not the only blood that had been shed, but he saw the danger of knowledge and held his peace.

When he had returned to the sick-room and George had gone off with Rachel, to drive him to Lass, we carried Casemate's body down to the second car, and Bell and Rowley and I drove up to the wood. And there we laid the fellow to such rest as a murderer has: and I trust he will lie undisturbed for the rest of our days, for, do what we would, we could not withdraw my knife, but were forced to bury the dead with this document fast in his back.

Until these grim rites were over, I could not rest, for, if dead men can tell no tales, a corpse can speak for itself, and I was determined to take no chances at all. George, who was very soon back, held the same view, and the four of us laboured like fury, until the business was done.

When we left the thicket, we took with us Punter and Bunch and cast them into the kitchen which they had turned into a gaol. When they saw their quarters, the two looked ready to burst: but, if they disliked their fortune, they had only themselves to thank. I do not suppose that hospitality was ever shown so grudgingly or taken so ill, but, though we hated their presence, we thought it wise not to enlarge them until we should leave the castle for good and all.

We then set the caretakers free.

As may be believed, these were half dead of apprehension. Indeed, their one idea was to fly the place, and, but for the bookseller, whom they had known for some years, we should have had no choice but to detain them by force.

'Rose' Noble, of course, had 'bought' them: and, once he was fairly installed, they could not go back. They could not betray his presence, without disclosing that they had betrayed their trust, and obeyed in fear and trembling their new and terrible lord. They had in the end made up their minds to vanish, but he had divined their intention and, coming upon them, whilst they were packing some traps, had cuffed their right feet together and locked them into their room. In this miserable state we found them, full of lamentation and the expectation of death and entirely persuaded that, even if they were saved, as the result of their bondage they would be lame for life. Indeed, when we cut the links, they both declared that they could not possibly walk, that the iron had set up gangrene and other faint-hearted rubbish that wearied us all. With infinite patience, however, the bookseller took them to task, and, when he had at last convinced them that they were whole, made it plain that they still had a chance of avoiding such penalties as they had justly earned. At this, they pricked up their ears, and within the hour it was settled that we would repair such damage as might have been done to the house and would hold our tongues, provided they served us truly so long as we stayed.

The terms were not to their liking, but, since beggars cannot be choosers, they had to agree, and the woman cooked us some luncheon that very day.

When George drove to Lass, to seek Rachel, that afternoon, he fetched from the inn what few belongings we had left there against our return, and, giving out that Mansel had crushed his foot and lay in a peasant's cabin in danger of losing his leg, sowed the seed of a story for Rachel to tell. Him we took back to a junction some miles below Lass and promised to meet him there at ten the next day.

The bookseller flatly refused to let us convey him at all, maintaining, that it was to our interest that he should go as he came and so be forearmed to affirm that, if there was trouble abroad, it was not at the Castle of Gath. His housekeeper, a notorious gossip, was aware that he had intended to visit the castle that day: any perilous rumours, therefore, were sure to be brought straight to him, and, if he was able to disclaim an acquaintance with strife, he would be able to crush them once for all. His one appearance in the car could be explained well enough: Hanbury had met him at the cross roads, in some distress, and he had offered to show him the surgeon's house.

The debt we owe to that man can never be paid. He had a heart of gold. Most brave, discreet and understanding, he threw himself into our venture, as though it had been his own, and would, I think, have cheerfully gone to the stake, rather than have spoken one word to our embarrassment. We had purchased the surgeons' silence, as well as their skill: the caretakers went in fear: but the bookseller held his tongue and gave of the best he had because he liked us and without, I am sure, any thought of any reward.

By dusk some sort of order had been set up. Rooms had been cleaned and prepared for Buchinger and Adèle; and each of us had his quarters and his particular charge.

That night a note went to Poganec.

*I am free and safe and sound – at a terrible cost. Jonah has been wounded and lies at the point of death.*

*Adèle.*

And there he lay for three days, as Buchinger had said, in the room that Adèle had once used in the south-west tower.

Then the mists parted, and they said he would live.

"I think," said Buchinger, "that he will recover fast. If all goes well, he can leave his bed in a fortnight, and in another week you may drive him home. But not before that. Tomorrow morning I shall return to Innsbruck, but shall visit him twice in each week until he is well. No doubt you will kindly convey me in one of your cars. Dr Rachel must still attend him twice in the day: but, when a week has gone by, once in the day will do. I have told Miss Adèle that now his servant may very well take the night watch, and, if you do not want another patient upon your hands, I recommend you to insist that this is done."

Here something touched his leg, and we both looked down to see Tester wagging his tail.

"Ah, you monkey. Yes, that is all very well. I come to save your master, and you fly in my face. You are carried off, breathing threatenings and thirsty to drink my blood. And now I have done it in your teeth, I am your very good friend and must be noticed and honoured—"

Tester rolled over and put his paws in the air: and, when the surgeon stooped, jumped up to lick his face.

I never saw the dog so use any other stranger, and he would not look at Rachel, for all his zeal. With this blunt discernment all his conduct was of a piece. We had set a box for him in the 'gallery of stone,' and there he had lain, like a mouse, since the day on which Mansel was hit, never going further than the terrace, the door to which stood open, for him to use. He never sought to enter the sick-room, but always rose and listened, whenever the door was opened by day or night, and anxiously scanned the faces of such as went. So for those three black days. After that he went out and about and took his ease and only kept his box when we went to bed. Then came the day when Mansel asked for him and, when I went to the door, to go and find him, there he was, standing on the threshold, with one paw raised and his eyes seeking confirmation of what he believed to be the truth.

I do not seek to magnify his instinct, but, well as we knew him, these things astonished us all, and, if speech was denied him, he had, I think, another and finer faculty.

There seemed little doubt that, so far, our secret was safe. We drew our supplies, not from Lass, but from towns in other directions from twenty to fifty miles off: since the day of Mansel's wounding, we had not been seen in Lass, and we fetched and carried Rachel by devious ways: when we left the drive, we did so with great circumspection, the castle gates were kept shut, and no lights were shown in the building or on the cars.

George had visited Poganec, had told the most of our story and had explained our case. The question of the Pleydells' coming had naturally arisen at once, but, after a while, they determined to stay where they were. Captain Pleydell could not be moved, because of his leg: and the others decided that, till Mansel was in a condition to be not only prepared for their coming, but satisfied that this move was entailing no risk, their appearance would only concern him and would do no manner of good. So soon, however, as Mansel began to mend, we were to fetch Daphne Pleydell, while it was dark, to spend a day in the castle and go back the following night: a day or so later Major Pleydell would come, and, when these two visits were over, Adèle would visit her husband in just the same way.

That all this precaution was needful, there is no doubt. Lass was big with rumour, and, though much of the gossip was wild, we were astounded to find how close some approached the truth.

Rachel maintained his story that Mansel had crushed his leg, and the bookseller quietly diverted suspicion from Gath; but neither could shut the eyes or stop the ears of a town whose sleep was seldom broken by anything more stirring than a chimney afire or an instance of petty theft.

The bookseller wrote to us daily, always directing his letter to a different village or town, from which we posted our answer, telling how Mansel did.

I cannot do better than make the first letter he wrote us speak for itself.

*Sirs,*

*You shall please take great cares. Yours fetchings of Dr Rachel cannot be too secretly made. It is said here that a priest is led into the mountains and there destroyed: that one man has met him to appointment in a house of the alley over against my shop and would lead him into the mountains, where three more men were lying ready to kill: that the priest was to seek a woman who had his love and was not of her own mind because she loved him so dearly: that the woman is lying still in his murderer's arms and that these had a great motor-car in which they drove themselves: that such car is now in Welsa, under the village's police, who wait for it to be demanded, but all in vain, because the murderers are afraid: that you came after the priest, to save his life, and are encamped in the mountains until the murderers shall move: that they are shut themselves in one of the castles, but you do not know which, and, because of your friend's misadventure, you are at a deadlock. And other things was said, that the woman wears the clothes of a man, that the priest is hanged to death, and many other untruths: but those of above will show upon you how clean you must pick your way.*

*All this, I learn, was said for two or three days, but was not come to my ears, because I sit still with my books: but, when I return from Gath, I find myself well awaited, and I am glad I was ready with my tale.*

*I trust and believe your friend is surviving his wound.*
*Your obedient servant*
*H.S.*

Still the days went by, and no one troubled us: the visits were paid, and the world seemed none the wiser: our curious heritage became a pleasant habit: and Mansel grew steadily better under the love of Adèle.

I was sitting on the terrace one morning, on a cushion of one of the cars, looking at the exquisite prospect and finding much virtue in sloth, when a hand came to rest upon my shoulder, and there was Adèle.

Care and her vigil had left her a little pale, but this only gave her beauty a delicate look which suited it very well.

Without a word, she sat herself down beside me, propped herself on an arm and tilted her chin.

"Have you drunk your milk?" said I.

"Yes," said Adèle. "Beautiful, fragrant milk – straight from the cow. Who travelled all night to get it – and drinks canned milk himself?"

"George Hanbury," said I.

Adèle sighed.

"I wonder," she said, "I wonder if ever a woman was so well served."

"You must thank yourself," said I.

"So Jonah says," said Adèle: "but I can't see why."

"You must take our word," said I, "for it's gospel truth."

And so it was. Without any thought of favour, we delighted to serve Adèle. I am not quite certain why. It was not because she was more bodily and mentally attractive than any girl that I have ever seen: it was not because of her dignity or because of her natural grace. She had a way with her. This was a royal way, and – it was the way of a child. She was full-grown, she was worldly, she was wise: but, with it all, she had never lost that golden flush of childhood which makes its way directly into the hardest heart. I have often wondered how 'Rose' Noble could have used her so harshly, but I think that he had no heart, and the others, I suppose, had no choice but to follow his monstrous lead.

"Do you remember," she said, "a question you asked me not very long ago?"

"Yes," said I. " 'What about going back?' "

She nodded.

"That's right. I think you saw better than I how very hard it would be. It would have been – awfully hard. But Fate's very wise. They say God tempers the wind to the shorn lamb. I'm sure He does – in His mysterious way. I've often wondered how such a thing could be done: but now I know. So soon as the lamb is shorn, He lets the wind blow for a moment *with ice in its breath*: and that moment's so dreadful that ever after that the lamb doesn't feel the wind... And that's our case. It would have been awfully hard. But that half-hour was so dreadful that now the rest seems easy, and I'm not a bit afraid. It's the old question of contrast. I've lifted the load that I might have had to carry. It crushed me – for half an hour. And then for three days and nights I stood waiting to know my fate." She drew a deep breath. "Can you wonder, William, that, after that experience, the future weighs no more than this necklace around my neck?"

"Thank God for that, Adèle."

For a little while she sat silent, smiling into the distance as though there were something there which I could not see.

"I'm very lucky," she said. "My love-affair's been so perfect – from first to last. I was taken because he loved me, and then he came in his strength, to pull me out. I shared the rough with him; and, whilst we were under the shadow, he slept with his head in my lap: when he was hurt, I was there; and alone I've had the glory of helping him back to life. And it's all been out of the world: we've never had to use the back stairs, or whisper, or put out the light. There's been nothing sordid about it, and nothing cheap. And, when it's finished, it'll go, like a painting, into the quiet gallery of which you and he and I have the only keys."

"I shall often walk there, Adèle."

She nodded gravely.

"I like to think that you will."

There was another silence.

Presently she knitted her brows.

"I'm upset about Boy," she said. "You can't get away from the fact that I'm letting him down. He is so good to me, and I love him so much. He's so proud of me and of Jonah, and he plays such a splendid game. When you took me to Poganec, he was so glad to see me, but they hadn't told him I was coming, because they knew he'd say that I mustn't leave Jonah's side. You can't beat that, can you?"

"As I live," said I, "I believe that he'd understand. Of course, you can't possibly tell him: but, if you did, I believe that he'd understand. So don't be upset, Adèle. It was nobody's fault. It was the most natural thing that ever happened."

Adèle turned a glowing face.

"William, tell me. All the world would say that Jonah and I were doing a rotten thing. How is it you don't think so? How is it you understand?"

"There's no one like him," said I.

"I know, but–"

"And, then – there's no one like you."

"Oh, William..."

"The page and the lady," said I. "It's often happened before. And I shall survive." I rose to my feet. "But that, I think, is the reason why I understand. I can look at him with your eyes, and I can see you with his, and – well, Kings and Queens go together, and, oh, my dear, I'm so glad I shall have that key."

Adèle put out a slim hand, and I lifted her up.

I would have loosed her fingers, but she left them in mine.

"You're a lot like him," she said quietly. "Rowley told me who fetched the milk."

Then she put her hand to my lips.

On the last day we spent at the castle, the bookseller came, by arrangement, to bid us 'goodbye.'

We made much of him, as was natural, but, when we had talked for a while and he had broken his fast, he begged us to let him ramble from room to room, "for my great desire," he said, "was to make my guide pages more full, and never again shall I have an occasion like this."

So we showed him the trick of the table – which afforded him infinite delight – and then let him go his own way, to discover and speculate to his heart's content. Ere it was sundown, he had a great book full of notes, and his voice was trembling with pleasure as he told over his hoard.

Then Mansel took him apart and did the delicate business of making him rich. I do not know what he said or how he said it, but, when it was over, the poor old fellow was quite unable to speak, and, though he shook hands with us all a number of times, and though George and I went with him as far as the porch, he never once opened his mouth, until the wicket stood open and he was about to step out.

Then—

"Sirs," he said shakily, "to some friendships there is no farewells."

Then he clapped his hat on his head and went his way.

We watched him pass up the spur, but, though we stood ready to wave, he never looked back, and at last the wood swallowed him up and we saw him no more.

When the dusk came in, George, with Bell and Rowley, went off with Punter and Bunch, to take them to Innsbruck, purchase their tickets for London and see them go.

The latter gave no trouble, comported themselves most humbly and touched their hats to their warders, if ever they spoke. Such piety suggested that their recent bodily affliction had chastened their souls; but Rowley, who was watching to see that they took the train, reported that, when they did so, Punter was burdened with a suitcase and Bunch with a dressing-bag, and, since, when they left the car, they had had no luggage and neither had upon him the price of a glass of beer, I fear that they were incorrigible and that honesty was, so to speak, beyond their element.

George was not to return to the castle, but to meet us at midnight at a point between Lass and Villach, some twenty miles from the hog's back from which we had scanned the country a month before. So, when we had dined and the terrier had had his supper, Carson and Tester and I went the rounds for the last time.

No sign of our occupation was anywhere to be seen.

The damage we had done in the antechamber had been repaired, the bullet-holes in the Dining-room had been stopped and such window-glass as was broken had been replaced. The rooms had all been cleaned, the floors shone like glass, the beds had been stripped: the caretakers had such linen as had been used, and this the woman would wash and return to store: what rubbish and litter there was had been taken the night before and sunk in a river we knew of ten miles away.

When we had finished our inspection and found all well, I sent Carson down, with Tester, to finish loading the Rolls, and walked by myself on the roof for half an hour.

The night was lovely, and, though October was in, the air was as still and gentle as that of a summer's eve. A fine moon was riding a cloudless sky and shedding enough pale light to lend the towers and bulwarks a fanciful air and all the world I could see the look of a fairy-tale.

I do not believe in Enchantment: but, if there be such a thing, it stood at my shoulder that evening upon the ramparts of Gath. Castle, spur and thicket, mountains and forests and the flash of the water below seemed all 'such stuff as dreams are made on,' and I could not shake off the feeling that we were about to quit a fantastic country which, search for it as we might, we never should see again.

When it was ten o'clock, I made my way to the courtyard. There all was in order: what luggage we had was in place, and the rugs and cushions for Mansel were piled in the back of the car.

Then I went to the terrace, as they had asked me to do, to tell Adèle and Mansel that it was time to be gone.

They had left the chairs, set for them, and were standing together up to the balustrade: his arm was about her, and her head was against his shoulder, and the two threw a single shadow upon the flags.

For a moment I stood, irresolute, at the head of the steps. Then I went heavily down...

They did not turn at my coming. Only Adèle stretched out a little hand.

I came and stood beside her, and her arm went about my shoulders and held me close.

So we stood, all three together, looking unto the hills...

Mansel was speaking.

"The very elements respect you," he said. "Was ever a night so lovely, to round a dream?"

"Our dream," breathed Adèle. "Our beautiful, shining dream. You gave it us, darling. By keeping my letters, you gave it. And your strength has been its glory, your gentleness its life."

"You wrote the letters," said Mansel. "Because of that, I loved them so very much. I never thought I should burn them... But then I never thought that, in their place you would give me something – something that won't go into words, Adèle, that all the ages must envy me, and that no thieves can steal."

Adèle's arm left my shoulders and came to rest upon his.

"Oh, Jonah – my love, my darling."

Mansel held her close, looking down on her upturned face.

"I love you," he said. "I love the stars in your eyes and the breath of your lips. I love your hair and your temples and the pride of your exquisite mouth. I love all your peerless beauty. But, most of all, my queen, I love your darling nature and the finest, bravest heart that ever closed a book at the end of one golden chapter – and put it back on the shelf."

He kissed her steadily, and I covered my eyes...

Adèle turned to me and put her arms round my neck.

"Dear William," she said, "you saw the beginning, and now you see the end. You've been with us in light and in shadow: you've given us freely the best that a man can give: and I can only tell you that the love that you have shown us is part and parcel of our dream."

With that, she put up her lips to be kissed, like a little child, and I kissed them a little fearfully, for my clay is common, but she and Mansel were spirits of another sort.

Then she returned to her lover, and I left them to the rustle of the water and the pale splendour of the moonlight and the motionless plumage of the opposing hills...

Very soon they came up to the 'gallery of stone': and I shut the door behind them and followed them down to the courtyard, without a word.

Five minutes later the Rolls stole up the spur and into the wood.

On the following day George Hanbury and I would have returned to Villach, if not to Town: but this Mansel would not hear of, and, when he discovered our proposal, Adèle and his cousins rose up in pleasant indignation against our leaving their roof.

We could not withstand such goodwill, but, while George was glad to give way, I was reluctant, and, indeed, I shrank from the visit, I think, with cause.

I need have had no fear.

We stayed at Poganec until October was old: every day was of summer, and, though the leaves changed colour, they did not begin to fall. But things other than the season were cordial, and the weeks I had dreaded so turned to my relief that, when we drove back to London, I was in higher feather than I had been for months.

Adèle and Mansel took up the thread of life as though they had never let it fall. If ever they made believe, I never saw it: and, when I was alone with either, neither by word nor look was any reference made to what had passed between them at the Castle of Gath. Indeed their passionate adventure might never have been. The old, easy relation was back in its seat: they were content – happy, for all the world to see: they avoided no ground, because to them it was tender: where others' fancy took them, thither they went, riding so straight and unconcernedly that I, behind them, caught something of their courage and found the formidable fences of no account.

I think this will show how very fine was their temper, how brave and notable their style. Handsome in all they did, in this supreme ordeal they gave full measure, and I like to think that with that same full measure it shall one day be measured to them again.

Not for some days did I remember that we had never replaced the stone slab which had sealed the entrance to the Closet from the archway below.

This will be found one day, where it lies beneath the King's bed: and one day the coverlet will be drawn, and men will find the blood-stain upon the quilt.

What curious interest will not these things arouse? The name of Maximilian will be in every mouth. Old annals will be re-read, old narratives revised and legends brought to bed of fine new tales of wrath and mischief and murder saved or done. And yet I cannot think that, for all their bravery, they will compare with the truth.

This I am never weary of recalling, and many a winter's night I have sat at Maintenance, looking into the fire of logs and giving my memory rein.

Our desperate drive to Poganec, and the red of Mansel's tail-light flicking into and out of sight: the roar of the waterfall, and the high-pitched laugh of the rogue that played with Mansel and lost his game: my perilous journey upon the roof of the car, and the first, stupendous survey of the Castle of Gath: our stealthy entry into the King's Closet, the ominous creak of the floor-board and then the frantic pounding upon the door: 'Rose' Noble at the head of the table, and Mansel's lightning move, and the crash of the shots: our vigil by the open window, and the enemy's hideous laughter floating into the night: Casemate's halting footfalls, and Mansel asprawl upon the terrace, with the rope by his side: and, then, the death of 'Rose' Noble, and Mansel on his knees in the passage, with Adèle, aghast and piteous, holding him up...

The remembrance of these things is precious to me, for I had my part in them, and the tapestry they make belongs to that quiet gallery of which Mansel and Adèle and I have the only keys.

# An Eye for a Tooth

# CONTENTS

# I

# SOME PERSON OR PERSONS UNKNOWN

This tale is one which could have been told before now: in other words, the events which I shall relate took place before some others which I have already set down. For this I am sorry, for order means much to me: but, as this book will show, I could not have told the truth while someone whom I shall mention was yet alive.

The first I knew of the business was when I was a guest at White Ladies – that was Jonathan Mansel's beautiful Hampshire home. George Hanbury and I were resting after our labours, by which I mean doing little but put up our feet: but Mansel took next to no rest, although God knows he had laboured as hard as we, and had, as well, directed our enterprise. Indeed he divided his time between White Ladies and Town, taking the road to London before we were out of bed and only returning in time to dress for dinner and, as he used to put it, to save his face as a host. And then at table one evening, after the cloth had been drawn, he bade us fill up our glasses and listen to what he said.

So far as I can, I will set down his very words.

"Ten days ago we three were in Austria." He glanced at his watch. "Very nearly ten days ago we were driving from Villach to Salzburg as hard as ever we could. Take your minds back to that drive. You two were in the back of the Rolls, and Carson was driving, and I was in front with him. Rowley and Bell were behind, in the second car. So much you know, but no more: for you were asleep. That's why you don't know what happened... some fifteen miles from Villach... very nearly ten days ago.

"I must have been dozing, myself, for the first thing I remember was that Carson was slowing right down. That woke me up all right, for, as you know, we hadn't an instant to lose. At once I saw what he'd seen – a man's body, lying in the midst of the way. He stopped ten paces away, and I left the car.

"Well, the man was dead. The body was cold, but not stiff: he might have been dead for three hours. A nice-looking, fair-haired man, with a slight moustache; age, about thirty-five. He looked – and his clothes looked – English.

"Before I did anything else, I looked for the cause of death. Up to then I'd assumed that he had been killed by a car. I found a heavy fracture at the base of his skull: so far as I saw, that was all, and neither his face nor his hands were so much as grazed. This showed me that my assumption was almost certainly wrong, and it was, I think, at that moment that I realized that I had assumed what I had been *meant* to assume. In short, the man had been murdered, and a clumsy attempt had been made to cover this up. I say 'clumsy,' because it was clumsy. The road, as you know, was not tarred, and, as soon as I looked for them, I found the marks left by the body which had been dragged from a wood.

"The next thing to do was to find out who the man was. The pockets seemed to be empty, but I opened the coat to make sure. The first thing I saw was the tailor's tab or label, protruding and half-unstitched. Well, that told me quite a lot. It told me the tailor's name and the name of the murdered man. But it told me more than that. Savile Row has its faults, but bad stitching is not among them; in all my life I've never had a button come off. And when they stitch their label into the inside of an inside breast-pocket, they stitch it with all their might. And so I knew at once that some stitches of that label had been cut and the label itself displaced. Why was this done? Because the murderer wished to ensure that the body would be identified. Unfamiliar with English ways, the Austrian police might have missed the tailor's label, stitched into place. And so he had cut some stitches and pulled it out. In fact, he lost his labour, for I cut the rest of the stitches and took the label away....

"Looking again, I found his note-case still there. This was empty except for a photograph – a small snap-shot of an English country house. I took the case and I took the photograph, too.

"Well, as you know, we were very hard pressed for time, and, since the poor fellow was dead, we couldn't help him by stepping into the ring. So Carson and I, between us, lifted his body and laid it down in the ditch. This was narrow and deep and lined very thick with ferns, and it would have made a beautiful grave; but of course we had no time to cover him up. Then we re-entered the Rolls and put her along. You two never woke up; but Bell and Rowley were out and were standing by." Out of his note-case he took a rectangular slip. "There's the tab or label I took from the dead man's coat. When you've had a look at that, I'll go on to Scene II."

Printed upon the tab were the tailor's name and address – *Tendon & Co., Savile Row*: and written in ink upon it was their customer's name – *Major J. D. Bowshot.* There was also the date on which the coat had been made, as well as some reference number, clearly of no account.

When I had looked at the label, I passed it across to George: he gave it back to Mansel, who put it away in his case. Then he continued quietly.

"When we arrived in England, the position was this – that a Major J. D. Bowshot had been murdered by some person or persons unknown: that whoever committed the crime had attempted to disguise it as an accident: that whoever committed the crime had also attempted to ensure that the body would be identified. It is this second attempt which is so enlightening. You see, it shows – to my mind beyond all doubt – that, unless Bowshot's death can be proved, whoever committed the crime will be no better off.

"Well, I couldn't let things slide. I had made it my affair by taking that label away – to say nothing of my failure to inform the Austrian police. And blood, shed like that, cries out.... But it was obvious that I must go very carefully, if for no other reason, because I had no desire to play into the murderer's hands.

"Once for all, let me make that point clear. If I had not interfered, the body would have been found and in due course Bowshot's people would have been informed of his death. That is what his murderer wanted and what he is waiting for. As the days go by, but no obituary notice appears in *The Times*, the murderer will grow suspicious. By now he probably realizes that someone has interfered. And if, as I believe, the proof that Bowshot is dead means much to him, he will institute furtive inquiries, in the hope of relighting the fuse which I put out. So that, if I start in too, there will be two people both making furtive inquiries about the same man. Well, that's the way to get a common denominator – which would be fatal, for common denominators talk. To conclude my digression, let me say this – when I talk of the murderer, I do not necessarily mean the fellow who struck the blow: I mean the person or persons who arranged for the blow to be struck.

"Well, now as to the action I've taken...

"In a sense, I'd a flying start, for Tendon's my own tailor: I've been there for twenty years. So I looked in to choose some clothes and to pass the time of day. To cut a long story short, in the course of conversation poor Bowshot's name cropped up, and before I left Savile Row, I knew quite a bit about him and where he lived. He was, a bachelor, lived at the Manor House, Beehive – that's in the Mendip Hills: very quiet bloke, cared for nothing but hunting and shooting, often summered abroad...

"Well, then I went down to Mendip.

"I found a fine, old house and a charming place: not too much ground – just right. Seventeenth-century building, in perfect state, five minutes' walk from the village, under the lee of a hill. It was, of course, the house of the photograph. I drove to the door and asked if Bowshot was in. An old-fashioned butler told me that he was away. I liked the look of the man. And his demeanour was cheerful, which showed that he had no reason to think that all was not well. I said the usual things – that it was of no consequence, that finding myself in the neighbourhood, I'd remembered I'd promised Bowshot to look him up, that I hadn't a card, but that, if he said 'Major Wilson,' Bowshot would know who it was. Now the time was half-past four and the weather was very hot, and so it was natural enough that, representing his master, the butler should beg me to enter and take some refreshment before I went on my way. After some decent hesitation, I said I would. I asked for a glass of cold water and said that I'd very much like to put through a telephone-call. I didn't want to, really. But I wanted to have a look at poor Bowshot's telephone-book – the list of numbers that he most frequently used. It was, of course, a bow at a venture, for he might not have kept such a list. But most people do. Well, he was no exception. He'd a list of London numbers – names of subscribers and all. I copied it down whilst I was speaking to Harrods – in Wilson's name, of course – about a second-hand car. I only hope they enjoyed the call more than I did: but that is beside the point. Against the butler's will, I paid for the call; then I bade him goodbye and made my way home.

"There were nineteen names and numbers. All but seven were those of tradesmen or clubs. Of the seven I washed out four: they were those of a bank, a well-known dentist, a doctor of Harley Street and a firm of bookmakers. The three that were left were these – Orion, Worsted and Co., and Shade.

"Of Worsted and Co. I knew something. They are a firm of solicitors and used to be very sound. But they are not what they were – or what they appear to be. In fact the firm consists of Messrs. Biretta and Cain. And they are extremely hot. They've still a lot of good clients whom Worsteds' forbears won. I quite expect that Bowshot was one of these. People are funny like that. They'll look damned hard at their rice, if their grocer sells his business to somebody else; but they take their solicitors for granted – I never know why. So much for Worsted and Co.

"Of Orion, I've found this out. He runs an East End hostel in Bedlam Row. And he moves about a bit, in his efforts to raise the money to carry the hostel on.

"Shade was a private inquiry agent. I say 'was,' because he is dead. He used to be at the Yard and I just remember his name. He died three weeks ago, by falling in front of a train on the Underground.

"That is all we have to go on.

"Now if I was to change my tactics and set inquiries afoot, I'm very sure they'd bear fruit. But my instinct advises me not to. Put yourself in the murderer's place. He desired and arranged that his victim's corpse should be found. That has not come to pass. He is, therefore, on the alert, because he knows that someone has put a spoke in his wheel. That is a danger signal. And so his eyes are skinned and his ears are pricked, to catch any sign of movement by anyone else. But that condition won't last. When he finds that no one is moving, he'll move himself. And my instinct says 'Wait upon him.'

"What, then, have we actually got?

"First, that Bowshot was known to Biretta and Cain, who are – disreputable. Secondly, that he was in touch with a private detective – lately, in touch. Shade's number was the last on his list. Thirdly, that three weeks ago that detective happened to die a violent death. Fourthly, that ten days ago Bowshot himself was killed, and his body so left that it must be identified. Little enough, I admit: but here is one thing more. I turned up the inquest on Shade. The principal witness was a man who was standing on the platform beside him and saw the whole thing. He said that he tried to save Shade, but hadn't a chance. He also swore that Shade was a stranger to him. But the name of that witness was Orion – James Belper Orion, of Bedlam Row."

Now from what Mansel said it was clear that he meant, if he could, to find out the men who killed Bowshot and bring them to book. I cannot remember declaring that I would come in with him nor that George Hanbury did so. Maybe we did. But in fact it went without saying, for we were ripe for action of any kind. Having lately concluded a matter of life and death, we had not yet settled down and were finding the days empty, and normal, peaceful pursuits of slight account. But I very well remember that there and then we made such plans as we could and we had the servants in and told them what was afoot. (I have mentioned the three by name a page or two back. Carson was Mansel's servant – a very good man. Bell was my servant, and Rowley was Hanbury's. All three had been with us throughout our late adventure from first to last, and I think that they felt, as we did, that running into danger was better than sitting still.) And then we went to bed, proposing to move the next day, for, thanks to our recent exploit, we were already equipped for any rough and tumble with desperate men. We were fit. We could work together, we could drive a car without lights and could stand up to any strain. We had arms and knew how to use them, and Mansel himself had taught us the virtue of discipline. And so, as luck would have it, we were all ready to move. And that was just as well, "for," said Mansel, "if we are to do any good, we must move at once. Poor Bowshot's servants knew nothing three days ago, but any moment now the news of his disappearance will be announced. And that will open the door to the sheep *and* the goats."

It was less than four days later, to be precise, on the fifteenth day of July, that George and Bell and I drove up to a village inn. Perhaps I should have said 'down,' for the hamlet was sunk in a valley between two very high hills, some twenty-two miles from Villach and well off the beaten track. It was a pretty place, which progress had left alone. Fine, upstanding timber lapped it about, and a swift, clear stream of water sang through its midst. Its name was Latchet – less Austrian than English, it seemed to me; and it boasted a score of dwellings, not counting its inn. These were pleasant to see, for they were plainly ancient, yet spick and span as pride or affection could make them, and, indeed, the whole place was as clean as any English village that I ever saw. It being the dinner-hour, there was not a soul to be seen, but without the forge, I remember, two magnificent bullocks were waiting, no doubt to be shod; they were neither yoked nor tethered, but stood there very quietly, swishing their tails and blinking their patient eyes. Across the stream hung two bridges of fine, gray stone, and, by the side of one, a cobbled ramp had been made, so that beasts could go down and drink. The inn was a good-looking house, standing back from the road; on either side of its door were a bench and a massive table of gray, old oak, and I know I was glad to accept this invitation, throw out my clutch and bring the Lowland to rest. (This car we had bought for our journey – or rather, Mansel had bought it on our behalf. It was not new, but had been carefully used for two or three months, and it did much more than its duty for many a day. And since Mansel, of course, had his Rolls, we were very well served.)

Now, unless the murdered man had been carried away by car from the district to which he belonged, it was clear that he must have been staying not far from where he had lain on the Salzburg Road; and Mansel had asked George and me to go on ahead of him and do our best to discover the inn or, maybe, the farm-house at which he had lodged. We were to ask no questions, but only to use our eyes and to play the role of tourists, fishing and enjoying the country and caring not where we went.

In the last three hours we had visited several villages all within a few miles of where, as near as we could make it, Mansel had found the body a fortnight ago; but Latchet was the first one which showed any promise at all, for the inns of most of the others were very rough, and few, I think, could have offered a decent bed. But Latchet's inn stood far above any of these, and, indeed, as soon as we saw it, we made up our minds we were home.

As we left the car –

"Not a shadow of doubt," said George, with his eyes on the house. "And very nice, too. You order the beer; I want to think out our approach. Why the hell can't we talk German?"

There he did himself less than justice, for he could, what is called, 'get along.' And I knew odd words and phrases, but that was all. Still, to converse in German was wholly beyond our power. Which was embarrassing; for, if there was to be nothing for us to see, only by idle conversation could we find out whether Bowshot had stayed at some house.

George took his seat on a table, and I walked into the inn. Bell had stayed with the car and was wiping the windscreen clean of the endless dust.

I was half-way down the flagged hall, when I heard a voice speaking English – and stood very still.

"I don't see what more we can do. He disappeared on the first and today's the fifteenth. Hopeless of course. When did they first report it?"

Another voice spoke in German, and a woman's voice made reply.

Then –

"She says on the eighth – a week ago today."

"Ask her again why she didn't report it before."

The question was put and answered.

"She says she didn't want to make trouble – that if Bowshot had come back, he would have been very angry to find they had made a fuss."

There was a pause. Then –

"She says that he carried a note-case. Can she say whether there was anything in that note-case besides money? Visiting-cards, for instance. She must have seen him use it time and again."

When the interpretation was done –

"She says he had a photograph in it, but she doesn't think anything else."

"How does she know that?"

"One day he took out the photograph and showed it to her. He said it was a picture of his home. And she said how lovely it was, and he laughed and said he'd give her the photograph to keep, when he went away."

There was another silence, broken by the sobs of the woman – no doubt, the hostess.

"Tell her not to cry. It may only be a case of loss of memory."

The translation was made, and the sobbing began to subside.

"How much does she consider that he owes her?"

"Seven pounds fifteen."

"Well, tell her this. If she wants to see her money, she'd better do as I say."

The interpreter spoke again, and the woman replied.

"She will obey implicitly."

"We're going to pack his things and to leave his bags here. I shall take his passport and cheque-book. If he should come back or communicate with her in any way, she is to wire us immediately. Better write down the address – just British Consulate, Salzburg. Oh, and if any letters should come, she must send them to me at once."

The translation was being made, when I heard the scrape of a chair.

At once I slipped out of the house, made a sign to George and ran for the car. Bell, on the watch, saw us coming and opened the doors.

As I took my seat –

"I want to know if we're seen. Keep your eyes on the inn."

Forty seconds later we had left Latchet behind. And had seen no one.

"Anyone see us, Bell?"

"I don't think so, sir. If they did, they never showed up."

"Inform me," said George. "And I want a damned good reason for being done out of my beer."

"Here it is," said I, and told him my tale.

When I had done –

"Good enough," said George. He sighed. "It's always the way. I sit still and flog my wits, and you walk into the grocer's and pick up the figs. And now what?"

"Salzburg and Mansel," said I, "as quick as ever we can. He may be there tonight. If he is..."

"Go on," said George. "Go on. I'm beginning to see."

"Well, the special idea is for us to prevent an announcement that Bowshot has disappeared. The very best way to do that is to give people reason to think that he is alive and well. Supposing tomorrow morning the hostess at Latchet goes into Bowshot's room – to find his luggage gone and, left on the table, *seven pounds fifteen and the photograph of his house?*"

"I hand it to you," said George. "I think I should make it ten pounds, but the photograph is the thing. That will be proof positive. For only Bowshot knew that he had said she should have it before he went away. Oh, very good indeed. An' then she wires to the Consul, an' he marks his file 'No action' and that is that." He slewed himself round in his seat. "You're growing quite cunning, Bill. It must be being so much with Mansel and me."

How burglars feel, I cannot pretend to say, but I know that I felt ashamed of the work that we did – not that, but the following night. The thing was too easy. Latchet slept like the dead, and the door of the inn was not locked. The whole business took six minutes from first to last. Mansel and I went in, while Bell stood on guard by the doorway and George remained with the car. The dead man's luggage was piled in a first-floor room – a trunk, two suitcases, a rug and a fishing-rod. I set the trunk on my shoulder and picked up a case, and Mansel brought down the rest. On the table we left an envelope, containing the photograph and ten pounds in Austrian notes. And then we were all four gone, like the thieves we were.

And about the time, I suppose, at which the British Consul received his telegram, the cloak-room at Salzburg station accepted the stolen goods. But Mansel lodged the receipt at a Salzburg Bank – under sealed cover and marked 'For Safe Custody.'

Here I should say that not until then did I learn that, while George and I were waiting for him at Salzburg, Mansel, Carson and Rowley were doing a dreadful duty some hundred odd miles away.

"It was always clear," said Mansel, "that it had to be done. In the first place, the dead deserve burial. In the second place, so long as it lay unburied, the body might well have been found, and, rightly or wrongly, it is our present aim to deny to those who killed Bowshot all evidence of his death. As things stand, we've done more than that, for we have convinced the Consul that Bowshot is still alive. And so his disappearance will not be announced. That will perplex the murderers: they will not know what to think: but they will be forced to the conclusion that for some reason or other the body has not been found.

What action they'll take, I don't know. But if, as I think, they are anxious that Bowshot should be known to be dead, they may pursue the matter. Putting myself in their place, if there was a lot at stake, I should have a stab. I may be entirely wrong, but I think I'm right. I can't get over that label's being pulled out. Why pull it out, if they only wanted Bowshot out of the way? They didn't only want that. They wanted more. They wanted proof that Major John Bowshot was dead. And it must be provoking for them, when they know he is dead, to think that they're losing their labour because the Austrian police don't know their job. So very provoking that they may feel compelled to come back. I mean, that's what I should do..."

It was two days after our raid that we took up our quarters at Goschen – a decent farm, some fourteen miles from Latchet and twelve from the fatal spot on the Salzburg-Villach road. This was very much better than any inn, for the house was agreeably placed and as private as we could wish. Though few would have guessed it, it was in fact served by two drives, the lesser of which ran out of the stable-yard: from there it passed through woods for a quarter of a mile, before slipping into a by-road which led to a hamlet called Talc. And here were cross roads. But the principal drive ran out of the Villach road. We, therefore, had a 'back door,' the approach to which was well masked; so that, if we took ordinary care, to keep a watch on our movements would be very hard. Then, again, there was a very fair trout-stream, five minutes' stroll from the house. But, best of all, the people were used to the English and had received them as guests before the Great War. It is, I think, common knowledge that during those four lean years their country was ranged against us largely against its will, and these poor peasants were not only plainly thankful to see some English again, but clearly most anxious to prove the goodwill which they felt. This was, of course, of great value; for our goings out and our comings in were pretty sure to be most irregular.

Still, fortunate as we were, it was no good sitting still and wondering what was toward. If things were going to happen, they were going to happen at Latchet or close to the Salzburg road. So within six hours of our settling down at the farm, Mansel took George and myself to show us as much as he knew. And Bell went with us.

Before leaving, we studied the map. This showed that, as the crow flies, Latchet lay less than three miles from where Mansel had found the body in the midst of the way.

"There may be a path," said Mansel, "but that is for us to find out. By road, as you see, it's nearly eleven miles; and it is not clear that Bowshot had the use of a car. You heard no mention of one. Now I said, if you remember, that his body had been dragged from the woods. That was going too far. I can only swear it was dragged from the side of the road. So he may have been brought there by car. But I don't think he was. If I am to speculate, I think he was on his way to or from Latchet, when he was done in. A path would bear out that suggestion. Assume that he was in the habit of taking this walk. The murderer finds that out and lies in wait close to the road. The rest is too easy.

"Now we're going to leave the car about a mile and a quarter from the spot where the body lay. This, for two reasons. First, we are out to observe – not to be observed; secondly, at that distance, there's a very convenient place in which to bestow the car.

"Tonight I shall show you round. Then we shall make for Latchet, of course on foot; and if there is a path, we should strike it at once. But, path or no, we must find the way there and back – and find it so well that we shall know it again. All this we must do in silence and without any light. Don't think I'm being foolish, because I'm not. I just don't want to be murdered, as Bowshot was. And in a show like this, you can shove your shirt on the man who sees, or even hears, the other man first."

That night there was no moon, but the sky was clear and the stars were luminous. Mansel drove slowly, so that we could study the way, and half an hour went by before he stole off the road and up a track into the woods. After about a furlong a second track crossed the first, and here it was very easy to turn the Rolls. This Mansel did forthwith, so that, when she stopped, she was facing the way we had come.

Mansel turned in his seat and spoke very low.

"I told you this place was convenient, and so it is. You saw that second track. Well, that leads back to the road; and it actually meets the road a short two hundred yards beyond where the body lay. So that is the way we'll go." Here he left the car and we followed him out. "Single file, if you please, and watch your step."

After about six minutes we came to the end of the track and the Salzburg road. All was very still, and, there being no wind at all, the silence of the woods all about us was that of death. The trees met over the track, which was therefore as dark as pitch; but the Salzburg road was lit by the stars above.

Mansel stood listening a moment. Then he made a gesture for us to come up with him.

"Before we go any further, I want us to wait for a car. I want you to see for yourselves, first, how its headlights show up the sides of the road, and, secondly, how very short is the warning of its approach. From either direction. This particular reach of road is about six hundred yards long. But at either end of this reach, there's a hell of a bend. The woods being very thick, unless your ears are pricked, you cannot hear a car coming until it rounds one of those bends; and, if it's moving, you've got to be quick and careful if you don't want to be seen. I don't mean, seen by the occupants of the car; I mean, seen by someone who might be glad of the sight."

As the words left his mouth, I heard a sudden snarl, and Mansel dropped. Instinctively, we all did the same. An instant later, the road upon which we had been looking was bright as day.... And then some car swept by, and the darkness came back.

As we got to our feet –

"You see," breathed Mansel. "These woods don't give you a chance. Still, it's not quite as bad as that, if you use your ears. I mean, you'd have heard it before, if you hadn't been listening to me. And now we'll cross the road – one at a time, of course. Over the ditch and into the bracken beyond. Then turn right and go on till you see a culvert ahead. If another car comes, there's the bracken. But keep your eyes on its beam: it might reveal something that you hadn't known was there."

We had all four crossed the road, before another car passed. This time, crouched in the bracken, I marked how its lights illumined the sides of the way. Had a man been standing there, I must have seen him. I saw the stone parapets of the culvert, one hundred and fifty yards off. There we came up with Mansel, who once again spoke very low.

"Thirty yards on from this culvert is where the body lay. If a path to Latchet exists, it won't be far from here. I'm going to see if there is one: I shan't be long."

As he moved away –

"Let us pray," said George. "Let us pray very hard indeed. Mansel's in the mood to move mountains – an exercise denied to weaker vessels like me. I've already fouled three roots and walked into two trees. And that in two hundred yards. And Latchet is three miles off. At this rate, therefore, if we don't discover a path, my face will want lifting before the night is out. So let us pray all we know that a path exists."

Be sure I agreed with him.

Whilst we were waiting, another two cars fled by. And then a lorry came pounding, defiling the sweet of the night with its sound and its smell. As the last of its rumble faded, Mansel appeared.

"Yes, there's a path," he said. I heard George sigh with relief. "And if you're as thankful as I am, that's saying a lot. I can't swear it goes to Latchet; but if it doesn't, I shall be much surprised. Any way, come along. It's not very far."

Mansel did well, I think, to find that path by night, without any torch. Even by day one could have missed it, for, where it met the ditch, there was no break in the bracken and what depression there was was of no account. But once you were on it, to keep to it was easy enough; and the four of us made good progress for more than a mile.

Then we met with a check, for the forest came to an end and we entered a sloping meadow, in which not even Mansel could find the track of men's feet. For a moment, he stood very still. Then I saw him lift his head, as a man who is straining his ears. And then I heard the whisper of water....

At the foot of the sloping meadow was flowing a decent stream; and, walking along its bank, we came to the little footbridge which we had been sure must be there. We climbed another meadow and entered the woods again. Here the path was as clear as it had been before, and soon more than one path joined it, to make it still more distinct. All this time we were rising, and, when at last we had surmounted some crest, we heard at once the song of the sturdy water which George and I had looked on three days before. That Latchet lay below us, there could be no doubt.

To make certain, we went on down; to find that the path ran into the place between walls, quite close to the inn.

It was now three hours since we had climbed out of the Rolls, and I was expecting that we should retrace our steps. But Mansel thought otherwise.

"I want," he said, "to have a look at the coach-house which serves the inn. I want to see what it contains. So William will stay with me, and George and Bell will go back and get the Rolls. Don't bring her into the village." He pointed South. "Do you remember cross roads just under a mile that way?"

"Yes," said George.

"D'you think you can get there all right?"

"Yes."

"Then pick us up there an hour and a half from now. And then we'll go home and spend a morning in bed."

"Every time," said George.

The next moment, he and Bell were out of our sight.

"The thing is this," said Mansel. "This inn is a magnet. It attracted the British Consul and it attracted us. I think it will attract others. Now I doubt if we can watch it by day – at present, at any rate. And to watch it by night would be futile. But we can check up on its garage. No car tonight; but two tomorrow, for instance. I mean, that would make us think."

An alley on the left of the inn brought us into a stable-yard, and there, on the right, stood a coach-house of a considerable size. It had two mighty doorways, each shut by two leaves of oak which must have been twelve feet high, and I think the place had been built to accept the berlines and coaches of bygone days. We could have opened a door, but we did not like to do this, for fear of making a noise: for one thing, the leaves had dropped and were resting upon the cobbles of which they should have hung clear; for another, their hinges were rusty and might well have lodged a protest which would have waked somebody up. But when we looked for a window, there was none to be seen. Since the coach-house ran all the width of the stable-yard, we could not approach its sides; for the yard itself was walled and the coach-house was really no more than a slice of the yard which had been fronted and roofed.

I glanced at Mansel, who was standing with a hand to his chin.

"How deep," he said, "how deep would that coach-house be?"

After a moment's thought –

"Say thirty-five feet."

"Thereabouts. Say fourteen paces. Let's measure the depth of the yard."

This was twenty-six paces dead.

"Forty paces in all," murmured Mansel, and led the way down the alley. As we came to the road, "And now how far from here to the mouth of the path?"

Together we paced the distance, making it forty-two paces or thereabouts.

"As I dared hope," said Mansel. "The path runs past the back of the coach-house wall."

"Now all we want," said I, "is the length of the alley."

"Twenty-two paces," said Mansel. "I took it as we came down."

I walked up the path behind him, looking up and straining my eyes....

Its height alone assured us that here was the coach-house wall, but, though we could make out the eaves, we could see little else; for here the path was a canyon some four feet wide, and trees which grew in some garden beyond the opposite wall, were stretching over their branches, to hide the stars.

At length –

"There's something there," I said; "about twelve feet up. It doesn't look like a window. It has the look of a shadow; and yet I don't think it is."

"Use your torch," said Mansel. "For one second only, of course."

It was the edge of a shutter that I had seen. And three feet below was foothold, upon the branch of an oak.

I mounted on Mansel's shoulders....

One minute later, I had my hands on the wood.

The shutter was not even latched. As I pulled it open, I saw that it hid a window that had no glass and no frame. I leaned well over the sill. Then I stretched down my arm and switched on my torch.

Three vehicles stood in the coach-house, which could have accepted twelve. One was a farmer's gig, one was an old landau and one was a very old car, with a tiller instead of a wheel and a tonneau as big as a sty.

I switched off my torch, swung the shutter to, found an easy way down and made my report.

Mansel nodded, and led the way back to the road.

Not until we were clear of Latchet did he open his mouth.

"We've had a goodnight," he said. "Fortune favours the patient as well as the brave. But one thing bothers me, William. It seems pretty certain that Bowshot had no car. And that seems strange to me. You don't want a car in a city, but Latchet is right off the map."

"We're very car-minded," I said, and Mansel laughed.

"That's true enough. All the same..."

"You don't think the car was pinched by the fellows who did him in?"

"Not on your life. They staged a running-down case. If he'd had a car, they'd have staged a smash, instead. No. Bowshot had no car; but I don't know why." I saw him shrug his shoulders. "And that's only a minor query. Except that some person or persons stood to gain by his death, when published, I don't know anything. And yet I feel there's a lot behind this case.... Well, we shall see – before long. Of that, I'm perfectly sure: 'for wheresoever the carcase is, there will the eagles be gathered together.'"

So we came to the cross roads.

And not very long after that, the Rolls slid out of the shadows and picked us up.

# II

## WHERESOEVER THE CARCASE IS

From that time on, every night we patrolled the path to Latchet from dusk to dawn; and every night we looked within the coach-house, to see whether any car-owner had come to stay at the inn. For such duty, two were enough: so Mansel and Carson did it one night, George and Rowley the second, and Bell and myself the third. In our spare time we took our ease, fishing and visiting Salzburg and getting to know the country round and about the farm. The weather continuing fine, we did very well: but, as the days went by, yet nothing took place, I sometimes wondered if Mansel's judgment was wrong.

Perhaps because I was doubting, I was the first to have something to report.

When Bell and I went out, our procedure was this. First, we inspected the road and the side of the road, and we proved the verge of the forest from the culvert up to the path. Then we followed the path to Latchet and, after inspecting the coach-house, made our way back. For the rest of the night, one was moving between the road and the meadow, and one was watching the edge of the Salzburg road.

It was my third turn of duty, and I was peering into the coach-house, about to switch on my torch, when I became aware of the presence below of a car that had been moving at speed and was not yet cold. For full three minutes I waited, straining my ears; then I lighted my torch, to see a wine-coloured saloon, all covered with dust. I could neither read its number, nor recognize its make: but it carried a 'G.B.' plate and one of its off-side windows was badly starred.

I put out my torch, carefully closed the shutter and made my way down to the ground.

When I told Bell what I had seen—

"Looks like we're off, sir," he said.

I agreed with him.

Instead of retracing our steps, we then stole on and round, to have a look at the inn; for, had some window been lighted, we might have been able to see the people who had come in the car. But here we were disappointed, for every window was dark. This was not surprising, for the hour was half-past eleven; and if they had come some distance, as like as not they had been glad to retire. So, after a careful survey from every side, we turned again to the path and our not unpleasant walk to the Salzburg road.

By the time we had reached the meadows, the moon was up, so, for what it was worth, I left Bell at the edge of the forest, to watch the open ground. He was to follow me in a quarter of an hour; if half an hour went by, but he did not arrive, I was to go to him as fast as I could.

There is a saying 'It never rains, but it pours.' Be that as it may, as I came to the verge of the woods, through which the road ran, I saw a car at rest by the side of the way.

Its lights were out, but the moon was showing it up and I saw it well. It was black or blue – a coupé, and looked American.

For a moment, I stood very still. Then, since I was still in the shadow and full thirty paces away from the edge of the road, I began to move on very slowly, keeping my eyes on the car....

And there I made two mistakes, which Mansel would never have made. In the first place, I ought at once to have left the path; in the second, I should have been careful to keep my eyes off the road, for, looking out of the darkness into the light, they were, of course, far less fitted to pierce the darkness itself, and anyone in the forest, with his back to the road, would have been able to see me before I saw him.

And that is just what happened.

I heard a gasp and a rustle: and, as I turned, two arms went about my neck.

"Oh, John, John! I'm so thankful. I—"

The sentence snapped off short, and the girl recoiled and stood peering, with one of her hands to her head.

"My God," she breathed. "Who are you? I – I thought..."

"I'm very sorry," I said. "It wasn't my fault."

"You're English. Have you brought me a message?"

"I'm afraid I haven't," I said.

"Then why are you using this path at this time of night?"

"Mere chance," said I. "I don't sleep well and I wander a lot at night. May I know who 'John' is? I might be able to help."

"You must be staying at Latchet. Is there anyone ill at the inn?"

"I'm not staying there, but I daresay I could find out. Won't you tell me who to ask for?"

I could see her looking at me and biting her lip.

"I suppose I can trust you," she said.

"I suppose you can."

"I want news of Major John Bowshot. He is – a great friend of mine. I – I haven't seen him lately, and I have a – a dreadful feeling that he may have been taken ill."

"I'll do my best," said I. "When and where can I meet you again?"

"Today is Tuesday. Can you be here on Thursday?"

"Not here," I said, quickly. I had the sense to say that. "Do you know the cross roads beyond Latchet?"

"Of course. But why not here?"

"I shall be tired on Thursday, and this is too far."

She looked at me very hard.

"Very well. The cross roads. Between half past ten and eleven on Thursday night."

"I will be there, I promise."

She hesitated. Then –

"He was staying at Latchet," she said, "and I had to go away. He knew that, of course. But when I got back and came here, he never came. And that's not – like him. If you could find out what's wrong..."

"I'll do my best," I said.

She turned and took the path, to go back to the car.

When she found me behind her –

"You needn't trouble," she said.

I took no notice and handed her over the ditch and into the road.

I saw a coronet painted upon the door of the car.

I opened this, and she took the driver's seat.

"May I know your name?" she said.

"Perhaps on Thursday," said I, and shut the door.

I felt her eyes on me.

"Why didn't you slam it?" she said.

"Till Thursday," said I, and stood back.

"You make me uneasy," she said. "Will you tell me only one thing?"

"On Thursday, perhaps."

"Do you know John Bowshot?"

"No," said I. "But I'll do my best for you both."

"Thank you," she said, and started her engine up.

As she let in her clutch, she inclined her head.

I made her a bow in return, and the car slid away.

Ten seconds later, I was once more out of sight.

Mansel was sitting upon the foot of my bed.

"I got your note," he said. "And I couldn't wait any longer. It's past midday."

"Sorry," said I, and, with that, I told him my tale.

When I had done, he rose and moved to a window and stood looking out.

"*Cherchez la femme*," he said. And then, "I might have known. Go and have your bath, William. You've given me food for thought."

But when I came back he was gone.

After lunch we discussed the matter – Mansel and George and I.

It was my desire – and I said so – that Mansel should come on Thursday and keep my appointment with me; but this he refused to do.

"Not this time," he said. "You are very well able to play the hand. All that you must be sure of is that the girl is straight. If she is, you can tell her whatever you please. And see what she says."

"I can't tell her that Bowshot is dead."

"I think it will be your duty. I'm very sorry, William, but, if you decide that she's honest – and of that, from what you tell me, there can be no doubt – I think you will have to tell her, there and then. And then you can tell her our mission – to find his murderers out."

"It's all damned fine," I said.

"I know. It's a hellish business. But we simply cannot lead her along the garden-path. Not even for twenty-four hours. If we did, she'd never forgive us – and she would be right. Once we are sure of her, we cannot have her on. What line she will take, I don't know. If she takes the bit in her teeth, we can but go home. But if she was in love with Bowshot, then she has a right to know that Bowshot is dead. Whether or no she can throw any light on his death, I've no idea. But she may be able to.

"And now for the strangers at Latchet.

"This may be a mare's-nest. Still, it's an English car, and Latchet is off the map. Any way, it's for us to make sure whether or no these are the fellows we want. So I think that tonight we should all go out on the job. And that, in good time. If they were concerned in the murder and mean to inspect the scene, I simply cannot believe that they will do it by day. A man's got to have an iron nerve to dispense with the cover of darkness on such an occasion as that.

"Now if they do visit the spot which we know so well, our principal object will be to overhear what they say. We are out after proof. Once they stand convicted by what we have heard them say, we have got to see what they look like. This may mean that we have to declare our presence. It may mean – anything. What is quite certain is that, once they know we are there, our relations will not be cordial. And, for that reason, I think we had better go armed."

That was as much as he said; but I know that I dreaded the appointment which I had made with the girl even more than I looked forward to the clash which might come that night. And that is saying a great deal.

I will not set down in detail the orders which Mansel gave before we set out; but I will make one point – that if the strangers at Latchet were indeed proposing to visit the scene of the crime, we could not possibly tell whether they meant to do so on foot or by car. It was, therefore, arranged that I should stay by the road, for I had seen the car and should know it again. And Bell and Carson with me. But Mansel and George and Rowley would answer for the path. George's post was to be in the meadows, and Mansel's by the side of the path, two hundred yards from the road. Rowley would move between them, playing connecting-file. Being, so to speak, in the centre, Mansel would be ready and waiting to move either way.

Carson and Bell would each carry a heavy chock. If the car I had seen were to stop not far from the path, and its occupants were to alight, they were to place these chocks beneath a front and hind wheel; so that, should the men take alarm and run for the car, although they gained it, they would not be able to leave.

The evening was overcast, and dusk came in soon after we left the farm. It was as good as dark when we came to the Salzburg road. We did not use our lights, but though I, who was driving the Lowland, was close to the Rolls, I could only just see her leave the road for the track and, once I had left it myself, I could see nothing at all. Carson at once alighted, to move in front of the car, taking with him one end of a cord which was tied to my arm. So long as this was drawn tight, I knew that the way was clear and that I could proceed. Five minutes later, both of the cars had been turned where the two tracks crossed, and had been berthed as usual, facing the road.

And then on foot and in silence we moved down the second track.

Arrived at the road, as usual, we crossed it one at a time. George crossed first, for he had the farthest to go; then Rowley; and, after him, Mansel. And I was about to follow, when I heard the sound of a car.

At once I left the track, stepping into the bracken which grew upon either side. And there I stood waiting until the car should have passed.

And then I suddenly knew that it was not going to pass.

Peering between the stems, I watched its lights approaching more and more slowly, until they stopped altogether, about a hundred yards off. Then they came on again at a walking pace. Twice more they stopped, as though the driver were looking for something he thought should be there. Craning my neck, I tried to follow their beam.... As I did so, this reached the culvert – or, rather, the twin parapets which showed where the culvert was. The car stopped again. Then again it came slowly on, until it was almost abreast of where – by this time – I was kneeling, by the side of the track.

And then it swung to its right, and I fell on my face.

I might have guessed for what the driver was looking; I should have been ready for what he was going to do.

Be that as it may, all the forest directly about me was suddenly bright as a stage with the footlights on, and the car swung into the track, whilst I lay four feet from its wheels, with my sleeves tight across my face.

The next few moments were among the worst I have passed.

I was not so much concerned about Carson and Bell, for they could be counted upon to do the right thing. But what made me want to cry out was the thought that the driver might do as we had and make for where the tracks crossed, in order to turn his car. If he did that – or even if he went too far up – his headlights would certainly show him the marks of our wheels, while, if he backed round to the right, they would show him the Rolls and the Lowland, some fifty paces away.

In this anxiety, I was, of course, not alone. Mansel, who saw the whole thing from the opposite side of the road, was on tenterhooks the whole time, and he told me later that George, who was crouching beside him, was praying aloud.

Whether George's prayers were heard, I cannot say: but the fact remains that, to my immense relief, the car stopped short of the cross, and, after what seemed an age, somebody switched off her engine and turned out her lights. And then I heard her doors opened and presently shut.

I was on my feet by now and was standing well back from the track by the side of a tree. This was as well, for somebody lighted a torch and threw its beam down the track and waved it from side to side.

"Keep that light on the ground, you fool."

The words were spat, rather than spoken – by one of four men: and since I was soon to learn that he went by the name of Forecast, I may as well set it down now.

His order was obeyed – under protest.

"Got to see where I'm goin'," said the man with the torch in his hand. "You ask me to—"

"See and be seen," snapped Forecast. "And damned well put it out when we come to the road. I don't want any cars stopping – to see what our trouble is."

"I always said," said a third man, "we oughter 'ave come by day. You wait till you're over the road. No—drives like this. Nothin' but ferns: an' trees with—great roots all over the place."

"What of the path you spoke of?"

"Well, wot of it?" said the other. "I said a path – not a by-pass. An' all hid up with the ferns."

"Boney," said Forecast, grimly, "if you don't mind your mouth, one of these—days I shall put you where you belong. As for coming by day, if you an' Gulf weren't lying, you've been here by night before."

"No, you don't," said Boney. "We never say that. Got 'ere by daylight, we did. On purpose to see our way."

"That's right," said the man with the torch.

"Well, you had to get back," said Forecast.

"Wot if we 'ad?" said Boney. "This is a drive, this is. But that's a path. An' it's goin' to take some findin', torch or no torch."

"Well, carry on. We've got to find more than that."

"Sez you," said the torch-bearer. "You wait till you see them ferns."

"—needle in a— 'aystack," said Boney, "if you ask me. An' I'd like to meet the—that done it. —interferin' body-snatcher."

"You've said it," said the other. "Took the words out of me mouth. A body-snatcher, that's wot he is. To think after all we done—"

"Easy now," said Boney. "This 'ere was an accident. Knock down an' killed, he was, by a runaway car."

"Quite so," said Forecast, "quite so. And perhaps the driver got wind up... and, after you'd gone, came back... and dragged the body into the forest... Or, if not the driver, then someone – some god-damned, meddling fool." I heard him suck in his breath. "Any way, show me the doings. And when I've got my bearings, we'll have a look round."

"Yes, an' wot if there's nothin' there?" said the man with the torch. "Just because some body-snatcher has stuck in his—oar, me and Boney's to drop four 'undred quid."

"Gulf," said Forecast, "I'll give you a piece of advice. When next you're arraigned for felony, don't go into the box. As sure as you do, you'll put the rope round your neck. And now lead on, you wash-out. I want to see exactly what happened and where it took place. If, after that, there is anything more to be done..."

"Yes?"

"You'd—well better do it," said Forecast.

The meaning with which he invested this blunt apodosis was unmistakable. Even I, an eavesdropper, found it most sinister: and I was not surprised when, after a little silence, the other turned on his heel and led the way to the road.

Now all this confirmed so precisely what Mansel had always said that I felt as though some nightmare had come to life and I wished with all my heart that he had been standing beside me to hear what had passed. And, with that, it came into my mind how very important it was that Mansel should know at once as much as I knew. Before, however, I ventured to cross the road, I must give the servants orders concerning the car.

By now the rogues had come to the edge of the road, and, though Gulf had put out his torch, I could see the four of them peering and looking to right and to left. So for a moment or two; then one – I think it was Boney – took the lead, and the others followed behind in a little bunch. Since they did not cross directly, but bore to the right, in two or three seconds they had passed out of my view.

At once I turned – to find Carson standing beside me two paces away.

He put his lips to my ear.

"Shall we chock the car, sir?"

"No," I breathed. "We'll have to do better than that. I want you to do in her lights. Don't cut the wires. Unscrew the dashboard connections and pocket the nuts. Use your torch if you need it; it won't be seen. But Bell must keep a look-out at the mouth of the track."

"Very good, sir," said Carson. "And then?"

"You both cross over the road and pick us up. I'm going to find Captain Mansel and put him wise."

"Very good, sir."

As Carson slid into the shadows, I made for the track.... I could not see the rogues, when I came to the road, but, in view of the line they had taken, I knew it was safe to cross. I did so at once. Then I turned to my right and began to move through the woods towards the path.

Now though Gulf was not permitted to use his torch on the road, I had no doubt at all that he would be encouraged to use it as soon as he and his fellows entered the woods; for to anyone not accustomed to moving in the country by night, the forest was by no means a 'joy-ride,' as he had foretold. But as the moments went by, yet no torch was lit, I began to think that caution had taken charge and that Forecast had made up his mind that no more light must be shown. I therefore stood still and listened, for I was perfectly sure that, light or no, their movements in country like this would give them away. And, as I stopped, I heard the approach of a car.

Automatically I took cover and stood by to use my eyes; and, as I looked, the head-lights made everything plain – in more senses than one.

Disliking the idea of the forest, the four had been walking along the crown of the road. So they had made good progress and had almost reached the culvert, when the beam swung round and caught them full in the midst of the way.

For a moment they stared at the lights, as though they were hypnotized. Then, as though the spell were lifted, they sprang to life.

To the scream of a high-pitched horn, they broke and ran, and two, to my great delight, fell into the ditch. Which goes to show what a guilty conscience will do, for they had but to stand to one side and suffer the car to go by. Still, in their defence, I must say that, on that particular reach, a car was upon you almost before you could think. For all that, when the car was gone by, the four fairly sacrificed caution upon the altar of rage; for they roared and cursed and swore like so many lunatics, and they very near came to blows, because Boney and Gulf had said nothing about the ditch. These two insisted with oaths that they had forgotten it was there, but the damning fact stood out that neither of them had fallen, but both had jumped clear.

As well as affording us pleasure – I frankly admit that I laughed till I could hardly stand up – this childish exhibition stood us in excellent stead; for, before the flurry was over, I had fetched a small compass and struck the path. And there I found Mansel and George, both of them weak with laughter, but both of them all impatience to hear what I had to tell.

But we none of us smiled when I had made my report and I often wonder how I could have laughed as I did, for here were two filthy blackguards seeking to prove to their master that they had done his bidding to put a poor soul to death: and here was the man who had ordered this pitiless crime, come like a ghoul in the night, if it could, to smell out its victim and ravage the field of blood.

"And the fourth man?" breathed Mansel.

"I've no idea. He hasn't opened his mouth."

"More than one torch?"

"I don't know. I've only seen one."

"All right. Steady. They're moving. From what you say, they're going to make for this path. I'm going over to join them, and you go up to its mouth. George and Rowley beside it, between there and here."

The four were now in the bracken, moving in single file by the edge of the ditch. Their progress was very slow, for Gulf, with the aid of the torch, would move a few feet and would then stand still and turn round and throw the beam down on the ground for the others to see their way. Even so, they tripped and stumbled and cursed aloud; and two more cars came by, to reveal them standing like dummies, watching them pass.

As the snarl of the second faded, Forecast burst out.

"Blind leading the — blind. Where is this blasted path? And put out that — torch before the next car comes by."

"I told you," said Boney, "it was all hidden up with the ferns."

"Either there's a path, or there isn't."

"We've walked the —," cried Boney, "Gulf an' me. It sort of goes on from the one that runs down by the inn. If we'd 'ave come that way—"

"God knows where we'd be," said Forecast. "You can't lead us three hundred yards, let alone four miles. You an' Gulf go on; and China and I'll wait here. And when you've struck it, come back and light us along."

By this time they were, of course, quite close to the path, for I could hear all they said, although I was standing upon its opposite side: with the result that Forecast had hardly sat down before Gulf declared in triumph that there it was. To make matters worse, both he and Boney agreed that 'that would be right' and proceeded by calculation to show that only a fool would have thought it lay anywhere else. And this, I suppose, was more than Forecast could bear, for he leapt to his feet and, disdaining the use of the torch, blundered to where this was shining as fast as he could. Then he snatched the torch from Gulf and flashed its light on the ground.

"Are you sure this is it?" he said, quickly.

"This is it right enough," said Gulf. "I always said—"

"— what you always said. Get down to it – both of you. Show me exactly what happened from first to last."

As may be well believed, neither Gulf nor Boney was anxious to do as he said; but Forecast was merciless. He cross-examined and bullied and lashed the two with his tongue, until the beasts had lost what spirit they had, and at last they threw in their hands and answered directly whatever he chose to ask.

From all they said it was easy to reconstruct the whole crime, and here, leaving out the detail, I may as well set it down.

They had followed Bowshot from Latchet one Monday night and had seen him met by a car on the Salzburg road. They had waited until his return, in about two hours, and had heard him make an appointment for just such another meeting in three nights' time. The next day they had taken their car and had reconnoitred the place. It was then that they had marked the track in which the car was now berthed. On Thursday they had arrived before the daylight was gone, had left their car on the track and had made their way to the path. It was after night had fallen that Bowshot had come. They had let him go by to his meeting, and, as before, had waited for his return. It was then that 'the accident' had happened – sullenly enough, the murderers showed the place.

"And then?" snapped Forecast.

"We pulled out the tab, as you said, and then we took him back an' laid him full in the road."

"Show me the place again."

In silence the four proceeded as far as the ditch.

Then –

"It was just along there," said Gulf. "Jus' short o' that culvert. We 'ad a job, I remember, to get 'im out o' the ditch."

There was a little silence.

Then –

"Have you any doubt he was dead?"

" 'E was dead all right," said Boney.

"That's right," said Gulf. "The – the car wot hit him done in his spinal cord."

There was another silence.

"Did you meet any cars when you left?"

"Nothing," said Gulf. "We turned at the first cross roads."

"He was found, of course," mused Forecast. "The body was found. But why wasn't it reported?"

Nobody answered, and presently he went on.

"Why didn't the inn report that he didn't come back?" In a sudden passion, he turned on the man called 'China,' "And you said that you could talk German!"

"So I can," declared China. "I learned it off of a deck- 'and wot came from Bruges. But they talk a dialec' here."

"You filthy liar," said Forecast. "You can't talk a—word. But that's for later. Some—shifted that body to suit himself. A gypsy, as like as not, that fancied his purse. But he didn' want no trouble; so, when he'd robbed him, he dragged him into the ditch. Give me that torch."

Now between where he stood and the culvert, the ditch was resembling a trench, being fully six feet deep and not more than three feet wide. Add to this that Nature had taken a hand and that the sides as well as the bottom were thick with ferns. It follows that, standing above, a man could by no means be sure what was lying below, and, after some fruitless endeavours to plumb the depths with its beam, Forecast handed the torch to China and told him to hold it whilst he got into the ditch.

Mansel breathed in my ear.

"Get hold of the others, William. Everyone back to the cars and wait there for me."

As I turned to the path, I saw China kneeling down by the edge of the ditch. Then the torch left his hand for Forecast's, and the light which it gave disappeared.

As I made the path, I felt a touch on my shoulder and there was Bell. (He was a splendid servant. Whenever I wanted something, he always seemed to be there: indeed, I think the truth is that in such a business as this he was always watching me with the tail of his eye and could interpret whatever movement I made.)

"Can you find the others, Bell?"

"Yes, sir. We're all in touch."

"Then pass the word – we're all to go back to the cars."

"Very good, sir."

As he moved away, I turned to look at the ditch. In that moment a match was struck, and I saw three forms together lighting their cigarettes. Then the match went out, and I moved again. I wondered how Forecast was faring – and whether Mansel had decided to take a hand. I reached the ditch and looked down it. Forecast was making good progress, for, not very far from the culvert, I saw the glow of the torch. But the others had not moved with him – their cigarettes told me that. And as I looked, they sat down....

I slipped across the road, made my way through the bracken and reached the track. And there I was standing, regarding the strangers' car, when Jonathan Mansel came limping up to my side.

"I'm inclined to think," he said, "they should have a flat tire. One of the back ones, William." I stooped to unscrew the valve. "I want to have a look at their luggage, and we don't want to be disturbed. They may be able to get along without lights, but changing a wheel in the dark is a hell of a job."

"They've got the torch," said I.

"It's broken," said Mansel, and laughed. "I followed Mr Forecast and laid him out. Then I did in his torch: then I lighted my own and went on – for the look of the thing. When I was close to the culvert, I had a look back. As you probably know, the three were sitting down, smoking, quite close to where Forecast went in. So that was all right. I doubt if they'll take any action before he comes to – that'll be in about twenty minutes. When he does, there'll be trouble to burn; and he'll have the deuce of a head for twenty-four hours. And here are the others. Before we move, we'd better go through their car."

The search revealed the car's papers, but nothing else. And those we left. Then we re-entered the cars, and ran without our lights for a couple of miles. Then Mansel put on his sidelights, as much to help me along as anything else, and twenty-five minutes later we stopped at the top of the hill below which Latchet lay.

Carson and Rowley stayed with the Rolls and the Lowland, with orders to turn them about, so that, if we had to leave quickly, the cars would be ready to move the way they had come. Mansel and George and I were to enter the inn: but Bell we took as far as the forecourt and posted him there.

As before, the door was unlatched, and there was no light to be seen. We passed upstairs quietly enough.

It was easy to guess that Gulf and China and Boney were sharing poor Bowshot's room: for a second, smaller bed was standing against a wall, and three dirty pairs of pyjamas had been laid out by some maid. As may be imagined, they travelled extremely light, and our disagreeable search was very soon done. We found no papers at all, but a clip of ammunition suggested that someone went armed.

On the opposite side of the landing we found a sitting-room, far too handsome and pleasant to lodge such villainous guests. That this room, too, had been Bowshot's, there can be no doubt; and the thought that its present tenants included the two who had actually shed his blood for some reason made me more angry than anything else. And here perhaps I should say that I was very much disappointed that, now that we knew the truth, no violence at all had been offered to those two men. That Mansel's judgment was good, I knew very well: but an hour ago all four had been at our mercy, if we had cared to strike, and, knowing what Fortune is, I doubted that such a chance would occur again.

It was in Forecast's bedroom that we found a battered dispatch-case, right at the back of a wardrobe, behind some clothes. The thing was locked, but we very soon had it open – to find what Mansel had hoped for, and more than that.

Mansel was after their passports: "for," said he, "without their passports, they cannot leave Austria. They dare not go to a Consul, men like this. And so they will stay – at our convenience. And before they go – *if* they go – I'll have the truth of this murder from bottom to top." And now their passports were there – the four of them tied together – and George slid them into a pocket and said, "What next?"

'Next' was a quarto envelope, such as some lawyers use. It was neither addressed nor sealed, and when Mansel drew out its contents, I saw him open his eyes. There were some typewritten sheets, and pinned to these was a map, very roughly done. There was also an envelope, addressed to Duke Saul of Varvic, which was unsealed.

Mansel flicked this open and drew out the sheet it held, and I looked over his shoulder, to see what it said.

I saw the heading, and that was enough for us both.

Solicitors head their letters with the name of their firm. And this particular letter was headed WORSTED & CO.

An ample supper was laid, awaiting our coming in, and the servants heated and served some excellent soup.

As we took our seats –

"And very nice too," said George. "Better than the picnic in progress by the side of the Salzburg road. But I shall always be sorry we didn't hear Forecast wake up."

I laughed.

"He'd better save something for Latchet. He'll feel the need of expression when he finds his papers have gone."

Mansel nodded.

"Till then, he won't be quite sure. Almost, but not quite. But then all doubt will vanish. More. The theft of the papers and passports will hit him over the heart. Of course he's played into our hands; but we've had a goodnight out."

"It's a rotten position," said George. "I'd hate to be in it myself. Up against someone who knows and who's out for blood: line of retreat gone; and three bloody-minded wash-outs round your neck. If I were Forecast, I'm damned if I wouldn't clear out."

"And leave them to it?" said Mansel. "He daren't. Those men are fools. Supposing they went to the Consul, to try and get home. No tale they could tell would wash. They'd find themselves in deep water almost at once: and then they'd let Forecast in. At least, that's how I see it. I think he's stuck good and proper, and I think he'll call for help. And that was why I let the brutes go tonight. I was more than tempted to blot out Gulf and Boney as soon as they'd said their piece. It would have been perfectly safe. But Forecast and China would have panicked. They wouldn't have called for help: they'd have faded away. But I want to know who's behind this. I think the papers will give us a good idea. But we've earned our supper tonight, and we'll eat that first."

George looked very hard at Mansel.

"You know who's behind this," he said. "You always have. But you want to get them out here – under your hand."

Mansel smiled.

"One of the truest things ever said is a jingle. This is how it runs. 'Oh, what a tangled web we weave, When first we practise to deceive.' In other words, criminals get involved. Say Gulf struck the fatal blow. But Forecast daren't let him down, because he is involved. And someone bigger than Forecast won't dare to let Forecast down, because *he* is involved. If we were to force the pace, all concerned would sit tight and do nothing but watch and pray. But so long as we leave a fair loophole – well, it's human nature to try and save the game. Oh, and by the way, did either of you see the swine? I had a good look at Forecast, but I couldn't swear to anyone else."

"I saw Boney," said I. "Gulf put the torch on his face. Clean-shaven and thin, with a nose a bit to one side."

"Forecast is ruddy and has a jovial face. You wouldn't think that, would you? But so it is. Bland to order, I'd say. Thick hair, and a hell of a jaw. A little bit under-hung. Quite decently dressed. Clean-shaven. Mouth turns up a little at either end. China, I imagine, has cheek-bones – hence his name. Oh, and what about his gift of tongues? I'd love to have heard him trying his Flemish on the hostess of Latchet's inn. Which shows that Forecast is a man of no education. And yet he looks one. You find astonishing fish in the waters of crime."

It was when we had finished our meal that we returned to the papers which we had found.

First we read through the letter from Worsted and Co.

*H.H. Duke Saul of Varvic,*
*Schloss Varvic,*
*by Villach,*
*Austria.*

YOUR HIGHNESS,

*This letter is to introduce Mr Forecast, who has all our confidence.*

*We are anxious to trace the whereabouts of our client, Major J. D. Bowshot, who was lately in your neighbourhood, and the delivery of this letter will mean that Mr Forecast, who has the matter in hand, is in need of your Highness' assistance.*

*Upon such assistance we feel that we may count, because of the interest in Major Bowshot's welfare which your Highness has more than once expressed. If, however, your Highness should feel that it would be more convenient for us to raise the matter with our Foreign Office, your Highness has only to say so. In that case Mr Forecast will place himself at the disposal of the British*

*Consul at Salzburg, who will, no doubt, communicate with your Highness direct.*

*We are,*

*Your Highness' obedient servants,*

*WORSTED AND CO.*

"How's that for blackmail?" said Mansel. "I told you Biretta and Cain were devilish hot."

"But I don't understand," said I. "How can the Duke find the body – any better than anyone else?"

"Only we," said Mansel, "know that he can't. But that's by the way. The last sentence of that letter is a definite threat. And now let's look at the notes; for that's what I think they are."

The sheets were not signed, but they contained Forecast's instructions, as they shall show. The typewriting was the same as that of the letter which I have already set out. Here and there they were altered in ink, and it was easy to see that the hand that had altered them was that of the man who had signed for Worsted and Co.

*To Mr Forecast.*

1. *I see no reason why you should not stay at Latchet. It might become expedient for you to visit the inn; and action by a visitor is always more open to suspicion than action by a resident. But in no circumstances will you try and pump the landlord or anyone else. If your interpreter is any good, he should be able to pick up information – by letting the people talk. But he must show no interest in what they may say about B.*
2. *First, you will satisfy yourself that the accident in fact took place, and that it was fatal. Eye-witnesses can report a thing like that easily enough; but take them to the place where it happened, and tell them to reconstruct it, and you will see at once if they're lying or not. This must be done after dark; and, except after dark, the spot must not be visited.*

3. *If you are not satisfied that a fatal accident took place, you will return at once alone, bringing the others' passports with you.*
4. *If you are so satisfied, you will consider the possibility of:*
   (a) *the body's having been carried into the wood,*
   (b) *and actually buried near by.*
   *This may be the explanation. A passing motorist, reluctant to be held for enquiries, may have carried it into the wood. A gypsy may have found it, robbed it and then buried it to avoid the consequences of his crime.*

   *Bearing these things in mind, you will make a careful search of the vicinity.*
5. *If and when you find the body:*
   (a) *you will immediately wire us saying – BUY FUNDING LOAN,*
   (b) *you will send the others home,*
   (c) *yourself, you will return to the spot by daylight, officially discover the body, and then report this fact to the local police,*
   (d) *as soon as the police allow you, you will follow the others home.*
6. *In the unlikely event of your being unable to discover the body, you will proceed to Schloss Varvic, present the accompanying letter and obtain an interview with the Duke.*
7. *The Duke will be difficult because he will be afraid of being involved. You will make it quite clear to him that only by helping you can he avoid being involved. He will try to avoid seeing that but he will see it in the end.*
8. *In all your dealings with him, never lose sight of the fact that what we must have is proof of B.'s death. That is all you are after. But he must not realize this, for, if he were to, he would wash his hands of the matter. He must be made to believe that we are acting solely in his interests. In fact, we are using him.*

9. *The line you must take is this.*
 *Insist that B. was put out at his instance. Stick to that, no matter how much he protests. Emphasize that failure to find a body will have disastrous results – that any day now B.'s servants may grow uneasy because he does not return. If they do, they will approach us, as B.'s solicitors, when we shall be forced to take action. This action can only take the form of approaching the Foreign Office and telling them all we know. In which case, as B.'s solicitors, we should be compelled to involve him.*
 *Point out that it is not a question of money; that, once a body is found, we should naturally expect him to fulfil his obligations, but that it is for his own security that the find must be made.*
 *Insist that the matter is urgent, as it is. Any moment now the servants or someone may move. And if they should approach the authorities direct, the matter will pass beyond our control.*
 *Put the wind right up him.*
10. *You will not wire to us (except, of course, as directed by paragraph 5), but in reporting you will use the ordinary post.*
11. *If we should have occasion to write or wire to you, we shall address you as WENSLEY, at 1645 Konigstrasse, Salzburg, which is an accommodation address. You had better call there once a week.*
12. *When you find the body, make sure that the tab is still there and is clearly legible. If it is not, put the attached envelope into one of the pockets of the coat. Any body which is to be found, must have this envelope in one of its pockets.*
13. *Also attached is a rough map, which will show you how to get from Latchet to Schloss Varvic.*
14. *You are to memorize the above instructions with great care. When you are satisfied that you have them by heart, you will*

*place them in the enclosed, addressed envelope and return them to us, before leaving England, by registered post. The attached envelope and the map, you will of course retain.*

When we came to the end of these instructions, each one of us drew a deep breath.

Then –

"Seeing's believing," said Mansel. "That's all I can say. And someone dictated those words, and someone else typed them out. Takes all sorts to make a world, doesn't it?"

"But fancy," said I, "trusting Forecast to send them back."

"Criminal folly," smiled Mansel. "They should have taken them off him, before he left. The probable truth of it is that Forecast has never read them – or never read them right through. Criminals are incurably lazy: that's why they so often fall down."

There were three more documents.

One was the map referred to. This was a pencil sketch, which showed that Schloss Varvic stood twenty-two miles from Latchet and some twenty-nine from our farm. It was not more than fourteen from the spot on the Salzburg road.

One was a crumpled envelope, bearing a stamp which had been post-marked and addressed to Major Bowshot, The Manor House, Beehive, Somerset.

And one was the foolscap envelope, which Forecast ought to have used. This was addressed to Miss Bauchen, of Gallface Mansions in Maida Vale.

"Who would she be?" said I.

"I rather imagine," said Mansel, "that she is a confidential clerk to Messrs Biretta and Cain. That of course is her private address. A hundred to one it was she who typed this stuff. And the letter to the Duke."

"We're learning quite a lot, aren't we?" said George. "And what's the betting that Forecast can't remember his accommodation address? The one in Salzburg, I mean."

"I should say," said Mansel, "about five thousand to one. Which means we can have his letters without any fuss. There's probably a wire there now, ordering him to return those instructions at once. And now let us think very hard. We've picked up a glorious hand, but I don't want to play it wrong."

"In other words," said George, "we've got to try and decide what Forecast will do."

"Exactly."

"Well, I know what I should do. I should murder Gulf and Boney and China without delay. Then I should wire to Worsteds, telling them where to find the bodies and asking for another two envelopes. Then I should repair to the nearest monastery and take the veil under another name. After all, when it was safe, one could always pinch the abbot and get the sack."

We all three laughed.

"That," said Mansel, "is exactly what he'll feel like doing; but I don't think it's what he will do. I think he'll go to Schloss Varvic – as soon as his head will permit. Anyone will tell him the way, and it's inconceivable that he has forgotten that name. He'll miss those instructions, of course; but he knows that the Duke's involved and roughly the line to take. And now he does want assistance. He's in a hell of a jam – with his passport gone."

"Will he write or wire to Worsteds?"

"I wish I knew. At a guess, I'd say that he wouldn't, unless he draws blank at Varvic. Without his letter, the Duke may have him chucked out. In his position, I'd try and save the game. And only when I had failed, would I break the unpleasant tidings to Biretta and Cain. I mean to say, he'll get no sympathy there. He has lost a paper which he should not have had to lose – a paper which lets them right in. Well, it isn't much fun reporting progress like that. Oh, no. I'm sure he won't do it, except in the last resort."

"If you want my opinion," said George, "he won't do anything for thirty-six hours. What with his head and the darkness and having to sit in the car till the dawn comes up; what with Gulf and Boney and China all swearing blue that he must have had a bad dream – why, he'll want about ten hours' sleep, before he has control of his brain. And even then he may not search his dispatch-case. And not until he does that will he know that the murder is out."

"I agree," said Mansel. "I think we have plenty of time. But that we must use. Don't forget what we're trying to do. To get the big fellow out here. We know who he is – now. It's either Biretta or Cain. And now let's look at those passports, and then we'll retire."

Passport photographs are seldom pleasing, but those of Gulf and Boney were damning documents. They looked what they were – I cannot say better than that. China's, too, was shocking; and if I had been a frontier official, I would have had them shadowed or, better still, turned them back. Forecast's was harmless enough, for the man was smiling broadly and might have been full of goodwill.

It was whilst I was studying his face that Mansel gave a cry and suddenly plucked the passport out of my hand.

"Oh, I'm a fool," he cried. "And the thing stood out a mile. Damn it, we'd better retire. If we find out very much more, we shan't be able to sleep."

I followed his pointing finger.

This was underlining Forecast's full name.

*James Belper Orion Forecast.*

"Like men, like master," said Mansel. "He shoved Shade under a train six weeks ago."

# III

## THE TRAIL OF OIL

The next night was fine and clear, and all the winds were still. Quiet-running though it was, I heard the coupé coming for half a mile.

As it stole up to the cross roads, I stepped down out of the shadows and up to its door.

"Goodevening," I said at once. "If we are to talk, I'd rather we moved from here. If you would drive on—"

"You named this place," said the girl.

"I know. Things have changed since then." I pointed ahead. "Three miles on, you'll see a lane on your right. Please take that, drive a hundred yards up it and wait for me."

"But you'll be ages, walking."

"I shall be close behind you. I have a car."

"Very well. But you lead the way."

I hesitated. Then –

"All right. I've a servant with me. I shall drop him at the mouth of the lane: and he will stay there out of earshot, to see that we are not disturbed."

"You didn't mean me to know that you weren't alone."

"That's quite true," I said. "I thought it might make you uneasy to know we were two. And now will you please drive on? I'll overtake and pass you before you come to the lane."

Without waiting for her to reply, I made my way to the Lowland, a hundred yards off. Half way there, I turned to look back. The coupé was gone. A few minutes later I passed it, as I had said I would do. At the mouth of the lane I dropped Bell, and then I drove slowly up it for a hundred and fifty yards. As I got out of the Lowland, the coupé came to rest six paces away.

I stepped to the near side door.

"If I open this door," said I, "you can stay where you are, and I'll sit on the bank."

"I'd rather get out," she said. "We can sit on the step."

"As you please," said I; and, with that, I opened the door and handed her out.

She did not sit down at once, but stood peering at me.

"May I see what you look like?" she said.

I drew my torch and put it into her hand.

"Put the light on my face," I said.

She switched on the light and did so.

Then she put out the light and gave me the torch.

"Thank you," she said quietly: "and now let's sit down."

In silence we took our seats.

Then –

"From the look on your face," she said, "I think you bring me bad news."

"I'm afraid I do," I said.

She began to tremble.

"Very bad news?"

"Major Bowshot has disappeared."

"What d'you mean, 'disappeared'?"

"He went for a walk one evening, and he – didn't come back."

I heard her catch her breath.

"When was this? How long ago?"

"It was on the first of July."

"But that was the last time I saw him. D'you mean to say that since then..." Her hands went up to her temples. "Oh, my God! And today is the twenty-ninth. But has no one tried to find him? What has been done?"

"Have you reason to think," said I, "that he had an enemy?"

She looked at me sharply, and a hand came down to her mouth.

"He – he might have had," she whispered. "There is a man who – who has no cause to love him. But I... could have sworn that he didn't know John was here."

"Who knew he was here?" said I.

"Only his Bank, I think. He – he wanted to be very quiet."

I braced myself.

"He... is... quiet... now," I said slowly. "He's gone to his long home.... That is why I am here – to lay by the heels the blackguards that took his life."

I dared not look at her, but I thought she would never move. With the tail of my eye, I could see that she was still sitting exactly as when I had seen her last – her head turned to me, and one hand up to her temples and one at her lips.

Then at last she turned away, and her head went down.

"I knew it," she breathed. "I knew when I saw your face."

Then her arm went across her eyes, and she burst into tears...

Her grief was terrible, and since I was shaken enough, I left her sitting there and passed to the back of the car. And there I paced to and fro, with the sweat running down my face. I felt that I should do something, but I did not know what to do. Indeed, as never before, I was out of my depth; for to make no move seemed inhuman, when there was a fellow-creature in such distress; yet no move which I could make could help such agony.

How long I walked up and down, I do not know, but at last I turned to see her standing before me, like any ghost.

"Will you please come back and sit down? I've some questions to ask."

In silence I did as she said.

"First, may I know your name?"

"My name is Richard Chandos."

"You told me you didn't know – him."

"I'm sorry to say I didn't."

"Then why are you interested?"

"We were the first on the scene. And it looked as if those who had killed him were going to get away with the crime. That seemed all wrong to us: and so we decided to – to put a spoke in their wheel."

"Who is we?"

"There are three of us in this show. And we've got a long way. I'll tell you all in a minute, but first I must ask you this. Are you content that we should do what we can?"

"To bring the crime home?"

"Yes."

She looked away for a moment.

Then –

"Are you sure he was – murdered?" she said.

"By two hired bullies," I said. "They watched him enter your car, and they knew he'd come back. So they hid themselves in the bracken on either side of the path. Sure enough, you brought him back. He said goodbye to you, and when your car moved off, he took the path through the woods. And as he went by, they struck him down from behind."

I heard her draw in her breath.

Then –

"I'm more than content," she said. "I don't know how you know this, but if the half is true, I'll pray for you all every night that you may be given the power to bring the crime home."

"Very well," said I. "Now, as I see it, you have a right to hear the tale I am going to tell. But we have a right to ask that you do not repeat one word of what I shall say. Had we known about you, we should not have done as we have, without consulting you first. But we did not know of you, and now we are very deep in. I mean – it's really serious. But the law would have done no good, so we've taken it into our hands."

I heard her sigh.

"You needn't worry," she said. "I've no one to talk to – now."

"I'm terribly sorry," I said.

After a little silence, I told her my tale.

I left very little out, but she never once interrupted and scarcely moved.

When at last it was done, she glanced at her watch.

"There seem," she said, "to be two who desired his death. Duke – Duke Saul of Varvic and Worsteds. Each on his own account."

"That's right."

"But the Duke doesn't know that Worsteds desired his death, and they will declare that they did what they did for him."

"Yes."

"But they couldn't have done it without him."

"Why d'you say that?" said I.

"How could they have known he was at Latchet? He was so terribly careful to cover his tracks. He wouldn't bring his car, lest that should give him away. And he never passed through Salzburg. He came by Trieste. But Varvic's not twenty-five miles from where we are sitting now. Oh, yes. The Duke must have known he was there. And he sent word to Worsteds – no doubt about that." Again she glanced at her watch. "Time I was going," she said, and got to her feet. As I rose too, "I'd like to thank you," she said. "You've been very good. I'm sorry I went to bits; but my life – isn't very happy, and John... was everything." Her voice broke there, but I saw her clench her teeth and take hold of herself. "One thing I must say, and that's this. I am so very thankful that you came into this for his sake, and not for mine. It just makes all the difference. It means I can cheer you on; it means I can wish you God-speed with all my heart. For every reason. You see, Mr Chandos, it's just what he would have done. I wish you'd known him. You would have got on together. If he had found you in the road, though he might not have known you from Adam, he'd never have rested until he had done his utmost to bring your assailants to book."

"I wish I had known him," said I. "And I'm sure we should have got on. But you have got to thank Mansel for all we've done. I don't count beside him. I've only followed along. I think you ought to meet him. He's twice my brain."

I think she smiled at that, but I cannot be sure.

"Perhaps you're right," she said. "But simplicity has its points. Never mind. I'd like to meet him. From what you say, I think you're staying at Goschen."

"That's right," said I.

"I can't come there by day. Sunday night, perhaps: but I won't drive up."

"Come here," said I. "You can leave the coupé here and I'll be here to meet you and drive you in. No one will know. You see, there's a second approach."

She seemed to reflect for a moment.

Then –

"That's understood," she said. "On Sunday at half-past ten. And thank you once again – for everything. You'd a rotten job tonight: and I only know one man who could have done it so well. And he... is... quiet... now. He's gone to his long home."

She opened the near side door and slid into the driver's seat.

As I closed the door –

"Will Forecast go to the Schloss?"

"I think he may," said I.

"I see. In that case beware of Varvic. From – from all I've heard, he can be a dangerous man."

"I'll bear that in mind."

A hand came over the door, and I bent my head and put it up to my lips.

"Till Sunday, then."

"Till Sunday. Don't put on your lights just yet. I'll guide you back to the road."

She put the car into reverse, and I walked with my hand on the door and guided her back. Bell saw us coming, stepped into the midst of the road and beckoned me on.

"Shall I go another way home?"

"I wish you would," said I.

"Very well."

She backed round into the road the way we had come. Then she slipped into first... into second... and then she was gone.

I turned to Bell.

"I'll get the Lowland," I said, "while you stay here."

"Very good, sir."

I was not very far from the Lowland, when I slipped and very near fell. At once I lighted my torch, for I was perfectly sure that I had stepped into some oil. And so I had. A small pool of very black oil was lying where the coupé had stood.

I regarded it, frowning.

Then I turned and began to walk back down the lane.

Two very fine trails of oil were easy to see – sometimes joined together, and sometimes separate.

It looked as though the coupé's crank-case was leaking; in which case, before she got home, her engine might seize. That was bad enough; but what I liked still less was the fact that to and from the lane she had left a definite trail.

An idea came into my head and I called to Bell...

Together we returned to the pool into which I had stepped.

"What d'you make of that oil, Bell? It looks very black to me."

Bell rubbed a little between his finger and thumb.

Then –

"It's not pure oil, sir," he said. "And it must have something mixed with it. If it had been pure oil, it would have soaked into the ground."

"Ah," said I. "And now let's decide where it came from."

Thanks to the print of the treads of the coupé's tires, we were able to say exactly where she had stood; and that at once showed that the oil had not come from her crank-case, but from the rear of the car.

Bell was shaking his head.

"That's not gear oil, sir. It's much too fine."

I fingered my chin.

"What about a drum in the boot – with a feed-pipe run through the floor-boards?"

"Fixed up on purpose, sir? To see where she went?"

"It looks damned like it, Bell. The boot looked very capacious; and one never opens a boot, if one's only running about."

"But who would do that, sir, to her?"

"God knows," said I. "But she was a friend of Major Bowshot's. And someone may think she's worth watching. In fact, it's quite clear they do. And we must do something about it. For one thing only, she's coming to meet me here on Sunday night. More. We'd better be quick. If somebody's trailing the coupé, they're sure to be here before long. Get that clothes-brush out of the Lowland. The first thing to do is to clean up the mouth of the lane."

Now it stood to reason that, when the man or men who were using the trail of oil came to a place where this seemed to come to an end, they would at once alight and examine the ground: it was, therefore, essential that we should do nothing to show that the trail had been covered up. Rough obliteration would be useless; the thing must be carefully done. Bell, therefore, collected dust and laid it by handfuls along the side of the trail, and I brushed this dust over the oil, as fast as I could. Still it was a slow business; and a quarter of an hour had gone by before we had hidden the fact that the coupé had entered and later emerged from the lane. And this was not nearly enough, for now the trail ended just short of the mouth of the lane and then began again on the other side. This, to a man who meant business, would be a significant fact; and if such a man entered the lane, though we had covered the oil, he would see the print of the tires.

I could not think what to do, for I felt that at any moment the following car might arrive. And Bell had no suggestion to make.

I remember standing there, frowning and biting my lip.

And then at last I did what Mansel was always doing to such effect. I tried to put myself in the other man's place.

At once I saw that, if I were driving with my eyes on the trail of oil and it came to an end, I should not immediately stop, but should drive on very slowly in the hope of picking it up. And when I did pick it up, I should account for the gap by supposing that for two or three moments the feed-pipe had become choked. So far as it went, I think that reasoning was sound, but I could not dismiss the fact that, when at last I came to the end of the trail, I should find it strange that only once, for ten yards, had the feed-pipe been choked. And if once I returned to the gap, I should never leave it until I had examined the lane.

And then I saw what we must do.

We must make some more gaps between the cross roads and the lane.

If we could make two or three, by the time the car which was following came to the lane its driver would be convinced that the feed-pipe had taken to working by fits and starts, and when, after passing the lane, he found the trail once more intact, he would assume that the pipe had now passed some obstruction and cleared itself.

At once I sent Bell for the Lowland and ran down the road myself for fifty or sixty yards. There I collected some dust and set to work again to cover the trail.

Bell was back with the Lowland before I had finished my gap, but I would not let him help me, but bade him stay at the wheel. For then, if we heard a car coming and I was quick, we should not be caught standing still by the side of the road.

But no car came. And when I had made three gaps in the trail of oil – and each of these between twelve and twenty feet long, I felt that Mansel himself would have said that was good enough. So I entered the Lowland and took the seat beside Bell – filthy with dust and sweating, because I had worked so fast. Indeed, so vile was my state that when Bell said "Back to the farm, sir?" I was immensely tempted to, as they say, call it a day. But – and here is the force of example – I could not do that. Had I gone home there and then, Mansel would have said nothing: indeed, he would have commended all I had done. But both he and I would have known that, had he been in my place, he would have done his best to get a view of the men who were trailing my lady's car.

And so –

"Not yet, Bell," I said. "Before we go, I'd like to pick up the wallahs whose game we've been trying to spoil. Of course, I'd like to see them without being seen; that's rather a lot to hope for; but at least we may be able to have a look at their car. What I do not understand is why they haven't rolled up. It's suited our book very well, but I find it strange."

"They might have been waiting, sir, till the lady got back. Say they're in the same garage. Well if they start before she gets back, when she comes in, she'd see that their car had gone out. And that might make her think."

"Good for you," said I. "That's the explanation, as like as not. Oh, of course it is. They must belong to her garage. That's how they had the chance of fixing her car."

"That's right, sir."

"I'm afraid it is. And I don't like the look of it, Bell. She's no one to count on – she told me as much tonight."

"You can't get word to her, sir?"

"I don't know where she comes from or who she is."

There was a little silence.

Then –

"You can find where she comes from, sir. You've only to follow the oil."

"Well done, indeed," said I. "Round we go, Bell. And we'll have a look at the others as they come in."

In a flash he had turned the Lowland, and then we were whipping along the way we had come.

Our lights were good; but only when they were dipped, could we see the trail – a black thread, shining a little, laid upon the white of the road. Still, as long as there was no turning, we knew that it must be there; so we drove with our headlights up, watching the road for a turning and taking the trail for granted, so long as no side road appeared.

Three times we slowed down, on seeing a turning ahead; but always the trail led straight on, until we came to a place where three roads met. Here it swung to the left; and another nine miles went by before we came to cross roads where again it turned to the left.

It was when we had covered in all some twenty-eight miles, that we saw we were approaching a by-road which seemed to climb up to a wood; and when Bell had checked the Lowland and dipped her lights, we saw at once that the coupé had gone that way.

Round to the left we went and up – a sharp climb – to the wood, and there, to an oak, was fastened a notice-board. Only two words it bore, and these were 'PRIVATE ROAD.'

Automatically, Bell slowed down.

"On you go," said I. "But dip your lights. Once we're out of the wood, we'll turn them out."

But the wood did not give way; and though we tried to drive without any lights, the leaves above were too thick. There was, therefore, nothing for it but to go on as before – but, of course, with our headlights dipped.

And then after more than two miles, in which we must have risen a hundred and fifty feet, I saw the moonlight flooding the meadows ahead.

And something more than the meadows.

No cathedral that ever I saw so dignified its precincts as did that splendid castle its simple curtilage. The forests walled it about, and the meadows made it a carpet on which to stand. With the silver light and the shadows, it made a picture fit for a poet's dream; and though thereafter I saw it more than once, I shall never forget my exquisite, first impression, for it had the fairy-tales beaten – and that is the honest truth.

Only one light was burning in all the pile, and that was showing low down by the castle gate. Presumably this was the light of the porter's lodge; for a place of such importance would certainly have a night-porter, to keep the gate.

Bell stopped at the meadow's edge and put out his lights, and I sat for a moment or two, regarding the lovely scene. Then I took hold of myself and began to consider the facts.

We had presumably run my lady to earth: but unless I could see her and tell her what was afoot, I should have done no more than obtain some information which she had not meant me to have. The castle was not very big, but, if indeed this was her home, to investigate such a building was more than I dared. As it was, we were badly placed, for we could not turn and go back down the private road, for fear of meeting the car which we knew must be following us; yet so far as I could see, the road we were using ran up to the castle's gate; and though, of course, there must be a second drive – for only one trail of oil had been laid upon this – I could see no sign of one and could only suppose that it, like ours, ran up to the castle itself. That meant that, if we were to reach it, we must drive for two hundred yards under the eyes of the watchman or anyone else who was up, right up to the castle, as though we desired to go in; and this was not at all to my taste; for, if our passage was reported, my lady, already suspect, might well be taken to task. Besides, to advertise our presence was the last thing I wanted to do.

After a little reflection, I told Bell to drive on a few paces until we were clear of the trees and then to back the Lowland on to the grass, keeping as close to the trees as ever he could. This he did very deftly; and we presently came to rest some thirty yards from the drive and so close to the wood that no one who had not been watching would have known that the car was there.

We were now all ready to leave by the way we had come and had only to wait for the following car to go by; but since we had now secured a fair line of retreat, I felt we should leave the Lowland and go on on foot; for if we could locate the garage before the others came in, we should stand a very good chance of seeing what they looked like; for we should be in the shadows, but they would be in the light. And they would be off their guard.

Since the moon was westering, the castle was throwing its shadow towards the east; as we were now north of the castle, the shadow lay on our left; we therefore left the Lowland and moved round the edge of the woods, until we were opposite the shadow the great pile threw. We now had about one hundred and thirty yards of moonlit meadow to cross, but on this side no light was showing, and I felt that here was a risk we could fairly take. Still, to walk upright, would have been the act of a fool; so we covered the ground on our bellies, until we had reached the shelter the shadow gave. Then we stole right up to the castle, and, turning left, began to move round its wall.

After some twenty paces we came to a postern-door. This was shut, but was clearly in use by day, for the dirt on the steps was fresh and someone had left a light crow-bar leaning against the wall. By now we were out of sight of the drive by which we had come, so we went on as fast as we could, sure that we should come upon some garage before very long and not at all anxious to find that, whilst we had been rounding the castle, the following car had arrived.

But luck was with us.

Before we had gone much farther, I saw the glow of some light, and after a few more paces, I knew we had won our race.

Some light within the castle was shining out of an archway on to a cobbled apron which must have been fifty feet square. From this apron a drive ran off, to curl with the castle's wall. That the archway led into the garage there could be no doubt, and the light had been left burning to help some car to enter on its return.

We had now passed out of the shadow and into the moonlight again, but no one above could see us because we were hugging the wall. And since it seemed unlikely that those who were now abroad would have left a man in the garage to witness their coming in, I ventured up to the archway and looked within.

The archway was really a tunnel which had been driven through the outer wall of the castle into the bailey beyond. And in the bailey a very fine garage had been made. All this I could see very well, for the light was not burning in the archway, but in the garage itself. I could not see any cars, for these were out of my view, but a mighty turn-table stood in the midst of the concrete floor, so that, once a car was on this, it could be headed exactly towards where it had to go. The depth of the garage was clearly that of the bailey, for its back wall curved and was built of the same coursed rubble as was the outer wall upon which I was resting my hand.

I then examined the door with which the archway could be closed. This was in two great leaves, each swung back against the wall. They were made in the ancient fashion and studded with iron, but they were but copies of leaves much older than they. They could be barred, but not locked, which meant, of course, that, while someone within the garage could let himself out, he could not put back the bars which he had displaced; but in one of the leaves was a wicket, and when I examined this, I saw that it had a Yale lock, which meant that it could be closed by someone outside.

At once I made up my mind to conceal myself in the garage and wait for the car to come in, whilst Bell stayed without the castle in case of accidents. If, after the car had returned, more than an hour went by, but I did not appear, he was to take the Lowland and drive to the farm, there to report to Mansel and tell him what had occurred.

"I'd rather come with you, sir. I mean, you don't never know with people like this."

"I'll be all right," said I. "I've no intention of—"

And that was as far as I got, for in that instant some headlights' beam fell on to the cobbled apron, to make it as bright as day.

By the mercy of God, we were both within the archway and so out of view, and that, I suppose, was why we had not been able to hear the approach of the car. Be that as it may, we both of us ran for the garage as hard as ever we could, and, whipping out of the tunnel, darted to right and left, to make ourselves scarce. Where Bell went I did not see, but finding myself beside a huge limousine, I opened one of its doors and stumbled inside. As I shut the door behind me, the drawl of the incoming engine increased to a roar, and I knew it had entered the tunnel, which was magnifying its sound.

At first I crouched on the floor-boards, afraid to move, for there were windows all round me and the garage was brilliantly lit. Then the driver switched off his engine, and I ventured to raise my head.

The car had been stopped on the turn-table, as no doubt was the custom in such a place. It was a powerful two-seater and must have been very fast. A liveried chauffeur was sitting still at the wheel, and a giant of a man was climbing out of the dickey, presenting his back to my eyes. Beside the chauffeur was sitting a slighter man, with a muffler about his throat and a flying-cap on his head.

When the giant was out of the dickey, he opened the off-side door and took off his hat. And the chauffeur, too, uncovered, as the other man left his seat.

I saw the latter well, and, though he was very handsome, there was that about him that made me clench my fists. His eyebrows were slightly lifted, and a faint, disdainful smile hung about his lips; but, most unpleasant of all, his eyelids drooped so low that his eyes were almost shut. His face was very pale and he wore a small moustache which was turning gray; and the whole effect was that of a cold and merciless pride – a cruel and pitiless type, accustomed to have its way. Indeed, I remember thinking that of such must have been that Pharaoh that 'hardened his heart and would not let Israel go.'

As he left the car, his coat parted and I saw that, beneath, he was wearing evening dress. The giant fell in behind him, until his master had come to a door in the wall; this he made haste to open; and then he stood aside to let the other pass through. He did not go through himself, but put on his hat and walked along the wall until he came to a wheel, like that of a ship. When he put his weight on its spokes, the turn-table began to move, and, after a moment or two, the car was perfectly placed to move to between two others upon the opposite side. At that instant the chauffeur cried out and the other stopped turning the wheel. Whilst the chauffeur was berthing the car, the other stood looking on, with his back to the wall. I, therefore, could see him well, and a grim-looking fellow he was. I put him down for a confidential valet, and that I later learned was the place he filled. That the chauffeur feared him was plain, for his manner was deferential, and the other gave him orders, though I do not know what they were. And he gave them offensively, as only a servant can. Then he turned on his heel and went out by the door in the wall. The chauffeur watched his going; then he turned and passed down into the tunnel to shut the doors. I heard the bars fall into place. Then he, too, made his way to the door in the wall. I saw him pass through and shut it. A moment later the light in the garage went out.

Before we left we had a look at the coupé.

No pool of oil was lying beneath the boot and indeed she had left no trail in the garage itself. But beneath the boot ran a feed-pipe, as we had thought. And then at the head of the feed-pipe, I felt the tap... That made everything clear. My lady had driven in and had left her car on the turn-table for another to put away. That other, no doubt, was the chauffeur whom we had seen. The moment that she had gone, he had turned off the tap; and, after berthing the coupé, had washed away with petrol such mess as the oil had made.

Examine the boot, we could not; for this was locked; and, since we could do no more, we let ourselves out by the wicket, to make our way home.

Before we left, we went on round the castle, until we could see the place where the drives came in.

There were in all three drives or private roads. And they all ran into a sweep in front of the castle's gate. And out of that sweep, or *rond point*, ran the drive which served the garage and skirted the castle's wall.

Since the moon was still up, though low, we retreated as we had come, past the garage and postern and into the lengthened shadow the castle threw. And so we came back to the Lowland; and forty minutes later we reached the farm.

Mansel was sitting up against my return, and Carson had soup all ready to serve to Bell and to me. And whilst I was eating my supper I told my tale.

When at last I had come to the end –

"You really have," said Mansel, "done awfully well. I suppose you realize that you have been into Schloss Varvic and had a good look at Duke Saul."

"My God," said I. "And it never entered my head."

"And I've no doubt at all that your lady friend is the Duchess. She was a Boston girl – Caroline Herring, by name. She was very lovely and charming, I've always heard. And she married Duke Saul of Varvic four years ago." He sighed. "And that is so often the way. The bigger the blackguard, the straighter the woman he gets."

# IV

## FORECAST GOES VISITING

Our hands were now pretty full, for we were watching Latchet as best we could. This, of course, by day only; for, now that they knew that some stranger had entered the ring, Forecast and Co. were not likely to work any more by night. Although, under cover of darkness, we could have approached the inn, that would have been of no use, unless we could hear what they said. But that would have meant going into the inn and upstairs, and "that," said Mansel, "would be to ask for trouble of a very unpleasant kind. The horse has been stolen, of course; but it's only human nature to watch the stable-yard for a week to come."

Of two things we wished to be sure – whether Forecast went to Schloss Varvic and whether, and if so when, he would send a telegram. And so, as I say, we watched Latchet as best we could.

Our method was this.

Three of us would drive to the cross roads which I have mentioned before. Two would then leave the car, and the third would drive to the lane, for this showed no sign of use and was the nearest place at which we could hide the car. The two would pass through the woods until they saw Latchet below them, sunk in its dell. From more than one point here, a man could see the Post Office as well as the inn, and from one particular spot he could look right into the coach-house, if only its doors were wide. With the help of binoculars, therefore, a pretty strict watch could be kept, and if anyone left the inn, we could see where he went without being seen ourselves. Every two hours one watcher would return to the cross roads, to meet the car and report; and if there was any news, the car could immediately carry it back to the farm.

On Friday this duty was done by George Hanbury, Rowley and Carson, while Mansel and Bell and I took the morning off. To be perfectly honest, Bell was washing the Lowland and Mansel was sitting beside me, busy with pencil and pad, and I was half asleep in the sunshine, listening to the murmur of the trout-stream and dreaming of Varvic in the moonlight and what a picture it made.

"I feel," said Mansel, "that we must send Worsteds a wire – in Forecast's name. If we don't send one, he will; and ours will be much more likely to bring someone out. He'll wire in the end, of course; but either he'll put it too low, in which case they'll send him instructions he can't fulfil, or else he'll put it too high, in which case he'll frighten them off. To bring the big fellow out, he's got to be made to believe, first, that there's something wrong, secondly, that the game can be saved, and, thirdly, that only he can manage to pull it off." He put the pad into my hand. "Bearing those facts in mind, d'you think that would do? Worsteds of course will believe it's been sent by Boney or Gulf."

I read the draft telegram through.

*Forecast still in hospital carried on but found nothing so went to see his nibs waited two hours then told to come back next week please send money say twenty quid.*

WENSLEY

I covered my eyes and began to shake with laughter. "I confess," said Mansel, smiling, "that it has its humorous side.

But business and pleasure do sometimes go hand in hand. Seriously, d'you think it's too hot? I'll never forgive myself if I frighten them off. The idea of Boney or Gulf's visiting Varvic and trying to bluff the Duke will send them half out of their minds, but they may feel that, since he's not seen them, they may be able, by coming, to keep the appointment instead."

"I think it's brilliant," I said. "And the 'still' is a masterly touch. I wouldn't alter a word. But I'd love to be there when they get it."

"So would I," said Mansel. "That's the worst of these shows. One takes certain action, unknown to the other side. And you'd give a month of your life to be there when it takes effect. And to hear what they say. But you never are. It's probably just as well; you'd laugh so much that you wouldn't be able to stand. Never mind. We'll send this wire this evening – from Salzburg, of course. The answer ought to be there by tomorrow midday. So we'd better spend the night there. I say 'we,' because I must go – I know how to deal with an accommodation address. But you and George must toss up as to who holds the fort."

"George goes with you," said I. "He's had no show at all, and a night in Salzburg will suit him down to the socks."

Mansel looked at me very hard.

"Right you are," he said. "But no funny business, William. You're not to go near Varvic. I mean what I say."

I wrinkled my nose.

"We don't want the Duchess followed on Sunday night."

"She won't be," said Mansel. "On Sunday night we shall picket all three of the private roads. She's bound to use one of them, and we stop her as she goes out. Then we turn off the tap on the feed-pipe and show her the way to the farm. And when she returns, we go with her, and we open the tap again when she reaches a private road. And then we come home."

"That's good enough," said I. "But we can't do it more than once."

Mansel shrugged his shoulders.

"Sufficient unto the day," was all he said.

And there I saw George Hanbury, strolling towards us with a comfortable smile on his face.

"All's well," he said. "They haven't been near the Post Office. But China and Gulf have been splitting themselves on the car. Talk about spit and polish. They might have been hoping to win her some beauty prize. And good old Belper Orion cheering them on. All dressed up, he was – a study in brown. With a glass in his eye – I saw it – and a very rude hat on his head. And when China answered him back, he socked him one on the jaw. And China lay down and rolled. And Belper went and kicked him up to his feet. He's a little caution, our Belper. He knows what he wants when he wants it, and that's a fact. Then Boney comes out, all dressed up as a chauffeur, in navy blue. And dear Belper rehearses him in the stable-yard. I tell you I laughed fit to burst. But he made him open a door and hold a hand to his hat. And China giggled and got knocked down again. It's a pantomime, I tell you. If you saw it shoved on the stage, you'd swear it was overdone. And I saw it with these two orbs. Finally, off they go – Boney driving and Belper sitting behind. And Gulf and China laughing to beat the band. That they're bound for Varvic, there can be no possible doubt."

"Good," said Mansel, laughing, and got to his feet. "And now let's think about lunch. You're spending the night in Salzburg, with me for chaperon."

"Well don't be too strict," said George. "I haven't walked into a night-club for more than three months."

I was at the cross roads at two – with the Lowland this time, for Mansel and George were going to take the Rolls. As I slowed to a standstill, Rowley stepped out of the woods, to say that all was quiet and that neither Gulf nor China had left the inn. I bade him take my place and drive to the farm, break his fast there and be back by four o'clock. And then I went off to join Carson. All Latchet was very quiet, and, since it was very hot, the two of us took it in turns to doze and watch. At twenty minutes to four I sent Carson off to the cross roads, to send Rowley back to me and do as Rowley had done.

By now I was something surprised that Forecast had not returned, for from Latchet to Varvic was less than twenty-five miles, and Boney and he had left at eleven o'clock. From what I had seen of Duke Saul, I should have said that, without his letter of introduction, a man like Forecast would not have been admitted, much less received. But in such a case he would have been back by two. And when five o'clock had gone by, yet he had not come back, it seemed pretty clear not only that he had been received, but that he had convinced Duke Saul that, unless he took action of some sort, he himself was certain to be involved.

Thinking things over, I saw that, if Forecast told him the truth – that some person or persons unknown had now stepped into the ring and had actually in their possession the letter addressed to Duke Saul, the latter would be very angry, but greatly concerned. Such a letter was dangerous. And wild as he would be with Forecast and Worsted and Co., if he was to save himself, he would have to come in with them and to do his best to help them to bring the intruders down.

(Here perhaps I should say that Mansel had carefully copied both the letter of introduction and the very damning instructions which Forecast should have sent back. But he had taken the originals to Salzburg, as well as the four rogues' passports and everything else. All this he was to lodge with the Bank in whose custody he had left the cloak-room receipt.)

And then another notion came into my head – a sinister notion that made me feel sick at heart. And all at once I knew that Mansel had had it, but, perhaps to spare my feelings, had not conveyed it to me. That was why he had looked at me so straightly and then had forbidden me to visit Varvic again.

Let me put it like this.

Mansel had heard my account of how I had met the Duchess and how we had hidden the fact that the coupé had entered the lane; of how we had driven to Varvic and had a look at the Duke. And he had asked very few questions; but one he had asked was this. "How long was the coupé in the lane?" And I had told him, "A little over an hour." Which shows that he saw at once that, though we had hidden the place where the Duchess had stopped, we could not conceal the fact, that *she had spent more than two hours on a run which, though you drove slowly, took less than one.*

The Duke would therefore know not only that she had stopped, but that someone whom she had met had observed the trail and had erased the portion which would, if left alone, have betrayed their meeting-place: and if he did receive Forecast and hear what he had to say, he would at once perceive that the Duchess herself was in touch with the people who now held the letter which Worsteds had written to him.

It seemed to me very likely that any moment now some storm or other would break; but I did not want it to break about the Duchess' head.

At twenty minutes to six I sent Rowley off, with orders to send back Carson, take the car to the lane and wait there until we came.

Carson then watched with me for over an hour; but when dusk began to come in, yet Forecast had not returned, I told him to follow me and go down to the inn: "for," said I, "I should like to see them arrive; and if we stay here, we shall only see the lights of a car."

But I hoped in my heart that we should do more than that. In a word, I wanted to learn how Forecast had fared, and, if he related what had happened, to overhear what he said.

It was a fine, warm night, but the sky was overcast; and as we approached the inn, we heard two men talking English, and they were without the house. In fact, it was China and Gulf, sitting, smoking and drinking, and waiting for Forecast to return.

They were sitting at one of the tables, to the left of the door of the inn, for though we could not see them, the glow of their cigarettes declared where they were. Since no one in Latchet could talk English – or so, no doubt, they supposed – they did not lower their voices or seem to care what they said, and as we stole into earshot, I heard Gulf mention 'the hostel' and then 'Biretta and Cain.'

Except for these two, we could hear or see no one at all, but Latchet was never busy, and after dark it was dead. And I think the truth is that, except for the people of the inn, the inhabitants rose with the dawn and were glad to retire with the dusk.

Now, glorious chance as this was, I could not forget that Forecast was overdue; and that if, when he did return, Boney drove the car up to the door, as he very well might, its lights would illumine the forecourt and make this as bright as day. Yet, if we were to hear what was said, we should have to enter the forecourt: for from where we now were standing – that is to say, in the road – we could only catch words here and there, and the conversation itself was out of our reach.

It was then that I remembered the benches, on one of which Gulf and China were sitting now. I had noticed these benches, when first I had seen the inn, and had marked that they were 'coffered' – that is to say, their fronts and their sides had been boarded from seat to ground. They were low, of course, but some seven or eight feet long, and, since they stood away from the wall, a man could lie down behind one and not be seen. As I have said before, one of these benches had been set on either side of the door. Between them, the steps ran down, so that the two were only some twelve feet apart. If, then, I could reach the bench to the right of the door, I should be able to hear what

China and Gulf were saying, yet, if the car came in, I should not be seen.

The door of the inn was wide open, and a lamp, which we could not see, was burning within the hall; but this was not very bright, and the light which it shed only reached the head of the steps.

I breathed in Carson's ear.

"I'm going into the forecourt. There's cover enough for one, but not for two. So you go along to the path and get up to the coach-house hatch. They may drive straight into the coach-house. And wait there for me."

"Have you got your pistol, sir?"

"I have."

"Then take the safety-catch off. You don't want to take any risks, sir, with men like this."

"I'll be all right, Carson."

"I know, sir. But don't you wait. If you're seen, you throw your lead as quick as you can."

My shoes, being soled with rubber, made no sound, and ninety seconds later I was standing at the end of the table to the right of the door of the inn.

China was speaking.

"I know, I know," he said. "I've heard talk of things before that was goin' to come out in the wash. But I don't want my washin' done in no Austrian jug. I want my — passport – that's wot I want. This ain't my line o' country, an' never was. He says he can fix the Dook. Well, Dooks ain't fixed, my lad. At least, not by trash like Forecast. Don't you make no mistake. I saw Forecast's face when he saw that them papers was stole. White as a — sheet. He knew wot he done all right. An' if only he'd got his passport, you wouldn't have seen him for dust. But now — he's well stuck. An' so are we."

"That," said Gulf, "is where the Dook comes in. He don't want us goin' to Consuls to try an' get home. So he'll use his influence to get us tempory papers to take us away."

"Sez you," said China. "If he's the big pot you say, I can see him vouchin' for us. More likely to send some butcher to take us out for a ride. God knows it's easy enough in country like this. An' why didn' *he* do in Bowshot?"

I suppose it was natural to stay where I was to hear the argument out. But it was very foolish. And I might have paid dear for such folly, for in that instant I heard the sound of a car.

Now I had expected that, since the night was so still, I should hear the car coming some time before it arrived: but the sound of Latchet's water had smothered the sound it made, and, as my head went round, I saw the beam of its headlights illuminating the road.

"Here they are," said Gulf, and got to his feet.

I felt for the bench and found it, and dropped like a stone. As the car swept into the forecourt, I dragged myself out of sight.

The car drew up to the steps, and somebody opened a door.

"You ain't so early," said Gulf. "We'd — near given you up."

"The — was shooting," said Forecast. "He never got in till six. But I saw him all right. Not for very long, but just long enough."

The man's voice was triumphant. I dared not think what he knew.

"Go on," said Gulf: "go on."

"He knows who stole those papers and laid me out. He didn't mention names, but he gave me a map. We're to meet him on Sunday evening – he showed me where. 'An' then,' he says, 'I'll deliver him into your hands.'"

There was a pregnant silence.

Then—

"Yes, but wot about our passports?" said China.

Boney laughed.

"Well, he mayn't have them on 'im," he said: "but, before we're through with him, I guess he'll be ready an' willin' to cough them up. Oh, an' tell 'em about the farm."

"Upstairs," said Forecast, setting a foot on the steps. "Besides, that may be a wash-out. But he must be staying somewhere, and they used to have people to lodge there before the war."

With that, he passed into the house, and China followed him in. But Gulf got in beside Boney, who let in his clutch and moved off.

As the car turned out of the forecourt, I got to my feet....

Carson had little to add to what I had heard, for, whilst they were in the coach-house, Boney had talked of the castle and nothing else.

But, as we walked back to the car, I kept thinking of Mansel in Salzburg and wondering at what time tomorrow he and George would get back.

We stayed at the farm the next day, for to watch the inn any longer would have been waste of time. Besides, I was not at all sure that the rogues would not visit Goschen: and if they were to do that, I felt it was better that we should be found at home. What line to take, if they came, I could not think; but I told the servants to be on the tips of their toes and that, though, if Forecast appeared, I would play the hand, they had better be within earshot, but out of sight.

I confess that I hoped against hope that Mansel would be back before any visit was paid, for, though I should have been very happy to offer the utmost violence to any that came, I was sure that Mansel would deal with them better than that. And so would George. Indeed, of us three, I was by far the least fitted for such an interview. Still, there was nothing to be done; so I spent my time at the trout-stream, cleaning a jolly sluice, and doing my best to divine the plans which the Duke was making for Sunday night.

This was an unsatisfactory exercise.

'He knows who stole those papers and laid me out.... We're to meet him on Sunday evening – he showed me where. *An' then*, he says, *I'll deliver him into your hands*.'

This was a positive statement, strongly suggesting that the man was sure of his ground. And yet I could not see how he could be sure of his ground....

He might have reason to know that the Duchess meant to drive out upon Sunday night. He could not know where she was going, and he could no longer rely on the trail of oil. True, he could follow her closely; but, if he did that, how could he communicate with Forecast? He could, of course, place the latter at the mouth of one of the drives; but how could he tell which drive my lady would take? And of one thing I was quite sure – Duke Saul had no intention of being involved. He would set Forecast on, but he would not appear himself.

To and fro my mind went, discussing these facts and fancies as best it could, but I never got very far, although I toyed with the thought of putting Forecast's car out of action on Sunday afternoon.

And then at half-past two that blackguard, with Gulf and Boney, drove up to the farm's front door.

Since he could speak no German, he had no change at all of the farmer's wife; but after some hesitation, he strolled across the meadows to where I stood in the stream.

"Good afternoon," he said. "I don't think I know your name."

I looked him up and down.

"That may be," said I, and went on with my work.

He threw back his head and laughed.

"It looks as though I'm unwelcome."

"Well, I am rather busy," I said, "and this is private ground."

"So's my room at Latchet," he said.

I straightened my back.

"Then I should go back there," I said. "I don't know where Latchet is and I care rather less. But at least you'd be *chez vous*, if you understand French."

I saw his eyes narrow at that.

"You don't seem to understand that I've come to call."

"If you understood German, you'd know that I wasn't receiving this afternoon."

"Cut it out," he said, biting his lip.

I frowned.

"Look here," I said. "I've come all the way from England to get away from people and be by myself. Does that make you think at all?"

"It makes me wonder why you should keep late hours."

"I retire at ten," I said, "if that's any good."

"And you don't know Latchet?"

I stared.

"I've never heard of the place."

He screwed a glass into his eye.

"I can't quite believe that," he said.

I stepped out of the trout-stream, turned my trousers down and stepped into my shoes.

As I bent to fasten my laces –

"Is my action suggestive?" I said.

"You'd better not try any rough stuff."

"What do you do," said I, "when a stranger first forces his company upon you and then calls you a liar, because you don't agree with the statements he chooses to make?"

Forecast's eyes burned in his head.

"I bide my time," he said.

"That's the difference between us," I said. "I deal with the matter at once." I raised my voice. "Bell."

"Sir?" said Bell, stepping out from behind an oak, seven paces away.

"Stand perfectly still," snapped Forecast, pistol in hand.

Carson was directly behind him, but not within reach.

"As you please," said I, with my eyes on his feet. "But I think if I were you I'd *look out for that snake*."

As the fellow started backward, Carson flung himself forward and caught his wrist; and, as he fired into the ground, Bell hit him on the point of the jaw and laid him out.

"Quick," said I. "His pockets – before he comes to."

Out of his inside breast-pocket, Bell plucked a map.

This was of a very large scale, and since it had been folded inside out, all ready for use, I saw in an instant the markings which no doubt the Duke had made. These were done in blue pencil, and showed the way from Latchet to a point between five and six miles from the castle itself. The point itself was a building, which stood in a wood, and was in fact approached from the road which Bell and I had taken when we were driving to Varvic on Thursday night.

I noted it carefully. Then I gave the map to Bell and he thrust it back into the pocket from which he had taken it out.

As he stood up and away—

"Nothing else, Bell?"

"No, sir. Nothing at all."

"Have you got his pistol?" I asked.

"In my pocket, sir," said Carson.

"All right. You two go and comfort Rowley. I'll watch him wake up."

(As I afterwards learned, they found Rowley holding the others on the edge of the drive. When the shot had been fired, they had turned to make for the meadows, only to find him facing them, pistol in hand. And there the three had stood, till Carson and Bell arrived and ordered Gulf and Boney into the car. But first they searched them for arms and took a pistol from Gulf.)

Forecast came to slowly, and then sat up with a start.

First his hands flew to his pockets. Then he looked hard at me: and then he looked over his shoulder and round about.

A hand went up to his chin.

"Three to one," he said. "No wonder you got me down. Never mind. I'll know you again." He began to search the grass just about him. "You don't see my eye-glass, do you?"

I shook my head.

"Well, if you should see it, keep it. I'm sure to be back."

I raised my eyebrows.

"Well, you'll have to be quick," said I. "I'll give you till midday Monday. If you're not out of Latchet by then, I go to the police. I think we come under Villach."

His eyes still searching the grass –

"I don't think you will," said Forecast. "If you weren't shy of the police, you'd go to them now."

"If I wasn't a fool, I should. But I came to this place to be quiet – not to get involved in proceedings which might keep me here for two months."

Forecast stood up and looked me full in the eye.

"You'll stay longer than that, my son. A whole heap longer than that. Unless, of course, they take you back to England – to bury you there."

"That'll do," said I. "You'd better be going now. Back the way you came. I'll see you into the car."

Forecast glared. Then he turned on his heel and made his way back to the drive.

In the car were Gulf and Boney, sitting with folded arms. The expression upon their faces was good to see. Gulf was sweating profusely, and Boney's lips were moving as though in prayer. They were sitting side by side in the front of the car, and Carson was standing by the window, also with folded arms. But, whereas their hands were empty, in Carson's right hand was the pistol which Forecast had used.

Without another word, their leader let himself into the back of the car.

As he slammed the door behind him, Carson glanced at me, and I nodded my head.

"Start her up and drive off," he snapped.

Boney's hands sprang to life....

Forecast leaned to his window.

"Don't forget that eye-glass," he said.

Then the clutch went in with a bang and pitched him back on his seat.

Two and a half hours later the Rolls, bringing Mansel and Hanbury, entered the stable-yard.

They had with them two telegrams.

Both were addressed to WENSLEY, and one was four days old.

*Instructions not received as arranged stop if you have not already done so you will post these to me immediately*

BAUCHEN

The other was eight hours old.

*Arriving Latchet myself Monday stop do nothing till then stop on no account go to castle*

And this was signed CAIN.

When Mansel had heard my tale, he called for the map.

"Show me exactly," he said, "the spot at which Forecast proposes to meet Duke Saul."

I showed him.

"And now the way there from Latchet, as it was marked in blue."

I showed him that.

After a moment's calculation –

"I make the distance from Latchet just about eighteen miles. That means half an hour by car. The meeting is to be 'in the evening'; and that means 'not before six.' So they'll turn out the car about five. We must try and put their car out of action about four o'clock. You see my point. If we do in their car too soon – and they find it out, they will have time to keep their appointment without the use of their car. And I do not want them to do that, because it is so much better that we should keep it instead.

"This may precipitate matters, but not very much. When Forecast rolled up here, you were quite right to put up a bluff. But he is dead certain to call it. He can have no doubt at all that the seat of opposition is here at this farm. When Rowley produced his pistol, that settled that – for tourists don't carry pistols and hold callers up. But Rowley could have done nothing else, for he couldn't take risks with blokes like Boney and Gulf.

"What worries me is the Duchess. She's safe at the moment, because the Duke means to use her tomorrow night. But, after that... I mean, he can have no doubt that she knows a great deal too much. However, we'll see what she says tomorrow night."

"Will he let her come?" said I.

"I'm sure he will. He means her to be their guide."

"But if we meet him at six?"

"If we meet him at six," said Mansel, "Duke Saul will stay where he is, till the Duchess has left the castle *en route* for the lane." He rose to his feet and started to pace the room. "It's on the drastic side, but I don't see another way out; for if Forecast keeps his appointment, he will also keep the appointment the Duchess has made with you. Of course, you know, if Forecast was worth his salt, he would drive to Varvic tonight – or, at latest, tomorrow morning. But he isn't worth his salt, so I don't think he will."

"Why tonight or tomorrow morning?"

"To put the Duke wise," said Mansel. "To tell him exactly what happened this afternoon – that he had visited Goschen, bearing upon him the map which the Duke had marked; and that, since he had lain unconscious for three or four minutes of time, *for all he knows,* you may have studied that map. If Forecast did that, as it is his clear duty to do, the Duke would immediately alter the *rendezvous*. But Forecast won't do that. Confessions of failure are never pleasant to make: and so he'll keep his counsel and hope for the best."

"He wouldn't do that," said George, "if he saw the breakers ahead. Talk about confessions of failure! What ever is going to happen when Cain drives up to that inn? I'd give a month of my life to be in on that scene. Confusion confounded won't be in it. They'll shout one another down for the first half-hour."

"I agree," said Mansel, laughing. "From the moment Cain arrives, there'll be the devil to pay. Cain, of course, will spread Forecast all over the floor. Then he'll go off to Varvic, there to be spread all over the floor himself. And then they'll take hold of themselves and get down to things." He hesitated, biting his lip. "We've had all the luck to date, but now we're going to come up against heavier stuff. Cain is no damned fool and Duke Saul is a powerful man. And both will be very frightened. 'Such men are dangerous.' We shall have to be very careful from Tuesday on."

"To be perfectly honest," said George, "I'm all for coming to grips. The party will be complete on Monday night. The big five – three wilful murderers and the two unpleasant beings who set them on. When do we begin the process of elimination?"

"As soon as they try to," said Mansel. "They're bound to try to get us, and that is our chance."

"You don't think that Cain will leg it?"

"I don't think so," said Mansel. "If he had known what had happened, I don't believe he'd have come. But once he's here, I don't think he'll run away. After all, the matter is grave. That letter and those instructions would make very awkward exhibits, if any inquiry was held upon Bowshot's death. Then again Forecast will watch him – and so will the other three. They may even pinch his passport. After all, he sent them here; and they will contend that he's got to get them out. And so, by God, he has. He daren't leave them here to go to the British Consul and spill the beans."

"You're right," said George. "He's in a jam and a half. And his only chance of escape is to wipe the three of us out."

"That's how I see it," said Mansel. He turned to me. "Was there anything else, William?"

I told him of my concern as to which of the private drives the Duchess would use, when she set out for the lane on Sunday night.

"But," I added, "that doesn't matter now. If the Duke isn't there when she leaves, he can't sit on her tail. Still, I'm sure that he knows which drive she is going to take, and I cannot see how he can know."

"Nor can I," said Mansel. "And yet I'm sure you're right. For how can he post Forecast, if he doesn't know where she'll emerge? And I don't agree that it doesn't matter now. It will simplify matters for us, if we know which drive she will take; for it's better to stop her by Varvic than to let her leave a trail which leads to the lane. But perhaps we shall be wiser before we go to bed. I'm sorry to be such a bore, but I want you to take us to Varvic as soon as we've dined. I want to see the layout and get a good idea of the lie of the land." He set a hand on my shoulder. "Don't think I don't trust your reports – they've been terribly good. But nothing's the same as seeing things for yourself."

My second visit to Varvic, I paid at ten that night.

Myself I drove the Lowland as far as the mouth of the northern private road, that is to say, the drive which Bell and I had taken on Thursday night. Mansel sat by my side, with George and Carson behind. Mansel and George and I alighted at the mouth of the drive, and Carson took my seat, with orders to berth the car in some convenient place and then return to the drive and wait for us. For we were to go on foot; for then, if some car came by, we should not be seen.

Nearly an hour went by before we saw the moonlight upon the meadows ahead, for most of the time we were climbing, and, though the road was dark, we showed no light.

Since again the moon was shining out of a cloudless sky, the castle and its surroundings showed up as well as before, and Mansel and George were both immensely impressed. When they had looked their fill, we turned to the right and began to compass the castle, walking in the meadows, but keeping to the edge of the woods.

After, perhaps, three hundred and fifty yards, we came upon the second or western drive, and at once we saw, looking down it, that this was under repair. From where we were standing, its surface looked very good; but nearer the castle loads of chips had been shot and drums of, no doubt, cold tar, were lying upon the roadway, ready for use.

"And there's the answer," said Mansel. "This drive is blocked. And when we come to the next one, you'll find that that's under repair. And there's the advantage of being an autocrat. On Friday Saul calls for his bailiff and says, 'Repair these two drives – the material to be in place on Saturday night.' And it is so."

He was, of course, perfectly right. When we came to the southern drive, we found that that, too, was obstructed, so that no car could pass. And yet, like that of the other, its surface was perfectly good.

We made the circuit of the meadows, but, since the garage was shut, we did not approach the walls of the castle itself. We then returned to where Carson had berthed the car, and drove from there to the mouths of the other two private roads. These we studied with care. And then we drove to the spot which the Duke had marked on the map, where he proposed to meet Forecast upon the following day.

It took me a little time to be sure of my way, for the map which Forecast had had was of a much larger scale than any that we could procure, and it had shown many details which did not appear upon ours. After a little, however, I stopped where a road on the left ran into a wood.

"It's down there," I said. "It must be. And not very far. What's more, we'd better walk, for I think it's a farm and that this is the road of approach. I know it's a building of sorts, for the map showed that."

So again we took to our feet, to walk for a long half-mile through very thick woods: the road of approach was more of a track than a road and had not seen regular use for a very long time. And then the woods gave way, and there stood a hunting-lodge.

A glance was enough to show us that it was desolate.

I have seen deserted habitations that still retained some charm; but this was sinister. It gave forth a smell of corruption – and worse than that: and the woods were advancing upon it as though they would swallow it up. Rank grass was sprouting between the cobble-stones, and a rabble of fungus was thrusting beside the door. From this the paint was peeling, as it was from the shutters by which the windows were hid, and stains on the walls swore to gutters which had been choked. At the back of the place, which was only two storeys high, was a lot of stabling which had not been used for years, where some of the woodwork was rotting and giving way. But, as I have said, it was not that the place was neglected and had been let go: there was about it a cold and dreadful air, as though it had harboured evil, and things which must not be talked of had happened within its walls.

"Ugh," said George, with a shudder. "I wouldn't come here alone for fifty quid. I'll lay a ducat it's haunted. It fairly reeks of murder and sudden death."

"I quite agree," said Mansel. "And it isn't imagination. There's something very shocking about this place. Any way, let's be going. We've done what we came to do, and we've had a full day."

Forty minutes later we were back at the farm.

# V

# A LADY FAILS TO RETURN

After breakfast the following morning we held a council of war. At this we reviewed our plans, "for yesterday evening," said Mansel, "I spoke in haste. And I'm not so sure as I was of the line that we ought to take."

The first conclusion we came to was that we must advance the time of our dealing with Forecast's car. Mansel had said four o'clock; but that was a dangerous hour, for Latchet would be at its quietest between twelve and two, and somewhere between those hours the rogues would be eating their lunch: but by three the village would be stirring, and, unless they took a siesta, the rogues might well be about.

The thing was this. We must enter the coach-house by the window which we had so often used; but this meant using a rope, made fast to the branch upon which we had always stood. All would be well, when once we were up in the tree, for the leaves were thick, and passersby seldom look up in the ordinary way. But we had to reach the tree by using the path, which not only offered no cover, when once it emerged from the woods, but actually ran between walls for the last fifty yards. So, come what might, we must choose the quietest hour.

Once the car had been dealt with, it seemed pretty certain that Forecast would throw in his hand. He could not telephone to Varvic, because on Sundays the Post Office was shut: and though he discovered at two that the car would not start, and so would have time, by using a horse and cart, to reach the hunting-lodge, he could only inform the Duke that he could not strike that night, for you cannot follow a car in a farmer's gig.

So far, so good. The car would be out of action by half-past one. And that would put Forecast out of the running that night. Then arose the question of bearding Duke Saul.

"Supposing," said Mansel, "the meeting has been appointed for half-past six. Well, that will mean that we have to hold him there until after ten. That doesn't matter to us; but, Saul being who he is, when he doesn't turn up for dinner, Varvic will be concerned. And that doesn't matter to us; but, if Varvic is in a state, the Duchess may feel unable to keep her appointment with us. And that would be the devil and all; for it is of the highest importance that we should see her tonight."

"That's a good point," said George. "And I'll tell you another thing. There was doom about that place – that hunting-lodge. I may be entirely wrong, but I'm not at all sure that Forecast has not been invited to a party from which it is intended that he should never return. I mean, he knows quite a lot; and they always say that dead men tell no tales."

"I frankly admit," said Mansel, "that that had occurred to me. But, upon consideration, I've turned it down. We are far more important than Forecast is. When we have been settled, then Forecast should watch his step. But we come first."

"That's right," said I. "Saul intends to use Forecast to wipe us out. And then he will wipe out Forecast – but not till then. But I do see Mansel's point. We simply must not prejudice the Duchess' visit tonight."

"Look at it this way," said Mansel. "Saul keeps the appointment, but Forecast doesn't turn up. Saul will be fed to the teeth, but I don't see what he can do but let the Duchess go out and follow her as before. There's no object in cramping her style, but a very considerable object in seeing where she goes. For then he can set Forecast on. In other and simpler words, Saul will make the best of a bad job. And so I propose that we should keep the appointment, but not be seen. At six o'clock we'll be at the hunting lodge. And keeping well out of sight, we'll see what takes place. But we won't declare ourselves."

"I regretfully agree," said George. "I'd like to have pulled Saul's nose. But don't lose sight of this – that, now that Saul is aware that someone is wise to the oil, he'll follow extremely close on the Duchess' heels. If he dims his lights, she'll never know that he's there. He'll fairly hound her tonight: in fact, as like as not, he'll keep her in view."

"That's very true," said Mansel. "And we must provide against that. The simplest thing to do is to place an obstruction of sorts in the private road. After she has gone by, of course, and before he arrives. That'll give William time to stop her at the mouth of the drive, and, if the oil is running, to turn off the tap. And then he can get in with her and drive all out for the lane. Not for the farm. The coupé must not go to the farm, for the farm is the place to which Saul thinks she may go."

"Good," said George. "Bill shall deal with the Duchess, and I will deal with the Duke. Leave the obstruction to me. I've seen that drive and I know the very place – where the road falls sharply and curls, and then there's a sudden rise."

"I know the spot," said I. "But then I've driven the road and I used my lights."

George smiled.

"The idea was in my mind when we walked that road last night. And it wasn't pitch dark you know. And I felt it was a promising spot, and I wished I could see. And then some tree-top waved, and the moon came through."

Then we settled times and movements and who should do this and that, and then we had in the servants and told them their several duties and all that we had arranged.

At eleven-thirty that morning, Mansel and Bell and I were once more using the path which led from the Salzburg road, on which, five weeks ago, poor Bowshot had met his death: and in rather less than an hour we were looking down upon Latchet, asleep in the midday sun.

Some cottage doors were open, and a man was leaving the village with a sack on his back; but that was all.

Moving rapidly, one by one, we left the woods and made for the spot where the path became an alley, that is to say, began to run between walls. There we waited a moment – not on the path itself, but on either hand, in case another should enter from the opposite end.

Then Mansel entered the alley and began to walk leisurely down, limping a little, as usual, because of the wound which he had had of the war.

With our eyes on his back, we waited – Bell and I...

We saw him come to the mouth that gave to the road, and we saw him glance to and fro. Then he put a hand into his pocket...

At once we entered the alley and ran as hard as we could.

Arrived at the back of the coach-house, Bell mounted upon my shoulders and swung himself on to our branch, and I leaped up and caught this and pulled myself up. Then we made room for Mansel, and two or three moments later, he joined us up in the tree.

By now Bell was out of his jacket, which he had handed to me, and was standing against the wall with a hand on the window-sill. He opened the shutter a little, looked down into the coach-house, and then set the shutter wide. So we knew that the car was below and the doors of the coach-house were shut.

Bell put out a hand for his jacket, which I meantime had folded into a pad. This he laid on the sill. Then he stood with his arms uplifted against the wall, whilst I unwound the rope which was coiled about his body from arm-pit to hip.

Directly I had this free, Mansel made one end fast to the branch upon which we stood, and Bell passed the other over the window-sill. Whilst they were so engaged, I put on some wash-leather gloves, the palms of which had been well rubbed with resin an hour before.

When the rope had been all paid out, Bell swung himself out of the way, and I took his place. And then I was over the sill and was letting myself down the rope. As I reached the coach-house floor, I raised my eyes to see Mansel framed in the window's mouth.

Pulling off my gloves, I stepped to the car: then I opened her bonnet as quietly as ever I could. I could not know on which side the distributor lay; but luck was with me, for there was the thing before me, all ready to hand. In a flash I had its cap off. Then I took the rotor away, slipped this into my pocket and clipped the cap back into place.

The distributor was dusty, which meant that my fingermarks showed; so I took my handkerchief and wiped the whole of it clean. Then I closed the bonnet, pulled on my gloves again and turned to the wall.

My gloves helped me very much, but the rope was none too thick, and I must confess I was glad to get a hand on the sill.

And then I was up and out and was standing once more on the branch.

Mansel had the rope loose before Bell had pulled it up, then he gave it to me to coil and, after a glance at the alley, let himself down to the ground.

Bell slipped into his jacket and pulled the shutter to. By then I had coiled the rope, and he took some twine from his pocket and tied it about the coil in case this should slip.

With the coil about my neck, I peered through the leaves, to see Mansel, leaning against the wall at the mouth of the path, with a hand in his jacket's pocket, to tell us the coast was clear.

I glanced at Bell, who was looking the other way. As I did so, his hand came out...

As soon as the leafage would let me, I followed his gaze. And then I saw China coming, full in the midst of the alley some twenty-five paces away.

I knew the man at once, from his photograph, for his cheekbones were very high, and he had the lowest forehead I ever saw. But the puzzled frown he was wearing was not at all to my taste – for I knew that he was staring at Mansel... who had his back towards him and was leaning against the wall.

I shot a glance at Mansel, for, if he did not look back before China had reached our tree, I knew I must fall on the man as he passed underneath. And, as I looked at Mansel, he turned...

With the utmost nonchalance, he regarded his watch. Then he shrugged his shoulders, stepped out into the road and turned to the left. That is to say, of course, away from the inn.

China broke into a run...

As China swung out of the alley and round to the left, Bell and I reached the ground, to run as hard as we could the way we had come. As we reached the end of the walls, I threw a look back, and there was Mansel behind us, but thirty paces away.

He signed to me to go on, and we ran for the woods...

I flung myself down in the bracken and waited for him to come up.

"Anyone behind me?" he panted.

"Not a soul in sight, sir," said Bell.

"But how did you do it?" said I. "Did you lay him out?"

"No," said Mansel. "The moment I'd turned the corner, I went over the garden-wall. And China and I passed each other – with the garden-wall in between. When you looked round and saw me I'd just climbed the wall again and got into the lane. Mercifully I was ready – I had it all cut and dried. Bad luck, of course; but it might have been very much worse.

He must have been having a sleep in one of those meadows down there – quite close to this end of the alley. Under one of those hedges, perhaps. That's why we never saw him, when he went by. And if he had seen us, it wouldn't have been so good. He'd have probably messed things up, but there might have been a bit of a fuss."

"I rather suspect," said I, "that there is a bit of a fuss going on at the inn."

"Which is why," said Mansel, rising, "we'd better be gone. But I don't think they'll look at the car. They may have a look at the padlock which keeps the coach-house doors: but when they see that's all right, they'll write me down as a spy and leave it at that."

"And when they find the car won't work?"

"They'll get it then," said Mansel. "But it doesn't matter much. It never would have been safe to use that way again. Have you got the rotor safe?" I produced it cheerfully. "Well, that'll make them sweat. They may find another in Salzburg: but I shouldn't be surprised if they have to go farther afield."

(Here perhaps I should say that it is of design that I have set down in such detail how we three went about the disabling of Forecast's car. That all went so smoothly was due to Mansel alone, for he had thought everything out, and before we set out from Goschen, we had rehearsed twice over the action which we were to take when we were up in the tree. Indeed, he always maintained that rogues, as a whole, were a very lazy lot, so that, if, when you stood against them, yourself you took infinite trouble and infinite care, the odds would be in your favour time and again.)

As though by contrast, the rendezvous which we kept at the hunting-lodge was unearthly dull. It was Mansel and I who kept it, standing in the shadows beneath the trees. Carson, somewhere without, had charge of the Rolls. George had gone off with the Lowland, as he put it, 'to do his stuff.' And Bell and Rowley with him...

We were at the lodge before six, but nearly an hour went by before the Duke's two-seater slid out of the ill-kept drive. Again, Saul was sitting in front and the valet behind.

It was at once perfectly clear that the Duke was late, for he seemed surprised to see the forecourt empty, and, when the two-seater had stopped, the valet alighted and hastened to the back of the house. When he returned, to say that no one was there, his master looked very black and curtly ordered the chauffeur to turn the two-seater about: then he told him to switch off his engine, and the valet climbed into the dickey and took his seat. The three men sat in dead silence for twenty minutes or so, and Saul smoked cigarettes which the chauffeur lit.

When seven o'clock had gone by, the fellow gave tongue.

Then he spoke to the point.

"I'll wait no longer," he said. "Take me back to the castle: I'm getting cold."

The two-seater sprang to life...

As it passed down the drive –

"And that is that," said Mansel. "And I don't mind admitting to you that I'm sorry we came. Still, one never knows. And at least it's clear that the man meant Forecast no ill. If he had, he would not have been late. I'd very much like to have met him, I must confess: but it would have been injudicious. Another time, I hope. But the Duchess must be permitted to keep her appointment tonight. That comes first every time. And now I think she will be, although dear Brother Forecast is off the map."

I glanced at my wrist.

"We've time to go back to the farm."

"And have dinner," said Mansel. "Why not? She'll never leave the castle before a quarter to ten. And George has desired to be left entirely alone. He has something up his sleeve; but, so long as he stops that car, I don't care what it is. In fact if the Duke was smashed up, it might be as well."

As Carson stepped out of the shadows at the mouth of the drive –

"Are you going home, sir?" he said.

"We are."

"Could you drop me, sir, at the mouth of the private road? Mr Hanbury said, if you could spare me—"

"Good God," said Mansel, laughing. "How many more does he want?"

"I'm sure I don't know, sir," said Carson. "I don't know what he wants me to do. All he said was, 'It's rather a lot for three.'"

"All right," said Mansel. "But mind – you must be where I drop you at half-past nine."

"That's understood, sir."

We made our way back to the Rolls, and, after setting down Carson, for the second time that day we drove back to the farm.

It was very still that night, and the sky was overcast.

Since five and twenty to ten I had been standing still in the mouth of the private road, with my eyes on the spot where this ran into the woods, straining my ears for the sound of the Duchess' car. Mansel was watching me – or rather the place where I stood; for he was some fifty yards off, and a hundred yards beyond him Carson was holding the Rolls in a gateway that gave to a field. For so she could move either way, without having to turn.

At precisely five minutes to ten I heard – not the sound of a car, but what I can only describe as a hollow crunch. It came from the woods, and, faint though it was, for I was some way from the dip, I knew at once that George Hanbury had had his way. And almost at that same moment I saw the lights of the coupé stealing out of the woods.

When this was but sixty yards off, I flashed my torch and then stood with its light on my face.

At once the coupé slowed down, and I ran to the near side door.

"What does this mean?" said the Duchess. "How did you know where to come?"

I moistened my lips.

"I've nothing to hide," I said, "and I'll tell you everything as soon as ever I can. But it will spare us both, if you will get out for one moment and watch what I'm going to do to the back of your car."

"Very well," she said, "but be quick."

With the light of my torch, I showed her the oil on the road.

"You're laying that trail," I said. "There's a tank in your boot; and a feed-pipe runs through the floor-boards. But the feed-pipe has got a tap: and if you'll get back in the car, I'll turn it off."

"My God," she said. And then again, "My God."

I lay down on my back and hauled myself under the boot. But when I looked for the tap, the tap was gone.

For a moment I stared at the pipe. Then I saw that the pipe had been changed... that another pipe had been fixed... with the tap inside the boot... And the boot was locked.

It was clear that the Duke had meant business. But it was also clear that he had not allowed for a man with strength like mine.

I took that pipe and bent it into a hoop. Then I twisted the end of it round – not once but thrice. And then I crawled out.

"Into the car," I said. "She won't leave a trail now. And please will you take me with you? I'll tell you all as we go."

"To the lane?" said the Duchess.

"Yes. Mansel will follow behind and pick us up there."

We entered the car there and then, and the Duchess drove for the lane.

After a moment or two –

"I feel rather dazed," she said. "Will you tell me how and what?"

I told her all that had happened, since I had seen her last.

When I had done –

"Well, you've cleared the air," she said. "You can't get away from that. And we're coming up to a show-down. What line do you want me to take?"

"That I don't know," said I. "But Mansel will. And I hope very much you'll listen to what he says."

"You seem to think he's a god – a *deus ex machina*."

"He's not far off one," said I. "He's the quickest and clearest brain that ever I knew."

"You've yet to meet my husband. His brain's on ice. He's a very indolent man, but, when he cares to get going, he's – more than dangerous."

Here she slowed down for the lane in which we had sat and talked three nights before.

"Drive well up it," I said, "as you did before."

As she turned in –

"It's all right to leave her here?"

"Surely," said I. "And I think it would be a mistake for you to take her to the farm."

"I quite agree. If anything were to happen, she'd give my presence away."

"That's what we felt."

She stopped, put out her lights, turned her engine off and took the key from the switch.

"And the Rolls?" she said.

"Is waiting at the mouth of the lane."

Then we left the car and I drew my torch and threw its light on the ground. And there I kept it, until we were close to the road. This time the coupé had left no trail of oil.

The Rolls was there in the shadows, but all her lights were out.

I saw Mansel, standing bare-headed, two paces away.

"Captain Mansel – The Duchess of Varvic."

Mansel bowed and put her hand to his lips.

Then –

"Please sit beside me," he said. "I'm going to drive. You don't mind coming to Goschen?"

"I'd like to."

He handed her to her seat...

So for the third time that day we drove back to the farm.

I cannot forget the first time that I saw the Duchess of Varvic as she was meant to be seen. She was tall and superbly made, and she had that classical beauty which is today so rare. And yet it was not the purity of her features – the short upper lip, the straight nose, the glorious temples, the delicate droop of her lips... it was not that perfection that struck you; it was the level gaze of her truly magnificent eyes, the infinite grace of her movements, the leisurely dignity of bearing that made you think of Old Masters and of famous, romantic figures of days gone by. There was nothing studied about her, and nothing stiff; her manner was very easy, and she seemed to be quite unconscious of the stately picture she made. But an ineffable sadness sat in her great, brown eyes, and her hair, which had been chestnut, was now iron-gray. She was simply dressed in tweeds, and a coat with a fine, fur collar fell to her knees; and her feet looked very small in a pair of gray, court slippers, as simply made as could be. Except for her wedding-ring, she wore no jewellery.

When she entered our sitting-room, she took her seat on a sofa before the fire, and Mansel stood by the hearth, with an arm on the mantelpiece.

"May I make this plain?" he said. "First that, as Chandos has told you, had we had any idea that you were concerned, we should have found some way to consult you before we moved. Secondly, that though we have got some way, we are ready to pack up now, if that is your wish."

"It isn't my wish," said the Duchess. "I'm very, very grateful for all you've done."

Mansel inclined his head.

"We haven't done much to date. The rough stuff's to come. Cain is on his way out; and when he and the Duke get together, I think they'll put up a good show. Well, we're ready to take them on. But I must be sure of two things. The first is your – goodwill."

"You have that in all you may do."

"All?"

"All." She looked him full in the face. "Yes, I know what I'm saying. In all you may do."

"I quite understand," said Mansel. "Well, that's the first. The second is – your safety."

The Duchess' eyes widened.

"They can't touch me."

Mansel wrinkled his nose.

"They damned near 'touched you' tonight. But for Chandos here, tonight you would have been in the firing-line. And what of that trail of oil? Besides, you know a great deal that they would give much to know. And Cain will see that in a flash. And he will tell the Duke that, unless he puts pressure upon you, he, Cain, will throw in his hand."

"What pressure can he put upon me?"

Mansel shrugged his shoulders.

"That I can't say," he said. "Any way, I've made my two points; and I rather think that Chandos has told you what we have done and, indeed, as much as we know. If there's anything you'd like to say, you know that we'd love to hear it. I don't want to press you at all; but it is sometimes a relief to talk to people you know will understand."

The Duchess took a deep breath.

"You're very easy," she said. "And so is Richard Chandos. I expect you know what I mean....

"You probably know that I married four years ago. My father and mother were dead, I was immensely rich, and my husband, when he pleases, can be an attractive man. I was just what he needed. I brought him two million sterling, and, what was to him as important, I looked the part. Well, we were married... He was worldly wise, and I was an *ingenue*.

"Never marry a German – for that's what he really is. His mother is German, and he is his mother's son. And a grandmother was Italian. On the face of it, I am the Duchess; and if anyone failed to show me the respect which is due to his wife, the Duke would break him at once. You see, it would be an invasion of his prerogative. I found that out very soon. To the world, I'm the Duchess of Varvic; to him I mean no more than one of his cars. One.

"This spring, when we were in England, I met John Bowshot at luncheon...

"Well, you know how these things go. If I'd met him before I was married, I should have been – his wife."

She said no more for a moment, but sat looking into the fire, with a hand to her mouth. Then, as though to banish dead dreams, she gave a little shake of her head.

"Well, we couldn't do anything about it; but John knew how unhappy I was, and he couldn't bear that. So we saw each other sometimes... It wasn't too hard, for I often drive out at night. I've never slept very well, and even before I was married, I used to take the car and drive for an hour or more before going to bed. And so it became a habit. I used to do it in London – drive all about the City, when all the traffic was gone. Your policemen knew me quite well... Saul couldn't stop that, for I had the doctors behind me – I'd done it too long.

"To cut a long story short, John knew I was due for Varvic and made up his mind to come, too. I felt it was dangerous, and yet he meant so much that to be with him twice a week was a prospect I couldn't forgo. You see, except for him, I'd no one at all. And he was terribly careful. But Saul must have known. He'd probably had him watched. And that was enough for Saul – that he should follow me out. No breath of scandal must ever touch his house...

"The rest I gather you know – a good deal better than I. So far as I understand, Worsteds were glad of a chance to put John down. Of that, I know nothing. And I don't suppose Saul does, either. But of one thing I am quite sure – that Worsteds would never have found him, if Saul hadn't set them on."

"I quite agree," said Mansel. "In fact, to be quite honest, I think that for quite a long time the car you drive has been laying a trail of oil. And that is how the Duke found that you were meeting John by the side of the Salzburg road."

The Duchess regarded him steadily, finger to lip.

"Of course," she breathed. "Of course. That's how it was done."

Mansel stood up there and folded his arms.

"It was," he said, "a cruel and barbarous crime. Wilful murder is usually wicked; but when men hire others to do it, and so contrive that they shall not be suspect, much less involved, it takes on a monstrous shape. But, by your leave, they shan't get away with it here. And now will you tell me this? Did John Bowshot ever mention Orion?"

"Not by name," said the Duchess. "But from what Mr Chandos has told me, he'd been in touch with him. As I daresay you know, John used to live at Beehive, in the house in which he was born. He was very fond of the village, and when the blacksmith died, there was no one to take his place. And he simply couldn't see Beehive without its forge. He tried to find a smith, but without success. So he advertised for one; and Orion rang him up, to say that he had in his hostel 'the very man.' How far matters went, I don't know; but I know that he met Orion – at least, I assume it was he – and took a dislike to the man. I remember his saying, 'I'm perfectly sure he's a wrong 'un; but I'm having inquiries made, and when I get back, I shall know.'"

Mansel nodded.

"That all fits in," he said. "John mentioned the matter to Worsteds, who put his advertisement in – and privately told Orion that he was to pick it up. So Orion gets to know John; and so, unknown to John, do Boney and Gulf. But John finds Orion suspicious, and so he turns on Shade, to find out what he can. And Shade does rather too well, so Orion puts him to death. And there, of course, we have another motive. The report of the inquest on Shade would have made John think very hard. So Forecast, too, had good reason to wish him dead." He hesitated there for a moment, as though absorbed in his thoughts. "And now let's return to you. I'm going to be very frank. The idea of your staying at Varvic is not at all to my taste."

The Duchess knitted her brows.

"Will you tell me exactly why?"

"Yes," said Mansel, "I will. Cain will arrive tomorrow, and we may be sure that on Tuesday he'll see the Duke. And they will review the position.

"Now their position is ugly. They are up against some people – that is, of course, us – who can make things more than awkward if they care to open their mouths. That is quite bad enough; but what is a thousand times worse, we have in our hands certain papers which can be used to substantiate all we say.

"Well, Cain will know that we are not like Forecast – in other words, that those very important papers are certainly lodged in some Bank. How then is he to get them?

"The only way to get them is by putting pressure on us. And he *can* put pressure on us by using you as a hostage...

by proving to us that, unless we return the papers, he will be unable to answer for, let us say, the state of your health."

The Duchess shook her head.

"Saul would never dare to agree to that."

Mansel shrugged his shoulders.

"Duke Saul is right up against it. Those papers prove that he was concerned in the murder. And if that fact comes out, our Foreign Office will insist that he should be brought to trial. I don't say that he'd be sent down; but I think he would dare a good deal not to stand in the dock."

"He'd kill himself first – twice over."

Mansel leaned forward.

"Exactly. And so I think we may take it that Cain will have his way. And if – say, on Thursday next – we are informed that, unless we return those papers, things will go hard with you... we shall have to return them. That wouldn't mean that we should have to throw in our hand; but our strongest suit would be gone. So far we've been twisting their tails, to make them show fight. Once they do that, then we can really go in. The papers, of course, were a godsend. I'd never dreamed of such luck. And if we were to hand them back – well, Cain would be out of the country before we could think and Forecast and Co. would scatter like so many frightened curs. What the Duke would do, I don't know; but he would not show fight. In fact, it boils down to this – that we might put Gulf and Boney where they belong, and possibly Forecast, too. But the two who deserve to suffer would probably go unscathed."

There was another silence.

Then the Duchess spoke again.

"I feel outside all this, though I'm really in. I've lost my darling, but that is beside the point. What life might have held for us, I cannot tell. We were both beginning to see that we couldn't go on as we were. John was all I had, and they – they put him to death. And I don't think I should be human, if

I didn't want them punished for what they had done. But that, as I said just now, is beside the point. Why did you come into this? Not because of me; but because your sense of justice had to be served. A decent, fellow man had been done to death; and his blood cried out to you. And because of that you're determined to bring his murderers down. And there I'd stand beside you, if I'd never set eyes on his face. One month of his life was worth all theirs put together, and if their death-warrants were before me, I'd sign the lot. Saul's, too. I should have no compunction." With a sudden, eloquent gesture, she pushed back her hair. "That sounds unnatural – smacks of Messalina, and women like that: but, except in the eyes of the law, I'm no more his wife than yours...

"On the evening of the day we were married, his mother came to my room and spoke these words. 'Saul has made you his wife. He is your lord and master from this time on. He can do no wrong in your eyes, and you will do none in his.' I thought she was out of her mind, and I went to Saul and told him what she had said. I shall never forget his reply. 'That is the first of the lessons you have to learn. When you have got it by heart, she will teach you some more. But, in view of this episode, you had better know this at once – that, except in public, it is not for you to address me, unless I have first addressed you.'"

There was a pregnant silence. I know that I was trembling and Mansel was white to the lips.

The Duchess continued quietly.

"Twice I tried to run away. Each time I was caught and brought back. On the first occasion, all my pets were destroyed – my three hunters, both my dogs, even a canary I had, that used to sit on my hand and take seed from my lips. The second time, when I got back, every servant that I had found friendly had been dismissed. An old man and woman, for instance, had been given a lodge to keep. They had been in the service of Varvic for nearly sixty years. They used to pick me flowers from their garden, whenever I stopped to talk. These two were put in the street before I came back. That there might be no mistake, on my return, on my table, I found a typewritten list. All it said was:

*During your Highness' absence the following changes have been made in the staff:*

*Hans and Freda Gottlieb, lodge-keepers, dismissed.*

"And so on. In all, there were seventeen names..."

She threw back her lovely head and covered her eyes.

"I despair of conveying to you what my life has been. It's only by telling such tales that I stand any chance of making you understand. But I don't want to seem unnatural.... And yet, in another way, I daresay I am. I sometimes feel as though I were one of those things you leave under dripping water for them to be petrified. And, after four years, the process is nearing completion..."

After a little, I saw Mansel moisten his lips.

"I think," he said quietly, "it's time to arrest the process."

"But how can I leave the castle? You've no idea—"

"You have left it," said Mansel. "I suggest that you shouldn't return."

The Duchess started up to her feet.

"Not go back tonight? That's hopeless."

"Madam," said Mansel, "if you go back tonight, you won't set a foot outside Varvic, until those papers have passed. You'll leave it then, of course, for your safe delivery here will be one of my terms."

The Duchess put a hand to her head.

"Is that your belief?" she said. "That I shall be used as a hostage?"

"It stands to reason," said Mansel. "I'm an honest man, but it hits me between the eyes. Is it likely that Cain will miss it? Cain who, if rumour is true, is a very high priest of blackmail?"

"But how can I not go back?" She glanced at her wrist. "I ought to be going now."

"Please understand this," said Mansel. "No one in this house is going to force your hand. I'm going to make a suggestion. But if you turn it down, I'll drive you back to your car, myself escort you to Varvic and see you inside."

"May I hear your suggestion?"

"My suggestion is simply this – that the Duchess of Varvic should enter a nursing-home."

"But not tonight?"

"Tonight."

"But– "

"Please hear me out. There's a nursing-home in Salzburg of high repute. The Englishwoman who runs it is a friend of a cousin of mine. I called upon her on Friday, and found her as nice as ever – and, I may say, just as much of a martinet. Visitors, for instance, who desire to see patients who are not fit to be seen, go empty away.

"Now, if, on your way home tonight, the coupé's steering broke and you ran into a tree... and a passing motorist found you – unconscious, of course... I think he would drive you to Salzburg as fast as he could. I mean, that would be natural. Salzburg's the nearest big town, and he wouldn't know who you were or where you lived. Those things, of course, they'd find out at the nursing-home.

"The Press would very soon have it; but the Duke would have it at once. And he would have something else, for two can play at blackmail. He would have it in black and white that, if you were to leave that home, certain papers would immediately be laid before the British Consul."

The Duchess took her seat upon the arm of a chair.

"That's more than clever," she said. "I should be suffering from shock."

"That's right," said Mansel. "And you have to be careful of shocks. They lead to break-downs. Say 'detained for ten days.' And I think you'd like Mrs Lane."

"But Saul—"

Here the door was opened, and George came into the room.

Mansel introduced him.

"The obstructionist?" said the Duchess, as George bowed over her hand.

"No," said George. "The wrecker. It'll take a break-down gang to clear your northern drive. You've no idea of the work which a drum of cold tar will do. I hope to God I never hit one. Nobody's seriously hurt. Walking wounded, you know. Walking back to the castle in single file. In a silence that could be felt. But the Duke gave it up at last, and sent the big fellow on to turn out another car. You see, on leaving the *voiture*, they all stepped into the tar." Mansel's shoulders were shaking, and the Duchess began to laugh. "And tar is so – er – attractive. To put it shortly, they gathered where they had not strawed. After a quarter of a mile, each of their feet must have weighed about seven pounds."

Mansel looked at the Duchess.

"You must admit," he said, "that I'm very well served. I ask for a car to be delayed. I didn't say for how long; but six minutes would have done. Hanbury puts it out for six weeks. And now what about my suggestion? If we are not to adopt it, I think we should be taking you back."

"Give me five minutes, please. It's a big decision to make."

"Of course," said Mansel, and stepped to the writing-desk...

No one of us spoke or moved for four or five minutes of time, but I saw that Mansel was writing – first with pencil and then with pen and ink. The Duchess sat still as death, with an elbow cupped in a palm and a hand to her mouth.

At length she rose, and Mansel got to his feet.

For a moment they faced each other.

Then –

"I have faith in your judgment," she said. "Do you sincerely believe that, if I go back tonight, I shall be held as a hostage, until you return the papers which you have won?"

"I do."

"And if they demand those papers, you mean to give them up?"

"In return for your delivery, safe and sound."

"In that case, to go back seems madness."

"It does. But please remember this. I haven't got second sight, and I may be wrong."

"I don't think you are, somehow. All right. I'll play. Stage your smash and take me off to the home."

Mansel inclined his head.

Then –

"Tell me," he said, "d'you set much store by the coupé?"

The Duchess shook her head.

"But oughtn't I to be shaken? And bear some mark?"

Mansel smiled.

"I'll see to that," he said. "The last thing that you will remember is driving your car."

We chose the Salzburg road.

Mansel preceded the coupé, driving the Rolls. And I followed on with the Lowland, with George by my side.

About thirty-five miles from Villach we stopped by the side of the way.

George and I alighted and walked to the coupé's doors.

As the Duchess leaned forward –

"Goodbye for the moment," I said. "I'm so very thankful you've taken Mansel's advice."

"Goodbye, Richard Chandos," she said, and gave me her hand to kiss. Her fingers closed about mine. "You've been sweetness itself to me, and I'll never forget. And now I'll tell you a secret. I think I'm just about ripe for a nursing-home."

"You don't look it," said I, "but you're very likely right. And I hope to God it does you a world of good."

Then she spoke very kindly to George, and he made her laugh. And then he, too, stood back...

"Drive slowly forward," said Mansel, "and pass the Rolls."

As she let in her clutch, he mounted the near side step and I mounted the off.

When we had passed the Rolls –

"Bear to the left," said Mansel.

I put my arm into the car and took hold of the brake.

"Now put down your foot," said Mansel – and flicked her under the chin.

With his words, I applied the brake, and the engine stopped.

Then we opened the doors, and Mansel and I together got the unconscious Duchess into my arms. I carried her to the Rolls, laid her upon the back-seat and covered her up. Then I got out of the car, and Mansel got in. Thirty seconds later, Carson was driving for Salzburg, and Mansel was sitting behind him, with his fingers about a slim wrist.

When I got back to the coupé, George had just turned her about. As soon as her wheels were quite straight, he slipped her gear into second and throttled her engine down. And then he got out and walked beside her, holding the steering-wheel.

When he had passed the Lowland –

"All clear," said I, looking up and down the road.

George swung the wheel to the left. Then he threw open the throttle and let her go.

The coupé leapt forward...

Thirty yards farther on, she scrambled over the ditch and crashed into a tree. And her engine stopped.

(For what it was worth, the place and the way she was facing combined to insist that the Duchess was returning to Varvic –

but not from the lane or the farm. Had she been on her way either to or from the lane or the farm, she would not have passed that place or been heading that way.)

As we turned away from the wreck –

"Pity," said George: "but you ought to see the two-seater."

"Tell me about it," said I.

And as we drove for Varvic, he told me his tale.

"I don't know what those drums weigh; but it cost us something to get one down to the dip. We rolled it as far as the woods – that was easy enough. But from there it had to be carried: that's why I wanted Carson – to make up a four. The point is, we got it there. Whilst we were waiting for the coupé, we dammed the sides of the dip, so that any tar that emerged should stay in the road; and we cut a trough for the drum in the midst of the way. Well, at last the coupé went by, and quick as a flash we hoisted the drum into place. We didn't leave it upright: we laid it down on its side, in such a way that the car would meet it end on. I'd already loosened the bungs, and I just had time to flick the two of them out...

"It was just round the bend, you know, and the chauffeur was driving fast and hadn't a chance. He applied his brakes all right, and that probably saved their lives: but he hit it fair and square, as I meant him to. The result was catastrophic. Saul met the windscreen, the chauffeur's face met the wheel, and the valet behind was chucked over on to their heads. He's no feather-weight, that wallah, and, quarters being close, the most fearful confusion reigned for some thirty seconds of time. The three seemed to writhe together, cursing and grunting and heaving, to beat the band. Then Saul forced open his door and fairly erupted into four inches of tar. The others of course followed suit: and the valet slipped and fell; so he was all over tar by the time he got up.

"At last they were all three clear, and the valet produced a torch. But he couldn't make it work, because of the tar on his hands; and Saul snatched it out of his grasp and, finding it all sticky, immediately let it fall. The chauffeur found it at last, and they had a look at themselves. It's as well they hadn't a mirror... Saul's nose was twice life-size and his mouth stuck out like some Triton's, blowing a horn. And his clothes will have to be cleaned. The chauffeur took one look and then went down on his knees, but the big wallah kicked him up, and they all set off.

"As I've told you, each step they took, they collected more of the world, and presently Saul gave in and sat down by the side of the drive. By his orders the others went on and after about half an hour another chauffeur appeared with a small motor-van.

"I watched the two out of sight. Then I went back to have a look at the car.

"You never saw such a show. The front axle had riven the drum and, in doing this, had assumed an elegant curve: but the upper half of the drum had put up a fight. It had torn the sump away and fairly jammed the fly-wheel against the clutch. The drum was not in two pieces, but gaped like a pair of jaws. In these the axle was wedged, and I doubt if they'll get it free without taking it down. So far as I could see, the steering had moved with the drum, for a rod of sorts was mucking in with the crank-shaft – and that seems wrong. You won't be surprised to hear that the wheels were out of truth: in fact, when I saw them, they made me think of a clown: you know, with his toes turned in – the traditional stance.

"And that's how these things work out. I set out to inconvenience: in fact I discomfited. And I'll lay Saul's kicking himself for having given the order to dress those drives. Talk about being hoist with his own petard. I warn you, those drums are a menace. Don't you ever hit one. You won't be the same again."

"Three cars in one day," said I. "It's enough to make them go to the police. But I don't see what else we could do."

"It'll make them think," said George. "Cain'll keep an armed guard on his, if he brings one along."

"To tell you the truth," said I, "I think we'd better watch ours. They may have a weakness for the Mosaic Law."

"If you ask me," said George, darkly, "they won't waste their time on our cars. Fear and a lust for vengeance will make them aim higher than that. Not very much higher, perhaps. I believe the abdominal wound is very much favoured by Gulf and Boney's class. And to think we're *en route* for Varvic, to leave a blackmailing note!"

"The night-porter won't know that."

"Oh, no. Nor will he know that he's going to be fired tomorrow – for failing to take your life. He'll bow and scrape, poor man – and apologize to you for the state of the drives."

Which is exactly what happened, when I walked up to the gate, to leave the letter which Mansel had addressed to the Duke.

This was much to the point.

*H.H. THE DUKE OF VARVIC.*

*This is to inform you that H.H. the Duchess of Varvic's car left the road some fifty-six kilometres from Villach in the direction of Salzburg. Except that she is suffering from shock, her Highness was unhurt. A passing motorist took her direct to Salzburg, where she is now in the Gastheim nursing-home. In the opinion of her advisers, for her Highness to leave the home for two or three weeks would be... dangerous.*

# VI

## ENTER CAIN

Up to this time, of course, we had had things all our own way. To be honest, that did us some credit, but not very much. We had had the immense advantage of being first in the field and the almost greater advantage of the enemy's never dreaming that he was to be opposed. Then, again, the rogues were small fry. They were careless and out of their depth and all abroad in the country, where we were at home. And Duke Saul did not know where he was, and Cain knew nothing at all. And so, our path had been smooth, and we had been able to do very much as we pleased. But at least we had done what we had set out to do – and that was to bring the principals into the ring.

I say that advisedly, for Cain arrived at Latchet on Monday afternoon.

Myself, I saw his car turn out of the village street and into the forecourt of the inn. Since he came from the south, he must, I think, have travelled by train to Villach and motored from there. I could not see him alight, for the forecourt was out of my view; but he clearly paid off his driver and let him go, proposing, no doubt, to use Forecast's car himself; for, after a moment or two, I saw the car leave the forecourt and turn back the way it had come.

An instant later came cries which actually reached my ears, and Boney, then Gulf and then Forecast erupted out of the forecourt, all running like so many stags the way the car had gone, and yelling and whistling like madmen in the hope that the driver would hear. Cain, most plainly bewildered, followed them into the road and stood looking after the three with his mouth a little way open and a hand to his head. He can have had no idea that, unless the car could be caught, neither he nor anyone else could move from the inn; for there was no time to explain, if its driver was to be stopped.

I was certain they could not catch it, for the driver had had a fair start; but the judgment of men who are desperate is often warped, and three or four minutes went by before the three reappeared, all of them streaming with sweat and looking ready to burst. That they were arguing fiercely goes without words, and when Gulf, who had clearly fallen, held out a palm which was covered with dust and blood, Forecast struck it aside like a naughty child.

By the time they reached the forecourt, Cain had withdrawn from my view, but I could not help feeling that what had just occurred would not raise the tone of the interview now to take place. Indeed, I was sorely tempted to try and approach the inn, but Mansel had made me swear that, unless Cain arrived after dark, I would do no such thing. So, since it was not yet three, I turned on my heel and made my way back to the car.

Cain was a long, lean fellow, sallow of face. He had stood, looking after the others, for full two minutes before he turned back to the inn – this, with his hat in his hand and little dreaming, of course, that he was being observed. So, since my binocular was powerful, I saw him extremely well. He was, I judged, about forty-five years of age. His hair, which was very black, had gone well back from his forehead, thus seeming to lengthen a face which was over-long. He was carefully dressed in clothes which befitted his calling more than the countryside, and a pair of spats was surmounting his highly polished shoes. The expression of his face never altered, whilst he was standing there; and this was a curious smirk, as though he were nursing some jest, which he meant to keep to himself. Since he could have had nothing to laugh at, I wondered then if he always looked like that: and I afterwards found that he did – that the grin upon his face was a fixture, as were the slightly raised eyebrows and parted lips. And then, I remember, I thought of how Shakespeare had said, 'That one may smile, and smile, and be a villain.'

Little happened during the next three days.

Cain hired a car from Villach, no doubt by telephone, and this arrived at Latchet on Tuesday afternoon. Directly the driver had reported, he was carried off by Boney to look at the rogues' own car; and after a short inspection, I saw him discover the trouble – namely, that the rotor was gone. Then Boney went off, to return with Forecast and Cain. Cain tried to question the man, who kept on shrugging his shoulders and shaking his head. Then they all looked up at the window by which I had entered the coach-house two days before, and Cain said something to Forecast which made him look very grim.

Very early the following morning Forecast was driven to Villach – at least the car went that way and was back at Latchet, without him, under the hour. I think Cain had sent him to Salzburg, of course by train, to obtain another rotor by hook or by crook; for he had a parcel with him, which might have been the now useless distributor. At ten Cain left for Varvic, as we had known he would. Since Carson was watching the castle, he saw him arrive. There he stayed until nearly four, and then returned to the inn. A train from Salzburg reached Villach late that night, and I think Forecast came by that, for early on Thursday morning the chauffeur and Boney were working on Forecast's car. Exactly what they were doing, George, who was watching that morning, could not see, but they seemed to be fitting another distributor. Since they had not the requisite tools, the work went very slowly and cost them a lot of sweat, and when some spanner had slipped for the fourth or fifth time, the chauffeur sat down on the step and put his head in his hands. Indeed, Cain had to be fetched before he would move; and after some consultation he left once more for Villach, no doubt to fetch the tools which he said he required. Still, at five o'clock that evening, the engine of Forecast's car was running again, and the hired car returned to Villach on Thursday night.

And here perhaps I should say that every two days we sent a letter to Salzburg, telling the Duchess exactly what had occurred. And the one which we sent on Thursday reported that the wreck of her coupé had been retrieved and presently carried away.

It was upon Friday morning that the enemy moved.

In a word, Cain came to Goschen and sent in his card. And Forecast and Boney with him.

"What is your game, Captain Mansel?"

"To see justice done."

"That's very vague," said Cain.

"I don't agree."

Cain fingered his chin.

"That sort of reply," he said, "is hardly conciliatory."

"I have neither need nor desire to conciliate people like you."

"I see. And Varvic? If Varvic likes to move, he can have you run out of the country in twenty-four hours."

"Then why doesn't he do it?" said Mansel.

Cain shrugged his shoulders.

"For all I know, he prefers to deal with you here."

"That," said Mansel, "will suit me down to the socks."

"He's a powerful man," said Cain.

"He's a first-class swine," said Mansel, "if that's any good."

Cain looked away.

"He happens," he said, "to be a client of mine."

"That," said Mansel, "does not surprise me at all."

"So is Major Bowshot."

"Then he can't know your reputation."

Cain looked away again.

"I find that remark equivocal."

"Few people would."

There was a little silence.

Then –

"You're not very helpful, Captain Mansel."

"Did you expect me to be?"

Cain shrugged his shoulders.

"I had hoped you might see reason. I should hate to have to go to the Austrian police."

"That I can well believe."

"And you?"

"I can go to the police when I please. My hands are clean."

"That," said Cain, "is a matter of opinion."

"On the contrary," said Mansel, "it is a matter of fact. I repeat, *my* hands are clean."

Cain regarded his finger-nails.

"A solicitor," he observed, "is sometimes badly placed."

"I'll take your word for it."

"A client errs: his lawyer must either desert him or – be prepared to soil his own hands."

"I see," said Mansel. "Which course do you usually take?"

"That depends upon the client."

"And his means."

There was another silence.

Cain looked at George and myself. Then he returned to Mansel.

"I should very much value," he said, "a few words with you alone."

"No," said Mansel. "But you can have Forecast in."

"I do not admit Mr Forecast to consultations like this."

"Is that so?" said Mansel.

Cain cleared his throat.

"I propose to speak frankly," he said.

Mansel said nothing, and presently he went on.

"The first that I knew of this business was when a wire signed WENSLEY was brought to me on Saturday morning last. Biretta, my partner, was cruising – is cruising now. I sent for his managing clerk and asked what it meant. Then the whole story came out. I was inexpressibly shocked – and determined to leave at once, to see what could be done.

"It was my intention, on arrival, to send Forecast and his satellites home. But since they had – er – lost their passports, I could not do that.

"Then I drove to Varvic, to see the Duke.

"These Austrians are not like us. The man's outlook is purely feudal. He holds the opinion that he is above the law. He regarded Biretta as an agent... an agent who had bungled his orders... orders which should never have been taken – which never would have been taken, if I had known what they were."

"Why did you go to see him?"

"To counteract any impression which Forecast might have made. To tell him that I would not act nor permit my partner to act one moment longer for such an impossible man.

"But before I had been with him two minutes, I altered my mind. The man was beside himself, and I had to play for time. He gave me orders, Captain Mansel, that you and your companions should be destroyed forthwith. When I ventured to demur, he declared that he would detain me until the deed had been done. He did in fact detain me for nearly four hours, behind locked doors. In the end he allowed me to go, because I pointed out that, unless he did so, I could not give orders to Forecast whom I had left at the inn. And so I received his instructions and presently left. But, before I did so, he took my passport away....

"Captain Mansel, the man is dangerous.

"I know the plans he has made – plans which, with or without Forecast, he means to execute.

"Now, in self-defence, I am ready to tell you these plans. You see, I'm being perfectly frank. I say 'in self-defence,' for the man has taken my passport, and once his will has been done, I shall be in great danger, because I know too much.

"You said a few minutes ago that you wished to see justice done. What exactly you meant by that, you declined to say; but I can tell you this – that, if Duke Saul were to come to a sudden end, no one on earth could contend that justice had not been done." The man leaned forward. "To you, once you know his plans, the Duke's – er – elimination will be child's play itself."

"Indeed," said Mansel. "And your passport?"

"I was coming to that. I can get another, of course – by applying to the British Consul. Before I took such a step, I should like to feel assured that I was not to suffer for what my partner had done."

Mansel said nothing to that, and presently Cain went on.

"You have, I think, certain papers; papers given by Biretta to Forecast, before he left. I understand that they bear the name of my firm. The production of those papers, coupled with the undeniable fact that I had been in Austria – undeniable, because of my visit to the British Consul – would identify me with action of which I knew nothing, much less ever took.

"And so, in self-defence, I ask for those papers back. In return, I'll tell you the plans Duke Saul has made, put Forecast at your service and lend you my utmost assistance to bring down this dangerous man."

"I'm sure you will," said Mansel. "To use your own expression, 'he knows too much.'"

Cain shrugged his shoulders.

"I told you," he said, "I was going to be perfectly frank. Thanks to Biretta, I find myself in a jam. Well, I want to get out."

"You don't mind 'deserting' your client?"

"The man is not my client. If Biretta had been in England, d'you think that I should be here? The man is Biretta's client, and the mess is Biretta's mess."

"On paper Duke Saul is a client of Worsted and Co."

"Naturally. But Biretta has his clients, and I have mine. And only if one is away, does the other deal with his business as best he can."

"I see. Tell me this, Mr Cain. Why are Worsteds so anxious to be able to prove beyond doubt that Major John Bowshot is dead?"

Cain shrugged his shoulders.

"I've no idea. I assume that the Duke was insisting–"

"You're wrong. The instructions given to Forecast make it quite clear that Worsteds – and not the Duke – desired most definite proof that Major Bowshot was dead."

"You amaze me."

"I don't think I do. Those instructions were type-written. Do you ask me to believe that no copy was kept?"

"If it was, I never saw it. Biretta being away–"

"Look at that," said Mansel, and gave him a telegram.

*Sunday, October 7th*

*Cain left Croydon at noon today Biretta came with him to air-port and saw him off*

Cain read it carefully, nodded, and handed it back.

"One to you," he said. "Never mind. My offer stands. In fact, I'll go further. Give me those papers back, and Forecast shall finish the Duke."

Such calm effrontery hit me between the eyes, but Mansel appeared to take it as a matter of course.

"I'm not playing, Mr Cain."

"Quite sure?"

"Quite sure."

"No counter-proposals?"

"None."

Cain got to his feet.

"In that case, I must be going."

"Sit down," said Mansel. "I haven't done with you yet."

Cain glanced at his wrist.

"I can give you another five minutes."

"You will give me as long as I please."

Cain looked very hard at Mansel. Then he sat down.

"Yes?" he said.

"First, I should like your passport."

Cain stared.

"My passport's at Varvic – I told you."

"I know," said Mansel. "I didn't believe you then and I don't believe you now."

Cain leaned back on the sofa and crossed his legs.

"D'you propose to search me?" he said.

Mansel nodded.

"Unless you hand it over."

"Then that's that," said Cain, rising. He lifted his arms. "I've never been searched before, but I have an idea that this is the traditional pose."

"It's good enough," said Mansel, and stepped to his side. "Will you do the searching, William? I'll see that he doesn't move."

As I took the man's left lapel –

"Try the right breast-pocket," snapped Cain.

I could hardly believe my ears; but, when I did as he said, I found his passport there.

I gave it to Mansel, and Cain resumed his seat.

"Your score's mounting up, Captain Mansel."

Mansel inspected the passport. Then he slid it into his pocket and folded his arms.

"What?" he said. "Oh, my score. Quite so. But it's going to mount very much higher – from your point of view. But that's by the way. Now one thing I wanted to say was that you and Biretta are very, very anxious to be in a position to prove that Major Bowshot is dead. So anxious, in fact, that you contemplate planting a corpse, upon which, when the police are called in, will be found his name and address." He pulled out Cain's passport, ran through its leaves and then held an envelope up. "Faked, of course; like the other. But it does bear out what I say. Well, now please get this, Mr Cain. If any such body is found, your instructions to Forecast will immediately be laid before the appropriate authorities."

Cain said nothing, but merely looked at his watch.

"Another thing is this. I received you today, but I shan't receive you again. Or any of your crew. So make no more advances. I want to make myself plain. Come again, and you come at your peril. I'll 'fire on a flag of truce,' and any attempt at bluff will be treated as it deserves.

"I can't say I'm sorry to have met you; for I'd heard a good deal about you, and I was glad of a chance to see for myself. But, to quote the Queen of Sheba, 'Behold, the half was not told me.' I've met a lot of blackguards; but, all things considered, I give you pride of place. That may be unfair to Biretta; but if he is less virtuous than you are, then, if he believes in Hell, he must be afraid to die.

"Finally, let me commend you to do your worst. We shall not swerve from what we set out to do. And that, if you remember, was 'to see justice done.'"

Cain looked again at his watch.

"Quite finished?" he said.

"Yes."

"Good." The man got to his feet. "You see, I'm lunching at Varvic at half-past twelve."

"I see."

"What's my best way from here?"

"I'm afraid I can't help you."

Cain laughed and turned on his heel...

With his hand on the door, he turned.

"Take care of that passport," he said. "Sooner or later, you see, I shall ask for it back. And if, then, it isn't forthcoming..."

"I'll put it with the others," said Mansel.

For the first time Cain showed emotion. Twice he tried to make answer, and twice he failed. Then, with a working face, he turned and flung out of the room; and Carson, who was at the front door, let him out of the house.

We heard the slam of a door and an engine leapt into life. And then the crunch of gravel told us the car had gone.

Mansel lifted his voice.

"Bell and Rowley," he cried.

A moment later the servants entered the room.

"Anything to report?"

Bell replied.

"Boney stuck to the car, sir, an' never moved."

"I don't blame him," said Mansel. "Go on."

"But Forecast got out, sir, and started walking about. Then he began to stray, so I stepped out and asked him to keep to the car."

"What did he say or do?"

"He asked if we'd found his eye-glass. And I said 'No.' 'Well,' he says, 'that eye-glass was very precious. There's twenty quid for the fellow that brings it back.'"

Mansel smiled.

"And what did you say?"

"I said I'd tell the farm servants."

"Good for you," said Mansel. "And what did he say to that?"

"Nothing, sir. But he gave me an ugly look and walked back to the car."

"Right," said Mansel. "Open the windows, will you? All of them – wide. By rights, the room should be cleaned. And, between you, you might keep an eye on the lane at the back. They're supposed to be going to Varvic; but Boney might lose his way."

"And if he should, sir?"

"Put him right," said Mansel, laughing. "Put all of them right."

"Thank you, sir," said Bell, with the ghost of a smile.

Then Mansel and George and I set out for a walk; for the day before I had come upon a man seeking truffles with the aid of a couple of swine, and Mansel, who had heard of, but never seen such a thing, desired to talk with the fellow and watch him and his helpers at work.

# VII

## THE RACE TO THE SWIFT

Cain had said only one thing that made us think; and that he said right at the last. Sooner or later, he had said, he should ask for his passport back. *And if then it was not forthcoming...* Now that was more than a threat, for it showed how his mind was working and proved how right Mansel had been to persuade the Duchess to leave before he arrived. In a word, Cain was out for a hostage. If he could take but one of us prisoner, he meant so to use that one as to bring us all to our knees.

So Mansel gave strict orders that from this time on no one of us should ever be left alone. If watching was to be done, then it must be done by two: if only one could be spared to stay with a car, then that car must care for itself. And so on. And never were we to go out unless we were armed.

That night Mansel and I went out on patrol, whilst George and the servants remained, not only to 'hold the fort,' but to keep a particular watch on the region at the back of the farm, "for," said Mansel, "if Saul has a map of this district and that map is of the same scale as the one you saw, they know by now that we have a second way home. And I'm all against an ambush, unless I've laid it myself."

We took the Rolls, and I drove; and Mansel sat beside me, pistol in lap.

First we drove to Latchet, of course without lights. As we stole down its only street, I shot a glance at the inn, to see that lights were burning in two of the first-floor rooms.

Then we made for Varvic, taking such roads as would bring us to the mouth of the southern drive. This we had never used, though we had reconnoitred its mouth.

(I am anxious to make this point clear. Schloss Varvic, as I have said, was approached by three several drives or private roads. One ran in from the north, one from the west, and one from the south. The northern drive was the one which we knew so well, on which George had wrecked the two-seater on Sunday night. The western drive was the one I had used that same night, when I had carried the letter which Mansel sent to the Duke. But we had never taken the southern drive. And for this reason, rightly or wrongly, we thought that, of the three drives, the southern drive stood least chance of being picketed.)

We berthed the Rolls in a meadow a mile away, and twenty minutes later we reached the mouth of the drive. Here we stood very still for five minutes or more, to give any man who was watching a chance to move. Since we had seen and heard nothing, we were just about to proceed, when Mansel touched my arm. An instant later I saw a flash in the woods which spoke to an oncoming car.

The car was coming from Varvic, along the drive: after perhaps one minute, we saw the beam of its headlights flicking from tree to tree. And when we saw this, we took cover without delay.

Where the drive ran into the road, its banks were high; and Mansel mounted the right one, and I the left. Lying there in the bracken, if it had only been day, we should have been perfectly placed, for we were some ten feet up and each was on one of the corners made by the drive and the road. But the luck we had had still held, for as it approached the road, the car began to slow down. And then it came to a standstill – this, directly below us, in the very jaws of the drive.

I recognized the car. It was the big limousine in which I had hidden myself, when the Duke had driven into his garage just over a week ago. It had seen a good deal of service, for I had marked at the time how its cushions were rubbed, but its engine was remarkably silent, and so was its drive.

And then –

"To the left," said Cain.

"What d'you say, Boney?" said Forecast.

"I dunno," said Boney. "I've never drove by this way."

"Give me the map," said Cain, and switched on the ceiling light.

This showed us at once that Forecast and Cain were sitting in the back of the car, and that Boney was driving, with China and Gulf by his side.

After the usual wrangle, Cain was proved right. So the ceiling light was put out and Boney turned to the left....

I found Mansel out in the road, with a hand to his chin.

"Very interesting," he said. "First point – the lights were left on at Latchet, to make us think they were in. Second point – why are they using a bigger and better car?"

"I know it," I said. "It's out of the garage at Varvic."

"Ah," said Mansel. "Saul lends them one of his cars – without a chauffeur to drive it. That's more than I'd do. Third point – they're all five present. That means that they're not coming back from an ordinary call, for I decline to believe that Saul desired the acquaintance of China and Gulf. Fourth point – why would you say that they were using this drive?"

"I've no idea," said I. "The northern drive is open: Cain drove that way on Wednesday – that we know. Is it possible they're going for Goschen?"

"I think it's for one or two reasons. Either they're bound for Goschen, which is not so far by this way; or else the northern drive is now reserved only for us."

"Goschen has it," I said. "That's why they've got a quiet car, and that's why they are all of them there."

We turned and began to hasten the way we had come.

"I agree. All the same, I'm not quite sure; for when I drive by night, I'd sooner use roads that I know than roads that I don't. The latter may be shorter, but they won't get you there so soon, if you have to keep on stopping to look at the map. Any way, we'll get back to Goschen, just in case." We broke into a run. "Not that George can't hold his own, but I'm all for biting the biter whenever we get the chance. But I think we should have a look at the northern drive. Not now, and not by night. In the early morning, perhaps, when there's just enough light to see."

In less than ten minutes' time we had reached the Rolls, but the moment I let in her clutch, I knew that we had a flat tire. I had thought she was down a little, as I came up, but had attributed this to the unevenness of the ground.

Before I had switched off the engine, Mansel was out of his coat; and, though he uttered no word, I saw the frown on his face. This was our first set-back – if you can give it that name. But we could not have had a flat tire at a more unfortunate time.

But worse was to come.

The spare wheels, of which we had two, were locked into place. Dust or dirt had entered one of these locks, for when I had put in the key, I could only turn it half round, and when I sought to withdraw it, it would not move. And we had no duplicate. It took us near half an hour to free that key, and five and thirty minutes had passed before we were out of the meadow and on the road.

Mansel was driving now, and he put his headlights on and went like the wind.

Neither he nor I said a word, but I knew that he was worried, and so was I. Our luck had begun to change; and, as I have said before, there is a saying, 'It never rains but it pours.'

Faithful to the doctrine he preached, Mansel went by a longer way than the rogues had gone; for that way we knew very well, but were less sure of the other which we had taken but twice – and that, without lights.

Fast as Mansel drove, it seemed, I remember, an age before we were nearing Talc – that is to say, the village which lay just short of a mile from the back of the farm.

As we approached, he slowed down and put his headlights out; and then we ran into the village, up to the cross roads where we must turn to the left.

We were, I suppose, some twenty-five yards from the cross, when a torch was flashed to and fro, and Mansel set a foot on the brake.

Then Carson was speaking – in a voice that I hardly knew.

"They've got Mr Hanbury, sir."

"Got?" cried Mansel. "*Got?*"

"Seized, sir. Carried him off. I don't know which way they went."

"How long?" said Mansel.

"Not more than eight minutes, sir."

"Into the car," said Mansel. "Talk as we go."

As Carson leaped into the back, Mansel put the car at the cross roads, brought her up all standing and backed her round to the left. Then he swung her round to the right – the way we had come. And then he switched on his headlights and let her go.

If we had come fast to Talc, the pace we were going now was that of the devil himself. In a word, Mansel called on the Rolls, and that splendid car responded as only a thoroughbred will. He never spared her at all, but drove as a racing driver who has the road to himself, and once, on a long straight stretch, I saw the speedometer-needle touch ninety-six.

From time to time Mansel spoke. Carson was kneeling behind us, to hear what he said.

"Did you see the car?"

"Not properly, sir. But I know it wasn't Forecast's. Too big and too quiet."

"Identify anyone?"

"Cain, sir. I heard his voice."

"Mr Hanbury hurt?"

"That I can't say, sir. I never heard him cry out."

There was a little silence, while Mansel whipped through a hamlet at seventy-five and sliced two bends to an inch without lifting his foot.

He never asked what had happened, though he must have been burning to know; but gave the whole of his mind to the possible rescue of George.

"They're bound for Varvic, of course. And with George in that castle, we're sunk. So we've *got* to get there first. I don't want to overtake them: that's why I'm going this way. To overtake would be hopeless. Our only chance is to be there when they arrive....

"They'll take the southern drive. I daren't take the northern drive – I've told you why. And so we must take the western.... You've driven the western drive, William. What is it like?"

"Quite straightforward," I said. "There's a right and left turn half-way, where you drop to go over a bridge."

"Tell me before we get there."

Here I saw a check coming, and Mansel saw it, too.

Ahead, a lorry was pounding, going our way. And ahead of the lorry was a bridge, some forty or fifty yards long. We knew it well enough and had crossed it many a time – *and been held up there before*; for the bridge was very narrow, and once a car was upon it, no other car could go by. And the lorry knew we were there, but it had come first to the bridge and so it refused to give way.

Mansel pulled out. At once our headlights showed that the bridge was clear. Mansel sounded his horn and put down his foot....

I think I tried to say 'Stop,' for I knew that it could not be done. There are times when you can cut in, and times when you can't. And this was one of the latter, for the lorry had reached the abutment and was closing the neck of the bottle, if I may put it that way.

And then we were through the gap, somehow... and the Rolls was over the bridge....

(Mansel said to me later, "You see, you did not allow for the speed of the Rolls. I dare not say what we were doing, but we were moving so fast that, compared with us, the lorry was standing still. And so the gap was *not* closing. But, of course, we had to be quick.")

Mansel was speaking again.

"The point is – which will they do? Drive straight to and into the garage, or up to the gate? Myself, I think the garage, provided it's open, of course. Opinions, please."

"I agree," said I.

"The garage, sir," said Carson. "But if we get there in time, you can set me down at the gate. Then if they should stop there, I can hold them till you and Mr Chandos come up."

"Very good – if there's time. In any event, I shall drive right up to the castle, past the garage and put the Rolls under the wall. Is the going all right there, William?"

"Quite good enough."

"Remember this. We've got to wait, if we can, till George is out of the car. In the car, we can't get at him. He'll be in the back – for a monkey; and Forecast will have a pistol stuck into his ribs."

The car tore on.

The rogues had had eight minutes start, and, if they had gone as they came, they were taking a far shorter route; for we had to go right round to the mouth of the western drive. And, though we were moving so fast, they would not be wasting time, for fear of pursuit. I began to feel hopeless....

By the mercy of God, the roads were empty that night. Two cars, as well as the lorry, were all the traffic we saw. As a rule, at such a time, there was little abroad; but tonight we were using main roads for most of the way.

"And, if we do it," I said: "I mean, if we get there first..."

"We're going to do it," said Mansel, quietly enough. "What happens then, I don't know. It depends upon what they do; upon where they stop the car, and how they get out. But they must not suspect our presence, till George is out of the car."

And here, at last, we came to the western drive....

Although he had never seen it, Mansel still maintained a tremendous speed, and this, I think, did him more credit than anything else. His driving that night was really wonderful: of course, he took risk after risk, but he had to do that; and he never lost a second or gave two inches away. But the drive was full of bends and was not very wide, and the woods were standing thick upon either hand; yet Mansel went up that drive, which was two miles long, at nearly a mile a minute for almost the whole of its length, only slowing down when I told him that the right and left turns were at hand. This demanded a lightning judgment and perfect control – the eye, the brain and the members working as one.

So for less than three minutes...

Then we tore round a curve, to see the meadows ahead in the light of the moon.

At once Mansel put out his lights and lifted his foot....

A moment later we saw the castle itself.

Since the archway which gave to the garage was facing south-west, this was clear to be seen from the western drive.

And now its great doors were shut; but the wicket in one of the leaves was open wide, for the lights in the garage were on and were shining out of the wicket on to the apron without.

I did not know what to think....

As always, a light was burning beside the castle gate.

Carson was out on the running-board, ready to drop.

Mansel drove on to the sweep in front of the castle gate. As he turned, to make for the apron, he slowed right down for a moment, and Carson stepped off. And in that blessed instant, I saw the lights of a car in the southern drive.

"By God, you've done it," I breathed. I saw Mansel glance to his right. "Over the apron, and round. We've just got time."

It was the nearest thing – for we had to bestow the Rolls.

Had we left her close to the archway, quite apart from the moonlight, the lights of the incoming car must have picked her up. So we had to drive on, round the castle, until she was hidden from view. And then we had to get back – *before we ourselves were caught by the lights of the limousine.*

"Say when," said Mansel, whipping over the turf and shaving the castle wall....

I think those were the worst moments of all that terrible night; for there was the limousine coming, yet we were increasing the distance we had to go. We were going away from the wicket. Yet, unless we could reach the wicket before the limousine turned, her lights would fall full upon us and we should have lost our race.

Not until we had reached the postern could I see the apron no more.

"Good enough," I cried.

And then we were out of the Rolls and were racing the way we had come....

The limousine was out in the meadows – with seventy yards to go. As we reached the edge of the apron, I saw her enter the sweep. For an instant, she seemed uncertain; then I heard

Boney change down, and, instead of holding straight on, the beam of her headlights began to come round to the right.

In a flash we were through the wicket, to find a man in the act of drawing the bolts of the leaves of the door itself.

There was no time for nicety. As he turned, Mansel hit him once, and the fellow fell down in a heap.

Mansel picked him up and laid him along the wall, quite close to the gate.

"We must play his part," he breathed, "and open the leaves. One to each leaf. We keep out of sight, as we do it. And as the car comes in, we close them again. Keep your eye on my leaf and the instant you see it move, bring your leaf over to meet it with all your might."

As the car passed on to the apron, we drew the bolts. Then we pulled open the leaves, keeping out of sight as we did so, backing towards the wall. Before my leaf was quite open, the car, which had come to rest, began to move forward again. Its headlights were making the archway as bright as day....

With a hammering heart, I waited for Mansel to move. Then I saw his leaf shudder, and that was cnough for me.

With all my might I swung the massive oak forward, to the tune of such shouts and yells as I never had heard.

It was the merest chance, but, had we rehearsed the manoeuvre, I cannot believe that the timing could have been better or the result improved.

Almost at the same instant the two great leaves struck the car – and that, directly in line with the steering-wheel.

Since the coachwork was all of wood, and each leaf must have weighed near a ton – for oak is heavy and they were studded with iron – the car gave way, till the leaves came against its side members which slowed them up.

Gulf, who had tried to get out, was killed on the spot; the door, which he had opened, returned to crush his head between itself and its jamb. And Boney was shouting like a madman, and China was trying to clamber into the back of the car.

My leaf was the left-hand leaf – that is to say, the one in which the wicket was cut. And so I found Mansel beside me, as calm as death, holding the wicket to and looking through the crack he had left.

"Here they are," he said, "with the prisoner. Let them come in. And then we've got to get out, as quick as ever we can. Any moment now, the castle will come to life."

I stood back against the leaf.

Then a hand pushed the wicket open, and George stumbled over the sill and fell on his face. His hands were tied behind him and he moved as a man who is drunk.

Then Forecast, pistol in hand, stepped over his body and cursed him and lifted a foot.

Now George was my faithful friend....

Before the kick fell, I had the man by the wrist.

For some reason, he never fired, but I bent his arm and broke it – I heard the bone snap. As he clapped his left hand to the break, with all the strength in my body I hit him between the eyes.

As he fell, somebody fired – and the archway magnified the explosion, so that my ears could not hear.

Mansel was looking past me, pistol in hand; his left arm was round George's shoulders, holding him up.

I saw his lips moving, but I could not hear what he said.

"Get the Rolls," he shouted.

As I stepped out of the wicket, I saw Cain standing beside me, with his back to the wall and his hands clasped behind his neck. Carson was dividing his attention between the man and the car.

This was dangerous – I knew now why Mansel had fired.

"Watch the car," I said.

Then I turned to Cain.

"Get into the car."

"I prefer," drawled Cain, "to—"

I took the man by the throat and shook him down to his knees. Then I seized the nape of his neck and kicked him into the car.

"Thank you, sir," said Carson.

I turned and ran for the Rolls....

As I backed her on to the apron, a bullet went by my head and Carson fired into the wreck of the limousine.

I turned the Rolls on the apron, and George clambered into the back.

Cain and China were shouting, and Mansel was backing from the wicket, which was now shut.

"Sound the horn, when you're ready," he cried.

I sounded the horn.

As he turned, the leaf was pulled back, to release a pack of servants who ran for the Rolls.

Carson fired at their feet and I let in my clutch.

As Mansel and he reached the Rolls, I put down my foot....

"The southern drive," said Mansel, taking the seat by my side.

Much less than one minute later, we had left the meadows behind and were into the woods.

"How d'you feel, George?" said Mansel.

"Well, I have felt better," said George, "but I'm not dead yet. And when Bill pushed Forecast's face, that did me a lot of good. Oh, and thank you all very much for saving my soul. If they'd gone on as they began, I should not have survived. And now please interrogate Carson, who knows rather more than I. It's not that I'm being churlish, but the pain in the back of my head embarrasses thought. I think I must have been struck with what the police would call 'a blunt instrument.' It's nothing to do with my fall, though I took the deuce of a toss."

"What happened, Carson?" said Mansel.

"They've a spy or spies in Talc, sir. They knew that the Rolls was out."

"Ah," said Mansel. "Go on."

"It was all very quick, sir. Two shots, one after the other, were fired in front of the house – to attract us, of course; but we didn't realize that. Then, from the other side, we heard the horn of the Rolls."

"What, this horn?" said Mansel.

"One just like it, sir. And of course we thought it was you."

"Very clever," said Mansel. "And that explains the use of the limousine. Same, very unusual horn as that of the Rolls. And how did they find that out?"

"They know quite a lot, sir," said Carson, "if you ask me."

"I'll say they do," said Mansel. "Get on with your tale."

"Well, we all of us turned and ran. We thought you were in a jam, sir, sounding the horn. And we knew it was some way off – say the other end of the wood. In fact, that's just where it was....

"Well, you know how Mr Hanbury can run, sir. He was leading by thirty yards when we got to the wood. And I was next; and then came Rowley and Bell.

"I saw him take the last of the bends, and I heard him fall. A wire, sir, six feet from the bend, clean across the road, made fast to a couple of trees. And, as I came round the bend, a searchlight comes on – they must have had one fixed on the back of the car. I was blinded, of course, and, as I dived for the trees, a bullet goes by my ear. And then the searchlight goes out and the car slips away. And when I try to find Mr Hanbury, he's not to be seen."

"Simple and neat," said Mansel. "You can't get away from that. But the smartest thing of all was their striking tonight."

"How so?" said I.

"Well, don't you think it was?"

"Well, we didn't expect them to."

"Why didn't we expect them to?" said Mansel.

After, a moment's reflection –

"Cain came with an offer this morning. We naturally thought that, when we had turned it down, it would take him a little while to think up something else."

"Exactly," said Mansel. "And why did I think that, William? Because I was *meant* to think it. Cain's visit this morning was camouflage – dust in my eyes. He'd already planned this attack, and he came this morning on purpose to put me off my guard. *As he did.* If you remember, I told you he was no fool." He sighed. "Well, it's over now. But it was a very near thing – right up to the last.... Strange that till Forecast appeared and you took hold of his arm, they never realized that we were behind those leaves."

"They'd no time to think," said I.

"Not so much that, I think. I think they assumed that the crash was accidental – as, of course, I hoped they would – that the fools who had opened the leaves had merely closed them too soon. That that assumption was suspect, they must have perceived, but to that assumption they stuck, because, since we had not passed them, they simply could not believe that we could have got there first."

"I'm damned if I blame them," I said. "I couldn't believe it myself."

"They assumed that we were behind them – for all they knew, close on their heels. And so, though the heavens fell, they had to get George inside before we arrived. Never mind. All's well that ends well. Gulf's come to the sticky end he had fairly earned. And so has Boney. Less sticky, of course. Still, an end. He was just going to kill you, William; when you were engaged with Forecast. But I saw him just in time, and that's why I fired. And Forecast's arm won't work and he won't see out of his eyes for a couple of days. Did you hit anyone, Carson?"

"I don't think so, sir. They dared not get out of the car; but I couldn't see in."

"Well, we're all very lucky," said Mansel. "Too many chances going in scraps like that. One does one's best, of course: but when nobody knows what anyone's going to do and when half the stage is in darkness and the other half in the light, survival is very largely a matter of luck. Oh, and if there's a spy in Talc, we'll go in by the front tonight. I've no doubt you're right. And the spy must be in with the post-master. And when he saw us go out, he rang up Varvic and said so. And if I'm right, we must be truly thankful that he didn't ring up Varvic when we left for the second time. For if Varvic had been ready and waiting – well, I don't think that we should now be on our way back to the farm. As it is, we can go to our beds and sleep as sound as we please, for it's Berkeley Square to a birth-mark they've had enough for one night."

So we came back to Goschen, to the immense relief of Rowley and Bell; for though, when they found Carson gone, they guessed that the Rolls had come back and gone off in pursuit, they found it hard to believe that she could be got to Varvic ahead of the limousine.

And here I should say that George had had in his pocket the Lowland's keys, and since her bonnet was locked, it would have taken two hours to get her on to the road.

Of such are the changes and chances of mortal life. From first to last, the thing had been touch and go. But from what I have said, I think I have made it clear that, if Mansel had not taken his life and our lives in his hand and cut in front of that lorry as it came up to the bridge, George must have been within Varvic before we could reach its gates.

# VIII

## IN WHICH I AM OBSERVED

The following morning we rested and George spent the day in bed. The whole of the afternoon we gave to the cars, and particularly to the Rolls, going right over them both from stem to stern, greasing, testing and adjusting with infinite care. This was a special overhaul, for the two were always given the very best attention that cars could have. And here perhaps I should mention that our petrol and oil were delivered to Goschen in bulk, so that, except at Salzburg, we never entered a garage or stopped at a pump.

Mansel had written to the Duchess the day before; but now he wrote again, and the salient part of the letter shall speak for itself.

*...None of us can leave here just now, and, so I must write what I would rather have said. I see from last Tuesday's* Times *that the lord of the manor of Beehive is offering his property for sale. This includes his residence, known as The Hall, the living of Beehive, some five thousand acres and, finally, the village itself. The property will be sold by auction in October, unless previously disposed of by private treaty.*

*Now you told us that John Bowshot was 'very fond of the village.' Have you any reason to think that he was aware of this impending sale? If not, what would have been his reaction, on reading last Tuesday's* Times ? *Even if you cannot answer either of these questions, please tell me anything you can think of which might have any bearing upon the point....*

I was mystified, but Mansel only smiled.

"When we get her answer," he said, "I'll open my heart."

The next morning, long before dawn, we again went out – Mansel and Bell and I, leaving George and Carson, and Rowley to keep the farm. George was quite recovered and would have gone out with us, but his fall and the blow on the head had shaken him up and Mansel insisted that he should do no more than light duty for another twenty-four hours.

Our intention was, if we could, to inspect the northern drive by the light of day, and, if we saw any movement, to observe it and follow it up. Needless to say, such a reconnaissance had to be made on foot: but we did not like leaving the car, for a berth which will serve at night, may be worse than useless by day – and Varvic knew the country by day; but we did not. And so it was arranged that Carson should drive us out and then return to the farm: that at eleven o'clock he should be where three roads met, not far from the hunting-lodge; and that there we should be waiting for him to carry us home.

It was half-past three in the morning when Carson set us down, roughly a mile and a half from the mouth of the northern drive. It had been raining, but now the sky was clear, and a fresh breeze was combing the tree-tops, to our content: for it meant that we could move without being heard, because the chorister branches would cover our footfalls up. (By night, a man may be heard, but he cannot be seen: but by day, he can be seen, too; and if he is to outwit the ear as well as the eye, the precautions he has to take may ruin his chances of seeing what he came out to see.)

By four we had reached the drive and had made our way along it as far as the notice-board; and there we sat down and waited till the dawn should begin to appear. This was as Mansel had planned, for a man who has known the darkness can see better and farther when the light begins to come in. And then the light began to come in....

At once we rose and, moving like ghosts, began to go up the drive.

We had gone about half a mile – and no one, I think, could have seen us because the light was so thin – when we saw that, across the drive, was lying a pole. This had been painted white and hung four feet from the ground, so that no car could go by until it was moved. It was slung from two posts, one of which had been planted on either side of the drive – that is to say, in the bracken, beyond the ditches which ran by the side of the road. With our minds on an ambush, we all stood as still as death, straining our eyes for any sign of movement of any kind. But when, after four or five minutes, we had seen nothing at all, Mansel signed to us to stay where we were and himself walked up to the pole.

I saw him regard it carefully. Then he laid hands upon it, as though to lift it up or set it aside. But the pole would not move. I saw Mansel glance at the tree-tops, as though he wished for more light: then he stepped to the side of the road and peered at one of the posts. Presently he looked round, whereupon I came up and joined him, to peer at the post myself.

"What do you see, William?"

"There's a hoop or hasp on the post, and that is holding the pole."

"I agree. That's why I can't lift it. But why can't I slide it along?"

"I think," I said, peering, "I think, because it is wedged. Shall I go and see?"

"Not on your life," said Mansel, catching my arm. I looked at him sharply. "You see, I'm almost certain that that's what you're meant to do."

"Good God," said I. "You mean..."

"I don't know," said Mansel. "And there's not enough light to see. In a quarter of an hour, perhaps..."

In less than a quarter of an hour, both he and I could see something upon the ground, at the foot of each post. They had been laid in the bracken and very carefully set. In fact, they were man-traps – the fiercest, most barbarous gins that ever were made.

I have seen such relics in England, but never so savage as these; for those had been made to take a man by the leg, but these had been made to kill. Their teeth were less teeth than spikes, and their jaws were made to meet at rather more than one metre above the ground. Now a metre is three feet three, so that, if a man touched one off, he would, if of normal stature, be pierced just above the hips, and, though some friend should release him almost at once, must certainly die of his wounds in a very short time.

Any man approaching a post, as I had proposed to do, to see how the bar was held or to set it free, must have walked clean into a trap and have touched it off; and when I considered these things and that, but for Mansel's instinct that something was wrong with this drive, one of us must surely have met with a shocking end, my knees felt loose and the palms of my hands grew wet.

"Saul's contribution," said Mansel. He spoke through his teeth. "Well, I'm glad to have seen one open, instead of closed. Think of hearing a scream and rushing up with a torch... to find – someone you knew torn in pieces... so mad with pain that you would have to shoot him, to end his agony.... Never mind. We've been spared – this time. But I expect he's got more than two."

He turned there, and we made our way back to the road, "for, if we went on," said Mansel, "we could not watch the garage without moving round the meadows within the woods. And that is an exercise which now we shall have to forgo."

But since we had plenty of time, as soon as we reached the road, we turned to the left and set out to walk the five miles which lay between us and the mouth of the western drive.

We could not talk as we went, for we moved in single file and kept to the edge of the road – Mansel and Bell to the right, and I to the left. So we always did, for then, if we had to be quick, we stood a much better chance of taking effective cover against some approach or attack. But, to speak for myself, I did not feel like talking; for Saul, by setting his man-traps, had hit us more hard than he knew. All the success we had met with had been due to reconnaissance. We knew how to move in the forest by day as by night: we had learned to take advantage of light and shade and sound; and I do not believe that we had been seen or heard on any patrol we had made or any watch we had kept. But now that valuable ground had been cut from under our feet; for to fall into one of those man-traps meant certain death. Visit Varvic by night, we could not, unless we kept to the roads: and even by day, when to use the roads would be madness, our approach and withdrawal must both of them be so cautious, and therefore so slow, that any observation which we could contrive to keep would cost more than it was worth.

We had covered, I suppose, a little more than two miles, when, still some distance ahead, we heard the sound of a car. At once we left the road and took to the ditch – Mansel and Bell to the right, and I to the left. From there we could see well enough, without being seen, for the ditches were deep and the grass beside them was high.

The car was no car, but a van. And China was sitting in front, by the driver's side. He was staring straight ahead, and his look of glum apprehension was that of the low comedian who knows his job. But, although I could not help laughing, I found it in my heart to pity the rogue. After all, so far as we knew, China was not concerned in John Bowshot's death: yet here he was deeply involved in the consequences of that crime. He had seen his two cronies come to a violent end and now had no one at all to whom to confide his forebodings, with whom to share his highly unpleasant lot: such stripes as three had endured, he now had to suffer alone: and yet he could not withdraw, for his passport was gone. Be that as it may, there he was, sitting beside a man I had never seen – a small thick-set fellow, wearing the Varvic livery of Lincoln green.

The van was a very big one, with double doors at its back: it had not stood in the garage, when I was there; and it was moving slowly – doing, perhaps, some twenty-five miles to the hour.

As it passed out of sight, Mansel left his ditch and I stepped to his side.

"And I wonder what that means," he said, with a hand to his chin. "Presumably bound for Latchet. But why such a van? I mean, the whole of their kit would go in the back of a car – Cain's and all. Then again I should have thought they would have collected it yesterday. I assume they're staying at Varvic – that's natural enough." He shook his head. "I don't understand it, William. Any way, there's a lead, and we'll follow it up." He glanced at his wrist. "A quarter to six. Perhaps we shall see them come back."

So we turned back the way we had come.

We had walked for some forty minutes and had in fact just passed the mouth of the northern drive, when we heard the van coming back. At once we made ourselves scarce; and the van went by as before, with the same man driving and China still by his side.

As it disappeared –

"Forty-two minutes," said Mansel, regarding his watch. "And that washes Latchet out. At the pace they're going, they couldn't have got there and back."

"Where then?" said I.

"Well, I may be wrong, but it looks like the hunting-lodge. That's about four miles from here; and if they spent a quarter of an hour there, it would work out about right."

"Of course," said I. "But why?"

"We'll go and see," said Mansel. "We've plenty of time. And I think the environs should be safe, for they have no reason to think that we know that the lodge is there."

We hastened now, in case the van should return; and we made the mouth of the drive in less than an hour.

"What about it, Bell?" said Mansel, pointing to the print of a tire.

"She's been here, sir," said Bell. "I looked at her prints in the road. They weren't too clear, but I saw they were Michelin treads."

"Good for you," said Mansel, and led the way up the drive....

The lodge had been opened. There seemed to be nobody there, but the shutters hung back against the wall and the front door and windows were wide. On the grass-grown cobbles was scattered the stuff that had lain in the van – four bedsteads and mattresses, two hooded 'watchman's chairs,' as well as blankets and basins and things like that.

"What lovely chairs," said Mansel. "They must have come out of England. Not many left now. I'd like to have them for White Ladies – and that's the truth."

"Too good for China and Forecast."

"Much too good. But that's who they're for – among others. We're looking at their battle headquarters – no doubt about that."

"They can have it for me," said I, and spoke no more than the truth.

The place was perhaps less dreadful beneath the light of the sun; but where other dwellings would have been warmed, this seemed to stew, and all the decay and rankness to burgeon as hotbeds will. The air was still and heavy, and there was about it an odour which I can hardly describe; but it made me think of old deaths, and though it was stale and faded, I think it must at one time have been unspeakable. Worst of all, there was still prevailing that atmosphere of evil which we had felt so strongly when first we had found the place. I am, I suppose, no more or less of a coward than most men are; but the spot made me afraid – and that is the very truth. I do not know what I feared. I was just afraid.

To my great relief, Mansel did not suggest that we should enter the lodge, but, using the greatest caution, we made our way round to the back.

Since we had been there, a car had been driven that way – lately, too, for the tracks it had made were fresh. Since the yard was cobbled, the tires had left no prints, but the weeds which had covered the cobbles had been laid low and we saw how the car had been turned and then backed to a riot of laurels, walling one side of the yard.

There had been a path – there was still a path through the laurels, for someone who knew of its presence had opened it up. With Mansel and Bell behind me, I took that path, marking the broken suckers and leaves that were bruised and torn.

To this day I do not know why I gave such a lead. I sometimes think that I did it by way of a gesture, as though to deny my fear. But vanity like that is expensive; and in all this time I have not yet paid my account, for to this day I dream of the picture that met my eyes.

Beyond the laurels lay a graveyard, confined by three low, stone walls and the back of the lodge. The boughs of advancing trees hung over the walls and the laurels through which I had passed were unusually high, so the plot, which was not very big, could receive no sun. There were no head-stones, but every mound was staked – that is to say, a black post had been driven through the midst of the mound, and so, I suppose, through the body that lay beneath. Many of the posts were leaning because their wood had rotted under the earth, and more than one had fallen across the graves. On the top of each post was some headgear – some hat or cap or bonnet, the dead had worn, but most were hanging in tatters, and some, except for fragments, had disappeared. One grave was new – mound, post and hat were quite fresh. I had seen that hat before – upon Boney's head. A legend was painted in German across the wall of the house: the huge black letter was faded, but was still easy to read.

*THESE SUICIDES LIE HERE BY THE GRACE OF VARVIC. CURSED BE HE WHO DISTURBS THEIR RESTING-PLACE.*

I often wonder how many of those poor souls in fact had taken their lives – and how many had had their lives taken and then, to spare their murderer, been branded with *felo de se*. Of such was the Duchy of Varvic. Where the Duke's writ ran, no questions were ever asked. And I can well believe that such as knew of the graveyard would not have come near the spot for any money.

Without a word, we returned to the stable-yard and had hardly come again to the front of the lodge, when we heard the van leave the road and enter the drive.

At once we stepped into the woods, which stood so thick and uncared for on every side.

This time a kind of tender followed the van, to disgorge four great big fellows, all wearing the Varvic green. One of these was plainly some foreman of the estate, for he knew how things should be done, and the others, including China, made haste to do as he said.

By his direction, four man-traps were taken out of the van, and then some coal and some firewood and boxes containing stores.

The traps were laid down well apart, and two men were set to oil them, because, I suppose, they were stiff. The other man and China were told to take up the gear and carry it into the house, and, when they were all at work, the foreman took off his coat and joined the men who were busy upon the traps.

Of course the traps were closed, but his workmen opened one, while the foreman was cleaning the springs. One upon either side, they pulled the jaws apart, easing them to and fro and gradually opening them wider, according to the directions the foreman gave. Such was the power of the springs that to force the jaws to their widest was almost beyond their strength; but at last, with a mighty effort, they got them flat, when the foreman engaged the lug which locked the jaws into place. This lug belonged to the foot-plate, the slightest pressure upon which would disengage it again. (In fact the foot-plate was less of a plate than a grid. This was for the sake of concealment. If the trap were laid in a meadow, the grass would pass through the grid and hide it from view; but a plate would have lain on the grass and so could have been seen.)

For two or three minutes more, the foreman worked on the springs, for now these were fully extended and so could be wiped and oiled as they could not have been before. Then he ordered his men to stand clear, and picked up a piece of dead wood. Standing back himself, he pitched this on to the foot-plate....

I never saw the jaws close, for their leap was too quick for the eye. One moment the trap was open: the next it was shut. But I heard the crash of the iron, and, though I knew this was coming, it made me jump. It made the two men jump, too. And the foreman said something at which the three of them laughed.

And there Mansel touched my arm, and I turned and followed him deeper into the wood.

As Bell came up with us –

"It's nine o'clock," said Mansel, "and Carson is coming to get us in two hours' time. He's coming too close to this place, for when we arranged what we did, we had no idea they were using the hunting-lodge. So he must be met and stopped. Which way he will come, I don't know; but there are only two ways, and each of you must take one. Whoever meets him should do so about six miles from here. He is to turn at once and take whoever meets him back to the farm. Ask Mr Hanbury to drive at once to Villach and purchase some luminous paint. It's Sunday, I know; but he knows the inn-keeper there and he'll help him out. Be here with the paint and a brush not later than three. You must leave the car four miles off and walk the rest of the way. And no uncertainty this time – you will approach from the south. Sometime today, you see, they are going to lay those traps. I shall watch where they lay them, and then we'll mark the places with luminous paint. But, if they lay them in time, I must do the job before dark. Whoever does not meet Carson will have to go on walking until he is met and picked up. Carson can do that job, as soon as Mr Hanbury is under way."

I did not like leaving Mansel, for if anything were to go wrong, the odds against him were heavy – five to one. Besides, it seemed more than likely that at any time now Cain or Saul would arrive, to say where the traps should be laid: and, if they came, they would not come alone. Still, there was nothing for it; for, luminous paint or no, Carson had to be stopped from approaching the hunting-lodge.

And so we set out, Bell and I. And when we reached the road, I sent him off to the south and turned north myself. This I did on purpose, because the way I was taking was that which the van had gone: and if I was right and others were coming from Varvic, they might come by whilst I was still on their road. The chance was very poor, for after about three miles, I should have to leave their road and turn to the right: but it was better than nothing, and so I did as I say.

I had just passed the place at which Carson was to have met us – the place 'where three roads met' – when, sure enough, I had to take to the ditch. I was hardly in before a tender appeared: but, as it approached, I saw it was slowing down, and it stopped fifty paces beyond me... at the place 'where three roads met.' Here it set down two men – presumably foresters, for one had a gun in his hand and the other wore a short axe, which hung down from his belt. As soon as they had alighted, the driver let in his clutch and the tender moved off; but they clearly had their orders, for, after a quick look round, they climbed to the top of a bank from which they could see all round them, and then lay down in the bracken and out of sight.

There was no doubt about it. Cross roads and turnings and switches were being picketed. Saul, with Cain behind him, was out for blood.

Two things were now clear. The first was this – that a picket had already been posted at the point for which I was making, at which I must turn to the right. And the second was that when I had turned back Carson, I must make my way back to Mansel, to tell him what was afoot.

Now so long as I stayed in the ditch, I was out of the sight of the picket up on the bank; so I went up the ditch on all fours, till I rounded a bend in the road. And there I sat down for a moment, to consider what I must do. So far as I could remember, there was not another turning for nearly two miles – that is to say, the point at which I must turn to the right. I could, therefore, use the road for a mile and a half, and then I must cut across country to gain the road on the right, by which Carson would come. The trouble was that, as I have said before, we did not know this country. Indeed, until this morning, I had hardly seen it by day: and since roads are seldom straight, but twist and turn like serpents, I knew how easy it was for a man who had left the road to miss his way. To cut off a corner sounds simple. So it is – in open country, where you can see your way: but the country hereabouts was very blind, and the sun would help me a little, but not very much. Still, one thing was very plain – that I had no time to spare; for Carson was sure to be early, the time was a quarter to ten, and I had three miles to go. Three miles, more or less. And perhaps I may be forgiven for pointing out that I had not an hour and a quarter, but rather less; for Carson was to meet us at eleven, but I had to stop him three miles from the *rendezvous*. And, as I have said, he was always before his time.

Since I had walked this road not three hours before, I was able to judge pretty well when I was approaching the turning I had to avoid. Soon after ten, therefore, I took a good look at the sun and left the road for a meadow which sloped to a stream. When I came down to this, I could see no sign of a bridge, so I took off my shoes and socks and waded across. The ground then rose again; but, as I approached the crest, from which I was hoping perhaps to see my road, I saw the tops of trees begin to appear, and, when I was up, there was a wood just below me, thick and high enough to obstruct my view. For fear I should lose my direction, I dared not enter this wood, so I bore to the left in the hope that the trees would give way. And so at last they did, to leave me at the head of a valley which ran to the right. Down the valley I went for a quarter of a mile: then I struck up its side, to find more woods and meadows, but never a sign of a road.

It was now nearly half-past ten, and in desperation I hastened across the meadows, bearing left; for so I must strike the road, though perhaps much nearer the turning than I was to like; but, if I held straight on, I might not come across it for half an hour. So for another ten minutes. Then the woods seemed to close in, and I had no choice but to enter the natural maze they made.

No path presenting itself, I simply thrust my way on as best I could, thigh-deep in a sea of bracken, and stumbling again and again. Fit as I was, the sweat was pouring off me, and when a brier caught my shoulder and would not give way, I shook myself free of my jacket and left it there.

And then I saw a break in the bracken....

Thirty seconds later I was sitting with my feet in the ditch, by the side of the road.

As I sat there, mopping my face, I wondered if I was in time. It was sixteen minutes to eleven, and where I was on the road, I had no idea. If I was close to the turning, the probability was that Carson had not gone by: but, if I was not, then he probably had gone by, while I was yet in the wood; for my progress had been so noisy that I should never have heard the sigh of the Rolls. I decided to stay where I was till five minutes to the hour. If by then he had not appeared, either I had missed him or Bell had stopped him, coming the other way.

And then I heard the Rolls coming – the brush of a tire, no more....

Carson shared with his master a very remarkable gift. For myself, I can fairly say that, once I have gone some way, I can always take it again. But Mansel and Carson could do much better than that; for, once they had used some road, they could, I think, have mapped it from memory and made very few mistakes. So Carson said at once that the turning which I had avoided was a short mile ahead and that round the next bend was a track in which he could turn the car.

Then I gave him the message which I was to have given to George and told him that I was returning, not only to be with Mansel but to tell him what I had seen.

"I hope Bell's all right," I said. "I saw a picket posted, and that put me wise. But he may walk into one."

"I don't think he will, sir," said Carson. "Bell's pretty fly. An' when the tender goes by, that'll make him think. But this picketing makes things awkward."

"It's more than awkward," I said. "You see what it's done to me. I got here somehow; but by the merest chance. The country's heart-breaking. If only we had Forecast's map.... Whoever brings that paint will have to be careful to stick to the line of the roads – move parallel to them and never let them out of his sight."

"Shall two of us bring it, sir?"

"Yes." I knew who the two would be. "And don't forget Bell. Mind you go after him as soon as you can."

"Very good, sir. And what about you?"

"Oh, I'll get back all right."

"Don't forget, sir, they're certain to picket the mouth of the drive to the lodge."

"I'd thought of that. It's just as well Captain Mansel is going to wait for that paint."

"I'll say you're right, sir," said Carson.

"Well, you get on," I said. "I'll see you again at three."

"That's understood, sir," said Carson, and set a hand to his hat.

The next moment he was gone.

I made my way back to where I had left my coat; and, when I had disengaged it, by wood and stream and meadow to the point at which, an hour and three-quarters before, I had left the road. I did not take to the road, but walked along beside it, through wood and field. Since I knew that the 'three ways' were watched, I was able to fetch a compass simply enough. But as I came back to the road, I heard Cain's voice.

"Do you mind if I walk on?"

"I should prefer it," said the Duke.

On my knees, I peered through the bushes which bordered the field.

Cain was standing, glowering, and Forecast, his arm in a splint, was standing rather behind him, with his eyes on the ground. His face was black and swollen, and when at last he looked up, I saw that his eyes were not straight. The Duke was sitting on a shooting-stick, watching two liveried chauffeurs changing a wheel. I should have said 'trying to change it,' for the bolts of the wheel in place had, what is called, rusted on and were resisting all efforts to make them move.

"I think," said Cain, "I think you said 'Ten minutes' walk.'"

The Duke appeared not to hear.

"I addressed you," said Cain, trembling.

"That," said the Duke, "is because you know no better. A man of your race should never address me first."

"You insult me," said Cain.

"Naturally," said the Duke, and lighted a cigarette.

With a manifest effort, Cain controlled his voice.

"If," he said thickly, "I am to go through with this thing..."

"Are you speaking as my agent? Or is this a soliloquy? If as my agent, I have already told you that you are dismissed. If, on the other hand, it is a soliloquy, whether you go or stay is a matter of indifference to me."

"Indeed?" said Cain. "And when inquiries for Bowshot are set on foot..."

"If ever they are," said the Duke, "that will be an unfortunate moment for you. I shouldn't let it arrive. For if you do, you will never see it depart. And now pray go on – with your expert. In view of his run of success, he must be chafing to – er – face the bowling again."

With that, he turned his back and began to stroll down the road, away from the hunting-lodge.

Cain regarded his back with smouldering eyes.

Then –

"Come," he said to Forecast, and strode the opposite way.

Now, though I was more than delighted to see such a rift in the lute, all the time the two had been speaking, my eyes had been fast on two maps. The door of the car was open, and the maps were stuck into a pocket upon the door. And since the chauffeurs were working upon the opposite side, I wondered if I could possibly carry them off.

If I was to take them, I had no time to spare.

With one eye on the Duke, I waited, till Cain was out of my sight. Then I crawled through the bushes and into the ditch....

The car, a great *coupé-de-ville,* was not on my side of the road. The road was not very wide. The wheel which was being changed was the off front wheel.

Carefully I measured my distance, moving along the ditch until, if I made my attempt, the body of the car would be between me and the chauffeurs, provided they stayed where they were.

Saul was coming back now, absorbed in thought....

But though, by now, the refractory bolts were off, the jack was giving trouble, and the new wheel was not in place.

Saul strolled on round the bonnet and glanced at the wheel. Then he shrugged his shoulders and turned on his heel....

I let him stroll thirty paces...

Then I rose out of the ditch and stepped lightly across the road....

As I turned with the maps in my hand, I saw that Saul was lighting a cigarette. Before he had thrown down his match, I was back in the ditch. And there I lay like the dead, not daring to lift my head, much less return to the field; for when Fortune has been most gracious, only a fool will ask of her something he need not have.

Still, I would have given a lot to make myself scarce; for, if Saul were to miss the maps, when he returned to the car, I had no desire, so to speak, to be in on that scene: and, since I no longer dared to use my eyes, I listened with all my might and hoped very hard for the best.

At last I heard hasty steps and then the clink of tools as they were thrust into their box. Then the engine was started, and after two or three moments the door of the car was shut.

As it moved off, I ventured to lift my head, and the instant it disappeared, I scrambled out of the ditch and took to the fields....

I hastened for a quarter of a mile directly away from the road; then I sat down under a hedge to examine my spoil.

Both maps were of a large scale, twice that of the map which Saul had given to Forecast. In fact, they were roughly of a quarter of a mile to an inch. The first was of Varvic. There were upon this six crosses; and these, I had little doubt, disclosed where man-traps were laid. The other showed the country immediately north-east of Varvic – that is to say, it showed the hunting-lodge and the country for six miles about it, except on the Varvic side.

At once I saw where I was and the compass which I must fetch, to skirt the woods which surrounded the hunting-lodge; for, unless I made my approach from the opposite side, to get to Mansel I should have to cross the drive; and that would have been to take a needless risk.

Forty minutes went by before I had made my detour.

I was now to the south of the lodge, two meadows away from the road and a hundred and fifty yards from the woods for which I was bound. I began to move towards them under the lee of a hedge....

It must have been a quarter-past one when I entered the woods and began to move to where I was to meet Mansel not later than three o'clock. He was not there, of course, for I was before my time; and so I went carefully on towards the lodge.

It was then that I became aware of some activity.

Two cars, one after another, swept up the drive, and orders were shouted in German not far from the house. By now I was nearing the forecourt, if you can give it that name; but as yet I could see nothing, although my ears could tell me that the five men that I had left there had been reinforced.

I still saw no sign of Mansel: but that did not surprise me, for when he was keeping observation, it was not his way to be seen: all the same, to proceed much farther was clearly dangerous, for, though the wood was thick, it was not a wall, and, with so many pairs of eyes such a little way off, my presence might be discovered before I knew where I was. And so I climbed into a tree, as well to look out for Mansel as to see what I could.

I found a very fair perch some fifteen feet up, but I could not see into the forecourt, although I could hear that the place was alive with men.

Then some order was given, as though by an N.C.O., and an instant later the men I had heard appeared, moving in single file out of the forecourt, directly into the wood. They precisely followed their leader – indeed each man had his hands on the hips of the man in front – and their way was that of a serpent, passing between the trees. There were twenty-two in all, of whom China made one, and what they were about I could not conceive. For a moment I thought they were going to beat the woods; but beaters move in a line – not in single file. They passed quite close to my tree, but no one looked up; and soon the lot had gone by, and all I could hear was the measured tramp of their feet.

There was still no sign of Mansel, and I was growing uneasy on his account. Since the forecourt seemed quiet, I wondered if I should come down and take a look round; but, because the forecourt was quiet, it did not follow that there was nobody there, and, if I was seen and somebody gave the alarm, with twenty-two men in my rear, I might very well be taken before I could make my escape. Indeed, to be perfectly honest, I did not know what to do. However, when I reflected that Mansel did not expect me for over an hour, I saw that it would be foolish to worry about him till then: if by then he had not appeared, I must go in his quest; but till then it was clearly my duty to take no risks. And so I stayed where I was. Still, I was far from easy, if only because today we had broken the rule we had made that we should hunt in couples, but never alone. With that, I need hardly say that I found myself thinking of Bell and greatly fearing that he had walked into a picket where two roads met.

And there I heard the sound of the file of men coming back....

In a moment or two they appeared, treading exactly the line they had taken before; and the leader had his eyes on the ground, as though to be sure that he did not miss the trail.

To see grown men so behave, I found remarkable; for even children, I think, would before now have tired of such an exercise. Since they seemed to be under orders, I could only suppose they were doing some sort of physical drill, though why they should choose such a place and such a time and how such conduct could benefit body or mind I could not conceive.

I soon saw China coming, looking more sullen than woeful and limping a little, as though he had hurt his foot. I was looking at him and smiling, because I was perfectly sure that the moment he reached the forecourt, he meant to fall out, when, without any warning whatever, the leader stopped. This caused collisions and laughter, but China only sighed and favoured his foot. Indeed, his whole demeanour was as good as a play in itself, and I was just regretting that George was not there to see, when the ruffian lifted his head and his eyes met mine.

I think the shock of that instant took a month from my life. One moment I had been laughing; the next I knew I was doomed. So abrupt a reversal of fortune hits a man over the heart, and I hung where I was, like some waxwork, unable to move.

China stared upon me with open mouth.... Then his fingers flew to his mouth to give the alarm.... But no whistle rang out... and after another moment his hand crept back to his side and he looked away.

Then the file began moving again; and off he went with the rest – and he never looked back.

To say that I was dumbfounded is putting it very low. Why China should have spared me, I could not think; indeed, I was quite unable to marshal my wits, and it was my instinct that told me to seize the chance of escape which he had bestowed. But, of course, I dared not move till the file of men had gone by.

Now my tree stood some twenty paces from where the forecourt began, so that, as the last man passed me, the first stepped on to the cobbles and out of the wood. Wild as I was to be gone, I was afraid to come down till the last man had disappeared, for my only way down was the way by which I had mounted, and that, as luck would have it, was on the wrong side of the tree.

In a fever, I watched the file dwindle, until about six men were left. Then some order was barked, and to my utter dismay, the six men turned about and the file began to come back.

I now gave myself up for lost, for, in my impatience, I had started to leave my perch; and, though more exposed than before, I could not return, for the eye will notice movement more quickly than anything else.

I remember shutting my eyes and waiting for the sudden exclamation which would mean that I had been seen.

But none came. I heard only the regular tramp of the file of men going by. And when at last I ventured to look, it was nearly gone....

As the last man passed out of my view, I began to count ten. I counted twelve, to be sure. And then I went down that trunk, as a fireman goes down his pole.

As my feet touched the ground, there was China beside me, finger to lip.

" 'Op it," he whispered hoarsely. "Now's yer chance. I don't bear you no malice. Besides, *I'm coming along.*"

And there the scales fell from my eyes. China had seen a chance of turning his coat.

"All right," I said. "Follow me."

When we were clear of the woods, I led the way over a meadow and through a gap in its hedge.

"And now," I said, "what's your game?"

China regarded me.

"I could," he said, "I could 'ave gave you away: an' you'd be mutton by now, or else tied up in a tender an' on your way to the Slosh."

"That's true enough," said I. "What I want to know is – why didn't you do it?"

"Twenty to one," said China, wagging his head. "You wouldn' 'ave stood an earthly – not if I'd gave you away."

"Why didn't you?" I demanded.

"Wot d'yer think?" said China. " 'Cos o' yer ruby lips?" He closed an eye and laid a hand to his nose. "Fair does, cully. I — well saved your life."

"My God," I said, "will you tell me why you did it?"

"Yes," declared China, "I will. When I see you up in that fork, my instink was to give the — alarm. An' then your guardiang angel stays my 'and. 'Don' be a B.F.,' he says. 'Don' kill the golding goose. You scratch this —'s back, an' 'e'll scratch yours. He's got your — passport. An' if you save 'is life – well, wot price the ole school-tie? 'Arrer an' Eting, they never let no one down.' Then again I seen you sock Forecast, an' I owed you one for that."

I tried not to laugh.

"We must talk this over," I said. "If we give you your passport back, you must open your mouth."

"Treat me fair, sir," said China, "an' I'll come clean. I'm smartin', I am, for I've had a — raw deal. Brought out here to interpret, an' tied up in bloody murder before I 'ave time to think. An' the —s can't speak their own language.... But you won't treat me like that."

"I won't ask you to interpret," I said.

"I've save your life," said China. "Are you goin' to let me down?"

"Certainly not," said I. "But, life or no, if you try to double-cross me, I'll break your neck."

"Naughty, naughty," said China, poking his chin. He threw a glance over his shoulder. "But I'd like to move on a bit, sir. I don' want no search-parties out."

And there I saw Mansel running – but not from the woods. And behind him were George and Carson....

I bade China stay where he was, and ran to meet them.

"A prisoner?" said Mansel, panting.

"A turn-coat," said I. "But, by God, he saved my life."

"You must tell me later. I'm not surprised to see him. I rather thought he'd rat if he got the chance. But I'm devilish glad to see you. When I heard you'd gone back to the lodge I got the shock of my life."

"Sorry," said I. "But I had a report to make."

"I know. You did quite right. But you might have met it badly."

"Tell me – is Bell all right?"

"Yes. He's safe at the farm." He raised his voice. "China!"

China shambled forward and touched his hat.

"I've got you covered," said Mansel. "Put up your hands."

"Look here..."

"Do as I say," snapped Mansel.

China did as he said.

"Go over him, Carson," said Mansel.

Carson went over China and took his pistol away.

"And now we can talk," said Mansel. "I understand that you saved Mr Chandos' life."

"In a manner of speakin' I did."

"Say 'sir' when you speak to me."

"I beg your parding, sir."

"That's better. And you want to leave the service of Mr Cain?"

"I'll say I do – sir."

"And you'd like your passport back – and twenty-five quid?"

"That's good enough, sir. I'm reelly better at 'ome."

Mansel's lips twitched.

"You shall have them both," he said. "And if you like to talk, you shall have a bit more. But no funny business, China, for before you can pull your stuff, I'll have ironed you out."

"That's all right, sir," said China. "I've seen the way you work, an' I know where I am with you. Give me 'Arrer an' Eting." He jerked a thumb at me. "They learn 'em to 'it, don't they? Forecast's got such a squint he's afraid to shave."

"That'll do," said Mansel. "Take him back to the car, Carson." As the two moved off, "Come on. Let's follow along. We may as well be out of range by the time that China is missed."

As we went, I told my tale and showed the maps I had taken out of the *coupé-de-ville*. And when George and Mansel saw them, they clapped me upon the back. And then Mansel explained the manoeuvres which I had seen in the wood.

"As you have reason to know, Cain and Forecast arrived at the lodge on foot. At once they began to discuss where the traps should go. They argued a bit and Cain threw his weight about, but they hadn't got very far, before Saul fetched up.

"Swine as he is, you've got to hand it to Saul. He's got a brain and he doesn't waste any words. He heard Cain out: then he called the head forester up.

" 'Am I right in thinking,' he said, 'that there are no paths through these woods?'

" 'Your Highness is right.'

" 'Then make four paths forthwith and lay one trap upon each.'

"The head forester stared.

" 'Make four paths, Highness?'

" 'Those were my words,' said Saul. 'Think for yourself, man. How is a path made? By a man who walks the same way two hundred times. By two men who walk the same way one hundred times. By twenty men who walk the same way ten times. Call in your pickets and make up your twenty men. March them five times to and fro and you have your path.'

" 'It shall be done, Highness.'

"So that was that. Having cut the Gordian knot in very much less than one minute, Saul declared his intention of moving on. Cain wanted to stay and have a look at the lodge; but on learning that, if he did, he would have to walk home, he and Forecast climbed into the *coupé-de-ville*. Saul's certainly twisting his tail: I've never seen a man offered such studied offence.

"Now I should like to have stayed and have used the luminous paint; but I didn't fancy sharing those woods with twenty foresters; still less did I like the idea of your coming back with the paint, not knowing that they were there: and as I had now been told where to look for the traps, I thought I had better get out while the going was good. And so I withdrew and moved south, proposing, of course, to meet you. George and Carson were early, for George found a painter just coming out of his shop. And I met them at a quarter to two, two miles and a half from here. And then I learned that you had gone back to the lodge." He sighed. "And so I – retraced my steps. I suppose I have moved faster, but I can't remember when."

And not until he said that, did I begin to feel tired. Yet, when we had worked it out, we found that, since we had left the Rolls, I had covered near twenty-five miles and he rather more than nineteen.

At seven o'clock that evening, when we were refreshed, Mansel sent for China and questioned him for two hours.

Much that he said was irrelevant; some, we were sure, was untrue; but he did make some things clear and gave us some information that we were very glad to receive.

Even if I could remember it, to set down all he said would be waste of time; and so I shall only record such parts of his cross-examination as we found valuable.

"You came out of the hostel?" said Mansel. "The hostel that Forecast runs?"

"I 'appened to be there, sir."

"At the time you were wanted?"

"Yes, sir."

"As were Boney and Gulf?"

"Yes, sir."

"All three of you old lags."

"Not me, sir. My record's clean."

"And Boney and Gulf?"

"I think they 'ad been in trouble once or twice."

"Is the hostel open to all?"

"I wouldn't say that, sir. I think you 'as to be known."

"Who is – eligible for admission?"

China shrugged his shoulders.

"Out-of-works, sir – like me."

"Out-of-jugs, like Boney," said Mansel.

"There were one or two."

"And when somebody wanted something rather – er – exceptional done, he got into touch with Forecast, and Forecast provided the men?"

"Biretta and Cain did that."

"On many occasions?"

"I know three or four."

Mansel addressed George and me.

"And this place posed as a charitable institution in the heart of London in the twentieth century. If you want a waiter, you ring up Harrods. If you want a burglar, you ring up Orion. The only wonder is they didn't advertise."

He returned to China.

"Now tell me this. Six weeks ago, more or less, Boney and Gulf were sent out to Latchet to bump Major Bowshot off. But they didn't do it, did they?"

"In course they did," cried China.

"Then what's all the trouble about?"

"Well, there ain't no body – sir. Boney an' Gulf, they left it out in the road – to give the idea that 'e'd bin knock down by a car. An' some body-snatcher pinched it."

"Well, what does that matter," said Mansel, "so long as they know he's dead?"

"Ah," said China, "that's wot we wanted to know – me an' Boney an' Gulf. Before we came out, I mean. We didn' fancy Latchet. If you iron a bloke out on Barnes Common, you don't choose Barnes for a picnic for two or three months. So we 'as a show-down with Forecast: an' after we'd called 'is bluff, 'e spills the beans.

"Wot Boney an' Gulf 'ad bin tole was that the Dook 'ad gone to Worsteds an' given them instructions to get Bowshot put away. Bowshot was after the Duchess, so 'e said, an' 'e didn' want no scandal, an' this was the best way out. Well they do the job an' come 'ome. But Worsteds won't pay up, because they 'aven't 'eard that the body's bin found. Well, Boney an' Gulf get sore. 'Body be –,' they says. 'Let the Dook enquire at Latchet. 'E'll soon see whether Bowshot's missin' or not.' Well, that's fair enough. But Biretta an' Cain says no. 'Missin's no good,' they says. 'The Dook must 'ave proof o' death: an' you got to go back an' get it – an' get it quick.' Well, that didn't make sense: an' when he sees we're not playin'. Forecast opens 'is mouth.

"The troof was this. It was Biretta an' Cain as wanted Bowshot outed – an' they didn' know 'ow to do it. An' then along comes the Dook an' plays right into their 'ands. They make a song an' dance fer the look o' the thing: but in fac' they're 'uggin' themselves, for the Dook's goin' to pay them big money fer 'elpin' them out of a jam. So far, so good. An' then some body-snatcher chucks a spanner into the works.... The Dook don't want no proof; but Biretta an' Cain *must 'ave it* – an' 'ave it quick. If they can't get it, they're sunk. Wiv proof of Bowshot's death, they can put over 'is will, an' no questions asked: but when a —'s missin', it seems you got to go to the Court: an' the Court appoints a busy to look after 'is affairs. An' Worsteds don' wan't no busies lookin' after Bowshot's affairs. 'Cos why? 'Cos they blown 'is fortune – the dirty dogs."

"And what of the will?" said Mansel.

"Easy money," said China. "It mayn't be wot Bowshot wanted, nor it mayn't say wot Bowshot said: but 'e won't be there to say so. Bowshot's cold. 'E can't rise up an' say, 'I never lef' five thousan' quid to the 'Ostel – an' the rest o' my worlly goods to Biretta an' Cain.'"

"Very illuminating," said Mansel. "They're a couple of lads, aren't they – Biretta an' Cain?"

China described them at some length.

"Listen," said Mansel. "Forecast told you all this: but how did Forecast know?"

China looked over his shoulder.

Then –

"Biretta's clerk tole him; but Cain don' know that we know. Lady confidential clerk. If you like to 'ave a dame in your office, that's wot you get."

"I see. And Forecast?"

"Forecast's sittin' pretty. 'Five thousan' quid to the 'Ostel.' An' if they don' double that, 'e's goin' to contes' the will."

"Very nice," said Mansel. "And where do you come in?"

"You gimme my passport," said China, "an' I'll show 'em where I come in."

"Tell me this," said Mansel. "Can Cain speak German at all?"

"Not like wot I can," said China. " 'E tried the landlady, but 'e very soon give it up."

"I take it he's worried," said Mansel.

"I'll say 'e is. First, you got them papers, an' 'e don' feel too good about that. Next, 'e knows any moment Bowshot's goin' to be missed. 'E don' put it like that, o' course: 'e makes out 'e can't wait, 'cos every day 'e spends 'ere is costin' 'im seventy quid. An' then the Dook treatin' 'im like somethin' the cat brought 'ome.... 'E's only got one idea, an' that is to iron you out. Wiv you ironed out, 'e's safe. 'E'll find the corpse the nex' day. 'E's keeping Gulf fer that. Goin' to plant 'im by Latchet any time now.... Gawd, the day 'e got here! Did you send that — wire?"

"Maybe," said Mansel, smiling. "I suppose there was some misunderstanding."

"You can call it that," said China. "We was talkin' differen' tongues for the first 'alf-hour."

"Tell me," said Mansel. "Who is to occupy the hunting-lodge?"

"We was," said China. "Me an' Cain an' Forecast an' four or five men. An' work from there – I don' think." He closed an eye and laid a hand to his nose. "Now this is worf fifty quid, but I'll leave it to you. 'Work from there' be —. They're out to draw you there. You know wot I mean – decoy. An' don' you do it, sir. If you miss them — man-traps, you'll foul the electric tape: an' then, 'avin' give the alarm, you'll come to a nempty 'ouse. An' a woman screamin' somewhere.... But if you go in, you'll never come out alive."

There was a little silence.

Then –

"Well, I'm much obliged, China," said Mansel. "You'll have your passport tomorrow and leave for England at noon. You'll have ten quid at the station, before you go; and a letter to an agent of mine. Take that letter to him, and he'll pay you a tenner a week for the next six weeks – provided you keep your mouth shut. If you don't, the money will stop, and still worse things may befall. I've got your finger-prints" – China started – "they're on that paper there that Carson gave you to read: and the moment you give any trouble, I send them and have them checked at Scotland Yard. And I'll give you a piece of advice. I should give the hostel a miss. It might be raided one day – you never know."

"Can't I touch Biretta and Cain?"

"Not for six weeks. If you do, you lose your dough."

"But if they put over that will..."

"They won't," said Mansel, quietly.

China looked at him very hard.

Then –

"Time I was goin'," he said. "I've lef' me goloshes at 'ome."

# IX

## THE NET IS SPREAD

Early next morning George and Rowley escorted China to Salzburg: and George drew China's passport and Rowley saw the rogue off by the midday train. Whilst he was at the Bank, in view of what China had said, George drew Gulf's passport as well: but he lodged that of Cain.

(Here perhaps I should say that in a note to the Bank, Mansel had directed that the papers there lodged for safe custody were to be handed not only to him, but to George or to me on demand: so long, therefore, as one of us three survived, the papers could be conveyed to Scotland Yard.)

Whether Cain ever knew of the action which China had taken, I cannot tell. So far as I know, except by the farmer's wife, he was not seen with us; and I doubt if he was found to be missing until night fell. By night no search could be made: and soon after dawn the next morning, China was well away. But I think that his disappearance must have troubled both Saul and Cain, for the rogue knew far too much; and I have little doubt that, had he stayed in their service and had they brought us down, they would have taken care that he never saw England again.

Whilst he was in Salzburg, George called at the nursing-home, spent half an hour with the Duchess and brought back with him her answer to Mansel's note.

*... I am quite sure that, had John been alive, he would have beggared himself to buy Beehive. I know that his solicitors had standing instructions to let him know if ever they had an inkling that Beehive was to come up for sale. He did not like the lord of the manor and always considered that the latter failed in his duty....*

When Mansel had read this, he nodded.

"And so," he said, "the last fragment of the jig-saw clicks into place.

"If China may be believed – and I think he may – Biretta and Cain have converted John Bowshot's fortune to their own use. Now, how do defaulting solicitors go to work? Nearly always like this. They choose an easygoing client, who, so long as he gets his income, is only too glad for them to look after his affairs. They then dispose of his capital. But they don't dispose of it all, for, unless his income is paid, the client will smell a rat. They dispose of, say, two-thirds. And they go on paying the income out of the third that remains. Of course when that third is exhausted, the balloon is bound to go up: but till then the defaulters are safe; and, before it happens, they sail for some destination which is unknown. In fact, there's only one snag – and that is that the client may say that he wants some capital. Which is, of course, precisely what Bowshot did – or was intending to do.

"One fine day he tells Biretta and Cain that he means to buy Beehive if Beehive is ever for sale. In other words, he warns them that he may require at short notice some thirty or forty or fifty thousand pounds. Well, Beehive isn't for sale, and they hope for the best. But they damned well keep their ears open, as Bowshot told them to do. And then this summer, the sword of Damocles falls; for it comes to their knowledge that Beehive will be in the market before the autumn is out.

"Well, something's got to be done, for penal servitude is looming unpleasantly close. No more years of grace for

Biretta and Cain. Less than six months, perhaps – unless they can manage to put John Bowshot away. And just as they're wondering how they can bring this off, Saul walks into their office and asks them to rub him out.

"And there you have the whole thing....

"They consent to do Saul's bidding – no doubt at a hell of a price. They fake a will. They tell Forecast to have the job done. And the only thing they need is proof of John Bowshot's death. That is essential, for China's law is good: and, as China put it, without such proof they are sunk.

"Well, we know that they're not going to get it; but, now that we know the truth, we may as well quicken things up. And so we'll send some wires – in John Bowshot's name. Give me a pad, William. I'll rough them out."

The telegrams he there and then drafted shall speak for themselves.

The first we sent that evening, addressing it to the lawyers whom the lord of the manor of Beehive had charged with the sale; for their name had appeared in the advertisement which we had seen in *The Times*.

*Messrs. Collard Brodie and Thane, New Square, Lincoln's Inn, London*

*Please let me know the very lowest price which your client is prepared to accept for the Beehive estate*

*John Bowshot*

*Poste Restante, Villach, Austria.*

The reply to this ran as follows:

*Major John Bowshot, Poste Restante, Villach, Austria*

*Very lowest price thirty seven thousand five hundred pounds*

Collards

That we received the next morning, when Mansel at once dispatched his second and third.

This was how they ran:

*Collards, New Square, Lincolns Inn, London*

*Very well stop will pay thirty seven thousand five hundred pounds stop please get in touch with my solicitors Worsteds of Jawbone Place stop I am instructing them by telegram to pay you ten per cent of purchase price forthwith and to take all steps necessary to complete sale stop acknowledge to me at Schloss Varvic, by Villach, Austria*

JOHN BOWSHOT

*Worsteds, Jawbone Place, London*

*Have arranged to purchase Beehive estate for thirty seven thousand five hundred pounds stop please pay Collards of New Square, Lincolns Inn, ten per cent of purchase price forthwith and sell out sufficient of my securities to pay balance on completion stop take all necessary steps to complete in conjunction with Collards stop writing*

JOHN BOWSHOT

To all the consequences of the dispatch of these telegrams, I cannot speak with any certainty: but I think it is fair to assume that the emotions provoked at Varvic by Collards' reply must have been almost as unpleasant as those already prevailing in Jawbone Place. For Mansel had brought a third party into the ring. And that party was Collards – a firm of the highest repute, who would be very pleased to have sold the Beehive estate by private treaty and so to have saved their client the expense of a sale by auction which might have been held in vain.

Be that as it may, it was clear that the blow would fall upon Biretta in Jawbone Place at least some three or four hours before it fell upon Cain: for Cain would know nothing until Collards' reply reached Varvic. And it seemed much more than likely that Biretta, so stricken, would instantly wire to Cain. It was less likely, but still quite possible, that Biretta was not yet aware that Cain had left Latchet for Varvic three days before; in which case he would wire to Latchet....

In fact, that was just what he did: and we picked the wire up, in Cain's name, at four o'clock.

This is how it ran:

*Cain, The Inn, Latchet, by Villach, Austria*

*Beg that you will return immediately stop things passing rapidly beyond my control stop report rendered by Forecast's people manifestly untrue stop our client is in touch with Collards and has agreed to purchase Beehive estate*

*Biretta*

To this frantic communication, Mansel replied at once, and Bell sent the wire from Latchet before that post office closed.

*Biretta, Worsteds, Jawbone Place, London*

*Your wire received stop everything satisfactorily arranged stop write Collards confirming agreement to purchase and leave for Latchet at once stop we can return together at end of this week*

*Cain*

"And there you are," said Mansel. "It may or may not come off. It certainly won't come off if Biretta is in his right mind. But I don't think he is. I think he's beside himself. And so he may do as he's told. And that will mean fun and games, for we can be at Latchet when he arrives."

It was upon Monday morning that George had driven to Salzburg and it was upon Tuesday evening that Mansel had wired to Biretta, bidding him leave for Latchet without delay; but during these two days we had not wasted our time. With the help of the large-scale map we had reconnoitred the country which neighboured the hunting-lodge: this, with infinite care and three at a time: in this way each one of us six had been able to make two full reconnaissances, each four or five hours long:

and I am ready to swear that, when night fell on Tuesday no man in Saul's service could have found his way in that region as well as could we. But we had not been out by night. And so on Tuesday night Mansel and George and I went out again to study that slice of country under the stars.

Perhaps because we were so well accustomed to moving by night, we found the exercise simple and made our way to and fro wherever we pleased: and so, at the end of two hours, we left the woods and meadows and took to the road. This, because for two days we had not gone near the drive which led to the lodge, and we felt that, if we could approach it, we might learn something that we should be glad to know.

Here perhaps I should say that, so far as we knew, the enemy was not aware that we knew of the lodge's existence; for this he can hardly be blamed, for, had I not seen Forecast's map some ten days before, we should not have known of the place, and though we might have remarked the mouth of the drive, this differed very little from scores of tracks we had noticed but had not explored.

We struck the road a mile south of the hunting-lodge; and we moved in absolute silence, in single file, "for don't forget," said Mansel, "that the foresters may be out, and their eyes and their ears are trained to catch the slightest movement of man or beast."

The road was by no means straight, and we had to round several bends before coming to the mouth of the drive. The last of these lay very close to the mouth, and as Mansel began to round it, I saw him stop. For a moment or two he stood still: then he returned and came back.

"There's a light ahead," he breathed. "It isn't moving, and I don't yet know where it is; but I don't think it's right in the mouth. And now let's go on. We'll walk in the middle of the road. I shall watch our front and our right; George will watch our left and William our left and our rear."

This made very good sense, for the drive lay to our right; if, therefore, there was an ambush, it would probably be to our left. But, since I did as he said, I did not see for myself all that I am about to relate. But Mansel told me later.

We moved forward very slowly, about four paces apart, until Mansel was very close to the mouth of the drive. There he stood very still for five minutes or more. Then we heard a man clear his throat. The sound came from the mouth of the drive, and at once Mansel turned to the opposite side of the road. There he lay down by the ditch, and we did the same. And then he began to move forward, until he could look up the drive.

The light he had seen was burning a little way up the drive, directly beyond a slight bend. The impression it gave was this – that some car, with its headlights dipped, was about to round the bend on its way towards the mouth of the drive, and, had we gone by in a car, instead of on foot, we must have observed the light and have so interpreted it. But in fact the light was not moving. More. When you studied the beam, you saw it was limited. It shone upon the roadway, but nowhere else: and so, to avoid it was easy; for a man could walk up the drive and then step into the woods, move on past the beam and then back to the drive. At least, it seemed that he could...

Many men know the value of waiting: but few, I think, are prepared to use that knowledge as Mansel always did. His patience was infinite – and was almost invariably rewarded as it deserved. On this occasion he knew that the man who had cleared his throat would eventually go away or would be relieved; to observe such a movement, he was ready to wait all night, because he desired to see how the man behaved as he went – whether he stuck to the drive or entered the woods.

For over an hour and a quarter we lay beside that ditch, always ready, at the sound of some car, to slip down out of sight; but in all that time nothing happened, except that now and again the sentinel cleared his throat.

And then at last a figure, moving towards us, whipped into and out of the beam a little way up the drive.

Now whoever it was did not proceed at once to the mouth of the drive. Though, of course, we could not see him, I think he was probably listening for any sound of a car. If I am right, I suppose he was satisfied, for after three or four minutes, he used his torch. He used his torch to examine the sides of the drive; and the light of his torch showed us that each of the sides was wired. They were wired waist-high with barbed wire; of this there were three strands, and all of the strands were strained. A man could step over them, but only by holding them down; he could pass between or below them, but only by holding them up.

The man did not touch the wire, but only examined it: then he came on down the drive and spoke to the sentinel. He spoke in German, of course: but while I could hear his words, Mansel understood what they meant.

"Has a car been by?"

"No, sir."

"Anyone on foot?"

"No, sir."

The torch was lighted.

"Look at your watch and tell me what time it says."

"Ten minutes to one, sir."

The torch was put out.

"Well, listen. You will now return to the lodge and report to Hans. You will tell him that at five minutes past one, according to your watch, I am going to test the wires by the side of the drive. If all is in order, the signal light should go out. He will not rouse the others, because he will know it is me: but he will at once send Kleiner to restore the connection which I shall have broken in two. If the signal light does not go out at five or six minutes past, then Kleiner and Boll will come out to find and repair the fault. And now repeat those instructions."

The sentinel did so.

"Off with you then, and be back at half-past two. And don't loiter about in that beam."

"Very good, sir."

With that, the fellow withdrew, and after a moment or two, passed into and out of the beam. And such is the way of the world that, as soon as his subordinate was out of the way, the other took out matches and lighted a cigarette.

Nothing could have been better – from our point of view, for now we could see where he was and watch every movement he made.

After a little he began to stroll up the drive – and before I could think, Mansel was over the road. George had time to join him, before the man turned; but I stayed on the other side, only moving forward, until I could see up the drive.

I saw the man turn and come back, and glanced at my wrist. It was almost one o'clock – by the sentinel's watch. Right down the drive he strolled and into the road. There he stood, with his hands in his pockets, looking to right and to left, four paces from where I lay.

And then he turned about... and, as he turned, Mansel hit him... right on the point... the very deuce of a blow.

George and I picked him up and carried him into the drive. It was Saul's valet – the great, big brute that I had seen in the garage, less than a fortnight before.

"Come," said Mansel, and led the way up the drive.

At exactly five minutes past one, according to the sentinel's watch, he set his foot on the middle strand of the wire, pressing it down firmly before letting it go. And then we moved up to the bend, and waited just clear of the beam.

The beam was thrown by a powerful acetylene lamp, attached to a tree. Over this a hood had been placed, and the hood had been so adjusted as to limit the beam to the drive.

Within ten minutes we saw the light of a torch coming down the drive from the lodge. That the man who bore it was

Kleiner there can be no doubt, for he threw its light on the post which was taking the strain of the wire which Mansel had touched. This post was of metal and was very carefully planted and heavily stayed. Three feet behind it, however, had been planted a wooden post; and from this wooden post ran a single, flexible wire. This was covered with rubber and lay on the ground. When Kleiner arrived there was nothing between the two posts, but at once he picked up two ends which he found hanging down. These he hitched together, thus making a rough connection between the two posts. Then he touched the metal post, and at once the connection gave way. Again he made his connection. Then he turned to examine the wire on the other side of the drive. But this was intact. And then he turned on his heel and began to walk back up the drive.

"Simple and effective," murmured Mansel. "Ah, well. One lives and learns. So much better to break than to make. So much more certain. And now we know. I rather suspect that these wires are China's 'tape.'" The light of Kleiner's torch disappeared round a bend. "Come along. Let's keep him in view."

We passed through the beam of the lamp and hastened along the drive, some fifty yards behind Kleiner, making his way to the lodge. Our shoes were soled with rubber, but his were not; so we closed to within twenty paces without being heard.

We saw him cross the forecourt and mount the steps of the lodge, and we saw that the door was wide open and that some light or other was burning within.

As the fellow crossed the threshold, we came to the end of the drive.

"You two, wait here," breathed Mansel, and went on alone.

Twenty seconds later, I saw the slightest movement against the glow of the light which was burning within the lodge....

Waiting there with George in the darkness, I was again assailed by that shameful feeling of fear. I was afraid for Mansel,

I was afraid for us; I felt we were probing something that ought to be left alone – trespassing upon ground that belonged to a jealous lord, who took no offence at our presence because he knew the doom that befell all trespassers. To put it another way, it seemed to me that the powers of evil were watching and, worse than that, were smiling a slow, sure smile. It was absurd, of course, for men could live and move in the house itself. And yet...

And so I was more than thankful when Mansel came back, after being gone a quarter of an hour – which had seemed like three-quarters to me.

He said nothing then and we made our way back down the drive, to find the valet still senseless and flat on his back.

This time I went through his pockets. He carried two heavy pistols, and both of these we took. And his name was Frederick Auger, as one or two letters showed.

"And now," said Mansel, "let's save the blackguard's face. Don't think I want to help him – I've seen his type before. He's German inside and out. But he is a moral coward, as every German is. And that is just what we want. So turn him over and drag him along on his stomach to the wire."

We did as he said.

Then Mansel took Auger's hand and hitched the palm on to a barb on the strand of the wire. And then he pressed the wire down.

"And this," he said, smiling, "is where we clear out at a run."

With that, he led the way; and George and I ran behind him, out of the drive and back the way we had come.

After half a mile or so, Mansel dropped into a walk.

"Tell me this," he said. "Do you both understand why I did what I did with Herr Auger?"

"I think I do," said George.

"So do I," said I, "but I'd rather you said right out."

"Those who find him," said Mansel, "are bound to observe the posture in which he lies. He is lying flat on his face with one hand caught up on the wire. That will at once suggest that, such was his sense of duty, although he was passing out, he managed to crawl to the wire and give the alarm. Now two alarms were given – one at five minutes past one and one at two o'clock. Those who find Auger wall assume that he gave the first, that then for fifty-five minutes he did his sentinel stuff and that then he was struck down from behind and gave his lovely performance of 'Faithful unto death.' Now if Auger told them the truth – that in fact he gave *neither* alarm, they would at once perceive that we knew a great deal too much. But, because he is German, he will not tell them the truth. Moral cowardice and vanity will have their way with him: and, rather than let himself down, Auger will let them believe what he knows to be false." He shrugged his shoulders. "I may be wrong, but I know the Boche pretty well. And if I am right, the enemy will assume that we were only on for two minutes – instead of for more than an hour.

"And now for the lodge.

"I didn't go in, but I had a good look at the hall. This is a strange apartment. It's some sixty feet long by thirty, and two floors high. The walls are tapestried and the floor is of polished oak. I couldn't see any doors except at the farther end, where there seemed to be two: but I think there must be others, cut in the tapestry, for I saw no sign of Kleiner and I don't think he had had time to go the length of the hall before I arrived. Right at the end of the hall there's a very grand staircase – a broad flight up to a landing some twelve feet high, and from there two flights, one running up to the right and one to the left. It would make a good place to dance in: the band could be up on the landing, out of the way. But it's not the sort of apartment which you would expect to find in a hunting-lodge. Of course there's no furniture, but that is natural enough."

"No watchman's chairs?" said I.

"Not there. That doesn't altogether surprise me, for the hall is without a fireplace, and watchmen like a fire. Besides, it was the reverse of cosy. Dank, gloomy, cheerless and colder within than without. I should think the tapestries were mouldering; but I couldn't see details like that, for the only lamp there was hanging down from the ceiling over the stairs. But the smell of decay was unmistakable.

"Well, then I left the steps and went round the house. Two cars – one of them Forecast's – stood in the stable-yard. But I really went to see if, supposing we came in force, we could approach that way. Quite apart from the man-traps, I don't think we could – by night. So I crossed the forecourt again and tried the other side. But I don't think we could make it, except by day.

"I should like to have placed the guard-room. I should say it's in one of the rooms on the right or the left of the hall – one of those looking on to the forecourt. And, as I said just now, its door is probably cut in the tapestry. But I could hear no sound, and I saw no light. If I could have used my torch, I might have been able to see where the wire ran in. But of course I couldn't do that. China didn't know, because I told Carson to ask him. He couldn't give any details of what was in store for us. He'd heard Cain and Forecast talking – which was how he knew as much as he did. Still, what we have seen tonight bears out what he said. Their object is to decoy us into that house. But it's no good getting us in, unless they are ready to receive us: hence the stratagem – the beam confined to the drive to force us to touch the wire. It looks very feeble now, because we have been conducted behind the scenes: but in fact it's rather clever, for nine out of ten would assume that somewhere or other a sentry was watching the beam.

"Any way, we've got a step farther, for, if we have done little else, we have at least assured them of what they were anxious to know. And that is that we are aware that they are to be found – not at Varvic, but at the end of that drive."

"To be perfectly honest," said George, "I dislike that place; and, to be still more frank, I don't fancy mixing it there. It is for me the very lair of foreboding. I don't wonder they've chosen it as a place of execution. As such, it has all the qualities. But I hope very much that you won't endorse their choice."

Mansel laughed.

"You needn't worry," he said. "If I can help it, I'll never do battle there. That place is accursed. They propose to decoy. Well and good. But they are up against time, while we are not. And when they find we're not playing, they'll have to do something else. And that will be the moment to help them. After all, two can decoy. And when we take that line, there are several suitable places within two miles of those woods. I confess that a thirst for knowledge took me up to the lodge tonight. And you two unfortunates with me. But in a show like this I set great store by studying the enemy's methods and all he does. If it does nothing else, it teaches you what to expect. Besides, one day we might have to go there – against our will. And now we know something of the lay-out."

"Every time," said George. "But from the casual way in which you pushed off all alone to smell out the curtilage, I felt that you must be proof against its horrid alarms. And so I felt bound to inform you that in that odious vicinity, do what I will, my morale is not at its best. I don't believe any dog would approach that place."

"The woods are birdless," I said.

"That's quite true," said Mansel. "I'd noticed that."

"Ugh," said George. "Let's talk about something attractive, just for a change. I expect Gulf's planted by now. When is the exhumation? I mean, I'd hate to miss that."

"I don't think," said Mansel, laughing, "we need go as far as that. But I'd like to know where he lies, for then we can add his passport to his remains. Wrap it up in a bit of oil-silk, and shove it under the turf. Just in case of accidents."

"Splendid," said George. "Just the job to do before breakfast. I'll tell you what. Let's try and locate the grave and wait till Biretta comes. If he's brought his spade and pail with him, we'll take him there for a run. And then when he's nearly home, we'll tell him it's Gulf."

"If he comes," said Mansel, "you shall do with him what you will. But don't take our luck for granted. One of these days the fine weather's going to break."

As though to deny this precept, some eight hours later. Bell drove into Latchet and picked up a wire for Cain. And this was from Biretta, to say that he should reach Villach at half-past two the next day.

# X

## AND SATAN CAME ALSO

Now though we had spoken lightly the night before, if China had told us the truth and Cain in fact intended to bury Gulf's body by Latchet, it was important that we should spoil his game. We had certainly told him that, if any body was found, we should go to the British Consul without delay: but we did not want to do that, if for no other reason, because, if we did, the case would pass out of our hands and persons other than we would deal with Cain and the Duke. And Cain was not now in the mood to care about threats. The man must be very near desperate: and the telegram from Collards might well push him over the edge. After all, Bowshot was missing: and if some body was found which bore his name and address, incriminating papers or no, it might be hard to disprove that that body was his.

China had said on Sunday that Cain was 'keeping Gulf' and was 'going to plant him by Latchet any day now.' And now it was Wednesday. All things considered, it seemed much more than likely that, during the last two days, the burial had taken place. And since we had nothing to do until Biretta arrived, George and I set out, with Rowley and Bell, to prove the ground we had proved when first we came, that is to say, the ground which neighboured the path which led from Latchet up to the Salzburg road.

As we had done in those days, we did again. We took the Salzburg road and we berthed the car in the track which nobody seemed to use. And then we walked up to where the two tracks crossed, to take the second track and so come back to the road. And there our quest was ended before it had fairly begun, for, a few feet beyond the cross, where the track turned into a ride, the turf had been sliced and lifted and then stamped back into place.

After all, it was not surprising that they had chosen this place. Forecast had excellent reason to remember the second track, and the spot was very private and favoured the work to be done, for a car could be driven right up to the very side of the grave.

"No doubt about that," said George. "Get the implements, Rowley. Oh, and take my coat, will you? And shove it into the car."

"That's all right, sir," said Rowley. "You and Mr Chandos, keep watch. Bell and I'll do it quicker than you."

And so it was.

As a matter of fact, the business was very soon done, for the body was covered by scarcely a foot of earth. Still, Bell and Rowley were men who never did things by halves, and when Bell came to ask for Gulf's passport, he gave me a dirty envelope bearing John Bowshot's address.

"Well done indeed," said I.

"It was easy enough, sir. It was in the first pocket we come to. Shall I put the passport there?"

"Yes," said I, and, with that, I took out matches and burned the envelope up.

Forty-five minutes later we were back at the farm.

Well before dawn the next morning, Mansel and Carson went out again with the Rolls. According to Mansel, they went 'to have a look round.' But when he said that he meant to leave the Rolls at Four Mile Point, I knew that once again he was bound for the hunting-lodge: for, when we had surveyed the country surrounding the lodge, we had always left the cars in a coppice four miles south-east of the place and, for the sake of convenience, had given this spot the name of Four Mile Point.

To my relief they were back by nine o'clock; but they did not say what they had done, but only that, just before seven, Cain and Forecast and Auger had left the lodge for the castle in Forecast's car. This left no doubt in our minds that they hoped to draw us by night to the hunting-lodge. And I think they had reasoned like this – first, that they wished to fight us upon their ground; then, that we were not such fools as to try to attack a castle with forty-foot walls; then, that the lodge was easy enough to enter; and then that, by night, it was easy enough to approach without being observed. This reasoning was good enough, so far as it went: but they were up against time, while we were not; and so there was no reason why we should do as they wished. In a word, we preferred to fight them upon *our* ground. Moreover, there is a saying, 'In vain the net is spread in the sight of any bird.'

George and I were upon the platform, when Biretta's train steamed in. But we were only in reserve. The duty of meeting the man had been given to Bell; and very well he did it, picking him out before I could and touching his hat to the blackguard and taking his suitcase and rug.

"Well, Saul may take to him," said George; "but somehow I don't think he will."

Biretta was truly repulsive. He was short and fat and greasy and overdressed. His skin was very swarthy, his hair was black and he had a way of pursing his heavy lips. His face was fleshy, his eyes were small and close-set, and his air was very pompous, as is the way of small fry when an unfamiliar greatness is thrust upon them. Indeed, he received Bell's attentions with great contempt, addressing him very rudely and walking out of the station as though resenting the fact that a man so far beneath him should have to show him the way.

Without, the Rolls was waiting, with Carson standing stiffly by one of its doors; but Biretta ignored his salute and entered the car. Bell put in his things, and Carson shut the door: then they took their seats in front and the car moved off.

Though Biretta did not know it, the Rolls was bound for Goschen, and Carson drove there slowly, that George and I, in the Lowland, might get there first. So all was in order before the Rolls arrived.

Mansel and George were in the parlour; and I was seated outside an open window, so that, though I could not be seen, I could hear all that passed. (In fact, I saw everything, too, for Biretta's back was towards me for the whole of the time.)

At last the door was opened, and Rowley ushered Biretta into the room.

The man stared upon Mansel and then upon George.

Then Mansel spoke with an accent.

"Be seated, Mr Biretta. I have some questions to ask."

"What does this mean?" said Biretta. "And where is Cain?"

"Mr Cain is in Salzburg," said Mansel. "His arrest was effected yesterday afternoon."

Biretta collapsed.

I do not mean that he fell, though how his legs held him up I shall never know. But his face and his body sagged, and the airs which he had put on fell away as a cloak falls away, when the fastening about the shoulders has been released. A hand went up, as though to cover his mouth.

Mansel indicated a chair.

"Be seated," he said.

Biretta swayed to the chair and sat down on its edge. He was breathing hard, and his face was shining with sweat.

Mansel stepped to the table behind which George was sitting, pencil in hand.

Then he spoke in German.

"The notes of the interview," he said.

George gave him the notes we had made of his conversation with Cain just six days ago.

Mansel returned to Biretta.

"Mr Cain," he said, "insists that he had nothing to do with – a certain affair."

"A – a certain affair?" said Biretta.

"Major Bowshot's attempted murder."

Biretta wiped the sweat from his face.

"I will read you his words," said Mansel. " 'The first that I knew of this business was when a wire signed WENSLEY was brought to me the Saturday before last. Biretta, my partner, was cruising. I sent for his managing clerk and asked what it meant. Then the whole story came out. I was inexpressibly shocked—' "

"It's a filthy lie," mouthed Biretta.

Mansel shrugged his shoulders.

"That remains to be seen," he said, coldly. "Mr Cain was most definite. He has made and signed a statement to that effect."

"May I see it?" said Biretta.

Mansel shook his head.

"That would not be in order. But he made it perfectly clear that, had you been available, he would never have come; but that, since you were not available—"

"I saw him off at Croydon – if that's any good."

Mansel looked at him sharply.

"But Duke Saul is your client?"

"He's just as much Cain's."

"But Mr Cain said—"

"I don't care what he said. He's a filthy liar, I tell you."

Mansel held up a hand.

"Restrain yourself, please. And listen. I first saw Mr Cain the day before yesterday. When he declared that he was deputizing for you, I said, that since you were not here to speak for yourself, I could not accept that plea: that I knew nothing of partners or partnership: that he was here on the spot and that he was deeply involved in a very serious crime. He then said this – that if I would postpone his arrest, he would telegraph to you and ask you to come. I confess I thought it unlikely that you would do as he asked. However, it seems that he was successful."

Biretta's face was working; his eyes were like slits.

Mansel proceeded, calmly.

"Unhappily, I had to order his arrest the following day. I will tell you why. A document came into my hands. This document satisfied me that some of the statements which Mr Cain had made were not in accordance with truth. This rendered the whole statement suspect, for, if what can be checked is untrue, how can we believe what we are unable to check?"

Biretta moistened his lips.

"You mean you don't believe that he wasn't in this business up to the neck?"

"I do not say that. I say only that I am not satisfied that Mr Cain is as innocent as he makes out."

Biretta mopped his face.

"D'you want me to make a statement?"

"That, Mr Biretta, will be a matter for you. But first, if you please, I have some more questions to ask. A Mr Forecast, I think, is in your employ."

Biretta swallowed.

"My firm was in touch with him."

"Please do not mistake my meaning. I said '*your* employ.' Mr Cain—"

Biretta sprang to his feet.

"For God's sake get this," he cried. "Cain is trying to climb out of this on my back. The Duke was *our* client, and Forecast was in *our* employ. I don't deny that I knew what was going on. I did. I knew everything. But this I will say, and that is that Cain took the lead. That is why, ten days ago, he came out instead of me. And now that he's in deep water..." With trembling hands, he dragged out a pocket-book and plucked forth a telegram. "Read that," he said, wildly. "Read that." Mansel took it out of his hand. "That is his lying enticement to make me come out. *Everything satisfactorily arranged... we can return together at end of week.* He doesn't say *Come out and face the music with me.*" His voice rose to a scream. "He's a treacherous hound, I tell you. And if you hadn't arrested him, he would have been over the frontier before I'd even arrived."

"I think, perhaps," said Mansel, "that that was in his mind. But, unknown to Mr Cain, I saw this telegram as soon as it had been dispatched. I found its wording suspicious. And from then, until he was arrested, his movements were watched. But that is by the way. Duke Saul of Varvic is also under arrest."

There was a moment's silence. Then –

"Has – has he made a statement?" said Biretta.

"No. He preserves complete silence. But Mr Cain, by his statement, has indicated his Highness as, what I will call, the prime mover in this most serious affair."

Biretta said nothing.

Mansel leaned forward.

"He says, shortly, that early this summer, the Duke instructed you to arrange that Major Bowshot should meet with a violent end."

Biretta wiped the sweat from his face. I observed that his head was moving, against his will.

Mansel continued quietly.

"Everyone knows that abnormal clients do give abnormal instructions. But what I could not understand was why you carried them out. I told Mr Cain as much. He replied that he could not answer for you" – Biretta stiffened – "but that he could only suppose that the Duke was to pay very well. I pointed out at once that you must have had some more powerful inducement than that: but he said that, if you had, he had no idea what it was. Now at the very time that Mr Cain was making this statement, unknown to him, his luggage was being searched. And there a paper was found – a paper which, I fear, Mr Cain had hoped to conceal."

Here Mansel spoke in German to George; and George picked up and brought him the copy of Forecast's instructions which we had made.

Mansel returned to Biretta.

"This is a copy of that paper – that is to say, of the document to which I referred just now."

He held it out for inspection. And Biretta peered at it, and then averted his eyes.

"Now when I had considered this paper, two things became clear. The first was that, as I have said, some of Mr Cain's statement was clearly untrue. And the second was that my instinct had not been at fault – that you had had some powerful inducement to carry out the instructions which you had received from the Duke. That inducement, it seemed, was this – that, quite apart from the Duke, you were only too anxious that Major Bowshot should die."

"I–I can't accept that," said Biretta.

"Can't you? Listen to this. *In all your dealings with the Duke, never lose sight of the fact that what we must have is proof of Bowshot's death. That is all you are after. But he must not realize this, for, if he were to, he would wash his hands of the matter. He must be made to believe that we are acting solely in his interests. In fact, we are using him.*"

With a manifest effort Biretta controlled his voice.

"As Major Bowshot's solicitors, it was obviously desirable that we should be in a position to prove his death."

"Convenient, desirable or – vital, Mr Biretta?"

"I–I said 'desirable.'"

Mansel's hand shot out.

"So 'desirable' that this man Forecast was to go to the length of producing some other corpse... which he had previously furnished with Major Bowshot's name and address."

Biretta made no reply. The involuntary movement of his head became more pronounced.

Mansel continued mercilessly.

"When I had read these instructions, I ordered your partner's arrest. But that was not all I did. I sent for Mr Forecast and had a conversation with him. And he, too, has signed a statement."

Biretta looked up.

"D'you know Forecast's record?" he said.

"Not yet," said Mansel. "I expect to receive it quite soon. But that is beside the point. His statement is not without interest. I'll tell you why.

"When Mr Forecast was instructed to leave for Austria to search for the corpse of a recently murdered man, he did not fancy the task. More. It seemed to him, shall we say, a work of supererogation; and, before he undertook it, he felt that he should know why he was asked to do such a thing. And so he inquired... and was told... by Miss Bauchen, your confidential clerk."

Biretta turned green in the face, made a hideous, gobbling noise, clawed at the air and slid to the ground in a faint.

Mansel loosened his collar, and George poured out some water and dashed it into his face. When he came to, they helped him on to a sofa and gave him a brandy and soda – half and half. But though that revived his flesh, his spirit was down and out: and when presently Mansel asked if he still wished to make a statement –

"You'll have to help me," he whimpered. "I'm not myself."

"Listen, Mr Biretta. I do not advise you to make one, unless you tell the whole of the truth. I wish to be frank with you. Mr Cain's statement will do him more harm than good."

"I'm glad of that," said Biretta, miserably.

"But that is not as it should be. A statement should do its maker more good than harm. And so, in my experience, it always does – provided that the statement discloses the whole of the truth."

A gleam of hope slid into Biretta's eyes.

"May I ask," he faltered, "may I ask what you mean by that?"

"I can make no promises," said Mansel. "But at present, at any rate, you are not under arrest. That is because so far, to the best of my belief, you have not told me a lie. And if we are satisfied with your statement, and if you give certain undertakings, it may – I do not say it will – but it may serve our purpose better not to put you under arrest. We have the Duke of Varvic and Mr Cain. The others are at our disposal. If the statement you make comes up to our expectations, that may, or may not, suffice – so far as you are concerned."

Biretta drained his glass.

"Tell me where to begin," he said....

I will not set out the statement, which took a long time to take down, for it said almost exactly what we had come to believe.

By his father's Will, Worsted and Co. had held Bowshot's fortune in Trust. The greater part of this they had stolen away, reserving a very small portion with which to pay the true income for several years. Then Bowshot had spoken of Beehive.... And then it had come to their knowledge that this very autumn Beehive would come to be sold. It was when they were at their wits' end that Saul had approached them and requested them to arrange that Bowshot should die....

George took the statement down. When it was finished Mansel gave it to Biretta and bade him read it through. When he had done so, he asked him if it was correct. Biretta said that it was.

"Then kindly initial each page." Biretta did so. "Now write at the foot these words – *I have read the above statement through and have found it correct.*" Biretta did so. "And now your signature." Biretta signed his name.

Mansel glanced at his writing and handed the statement to George. Then he returned to Biretta.

"And now may I have your passport?"

Without a word of protest, Biretta yielded it up.

Mansel glanced at this and gave it to George.

Then he looked at his watch.

"You are now at liberty to go to Latchet," he said.

Biretta stared.

"But I thought this was Latchet," he said.

"This is District Headquarters," said Mansel. "Latchet is several miles distant. The plain-clothes men who brought you will take you there." There he nodded to George, who left the room. "But I must make this request – that you will not abuse this licence, that you will not quit the inn without letting me know."

"That is understood," said Biretta, and got to his feet. "But I trust you will see your way to – er – to..."

"Mr Biretta," said Mansel, "I have already said that I can make no promises. It would not be right. But that you have made a full statement is in your favour. Had Mr Cain done the same, I do not think he would now be under arrest."

Biretta bowed.

Then –

"Is there any question," he said, "of Cain's being let out on bail?"

"Not at present," said Mansel, gravely. "Should he be released on bail, I will let you know. But if you would like to see him—"

"No, no," cried Biretta, recoiling. "On no account. It would only lead to unpleasantness." He swallowed. "I feel very strongly about it. If I knew he was coming to Latchet, I should prefer to leave before he arrived."

"I will bear that in mind," said Mansel.

"If you would," said Biretta, blinking.

Here George re-entered the room.

Mansel asked him in German whether the car was without, George ventured to say "*Ja wohl*" and held open the door.

"Then, Mr Biretta," said Mansel, "I will bid you goodday."

Biretta bowed.

"Er, when," he faltered, "may I expect to hear from you?"

"In a few days' time," said Mansel. "Till then, as I say, I must ask you to stay at the inn."

"Quite so," said Biretta, thoughtfully. "Any way, you have my passport."

"Yes."

Biretta moistened his lips. He seemed to be steeling himself to say something else. But Mansel nodded to George, who touched the man on the arm.

Biretta started violently.

Then –

"Er – quite so," he said....

With bolting eyes, he turned and passed out of the room... out of the hall and once more into the Rolls.

As the car stole down the drive, I bent my head and threw a leg over the sill.

Mansel and George were busy with the statement.

"Write *Witnessed by*," said Mansel, "and then sign your name and put your London address."

"You first," said George. "You led the horse to the water and made him drink. But why on earth did he do it? He's damned well scuttled himself."

"Demoralization," said Mansel, appending his signature. "The moment I saw him I thought we ought to get home. So, as you observed, I kept hitting him over the heart. And the Bauchen punch finished him. Of course he had a great fall directly he entered this room. He'd assumed that the Rolls was from Varvic – that Saul had sent two of his chauffeurs and one of his cars to carry Biretta the Great to where he was going to lodge. That had made him feel pretty good. And then he realized that the car had been sent by the police.... That brought him down with a run. And then he was glad of a chance to get back on Cain." He passed the statement to George and laid down his pen. "And that is the end of Worsteds. At least, it will be the end, when that confession is read at Scotland Yard. And by the way, it has got to be safe in Salzburg tomorrow at nine o'clock. I think the Banks open then. To keep it here would be foolish, for we've nowhere to lock it up: and if Cain did blow into Latchet – well, he'd burn this house over our heads to get it back."

"I wish he would," said George. "Goats and monkeys! I'd like to be on in that scene. Talk about misunderstandings! When Biretta says he's been at District Headquarters... and Cain asks what it looks like... and Biretta says it's a long, low house, with a porch..."

"I'm afraid it's unlikely," said I. "Cain's nothing to take him to Latchet nowadays."

Mansel sat up.

"You're right," he said. "He hasn't. And Biretta will stick to Latchet. And so they will not meet. But, if they did meet, and Biretta confessed to the statement – well, as I said just now, I'm perfectly certain that Cain would attack in force. *And that is just what we want.* We want to draw them: we do not want to be drawn. Very well. We drop a hint to Cain that Biretta is now at the inn. And then we take off our coats and await the assault."

"Oh, very good," said George. "Very good indeed. I – I can't be too warm about it. I'd rather be shot dead here than winged at the hunting-lodge."

"That's settled, then," said Mansel. "But at dawn tomorrow you take that statement to Salzburg. And not until you are back and produce the receipt, will I send word to Cain that Biretta is here."

"I'll be back at noon," said George.

He was as good as his word.

At half-past five the next morning he took the road, and he and Rowley were back at a quarter to twelve. He did not even call on the Duchess, but only broke his fast before walking into the Bank at nine o'clock.

Immediately after lunch Mansel drove into Villach and telephoned to Varvic from there. He spoke in German and asked if the Duke was there. I forget what name he gave, but a secretary replied, to say that the Duke was out.

"Have you a pencil?" said Mansel.

The man said yes.

"Then take this down."

*"Mr Biretta presents his compliments to his Highness and begs to say that he has arrived at Latchet and is only prevented from calling upon his Highness because he has no car. Mr Biretta would be grateful if his Highness can inform him of the whereabouts of his partner, Mr Cain."*

When the secretary had read this through, Mansel rang off.

Half an hour later he was back at the farm.

"The fuse is burning," he said. "But we don't know how long it is, and so we must be on our toes from this time on. Say from nine o'clock tonight, for they've got to have their show-down and then they must alter their plans. And that gives us time for a stroll – and a talk about Oxford and trout: for a world without Oxford and trout would be a cheerless place."

We walked farther than we had intended and did not get back to Goschen till nearly eight o'clock.

Carson was waiting on the steps, with a telegram in his hand.

"When did this come?" said Mansel.

"Two hours ago, sir. Rowley and Bell went out, sir, to find you at once: but they had no luck and they've not been in very long."

Mansel ripped the envelope open with a frown on his face.

The telegram was from the Duchess.

*Yes, of course. Will be with you almost as soon as this wire.*

CAROLINE OF VARVIC.

George and I stared at each other, but Mansel clapped a hand to his head.

"My God," he cried. "They've taken a leaf from our book."

And then I realized that Cain had sent a wire to the Duchess and had signed it with one of our names... and that his wire had asked her to come to Goschen at once.

# XI

## WE ENTER THE HUNTING-LODGE

We had the servants in and held a council of war.

"There can be no doubt," said Mansel, "that the Duchess of Varvic has been decoyed from Salzburg and is by now either at the castle or at the hunting-lodge. But I don't care where she is, for we're going to get her out. Up to now, as you know, we have never shown our teeth; yet we've done what we liked with the brutes. So now we shall go all out and shall make an end of them.

"I think we should try the lodge first, for the lodge is easy of access, but the castle is not. Does anyone think otherwise?"

Nobody did.

"Very well. Now we can hardly surprise them, for they will be waiting for us: but they will expect some warning of our approach. That warning I propose to deny them: indeed I propose to mislead them, so far as I can.

"Early yesterday morning Carson and I inspected one of the paths which the Duke had made – a path running through the woods on the southern side and into the piece of country we know so well. Sure enough there's a trap on that path: and we've marked the spot where it lies with luminous paint. To make sure of missing the trap, look out for a tree on the left which we marked with a cross: leave the path and pass to the left of that tree: as you pass it, you'll see another, marked with a ring: pass to the left of that, too, and then return to the path.

"By using this path we shall deny them warning of our approach, for the path won't be watched or guarded, except by the trap.

"Now how do we reach the path? We can, of course, reach it by leaving the car at Four Mile Point as usual and crossing the fields. But that will take a long time. And so I suggest that we all get into the Rolls and come down from the north... past the mouth of the drive and apparently on after that. In fact we shall stop half a mile from the mouth of the drive. There five of us will alight and enter the fields, and ten minutes later we shall be treading the path. Carson will take the Rolls on and berth her at Four Mile Point and will then make his way to join us as fast as ever he can. The sentry at the mouth of the drive will see us go by and will doubtless report this occurrence. And I don't think they'll know what to make of it. To be perfectly honest, I know that I shouldn't myself.

"Well, that's the best I can do. But, if it turns out as I hope, at least we shall reach the forecourt before they know we are there. And that should be a great help. Further than that I can't go, for not until we are there can we see what's what. But tonight, if you please, we shall take no chances at all. These fellows are out for blood, so I'm going to shoot at sight and you'd all better do the same."

Ten minutes later the Rolls was upon the road.

It was a quarter to nine when the five of us entered the woods surrounding the hunting-lodge. Mansel was leading and I brought up the rear, so I had but to follow the others to miss the trap; but the luminous paint showed well and, had I been alone, by observing Mansel's directions I could have reached the forecourt without mishap.

That I was more than uneasy, I here most frankly confess. I could not get away from the fact that we were about to do exactly as the enemy wished; we had watched him work to this end and had smiled in our sleeve: and now here we were about to play into his hands. We had, of course, no choice, for the Duchess had to be saved at any cost: in other words, our hand had been forced: but, because of this, we were going against our judgment and flying in the face of the warning which China gave. Worst of all, I was sure that we were to try a fall with something far more dreadful than blackguard flesh and blood, with some abomination which could not be seen, upon whose domain we were about to trespass against such orders as Instinct seldom gives. Still, there was nothing for it. I had very little doubt that Mansel and George were beset by the same foreboding and were determined to put its endeavours to shame: and so I took hold of myself, cursed my imagination and forced the whole of my mind to the business in hand.

Thanks to the path, we were able to move in silence, yet at a fair speed, and before very long I was able to see ahead the glow of some light. As I had expected, this came from the open door of the hunting-lodge.

All was quiet in the forecourt: indeed, all seemed the same as when we had seen the place three nights before. Only the hall was lighted, and the doorway stood out of the darkness – a tall rectangle of luminance, rather than light.

Mansel was whispering.

"Mr Chandos comes with me; the others stay here."

Together we moved like shadows towards the steps....

By one consent, we made for the wall of the house, one upon either side of the open door: and when we had gained the wall, we turned to the steps. These were four in number and very low: they were kept by no balustrade, but were splayed as they descended, so that the bottom step was twice the length of the top. Since the latter was longer than the sill, it was easy to crawl to their head, yet keep clear of the open door: and this was what we did. And then we looked over the sill and into the hall.

All was as Mansel had found it, three nights before. The only lamp was hanging above the staircase right at the farther end. Broad and low, the stairs led up to a landing which would have accepted a dance-band, piano and all; from there, as Mansel had reported, two flights of stairs ran up and into archways on either side. But tonight there was something else – something which had not been there three nights before. Hanging over the balustrade was the coat with the fine, fur collar which the Duchess of Varvic had worn when I saw her last.

I glanced at Mansel for instructions, but he was lying quite still, looking down the hall.

Forecast emerged from the archway up on the right, passed down the stairs to the landing and then up the other flight which led to the left. His arm was still in splints and he seemed to be growing a beard. After a moment or two, he reappeared with Auger. That the latter was in high spirits was easy to see. He was laughing and rallying Forecast, who looked very black, and he minced down the steps, pretending to be some great lady, flirting her fan. As he passed, he picked up his mistress' coat, flung it over his shoulders and strutted to and fro on the landing, alternately ogling Forecast and rocking with silent laughter at his own drollery. And then Cain appeared from the archway up on the right.

If Forecast looked black, the look on Cain's face was plainly murderous. That awful smile was still there, as though to mock the glare that burned in his eyes: but his face, no longer a mask, seemed the very seat of hatred and savage enmity. That the man had spoken with Biretta, I did not have to be told. He knew what had happened. He knew that his race was run. And his one idea was to wreak the most horrid vengeance on the men who had brought him low.

I could not hear what he said, but he spat out some scathing comment upon the revolting performance which Auger was giving below. The German took this badly and made some offensive reply, perhaps because he knew how his master treated Cain: still he took the coat from his shoulders and put it back where it had been, upon the balustrade, and then, with a very ill grace, he mounted the flight with Forecast and followed Cain, who had gone the way he had come.

Mansel was by my side.

"Now," he breathed, "is our chance to get up those stairs. I'm going to get the others. We shall, all four, go in, but you must stay here, out of sight. I'm sure there are doors in the tapestry up at this end of the hall. There may be peep-holes, too. And I should think their idea is to let us get to the stairs and then come in behind us and mop us up. If they try that, open fire, and we shall know where we are; but until I hear a shot, I shan't worry about our rear."

With that, he was gone – to be back in less than two minutes with George and Rowley and Bell.

"Any more movement, William?"

"Nothing at all."

"Good. Once we are in, you can come a little closer, for I want you to see as much as you can of the hall: but don't go over the sill. And don't forget that now you have no one behind you – except the enemy."

With that, he lifted his hand, and the four rose up together, passed through the doorway and ran a-tip-toe for the stairs....

They were half-way down the hall, when, with no warning whatever, *they disappeared... and not only they, but the hall and everything*.

As I live, I am telling the truth.

I was lying there watching, with my eyes just above ground level and my chin just touching the sill of the open door. And one moment they were crossing the hall... And the next there *was* no hall... no hall, no staircase, no light – the lot were gone.

As though by some stage magic, a transformation of scene had taken place. The scene which I had been watching had disappeared, and nothing, except pitch darkness, had taken its place. Yes, something else. A wave of well-damp air, foetid and noisome, the very breath of corruption, broke on my face, and I knew, though I could not see, that I was lying on the brink of some deep and terrible pit. A rumbling, slithering sound came to my ears...

I think the hair rose upon my head.

So for perhaps ten seconds... twenty, perhaps... I cannot swear to the time.

And then the foul breath of corruption rose to a breeze... to a blast... I remember, I quailed before it: and, as I quailed, directly under my nose there came a thunderous crash... and there was the hall before me... hall and light and staircase, as they had always been.

There was no mistake about it.

Cain and Forecast and Auger were standing above the landing, at the top of the flight of stairs which ran to the right. Cain was smiling, Auger was pointing and laughing, and Forecast had a hand to his mouth. But the hall was empty. Mansel and George and the servants had disappeared.

I despair of describing my emotions.

For a moment I wondered if I had lost consciousness – if the things I have just related belonged to some awful dream, for indeed they were of the stuff of which nightmares are made. And then I knew it was true... that Cain and the German were gloating over their triumph... gloating over the fact that Mansel and George and the servants had been – swallowed up.

To say that I was shaken means nothing. In body and mind I had been profoundly shocked. I felt very sick of my stomach and grievously sick at heart. Indeed, I felt very faint; and had I been standing, I should, I think, have had to sit down. As it was, I laid my forehead against the stone of the sill. It was then that I found that I was trembling...

How what had happened had happened, I could not tell. I supposed some trap had been laid. And China's words kept hammering on my heart – *But if you go in, you'll never come out alive.*

Strangely enough, it was the enemy that lugged me out of the depths and set my feet on the ground.

Auger was shouting for Hans, and the sound of his voice cleared my brain.

I had seen what happened, and I was safe and sound. I must wait and watch and make the most of my wits; and then, when Carson came, he and I together would save the others if they were still to be saved, and, if they were not, would take such a vengeance upon Cain and Saul and their fellows as would make them curse the days on which they were born.

Indeed, from being confounded and, so to speak, knocked out, I became strong of body and cool of mind: my brain seemed ice-cold and I felt I had the strength of two men. Of such is the lust for vengeance, for I had next to no hope that Mansel and George and the servants were yet alive.

"Hans," shouted Auger. "Hans!"

I lay still as death, with my eyes just above the sill.

I heard a man enter the hall.

I could not see him enter, for the entrance was out of my sight: but he came from the left, and as he passed into my view, I heard the thud of a door. This showed that the door was self-closing – that is to say, was controlled by a heavy spring.

With his back to me, he walked towards the staircase – but not very far. He stopped, I should say, a third of the way down the hall. I recognized him at once. It was the burly foreman, whom Mansel and I had watched adjusting the traps.

Cain spoke up.

"Did the signal light go out?"

Auger translated his words, and the foreman replied.

"No. It is still alight."

"So much for your sentries," sneered Cain. "How many of the English went down?"

"Four or five – we cannot be certain which."

"Why not?"

"We had no warning. The signal light was still on. But Kleiner got to the peep-hole just in time."

"Just too late, you mean."

"In time to see there were four and possibly five."

I saw Cain finger his chin.

Then –

"Get back to your post," he said. "The others will come."

The foreman hesitated.

"It occurs to me," he said, "that the sentries may have been hurt."

"Serve them right," snapped Cain.

"I propose to leave Kleiner here and take Boll to the mouth of the drive."

"What for?"

The foreman spread out his hands.

"The sentries," he said, "may be at the point of death."

"What if they are?"

"One is my son," said the foreman.

"I can't help that. They have failed in their duty. Get back to your post."

Auger did not translate this, but argued with Cain. I do not know what they said, but apparently Cain gave way, for Auger addressed the foreman who nodded his head. As he turned, I sank out of sight. But I heard him cross the hall and then the thud of the door. And when again I lifted my head, Auger had left the others, had crossed the landing and was mounting the opposite flight.

That was as much as I saw, for if I was right and Hans and Boll were to leave for the mouth of the drive, I must be gone before they came to the door. And so I withdrew to the right, slipped off the edge of the steps and lay down against the wall.

Except to join forces with Carson, I had, of course, no plan. Since the odds were six to one, until Carson came I dared not launch an attack. But the enemy had no idea that I was at hand, and I meant to take advantage of any opening he gave. It was now just half-past nine, and Carson could hardly arrive before ten o'clock. Still, if Kleiner was alone in the guard-room...

And there I heard Auger's voice.

The man was not shouting from the staircase: he was talking and laughing somewhere, quite close at hand. And then again I heard the thud of a door.

At once I saw what had happened.

When Auger had argued with Cain, he had suggested that Hans should be suffered to go and that, whilst he was out of the guard-room, he (Auger) should take Hans' place.

Sure enough, almost at once, Hans and Auger and Boll emerged from the hall.

Now almost all I had witnessed since Mansel had disappeared, goes, I think, to show what very poor soldiers the enemy would have made. All the calling and bawling for Hans, the questions and answers shouted across the hall and now all this talking and laughing at the head of the steps – these things were so much folly, when one or two of us remained to be trapped. I can only suppose that they were intoxicated with their success – which was, indeed, handsome enough – and were now so sure of themselves that they felt they could afford to take risks. Auger should have known better; but he was the worst of them all. Some people will never learn.

Hans and Boll said nothing, but Auger went laughing and talking down the steps: and, when the two had left him, he did not turn back, but stood, with his hands in his pockets, looking the way they had gone and whistling under his breath.

He never heard me rise and step to his side...

It was no time for niceties – there was too much at stake.

With all my might, I hit him with the butt of my pistol behind the ear, and, as his knees sagged, I caught him and picked him up. I cannot think what he weighed, but I managed to get him out of the forecourt and round to the side of the house, and there I laid the man down to die when he pleased; for I knew how hard I had hit and that, though he might live for an hour, he never would move again.

So much I had done on impulse. But now I stood still for a moment, and thought very hard.

Twenty or twenty-five minutes would pass before Hans returned. Then Auger would be missed and the hunt would be up. Meanwhile the man called Kleiner was in the guard-room alone. The trouble was he had his eye to the peep-hole...

And then I saw what I must do.

Auger had been wearing a hat. When I struck him, this had fallen, but I had managed to catch it and carry it off with him. I sought for this and found it and put it on. And then I made my way back to the foot of the steps.

I had not all Auger's inches, but I am not a small man and, as I have said before, the light at this end of the hall was very dim. So I put my hands in my pockets, assumed the German's demeanour, and sauntered up the steps and into the hall....

Now the instant I entered the hall, I knew that the floor was not fixed. It was solid enough, but there was a ghost of a tremor, such as you may feel in a ballroom, the floor of which has been slung. Still, I knew it was safe to tread, for Hans and Auger and Boll had been by this way.

A glance at the staircase showed me that there was nobody there.

Still strolling and humming aloud, I turned to the left, but to my dismay I could see no sign of a door. Mansel was right – it was cut in the tapestry. I walked as slow as I dared and went so far as to dance a pace or two – all to gain time, of course, for my eyes were raking the wall for any sign of a cut.

And then something caught the light....

The door-handle was of cut glass, and, as I danced to the right, one of its facets had rendered a sullen gleam.

I was just about to grasp it, when Kleiner played into my hands.

No doubt, because of his position, Auger was feared. Five nights ago the sentry had called him 'Sir.' And so Kleiner thought it expedient to save the fellow trouble and open the door. And since it would close on its own, Kleiner held the door open, for me to pass in. Everything indeed was against him, for I was in the darkness, but he in the light.

I clenched my fist and hit him as hard as I could.

It was a clumsy blow, for I hit him full in the face, instead of under the jaw; but, as luck would have it, he was standing against the jamb – and that was of stone. So the back of his head met the stone, and once again I had a body to catch.

I laid him down in a corner and glanced at my watch.

Twenty-two minutes to nine. And Hans and Boll would be back in a quarter of an hour. And Carson...

I gave myself ten minutes to see what I could.

The room was small, but high-pitched. I would have said that it was an ante-room. The window was shrouded with blankets. A slow fire burned in a grate, beside which were the watchman's chairs. On a table in the corner was burning the signal lamp. On a hook on the wall an acetylene lamp was hanging, to light the room. There were three doors – one by which I had entered; another opposite that; and a third, which was slightly open, facing the window – that is to say, on my right, as I had come in.

This third door had been cut in the panelling, and when it was closed, you would not have known it was there. It was clear that this was the door by which Auger had entered the room when he had come down from the stairs, for the other door could not have been opened unless the signal-lamp's table had first been moved.

I set the third door wide, to see where it led.

All was dark and I ventured to use my torch.

The doorway admitted to a passage, not six feet wide – a passage all of stone, running as straight as it could by the side of the hall. But the passage was lower than the hall by at least three feet, for, from where I stood, a short flight of steps ran down.

With another glance at my watch, I passed down the steps...

I had taken four or five paces, when on the right of the passage, I found a recess, such as you see in tunnels into which a man may retire upon the approach of a train. In this recess had been planted a massive crutch or cradle of solid iron. This was some two feet six or three feet high and was bearing the end of a giant, steel spindle, which was itself protruding out of a hole in the wall. Both spindle and cradle were fairly plastered with grease, some of which had been lately added, as a tin of grease, newly opened, most plainly showed.

For a moment I stared at these things, remembering the others' disappearance and the tremor I had felt in the floor. And then in a flash I knew that I had the truth of the matter between my hands – that I had conducted myself behind the scenes and was at this moment regarding the cruel and treacherous device by which he who had built the lodge had been used to rid himself of his unsuspecting guests.

The floor of the hall was in fact a limited see-saw – that is to say, it pivoted on a spindle, just as a see-saw does – with this one difference, that the staircase end could fall, but could not rise, while the other end could rise – but could not fall.

It was, doubtless, perfectly balanced, so that the instant a man passed beyond the centre, and so found himself nearer to the staircase than he was to the door, his weight would tip the scale and would bring down his half of the floor, while the other half would rise up. Since the floor was so highly polished, the victim would have no chance: he was bound to fall or slide forward, thus actually sealing his doom, for the farther he went, the sharper, because of his weight, the tilt would become, until at last the floor from having been horizontal would become vertical and he would simply fall headlong into the depths below. And then, relieved of his weight, his end of the floor would rise up, while the other fell down, thus locking him into his prison, for what that was worth.

There could be no doubt about it.

This was the dreadful way which Mansel and George and Rowley and Bell had taken: it was the weight of their bodies which had lifted my end of the floor, thus hiding the hall from my eyes and revealing the awful depths of that noisome pit: here was the explanation of the tremor which I had felt when I entered the hall; and here the reason why Hans had kept his distance, when he had stood in the hall, conversing with Cain.

And then I remembered the 'rumbling, slithering sound'... the sound I had heard when everything had gone black...

I knew now what had made that sound – and the palms of my hands grew wet...

Then something occurred to me.

I had found that the floor was a trap and I knew how it worked. But a floor which was *always* a trap would be inconvenient indeed. And in this particular case it would be absurd to suppose that the hall could never be used except by those whom Varvic proposed to destroy. This being so, there must be a locking device, so that the hall could be used – by the sheep as well as the goats. And the locking device would be at the staircase end.

I hastened along the passage, still using my torch.

The passage ran into a chamber, some twelve feet square. On the left rose a flight of stone steps, and on the right I saw the locking device. This was most simple.

A steel beam or girder had been let into the wall, as a safe is let into a wall: but whereas a safe is fixed, the beam could be moved to and fro. It ran, of course, on a carriage which did not move; and a toothed wheel, controlled by a windlass, could force it to right or to left. At the moment it was clear of a hole in the massive wall on the right; but there could be no doubt that, if, by the use of the windlass, it was made to pass through this hole, it would jut out beyond the wall and under the floor of the hall – for it hung at the height of the spindle or thereabouts. The whole was smothered in grease, as the spindle and its cradle had been. There was just such a beam, no doubt, on the opposite side; and when the two were protruding, instead of withdrawn, the floor of the hall would be safe for fifty men: but, with only one beam engaged, the floor could not give way unless a tremendous weight were put upon it.

I was now abreast of the spot at which Mansel and George and the servants had been cast into the pit, so, for what it was worth, I put my arm through the hole through which the beam, when advanced, would have to pass, and flashed my torch three or four times, that if they were living and conscious they might believe that help, if not at hand, was going to come. I would have liked to call, but I dared not do that: but, when I had drawn back my arm, to my inexpressible joy, I saw through the hole in the wall a flash in return.

At once I plunged in my arm and flashed my torch again. Then I drew it back, again to receive a reply. And I was standing, thanking God and trying my best to remember two or three letters in Morse, when I heard a sound I had heard three times before. It was unmistakable. In fact, it was the thud of the ante-room door.

# XII

# THE WAGES OF SIN

So do plans go awry.

What had happened, I never knew – except that Hans had not gone so far as the mouth of the drive. Maybe he had met a sentry when he was half-way there. Be that as it may, he was back – and by now had seen Kleiner's body, which I had meant to remove before his return. This was unfortunate, for it meant he would raise the alarm; but what was very much worse, my retreat was cut off. And Carson...

For an instant my brain zig-zagged. Then I saw all things clear.

I must be out of the passage before the alarm was raised. Otherwise Cain and Forecast would hold the head of the steps which rose from the left of the chamber in which I stood; and with Hans and Boll in the guard-room, I should be trapped.

*But before I left I must lock the floor of the hall.*

Thus, unknown to the enemy, I should have a line of retreat – a line of retreat of which they would never dream.

All this time I was watching the guard-room's door. I had left this ajar, as I had found it, and so far it had not been moved. Hans and Boll were probably ministering to Kleiner....

I whipped to the windlass and hoped very hard indeed that no sound would give me away.

Thanks to the grease, the beam moved forward in silence, and though it went very slowly, a child could have done the work.

I dared not use my torch, but at last I could turn no more, and when I put up a hand, I found that the hole was gone, for the beam was filling it up.

At once I turned to the left, to make for the steps, and then I saw that the door of the guard-room was shut.

This made it clear that Hans was taking no risks: he had closed one end of the trap.

At once I lighted my torch and sprang for the steps....

These wound up in a spiral, and since the spiral was small, they were very steep: but I mounted as fast as I could, for if Forecast or Cain were before me, my cake was dough.

At the top was a heavy oak door, and my hand was upon the latch, when on the spiral below me I heard a man miss his step.

In that instant I realized that Hans was by no means a fool. I had thought he was out to trap me – as he had meant me to think. In fact, he was out to kill me; for, before he had shut the door, he had entered the trap.

But two could play that game....

Quick as a flash I opened the door before me. But I did not pass through. I slid my torch into my pocket and shut the door.

Believing that I had gone on, Hans was now less careful to make no sound. He trod the last steps squarely, feeling his way. And as he came to the top one, I flashed my torch on his face.

Surprised and blinded, he recoiled – instinctively. But a steep, stone, spiral staircase is not a good place to recoil, and, as luck would have it, his weight was upon the wrong foot. He tried to save himself by throwing his back to the spindle round which the staircase curled; but against the spindle, of course, the steps had tapered to nothing, and when he put out a foot, no foothold was there. Before I could strike, the fellow toppled sideways and backwards, his great hands clutching the air: and, as he fell, he gave a terrible cry, for I think he knew what it meant for a man of his weight to fall badly in such a place.

In fact, his body landed out of my view, but such was the sound it made when it struck the stone that I knew as well as had he that he would not move again. Hans, the burly foreman, had broken his neck.

At once I re-opened the door, to see on my right the archway which stood on the left of the staircase at the end of the hall.

And then I heard Forecast's voice.

"I'll lay it was another," he said. "And that makes five or six."

"I'm not so sure," said Cain. "I don't say the floor didn't move, but we never heard it fall back." He raised his voice. "Auger!"

There was a little silence. Then –

"Rot the fellow," snarled Cain. "By God, I do hate that man."

"Hans," shouted Forecast. "Hans!"

There was no reply.

"Hans won't be back," said Cain. "It's that — Auger we want."

Again he shouted for Auger – of course, in vain.

Then I heard Forecast exclaim and once again the thud of the ante-room door.

"That's Boll," said Cain. "What's that mean? Boll was to have gone with Hans to the mouth of the drive." He raised his voice. "Where's Auger?"

Boll, who could speak no English, was shouting excitedly.

"Damn the fool," said Cain. He shouted again, "Where's Auger?"

"He doesn't know," said Forecast. "That's what he's trying to say."

"Where's Hans?" cried Cain.

What gestures Boll made, I was unable to see, but I heard him imitate the death-cry which Hans had made.

"My God," said Forecast, "they've got him."

His voice was hoarse.

"I said so," said Cain. "That yell we heard was Hans. You'd better get down to the guard-room and see what's what." He raised his voice. "Get back to the guard-room, Boll."

Apparently Boll understood, for a moment later I heard the thud of the door.

"Go on," said Cain to Forecast. "You heard what I said. Slip down to the guard-room and—"

"All right, all right," said Forecast. "An' not so much of the 'slip.' I've only one arm, you know; an' if one of these Willies gets rough—"

"What then?" said I, stepping into and out of the archway, pistol in hand.

The two of them turned to run, and had I hit Cain, who was leading, I should have had them both: but I am not a crack shot and Forecast was in my way: and so I fired and hit Forecast full in the back.

Forecast fell down on the stairs, but, before I could fire again, Cain had whipped back through his archway and out of sight.

In a flash I was down the stairs, across the landing and up the other side: but when I had reached the archway, Cain was gone. Immediately on my right was another oak door like that through which I had lately come, and I had no doubt at all that this gave to another stone staircase, and that, in turn, to a passage exactly like the one I had left.

Now it stood to reason that, if Cain had gone that way, he could probably gain the hall from an ante-room like that on the opposite side. In this way he could give me the slip, for while I was yet in the archway at the head of the stairs, he could whip out of the hall and into the night.

I therefore swung round, to go down and cut off his retreat – and that was very nearly the last thing I ever did.

Forecast had dragged himself up and had got his right arm over the balustrade. While he thus supported himself, his left hand had drawn a pistol out of his coat, and he was about to fire when a shot rang out from below, and the fellow collapsed and rolled over on to his back.

Carson.

It was a lovely shot, for he fired at eleven paces and shot the man clean through the brain. And had he not aimed so truly, I must have died; for I had no time to think and Forecast's range was point-blank – I was less than four feet away.

And then I was down the staircase and in the hall and was haling Carson out and on to the steps....

"I'm much obliged, Carson," I said.

"That's all right, sir," said Carson. "I'm glad I was there. And Captain Mansel?"

"They're all of them trapped," I said. "They're under this floor. I'll give you the details later. But to get them out, we've got to work undisturbed. And that we cannot do until we have bumped off Cain. And now listen to me."

As shortly as ever I could, I described to him the layout and showed how Cain could not escape, unless he went out by a window or some back door.

"If you ask me," I said, "he's in that ante-room now – the one opposite the guard-room – gluing his eyes to a peep-hole, and trying to screw up his courage to make a dash for this door."

"And Boll, sir?"

"Boll must be dealt with, too; and then, except for the sentries, we've got the lot."

"And the Duchess, sir?"

"God knows. When we've got the others out, we'll set about looking for her. But Cain comes first. For one thing only, unless we can iron him out, he'll go and get help."

Now when I had last seen Cain, he was passing through an archway at the head of the stairs. To reach the forecourt from there, he had a choice of three ways – one by the hall, which I had now made safe, one by the right-hand passage and one by the left. Add to this that from either ante-room he could go out by a window and so avoid using the hall.

I decided that, one by one, we must close these ways of escape. I, therefore, arranged that Carson should stay on the steps, from which he could watch the windows on either side, whilst I approached the ante-room on the right. I supposed that this resembled the guard-room, that is to say, the ante-room on the left: if so, and if I could do it, I meant to bolt the oak door which led to the right-hand passage down which I had never gone.

Now though, in this way, we should presently run Cain to earth, the operation seemed likely to prove very slow, for we had to be careful of Boll and one of us must always stay at the door: and since, as I had told Carson, I firmly believed that Cain was now in the ante-room watching the hall, I determined to try and mislead him – to make him take what he thought was a way of escape.

Cain could have reached his peep-hole within a very few moments of Forecast's death. And, if in fact he had done so, he was aware of two things – first, that Carson had joined me, and, secondly, that the floor of the hall was now locked. I therefore proposed that, just before I approached the ante-room on the right, Carson should approach the ante-room on the left. If Cain was watching, he would at once assume that we meant to clear the passages and meet at the head of the stairs; in which case, since the floor was locked, the hall would be at his disposal for him to make his escape. He would, of course, be wrong, for Carson would not enter the ante-room, but would return to the steps outside the front door. But Cain would not see this, for by then he would be in his passage, making his way to the stairs.

As we arranged, so we did: and the moment I entered my ante-room, I knew that I had been right; for the door which led to the passage was ajar and I heard the whisper of footfalls going away. At once I gave chase, but the man had reached the chamber before I was past the oak door, and the beam of my torch just caught him about to climb a staircase like that on which Hans had died. Be sure I ran like the wind, but, as I reached the foot of the spiral, I heard the door above close.

Playing the part of beater, I leapt at the stair, for I was now quite certain that our ruse was about to succeed and that Cain would dash through the hall and run into Carson's arms.

In a flash I was up the spiral, and as I flung open the door, I heard the man scream....

Two steps, and I was in the archway – and looking down upon a spectacle which was over and done in less than a tenth of the time which it will take to describe.

In a word, Boll, whom I fear I despised, had sought to put a spoke in our wheel by unlocking the floor of the hall.

Now when Cain took to the floor, he was running towards the door, but Mansel and the others had been running towards the stairs. It follows that Cain was running towards safety, while Mansel and the others were running downhill to their doom. So they had no chance at all: but Cain had a chance.

The fellow was moving so fast, that, though the floor gave below him the moment he set foot upon it, his impetus carried him on until, though running uphill, he had almost reached the spot beneath which the spindle lay. Indeed, when he threw himself forward, I think his frantic arms fell over the half-way mark, for the floor seemed to hover for a moment before deciding to continue its sweep to the vertical. But all the weight of his body was on the wrong side, and so it held on its way and Cain, who was scrabbling like a madman to gain the point of safety he must have known was so near, gave a second, ghastly scream and then slid smoothly and swiftly into the depths below.

The depths looked less black than gray, and Cain seemed to disappear in a cloud of dust. This showed that there was no water, to my surprise and relief. But, perhaps because of the dust, I could see no one of the others, although, as the floor was closing, I roared "Hang on."

And then, with a crash, the floor fell back into place – to show Carson framed in the doorway, down on his knees on the threshold, with a hand to his head.

I signed to him to stay where he was: then I made my way back by the way I had come.

Poor Carson looked very shaken, as well he might.

"Is that," he faltered, "is that what happened to them, sir?"

"Yes," said I. "And I was exactly where you were. Not very nice, is it? Never mind. When we've mopped up Boll, we'll get them out."

"My God, that stench, sir. I thought I was going to faint. And the Captain's down in the thick of it...."

"That's all right, Carson," I said. "It'll take more than a smell to get him down."

Carson wrung the sweat from his face.

"We'll need some rope, sir," he said.

"We've got it," said I. "There's a coil in that ante-room. And now for Boll. He's in the left-hand passage – possibly in the guard-room: the point is that, if we are quick, we've got him cold. I'm going back to the staircase. When you see me cross that landing, approach the guard-room door. I don't know whether he's armed, so watch your step. By the time you are in the guard-room, I shall be on the spiral staircase. And if he is not in the guard-room, he soon will be, for I shall drive him towards you. Don't kill him, if you can help it. He may be useful before the night is out."

The thing worked out very well; for when Boll saw Carson coming, he took to the passage at once. I heard him coming, of course, and as he entered the chamber, I lighted my torch. This showed me at the foot of the spiral, pistol in hand, and when I said, "Put up your hands," he knew what I meant. So

I marched him back down the passage, with his hands in the air; and Carson took his belt and Kleiner's and bound him hand and foot.

"And now for the others," said I.

While Carson ran for the rope, I shut the double front doors: and then, by way of a passage, we made our way to the staircase at the farther end of the hall. As we went by, I showed Carson the locking device.

When we had reached the landing, Carson fastened one end of the rope about my waist, and he took a turn round the newel at the foot of the stairs. He left me some three feet of slack and stood ready to take the strain. Then I took my seat on the bottom stair and put my feet on the floor. The instant I touched it, it gave – as was natural enough. I kicked it, and it swung open, but not very far.

"We must have a bedstead," said I. "In one of the rooms on the right."

While Carson ran for this, I held the floor down with my feet, and called Mansel's name.

He replied directly.

"Good for you, William," he said.

"Thank God," said I. "Tell me, are you all right?"

"Except that Bell's broken his wrist, we're perfectly sound. But the atmosphere's hitting us hard, so be as quick as you can."

"And Cain?"

"He's shamming dead. I've got his pistol all right. What of the others?"

"Boll is tied up," I said, "and the others are dead."

"Very good indeed. And the sentries?"

"Still keeping watch, I hope."

Here Carson arrived, with a small iron bed on his shoulder.

"Stand clear, Mansel," I cried. "We've got a bedstead here, and, when it's served its turn, I shall let it go."

There was a moment's silence.

Then –

"Carry on," said Mansel.

At once I leaned back till my head was touching the stairs. Carson set down the bed and pushed it down over my body, until I was lying beneath. I then laid hold of the legs, and, together, we pushed it farther until I could once more sit up. The floor was now well open, for while one end of the bedstead was lying across my thighs, the other was touching the floor and, because, of course, it was rigid, was holding it down.

"D'you think you can hold it, sir?"

I shifted my grip to the rail.

"Now let me try."

Carson released his hold.

"Yes, I can do it," I said. "But shout when you're through and be as quick as you can."

Carson fled for the passage, to use the locking device.

My muscles were trembling when at last I heard him shout.

"Stand clear below," I cried – and let the bedstead go.

The floor swung back to admit it: then the floor lifted and checked. A gap remained – a gap some four feet wide, for because of the beam which Carson had just wound forward, the floor could not close.

The mouth of the pit was now open and the rope we had found was long and strong enough to carry the prisoners up: but the foul air had sapped their strength and Mansel at once announced that to climb the rope was wholly beyond their power. I had expected this, for, unless it is very thick, to climb thirty-five feet of rope is a feat for a strong, fit man: but, though Carson and I had the strength to pull them up, we were badly placed for such an exercise. And then I saw what we must do.

The staircase upon which we were standing ran up, as I have said, in one broad flight to the landing from which two flights went on. It follows that upon either side of the flight below the landing there were a few yards of floor which did not move: in other words, if I had stepped straight off the staircase, I should have stepped into the pit; but if I took hold of a newel and swung myself off the last step to left or to right, I should not step into the pit but on to a morsel of floor which was perfectly safe. And here were two doors – one upon either side.

I sent Carson off for a mattress and swung myself round a newel and on to a patch of firm floor. Then I threw open a door. I fancy this led to the kitchens, but that is beside the point. If Carson and I were to stand within this door, we could easily haul up the others, because, when we took the strain, we could brace ourselves against the jambs of the door.

And that was what we did.

The mattress we laid on the brink, that the rope should not fray. Then we let the rope down and I called to Mansel and told him that we were now all ready to pull them up.

At once I heard a flurry down in the pit: then the rope was jerked to and fro; and then I heard the howl of a man in pain.

"What's the matter?" I cried.

"Nothing," said Mansel. "Cain tried to rush the boats, and I've knocked him down. Bell's coming up first, and Cain last – if he comes at all."

One minute later he told us to take the strain...

Now that the pit was open, the awful stench was rising into the hall, and I felt that we must work quickly, lest we, too – Carson and I – should be overcome. Indeed, to this day I do not know how Mansel and the others were able to keep their senses, for they were within the pit for more than an hour.

I shall never forget Bell's appearance, as he rose out of the depths. His face and head and shoulders were powdered most thick with dust – a very white dust that would not be shaken away. In fact, he looked like one that had been raised from the dead. And when we had pulled him right up, we found he was white like that from head to foot. So were they all. Indeed they looked like four spirits that had the shape and semblance of men we knew: they did not seem to be human or clad as men are clad, for the dust lay so thick on their clothes that all their detail was gone.

Mansel came last of the four, and before he was fairly up, Cain began shouting like a madman for us to let down the rope.

Be sure we let him shout, while Carson ran for some water that he had seen in the bedroom from which he had brought the bed. They dared not drink the water, but cleansed the dust from their faces as best they could: but whilst they were doing this, I found a glass and three siphons, and so, when I got back, they were able to rinse their mouths. And then Carson found a bottle of whiskey...

"Quick lime and bone dust," said Mansel. "Or something equally foul."

"Lime?" said I. "Lime? That's what is in those sacks. There are six sacks in the ante-room on the right."

"Waiting for us," said Mansel. "The old order prevaileth: a sack of quick lime per man. Quick lime destroys, you know – eats up the flesh and the bones and brings them to dust. But it does not devour the gases – you can't have it every way. And we have just had a close-up of the substance which is produced when quick lime has digested the dead." Again he rinsed his mouth. "This place is a charnel-house. We fell on a kind of dune – a reeking mound of corruption, and that is what broke our fall. Of course, we didn't fall straight; we slid for a lot of the way. But that stench was what did us in. I don't think we could have lasted another half-hour. Our senses would have left us, and that would have been the end. It was because of that that I thought we were done. I knew that you and Carson would pull something out of the bag, but, in view of the odds against you, I could not believe that you could reach us in time."

"But they did, God bless them," said George. "You know, I always told you I didn't like this place." A howl from Cain interrupted him. "Damn the wallah," he added, and pitched an empty siphon into the pit. "I felt that it had some drawback. But now that I know what it is, I am no longer afraid. All the same, the sooner we close that abyss, the more at ease I shall feel. Are you really going to draw up that murderous swine?"

"Well, I think we can use him," said I, and told what was in my mind.

When I had done –

"It's well worth trying," said Mansel; "but I think you must carry it out. I shall be fit for nothing until I've had some fresh air."

I leaned over the pit and called to Cain.

"Listen," I said. "We are not going to spare your life. Would you rather stay down there or come up and be shot?"

"I'd rather come up," yelled Cain.

Once more Carson and I laid hold of the rope...

When Cain's head was just to be seen –

"Tell me," I said, pausing, "in which room is the Duchess confined?"

"She isn't here," panted Cain. "She was taken straight to the castle. If you spare my life, I'll—"

"Her coat's hanging here," I said.

"I know. It was brought here to – to mislead you: to make you think she was here. If you spare my life I'll—"

"We are not going to spare your life. Nothing can alter that. Only the Duke will survive, of all your crowd."

"But that's not fair," screamed Cain. "It's damned unfair. Why should the Duke go free, while I go down?"

"Because we can't get him," said I.

"I'll get him," gasped Cain. And then, "My God, this rope. It's cutting me almost in two. Don't torture me. Pull me up."

"Listen," said I. "Get the Duke here, and you'll die a good clean death. If you don't, we'll chuck you back."

"I think, if I get the Duke here—"

I spoke to Carson.

"Lower away," I said.

As Cain began to go down –

"No, no," he screamed. "What you like. Don't put me back in that pit."

"Will you get the Duke here?"

"If you'll promise to kill him, I will. But I think, in return, you should—"

"Have no hope," I said. "Get the Duke here, and I'll send him to hell with you. If not, you go alone: and your jumping-off place is that pit."

We let him down another six feet.

"Stop!" screamed Cain. "I won't have it. I mean, I'll do as you say."

"I'll see to that," said I, and we hauled him up.

Once up, we bound his hands and made the blackguard fast to the balusters. Then Carson went off to the passage and drew back the beam: and, when the floor had settled, he wound it back. So the hall was safe. But, in case of accidents, he went to the other passage and shot the second beam. And then, at last, we were able to cross the hall, and Mansel and George and the servants were able to sit on the steps and to breathe fresh air. Not that the air by the lodge was truly fresh: but it seemed like attar of roses after the stench of corruption which laded the hall.

But Carson and I conducted Cain to a bedroom, found a pen and paper and bade him write.

"Use your own words," said I. "But tell the Duke this – that we are all dead: that two were shot and four fell into the pit: that, before we died, we killed Auger: and that, as a result of his death, you can give no orders, because the men who are left cannot understand what you say. Ask him therefore to send an interpreter, or, better still, come himself, for the sooner things are cleaned up, the better for all concerned."

"And how will you send this letter?"

"That's my affair," said I. "And you'd better write a letter he won't suspect: for if he doesn't fetch up, I'll shove you back in the pit."

"He won't come at once," said Cain.

"I'll give him till dawn," said I.

Cain picked up the pen and wrote...

I left Carson with him and went back to Mansel and George. But they and Bell and Rowley were fast asleep. I was not surprised at this, for, crossing the floor, they had staggered like drunken men: and I think that the foetid air had acted upon their systems as some intoxicant and that the fresh, night air had, so to speak, knocked them out.

Almost more than anything else, this showed me what they had suffered down in that pit; for Mansel possessed an endurance which was not of this world, and to see him yield to Nature before some business was done was proof of the savagery of the ordeal through which he had passed. But, Cain, of course, had suffered for a very much shorter spell.

By the time I was back in the bedroom the letter was done; and I must say it read very well.

I took and folded the sheet, which Cain had addressed to Duke Saul.

"I think that should do it," said Cain. "If it does, I like to think—"

"If it does," said I, "as soon as he's dead, you'll be shot – and thrown into the pit. If it doesn't, you won't be shot: but you'll still be thrown into the pit."

With that, in spite of his protests, we bound him hand and foot: and we left him there in the bedroom, for we had a lot to do.

Before we did anything else, we went the rounds of the house, opening every room and searching both high and low; for, although I was very sure that Cain had spoken the truth and that the Duchess of Varvic was not in the lodge, I dared not take the word of such a father of lies. But when we had done, we knew that she was not there.

For all that had happened, the night was not far advanced. It was ten minutes past twelve – almost exactly four hours since we had set out from the farm. And in that time four men had died, and four had been raised from the dead.

Between us, Carson and I performed the unpleasant task of fetching the bodies and laying them down on the floor at the foot of the stairs. We covered them up with some blankets which Carson brought down from above; but, I must confess, my heart smote me for the deaths of Kleiner and Hans, for they were guiltless, compared with Forecast and Cain. Still, they had consented to our destruction, and, if they had not died, five out of six of us would have lost their lives.

At half past one I roused Mansel – against my will: but I felt that the time had come to send the note to Duke Saul, and this I could not arrange without Mansel's help; for, though I was clear as to what I wanted to do, because I could not speak German, I could not further my plan.

To my relief, however, Mansel sat up and yawned and declared that his sleep had refreshed him beyond belief, that, except for a taste in his mouth, he felt perfectly well. When I told him what I proposed, he listened carefully.

"I can't better that," he said. "I wish I could. But I think it ought to come off. Let me see that note."

Calling for Carson, he led the way to the guard-room, shot a glance at Boll and read the note by the light of the hanging lamp.

"Couldn't be better," he said. He nodded at Boll. "Untie his ankles, Carson, and get him up to his feet."

Boll was upon the edge of panic.

With starting eyes, he shrank from Mansel as though from an apparition; and I must say I do not blame him, for that was precisely what Mansel appeared to be, and I am quite sure that, had he strolled down some lane, any being he happened to encounter would have turned and run for his life.

Mansel addressed him in German.

"You see this note?"

Boll tried to say that he did.

"You will take this note to the sentries at the mouth of the drive. And you will use these words – *Hans orders you to take this note to the castle as fast as you can. You will both go and, once you have delivered this note, you need not return. All the English are dead and Auger has lost his life.* Now repeat that."

Three times he made Boll repeat it, until he made no mistake.

"You will say nothing else – not another word. If they question you, you will not reply: but the moment you have said your piece, you will turn on your heel and come back. You will not go alone. This servant of mine will go with you. In one hand he will have a pistol: in the other, the end of a cord which is fastened about your waist. If you try to escape or if you say anything else than the words you have learned, he will shoot you dead. And now repeat them again."

Boll did as he said.

"Perform this task faithfully, and I will spare your life. This you do not deserve, for by unlocking the floor you sent Herr Cain to his death. But of that I shall say nothing so long as you hold your tongue."

We had no cord, but I cut a length of wire which ran from the drive and this we tied round his waist beneath his blouse. Then we cut a hole in his blouse and passed the end through. Then Carson untied his hands and we gave him the note. And then the two set off for the mouth of the drive – with ten feet of wire between them; and since the night was so dark, I could not see Boll when Carson began to move.

I must confess I was glad to see them return, but Carson reported that all had gone very well. Boll had delivered his message and said nothing else, and the sentries had taken the note and had left at once.

"All the same," said Mansel, "I'm not too easy about him. We cannot bump the man off and, once Saul is dead, there will be no one to make him hold his tongue. Of course, Saul may not turn up; in which case it doesn't matter, for Saul will see to it that he doesn't talk. But if Saul does turn up and we put him where he belongs, an inquiry into his – er – disappearance, is simply bound to be held. And that is where Boll will come in."

"Except for him," I said, "there's no one at all."

"I know – all thanks to you. You've done a wonderful job. Let nothing worry you, William. You had your back to the wall. And all you did was to get them before they got you." Here he glanced at his watch and got to his feet. "It's now nearly half past two. Those sentries won't reach the castle before half past three. Probably not before four – but say half past three. And if Saul turns out at once, he won't be here before four. If he comes at all, I should say he'd arrive about six. Any way, we've plenty of time, and so I think I might have a talk with Boll. You have a look at Cain – just to see he's all right."

With that, he walked into the guard-room, while Carson stayed on the steps, and I went off to the bedroom where Cain was lying bound.

About Cain I felt uneasy. I knew that I should not shoot him – that Carson or Mansel would play executioner. But, though he was worthy of death, I did not like the idea of killing him in cold blood. Five hours ago I could have torn his throat out, and so I would have done if I could have got to his side. But now that the others were saved, my rage was gone. I knew that he had to die – if for no other reason, because we could not afford to let him live. But I did not like the business, and that is the truth.

Looking back, I think that my trouble was that I had saved him alive. I would not have minded shooting him while he was down in the pit; but to spare him only to kill him savoured to me of the way of a cat with a mouse. And as I walked up the staircase, the bedroom for which I was making seemed to take on the horrid atmosphere of a condemned hold.

I remember bracing myself before I laid hold of the door-handle....

The handle turned, but the door itself did not yield.

I set my shoulder against it and burst the rotten woodwork apart. Then I used my torch, which showed me that Cain was gone.

I let out a yell for Carson and smashed my way into the room.

Its window was wide open, and flinders of glass on the floor showed me how the prisoner had managed to sever his bonds.

At once I leapt for the window – to see Cain clinging to the gutter some ten feet away.

The light of my torch revealed his terrified face.

"Help me," he whimpered. "I can't move either way and I'm nearly done."

His plight was hopeless. He was hanging some forty-two feet above the stable-yard. The gutter which he had been using had given way and was hanging and swaying between myself and him. Above him one piece remained – I know not why – but the down-pipe for which he had been making, had left the wall and now leaned drunkenly outward, only prevented from falling by some staple I could not see. Upon the remains of a staple Cain had his foot, and this and the gutter above him were holding him up, but unless he could gain the next window, only a ladder could save him from breaking his neck.

The man had been mad, of course, to try to escape this way. He had seen the lodge by daylight, and so had I. And nothing on earth would have made me essay its gutters or put my weight on a down-pipe, whilst there was another way. He could have taken a passage, watched from a peep-hole and made a dash for the door. He could have gained the ground floor and opened a window there. But only a fool in his folly would have put his faith in a structure which had been so plainly neglected for God knows how many years.

As I turned, Carson arrived.

"Look out of the window," I said, and ran for the room next door.

But when I had opened its window, I saw there was no hope there, for the gutter above was drooping and when, standing up on the sill, I stretched out my arm and took hold, a piece two or three feet long came away in my hand.

"For God's sake be quick," cried Cain.

"D'you know of a ladder?" I said. "Have you seen one here?"

"The rope," screamed Cain. "My fingers are giving way."

For what it was worth, I told Carson to run for the rope.

It was a chance in a thousand – slighter than that. An ape could have caught the rope and shifted his grip and then launched himself into space – and not let go. But I doubt if I could have done it, and I was much younger than Cain and twice or three times as strong.

"For God's sake be quick," cried Cain. "D'you want me to die like this?"

"The rope is coming," I said. "That's all I can say."

Here Carson came into the room, with the rope on his arm.

"He'll never do it, sir."

"I know," I said. "Never mind. I'll hold the torch and you chuck the rope over his arm and under his chin, but make it fast first."

"I've made it fast – to the top of the banisters."

"My God," screamed Cain, "I'm going. I can't hold on."

"Five seconds more," I cried. "Here comes the rope."

Carson threw it deftly: it landed across the man's arms and under his chin. At once I picked up the slack and bent it over the sill. And Carson laid hold.

Again I leaned out of the window, torch in hand.

"Take hold of the rope," I cried. "Let go and take hold of the rope."

And then, before my eyes, Cain took his chance in a thousand – and threw it away.

Reluctant to shift his grip and trust himself to the rope, he made a desperate effort to get his elbow into the gutter first. So he would have one hand free to lay hold on the rope. Somehow, he brought it off: but, as an immediate result, he shifted some weight from the staple on which he had set his toe and added this to the gutter which had already more than enough to bear.

As his elbow sank into the gutter, the gutter began to give way, and Cain in his frenzy, instead of seizing the rope, snatched at the slates above it, as though they would help him up.

"The rope," I roared. "The rope. It's your only chance."

But I think the man was past hearing.

His smile twisted into a grin, he clawed at the slates, while the gutter bent slowly downwards beneath his weight.

And then, at the last, I think he took leave of his senses; for he abandoned his foothold and, with a most frightful contortion, tried to set foot in the gutter, as though he were some urchin, idly amusing himself three feet above the ground.

So the camel's back was broken.

With a rending sound, what was left of the gutter gave way, and, letting a cry which rang far into the night, Cain fell into the yard with the old iron still in his hands.

That he was instantly killed, there can be no doubt. And though I could not have wished him so disagreeable an end, I was greatly relieved to think he had done the duty which otherwise must have been ours.

At once I ran to meet Mansel, who, I knew, must have heard the cry, and I found him at the foot of the staircase with Boll on his lead.

"All well," I said. "He tried to escape and a gutter let him down."

"Just as well," said Mansel. "I'll take this fellow back to the guard-room; and then you and Carson had better collect, the corpse." He glanced at the blanketed figures, waiting to be interred. "Yes, Boll," he said, using German. "Let this be a lesson to you. 'The wages of sin is death'. And I think you'd be well advised to do as I say."

"I believe, sir," said Boll, saucer-eyed, "I believe that your counsel is good."

By the time we had 'laid out' Cain, it was past three o'clock.

Then Mansel called Carson and told him to pinion Boll, "for though," he said, "he is going to do as I say, there is, I hope, another scene coming, and I don't want him on in that."

Together we walked to the steps, where George and Bell and Rowley were still asleep.

"Boll's going home," said Mansel. "We're going to take him to Villach and put him on board the train. He lives not far from Innsbruck – at least, his people do. He's very badly frightened, and I think he'll be glad to get out while the going is good. When he's asked why he cut and ran, he's going to say that the setting of all the man-traps got on his nerves. That happens to be perfectly true. He finds them barbarous – as do all the foresters. And when you come to think, that's natural enough, for nine out of ten of them come of a poaching stock."

"You don't think he'll talk?" said I.

"He may – later on. But by then we'll be out of the way. And I don't think they'll run him to earth. I don't think they'll look for him. I think they'll assume that he is with Auger and Hans, wherever they are."

Here Carson arrived, to say he had bound Boll's hands and had put him into the passage and locked the doors at each end.

"Good," said Mansel. "And this is where we wait. I think that note should fetch him – Saul, I mean. But I hardly like to wait after half past six. We mustn't be caught here, you know. And now let's think out his reception. I'd like to do him well; but we mustn't make any mistake."

Duke Saul of Varvic arrived before the sun was up. It was that cold hour when men can see and be seen, when the rear of darkness is thin. I think perhaps he came early, because, knowing what he had done, he hoped to be back at his castle before the world was awake. Be that as it may, he came – and he came alone. We heard his new two-seater before it had left the road.

We heard it slow down, to enter the mouth of the drive. And we heard it stealing towards us – towards the lodge and the forecourt, where we, and not Cain, were waiting to play out the final scene.

I was standing close to the forecourt, within the wood, near to the path we had taken the night before: and the others were likewise concealed, but ready to enter the moment they had their cue. And the lodge seemed to be deserted; only the lamp was still burning above the stairs.

Then the fine two-seater slid slowly into the forecourt, and we saw that Saul was driving, and driving alone.

He brought the car to a standstill: then he switched her engine off, opened the door by his side and slid to the ground. For a moment he looked at the lodge: then he put his hand back to the wheel and sounded his horn. And then he moved to the steps...

At the foot of the steps he stopped and lighted a cigarette: then he looked up to see Mansel, standing framed in the doorway, with folded arms.

Now, though I knew very well why Mansel looked as he did and though I had been by his side for the last four hours, I must confess that the white figure, standing there in that curious light, made my flesh creep upon my bones. And so I despair of conveying the effect that it had upon Saul.

For a moment he stood, as though he had been turned into stone. Then he clapped his hands to his mouth and he made a noise like that of a man in pain that is not to be borne, a sobbing, wailing sound, that might have been a prelude to something worse. And so it was. With staring eyes, he turned to run for his car; but, whiter even than Mansel, Rowley rose up from behind it, before he had reached its door. With a scream I shall always hear, Saul turned to make for the drive; but there he saw George standing, barring his way. Again he recoiled, and let out that frightful scream – a scream which seemed to echo the laughter of the damned. It was a maniac sound: and, indeed, I think at that moment the man was out of his mind. Be that as it may, he turned to run for the yard. There Bell was waiting for him, but he never got so far; for, as he went, he saw the mouth of the path – the path which we had taken the night before.

As he took the path, a bough twitched his hat from his head.

I turned and ran behind him...

Whether he heard me or not, I do not know. Sometimes I think that he was past all hearing and that his one idea was to leave the hunting-lodge. Sometimes I think he did hear me – and thought that one of his dead was in hot pursuit. All I can vouch for is that, fast as I ran, the man outdistanced me, and so he was out of my sight when he entered the trap.

For a shocking reason I never heard its jaws close; but I knew very well what had happened, for all of a sudden a cry which beggared the others rang out ahead. And not one cry only. Scream upon scream – to make the blood run cold.

I stopped and drew my pistol and braced myself: for I meant to end his torment, by shooting him like a dog.

But Mansel's hand fell on my arm.

"Come," he said. "We must leave him. I'd like to have ended it, but, for our own protection, we must not put him out."

I preceded him – mutinously.

Before we had reached the forecourt, the sounds had stopped.

"I'm sorry," said Mansel, "but, you see, we're not dealing with Cain. The death of Duke Saul of Varvic is going to be head-line news. I meant to have shot him and chucked him into the pit. But now he's done very much better, for, as we have reason to know, disappearance is unsatisfactory, but 'death by misadventure' is a verdict that none can contest."

Mansel was right, of course. Once again Fortune had played clean into our hands. Yet, as I looked at Saul's hat, hanging up on the bough, I remembered those other hats that had been hung upon poles not very far off; and when I remembered them, I could not help feeling that something greater than Fortune had taken a hand in the game.

Whilst we had been waiting for Saul, Carson had found some water and had washed the blood from the staircase and had cleansed the guard-room of the stains which Kleiner's body had left. Then he and I, between us, had stripped that room and the bedrooms of the little furniture there and had taken and laid it upon the floor of the hall. So now we had nothing to do but to draw the bolts of the floor, and this we did together, as soon as I reached the lodge.

Once again the floor tilted, to shoot its burden of dead men and their effects, and once again I heard that rumbling, slithering sound: then the floor crashed back into place, and Carson and I, between us, shot the bolts.

After that, we all turned to and dragged the sacks of quick lime on to the floor, and there we opened their mouths and poured their contents out. And when this was done, for the last time we drew the bolts, to hear the lime go down: and when the floor had settled, we locked it once more into place.

Then George and Rowley took Boll and bound his eyes, that he might not see the two-seater, as he went out. Then we locked the passages up and we took the keys.

Once more I climbed the staircase, to lower and put out the lamp and pick up the Duchess' coat, and as I came back down the hall Carson was making ready to close the doors of the lodge.

Together we pulled them to and passed down the steps.

"Where are the others?" I said.

"Just in the drive, sir," said Carson. "They've taken Forecast's car."

"Good for them," said I. "I'd forgotten that."

As we were leaving the forecourt, I hung on my heel, to look my last on the place against which our instinct had warned us, in which we had so nearly come to a dreadful end. For it had been a very near thing – a matter of two or three moments... no more than that. Had Carson not arrived when he did – had he come *but one second later*, the rest of us must have died. Nothing on earth could have saved us; for Forecast could not have missed me and, except by being cast down, Carson would never have learned that the floor was made to give way. And nobody could have survived for more than two hours in that pit.

I did not fear the place now, perhaps because I knew the awful secrets it kept, but I think I shall always see it, standing deserted and silent, sunk in its birdless woods.

It was a true charnel-house. God knows what Varvic had built it, but it must have been two hundred and fifty years old: and God knows how many poor souls strode into it cheerfully, some tired, perhaps, with hunting, to meet a horrible doom. For it was most horrible. Death is grim in whatever guise it comes but the death the hunting-lodge offered was surely the foulest ever devised by man. Its victim was cast alive into a common grave, to spend his last moments stumbling on a mound of corruption that once had been men like himself, which soon he was going to swell, and breathing that frightful odour which his poor corpse must presently aggravate.

And then I remembered the graveyard that lay behind...

Little wonder the woods were birdless. Indeed, I found it strange that the trees should put forth their leaves about an acre which man had made so monstrous: but Nature always remembers the pitiful dead.

As I entered the car –

"I'd forgotten this," said I.

"Out of sight, out of mind," said Mansel. "So had I. But George remembered it – mercifully. We've cleaned up so very well that it would have been grievous to leave a pointer like this. We're not concerned with Saul: all the world can see how he came by his death. But a car without any owner would give the police ideas. Well, let it give them ideas – but not near the lodge. We'll shove it into a meadow some twelve miles off."

And so we did. But first we picked up the Rolls at Four Mile Point.

On the way we stopped by a stream and dropped the keys of the passages into a pool, and then we drove for Goschen as hard as we could.

# XIII

## ROADSTEAD

Since an Innsbruck train left Villach in less than an hour George and Rowley made haste to bathe and change, for they were to take the Lowland and see Boll off. But long before they were ready, Carson and I were once more out in the Rolls.

We drove for Varvic, using the southern drive.

We took the car right up to the castle gate, and there I demanded to see the Duchess at once.

After two or three minutes, a personal maid appeared.

She looked at me very hard, and then she asked me in French what reason I had to think that the Duchess was there. I showed her the telegram which had been delivered to Goschen the evening before.

At once she nodded and asked me to follow her.

She led me upstairs to a boudoir, full of the morning sun, and there the Duchess was standing, wrapped in a dressing-gown of black and gold.

As the door closed behind me –

"Oh, my dear," she cried, "but what are you doing here? He's out; so they take my orders, except that I may not leave; but the instant that he returns – "

"He will never return," said I. "Nor will Cain, or Forecast or Auger."

She started back and a hand went up to her mouth.

"We never touched him," I said. "He died in a trap which he had had set for us. And there, when they search for him, will his body be found. The others – will not be found. In a word, we have done what we set out to do. And now we are going, because Mansel thinks it wiser that we should go at once. Not one single thing can be proved: but we don't want to be involved, and we may be involved if we stay. You, of course, must know nothing of all these things. But as soon as you can, we hope you will come to England, and two of us will meet you in Paris, whenever you like. And there we will give you back your pretty coat. There's Mansel's address." I gave her a slip of paper. "If you are in any trouble, wire there at once: but put at the end of your wire the three words *love to Jill*. Jill is Mansel's sister. You do not know her, of course, but that will prove to us that the wire is from you."

The Duchess stepped to the window and stood looking out.

"I wish to God," she said, "I could leave with you. But, of course, I can't do that. Still, I shall leave for Paris within the week. D'you know the Hôtel du Rhin in the Place Vendôme?"

"Yes."

"Today is Saturday. Let's say that I shall be there on Thursday next."

"May we call there on Friday morning?"

"Yes, if you please. We've got such a lot to say. And I can't say it here – in this house. Besides, I mustn't keep you. I'm sure it's important that you should leave the country at once."

"I think it is better," I said.

She turned about.

"You shouldn't really have come here."

I shrugged my shoulders.

"There was no other way of letting you know. Besides..."

"Besides what?"

"Do you really think we'd have gone until we had known you were safe?"

She smiled at that, and put out a hand for mine.

"When they stopped me upon the road, I knew that you'd come. I saw in a flash that I was to be the decoy: and so I had fear for you – but none for myself."

"And when the hours went by, but we didn't come?"

"I knew you would – in the end. I never feared. You see, you are so like John. And in the short time that I knew him – well, he cast out fear. Perfect love does, you know." She cupped her face in her palms. "I'm not like most women I know. Most women would like to think that you had done this for them. But I rejoice to think that you have done it for him. Of course, I've come into it, because I was part of him. And it was for my sake that you went out last night. But if the triumph is yours, the tribute is his."

Her words were true enough, for though she had not existed, we should have done our utmost to bring Bowshot's murderers down. For all that, I bowed my head, that she should not see my eyes, for, since we had come to know her, I think we all confused what we had felt was our duty with what we knew was her wish.

Then she put out her little hand, and I put it up to my lips. But she leaned forward and set her cheek against mine.

"God bless you all," she whispered. "And you especially, Richard, for you were so sweet to me that night in the lane."

I kissed her hand again and held it fast.

"Till Friday?" I said.

"Till Friday."

I took my leave.

By now I was very tired, but if I had thought to rest, when I got back to the farm I was undeceived; for Mansel and George and Rowley were packing like men possessed. By the time I had shaved and bathed, the cars had been laden and we were ready to leave. All this, that we should reach Salzburg before the Banks had closed, and so withdraw the papers which we had lodged.

I was descending the stairs, when the police drove up to the door.

"Yes?" said Mansel.

"Sir," said the inspector, "I have some grave statements to make."

Mansel leaned back in his chair and looked rather bored.

"Pray let me hear them," he said.

"Wilful murder has been committed. We do not know how or why. But we shall find out – never fear. And we shall bring to book the men who committed the crime."

"I'm sure you will," said Mansel, comfortably. "And how can we help?"

"You are English," said the inspector.

"Certainly," said Mansel. "And what of that?"

"Do you know a place called Latchet?"

"I've never stopped there," said Mansel. "I've passed through the village. If I remember, it's built by the side of a stream."

"Ten days ago five Englishmen were staying at Latchet. We know where one of them is, but where are the other four?"

Mansel frowned.

"How should I know?" he said.

The inspector looked away.

"A conversation," he said, "was overheard. In the course of that conversation, a proper name was mentioned – not once, but several times. The name was Goschen... And that, as you are aware, is the name of this farm."

"That," said Mansel, "is very interesting. And what was said about Goschen?"

The inspector lifted a hand.

"One moment," he said. He took from his pocket a passport that I had seen before. He opened it and gave it to Mansel. "Regard that photograph, please."

"*Benjamin Gulf*," said Mansel, reading aloud. "Unattractive-looking fellow, isn't he?"

With his eyes fast on Mansel's face –

"Have you," said the inspector, "have you ever seen that man?"

"Good heavens, no," said Mansel. He handed the passport to me. "Take a look at that, William. Have you ever seen that bloke?"

Gulf's face stared out at me, as I shook my head.

"Never," I lied, and handed the passport back.

Mansel gave it to George.

"And you?"

George inspected the portrait.

"I'm glad to be able to say he's a stranger to me."

"Show it to the servants," said Mansel, "and see what they say."

George nodded and left the room.

Mansel returned to the inspector.

"Is that one of the men that you are anxious to find?"

The inspector shook his head.

Then he leaned forward.

"That man's body was found by Latchet. He had been rudely buried. Some days ago he died a violent death. His head had been crushed."

"How very unpleasant," said Mansel. "But what's this to do with me?"

The inspector cleared his throat.

"I will tell you," he said. "That man had been staying at Latchet with four other Englishmen. A week ago today the five of them left. In fact, they left without warning the day before: but two came back the next morning to pay their bill and pack what luggage they had. But Gulf was not one of these."

"Can't you trace the others?" said Mansel.

"We hope to very soon by means of their car. But that is not all. At the moment there is at the inn another Englishman. At least, he says he is English: but he bears an Italian name. And when we ask for his passport, he has it not. He did not arrive until Thursday – long after this man was dead. But the curious thing is this, sir – he denied all knowledge of Gulf, but when I showed him Gulf's passport, I saw that he knew his face."

Mansel fingered his chin.

"That's very strange," he said.

"More. Yesterday afternoon this man was visited by one of the four: and there was a terrible scene, the resident weeping and wailing and the visitor shouting him down. The landlady speaks no English, so she could not understand what was said, but again and again she heard the name 'Goschen' used: and Goschen, as I have said, is the name of this farm."

As though in excitement, Mansel leaped to his feet.

"Describe these men," he cried. "Is one of them tall and dark – with an everlasting smile?"

"But that is right," cried the inspector, starting up.

"Calls himself 'Cain'?"

"Yes, yes. That is one of the four. It was he who visited Latchet yesterday afternoon."

Mansel stretched out an arm.

"That is the man that came here ten days ago. He came in a car and he said he was staying near here. He was undoubtedly English, but I didn't like his looks. When I asked him what he wanted, he would not say: he tried to make me believe that he had come to call: but, whilst he was here, his driver was found by the servants inspecting the back of the house. In the end I had him shown out; for I didn't like his looks or his manner and I was perfectly sure that he was up to no good."

"And that is all you know, sir?"

"That's all I know. But I'll tell you what I will do. I have friends at Scotland Yard; and as soon as I get to London, I'll ask them to look up his record and let you know."

The inspector was deeply impressed.

"That would be most kind of you, sir."

"Not at all," said Mansel. "The man should be laid by the heels. He may or may not be concerned in the death of Benjamin Gulf: but the fact that he mentioned Goschen suggests to me that he has designs upon us. So it's just as well we're going. Any way, Scotland Yard may be able to help." Here George re-entered the room. "Any luck with the servants, George?"

"None," said George.

The passport was handed back.

The inspector bowed.

"I am in your debt, sir," he said. "And may I be permitted to wish you a pleasant trip?"

As he drove away –

"And that," said Mansel, "took fully a week from my life. If they'd thought of testing that passport for finger-prints..."

"My God," said George. "That's why you gave it to me."

"That's why," said Mansel, and smiled. "Well, we're safe enough now. But I don't think we'll wait any longer. Today or tomorrow they're going to find Forecast's car. They've nothing on us of course. But I'd rather not be questioned again. When one knows as much as we do, it is so very easy to put a foot wrong."

Be sure we agreed with him.

So we drew the papers from Salzburg that afternoon and before night fell we had entered Germany. We lay that night at a village whose name I forget, and the second night after that we spent at Mansel's flat in Cleveland Row.

So we came back to England, exactly seven weeks from the day we set out: and, except for Bell's broken wrist, we were not one penny the worse. (I should have said that his wrist was set at Salzburg, as we came through, and the London doctors said that it had been perfectly done.)

On the following day, which was Tuesday, Mansel sent a letter to Scotland Yard.

DEAR GEOFFREY,

*Major John Bowshot, deceased, of*
*The Manor House, Beehive, Somerset.*

*This poor fellow was murdered on 1st July last, three miles from the village of Latchet in Krain, Austria. I discovered his body and buried it not very far from where I found it lying upon the Salzburg road.*

*The blows were struck by two hirelings, Frederic Ernest Bones and Benjamin Gulf. Both these men have since died.*

*As I had intended it should, my disposal of Bowshot's body caused those behind the crime considerable inconvenience and within a month of the murder they dispatched James Belper Orion Forecast to Latchet with certain instructions, the original of which I enclose, and a letter of introduction to the late Duke Saul of Varvic, also enclosed. Forecast was accompanied by Bones and Gulf and one other man.*

*On 2nd August these four were joined by Joseph Cain, junior partner of Worsted and Co., of Jawbone Lane.*

*Unable to locate Bowshot's body, Cain interred that of Gulf, in the hope that, when found, it would be mistaken for that of Bowshot. The police, however, finding his passport on the body, identified it as that of Gulf.*

*In response to a telegram, purporting to have been sent by Cain, his senior partner, Aaron Biretta reached Austria on August 12th, on which day he signed a statement, the original of which I enclose.*

*A perusal of this statement will show you why Bowshot died.*

*I have reason to believe that Cain and Forecast are dead. Biretta was alive at Latchet on August 14th.*

*I enclose:*

(*a*) *Biretta's statement,*
(*b*) *Forecast's instructions,*
(*c*) *letter addressed to Duke Saul,*
(*d*) *the envelope and map referred to in* (*b*),
(*e*) *a second, similar envelope, found upon Cain,*
(*f*) *the passports of Biretta, Cain, Forecast and Bones,*
(*g*) *the cloak-room receipt for Bowshot's effects.*

Note: –

(*i*) *Under the name of Orion, Forecast was running a hostel in Bedlam Row. I think that, if this hostel was visited, it would be found that admission is limited to convicts who are for hire.*

(*ii*) *His Britannic Majesty's Consul at Salzburg has Bowshot's passport: he also has reason to believe that Bowshot was still alive on July 16th: in fact, this belief is ill-founded and may be ignored.*

(*iii*) *I am prepared to prove John Bowshot's death to the satisfaction of the Court, for I have in my possession his note-case and the tailor's tab or label which I cut from his coat.*

*It is not for me to make recommendations, but I think I am right in saying that, for some time past, the Director of Public Prosecutions has been uneasy about Worsted and Co. and I hope that Biretta's statement will enable him to take such action as he may think desirable.*

*Yours ever,*

*Jonah.*

P.S. – *The Austrian police are looking for Cain. They won't find him, but they would love a line from you, to say that, although his name does not appear in your records, you are about to proceed against his firm.*

What answer Mansel received, I do not know: but I know that on Wednesday night Geoffrey dined with Mansel at Cleveland Row. I know that, because he told us that 'Geoffrey' was going to come: then he set his hands on our shoulders and this is what he said.

"It is a real grief to me that I cannot ask you as well. Without you, I could have done nothing, and I shall tell him so. But he is within the law and I am without the law; he is the right hand and I, sometimes, am the left: and the right hand must never know what the left hand does. That is the golden rule – which now and again we break. *But no one must know that we break it.* Whilst he is here with me, Carson will be standing outside the door and one of his men will be watching the door of the flats."

This was easy to understand, and we said as much; but Jonathan Mansel was the most generous of men and I very much doubt if he did himself justice that night. For to him must go the credit for all we did. Of the actual thrust and parry, I had a very fair share; but, but for Mansel's brain we should never have come to blows. I have often worked with him since, but I never saw his precious gift of vision displayed to more advantage than in this case. How many men would have seen that Bowshot had been murdered? And how many professional detectives would have read aright the riddle – or seen that there *was* a riddle – set by the fact that the tailor's label was loose? Yet, weary to death as he was when he found the corpse, he saw that for some good reason the murderers needed proof that their victim was dead: and so he hid the body and put a spoke in their wheel. That they needed such proof was the only card he had, but he played it again and again – to take trick after trick. He had next to nothing to go on, till Forecast came: and then, though we might have struck, he had the wit and the patience to hold his hand. One by one he lured the principals into the net, and though, at the last, they nearly brought us down, they only got as far as they did by deceiving and showing violence to a lady who had suffered enough. And that was the kind of card which, though he had picked up a handful, Mansel would never have played.

So 'the right hand' dined with 'the left' on Wednesday night: and Mansel and George and I left by air for Paris the following day.

Caroline, Duchess of Varvic regarded her excellent hands.

"First," she said, "let me tell you as much as I know. And then you three shall tell me as much as you please. I think, perhaps, it's better that you shouldn't tell me too much. You see, you have managed so well that, so far as I can make out, between Goschen and Varvic I am the only link. That link is very slender. Well, we don't want to make it strong – in case it should presently be tested. I don't think it will be tested; but I'd rather not know too much, just in case it is."

"I entirely agree," said Mansel. "Besides, inquiries apart, the less you know, the less you will have to forget: for I hope you will forget a great deal that is past. That, of course, will take time: but I've thought of a way which would shorten that time for me; and so, before we go, I'm going to suggest it to you. And now please let us hear what you have to tell."

"Richard left me," said the Duchess, "about a quarter to eight, and I knew nothing more till they came to me for orders at a quarter to twelve. Saul, they said, had gone out, but had not returned. He had gone out very early, driving alone. I asked where he had gone to: but nobody seemed to know. I waited till one o'clock and then I sent out three cars to scour the countryside. The cars were back by three, but they brought no news. I then informed the police.

"Saul's body was found on Sunday, just before noon. He had been killed in a man-trap, about six miles from the castle, in a quarter of the estate which I have never seen. There is, I believe, an old house, in the heart of some very thick woods; but the place has been abandoned for many years. Very few, I am told, will go near it, for suicides are said to be buried there, and they say that the woods are shunned by birds and beasts. Locally, it is known as Golgotha. Why Saul should have gone there nobody seems to know. His car was found close to the house. The man-traps were in the charge of a foreman called Hans: it seemed likely that he would know something; but Hans had disappeared. So have two other men who were known to be working with him. A suggestion has been made that Saul drove out privily, because he wanted no one to know of the man-traps which he had had set – that they were barbarous things is very plain – and that, when he walked into one, Hans and the others were frightened to death and fled. Hans is not regretted; he was a brute of a man. That Auger was Saul's confidential valet, I think you know. His disappearance has been noted, but not pursued: the man was detested and feared by high and low. Of Forecast the police know nothing, but I understand that they were looking for Cain. A car he had used was found, not very far from the Salzburg-Villach road. Cain was known to have been in touch with Saul.

"An inquest was held on Monday, without result. Saul was found to have died by misadventure: the police were careful not to produce the trap. It seems that such things are illegal and may not be set. For the honour of Varvic, therefore, the matter will not be pursued. For the same reason, search for Hans and his fellows will not be made. The police do not want revelations which would reflect upon Saul. But they are hot to find Cain. They have the impression that Cain could give them the answer to many things. They think that Cain is the villain of the piece. They believe that Saul visited Golgotha in response to a summons from Cain. A summons in the shape of a note; but that note cannot be found. They have the two men who brought it: but, except that they were told to bring it, these men pretend to know nothing of what occurred. But they brought it from Golgotha, which argues that Cain was there. Yet his car was found miles away. So the police are mystified. There is an Italian at Latchet, whom they have put under arrest. He weeps and wails all the time, but he will not talk. He denies all knowledge of Cain, but the police insist that Cain visited him on Friday and that a quarrel took place. In fact, the whole business is wrapped in mystery. It is thought that certain foresters could talk, if they pleased: but Saul's death has frightened them all, and the word has gone round for them to hold their tongues. And I think the man-traps upset them. It seems that the one Saul died in was one of ten or twelve: and they should not have been set. So no one knows anything, for fear of being involved.

"Working with poles, they found four traps in the meadows and two by one of the drives. The remaining three or five, as the case may be, are thought to be in Golgotha: but no one, the police included, likes looking for them, so the place will be fenced about and marked with DANGER boards.

"The funeral took place on Tuesday. The heir attended – Saul's cousin: he's not too bad. He is now Duke Rudolph of Varvic. Saul had next to nothing, except from me: and now that he's dead, my income is mine again. But Rudolph has money and so will keep up the estate. He asked me to stay, if I pleased, for the next three months, but I've said goodbye and I shan't go back again.

"Well, there you are. That's really all I know – apart from what Richard told me, and he didn't say very much. But he said enough to show me that you three have done such justice as the law could never have done. And so I am very sure that John sleeps in peace. But one thing worries me – that wretched Italian that they have put under arrest. There's some mistake there, of course. And I'd hate to think—"

"He's not an Italian," said Hansel, "though he bears an Italian name. He is Cain's partner."

"Ah!"

"He's served his turn, but he wasn't worth putting to death, and that's the truth. But the rope is round his neck. Yesterday morning at Bow Street an information was sworn and two men left for Austria yesterday afternoon. So he will return to England under arrest. He will not be charged with conspiring to cause John Bowshot's death: he will be charged with converting his and other fortunes. He will certainly go to prison for at least ten years.

"We saw him eight days ago: and we took a statement from him. I brought a copy with me for you to see. It's rather illuminating – confirms a good many suspicions and ties some ends up. And I'm going to show it you now, because it introduces the suggestion which I said I was going to make."

With that, he put the copy into her hand.

The Duchess read it carefully, finger to lip.

As she handed it back –

"How on earth did he come to sign this?"

"We suggested that, if he did, he might escape arrest on a capital charge."

"It sounds very easy, when you put it like that. In fact you make light of everything. The notes you used to send to the clinic... Yet, what is the truth? You started from scratch, you've unravelled every inch of theaeoemystery and you've brought to book every one of the guilty men. I wish I knew how to thank you."

"We want no thanks," said George. "To be frank, we don't even deserve them. We have simply met the demands which our sense of justice made. And now please listen to Mansel: as I think you know, he's always getting ideas; but this one appeals to me."

"Well?" said the Duchess, smiling.

"We don't know your plans," said Mansel, "but Beehive is in the market and, before very long, you would, I think, be able to purchase The Manor House. As it stands. As it was left by its owner a month or two back. I should think you could buy the lot for fifty thousand pounds. If you felt like making your home there..."

The Duchess closed her eyes and put her hands to her face.

After a little –

"Will you help me to do it?" she said. "I mean, I should like it better than anything in the world." She rose and stretched out her arms. "What should I have done without you three good men? To live in the home he loved! D'you think his servants would stay? The butler and cook, I mean. They were man and wife. Curly, their name was: and I know they were devoted to him."

"Once they've seen you," said George, "you won't get them out of the house."

Then and there it was settled that Mansel should see his solicitor – Forsyth, by name – and that he should then wait upon the Duchess and take her instructions to purchase not only The Manor House but the Beehive estate. Indeed, it did our hearts good to see how the prospect pleased her. I cannot say that she was gay, but Mansel had set a light in her wonderful eyes.

We did not say goodbye, for she was to come to England within the week, and she made us promise to dine with her in London the day after she arrived.

And that is very nearly the end of my tale.

Upon Mansel's affidavit, the Court gave leave to presume John Bowshot's death. He was found to have died intestate and Letters of Administration were taken out. Six weeks later the Duchess entered his home. She had already bought Beehive, and so the Lady of the Manor dwelled in The Manor House.

And the village was mad about her: no estate in England was more considerately run.

Biretta stood his trial at the Central Criminal Court. He pleaded guilty to conversion and was sentenced to twelve years' penal servitude. John Bowshot was but one of the victims of Worsted and Co. Investigation showed that Biretta and Cain, between them, had stolen from their clients more than one hundred and eighty thousand pounds. And since they had been speculating in foreign currency, the lot was gone.

The 'hostel' in Bedlam Row was raided and closed.

The Austrian police continued their search for Cain for several weeks; then they made up their minds that he must have left the country, and directed their attention to other things.

Of Varvic I know no more than the Duchess said, but I like to think that Rudolph is a worthier master than Saul.

But I often think of those seven crowded weeks and how on that dreadful night we nearly lost the game and our lives and everything. I remember the first quiet nights when we watched the path to Latchet, but nobody ever came: I remember the grim reconstruction of poor John Bowshot's end: and I see Forecast lying senseless, beside the stream, whilst I strove to memorize the map which the Duke had marked: I can hear the Duchess' quick breathing, as we sat on the step of her coupé and I told her the wicked truth: and I see Cain lounging at Goschen – lounging and lying and smiling, with his eyes fast on Mansel's face. I remember our race to Varvic, to rescue George, and how Mansel beat the lorry with less than inches to spare; and I see Hans oiling the man-traps and China's startled gaze; and I hear Biretta's whimper and watch him making his statement with bolting eyes. And then I remember the lodge... with the birdless woods about it... and the devil's acre behind... I feel again the instinct that warned us off, in whose face we were forced to fly on that terrible night; and the burden of those few hours is as sharp and clear in my mind as though it were yesterday's. I see Cain fall with the gutter fast in his grip; I hear Saul's screams, as he paid the wages of sin; but clearest of all is ever the awful event which neither eye nor ear can be said to record, when the hall of the lodge disappeared, when the darkness gaped upon me, when the very breath of corruption blasted my face... I have ridden storms since then, but never like that: for then my soul was shaken and for two or three shocking moments the powers of evil sat on the throne of God.

George Hanbury shall sum up.

"I wouldn't have missed it for anything in the world. It was a great experience: and taking it by and large, we had less rough than smooth. But that merry-go-down was a dirty bit of work, and the wallah that thought it out had a nasty mind. Still, I'd almost face it again to see Caroline ruling Beehive, and the look upon Curly's face when she says, 'Is the port all right? Good. That's Curly. I'm not a judge of wine, but he is a connoisseur.'"

Caroline could have remarried time and again: but John Bowshot had all her heart, so she never did. Unkind as had been her fortune, the years which she spent at Beehive brought her as close to happiness as she could ever come.

And then, six months ago, as I came in from hunting, Bell brought me a telegram...

Caroline had been driving at night, as she still so often did, and she had been hit by a lorry whose steering had given way.

She was sinking, when I got to her side, but, as once before, she set her cheek against mine.

"Soon happier still," she murmured. "And you shall say of me what you said of him. 'She... is... quiet... now. She's gone to her long home.'"

121. The Problemist by Clinton H. Stagg
122. The Dorrington Deed-Box by Morrison, Arthur
123. The Lone Wolf by Vance, L. J.
124. The Complete Martin Hewitt Collection Vol 1: Martin Hewitt, Investigator & Chronicles of Martin Hewitt by Morrison, Arthur
125. The Complete Martin Hewitt Collection Vol 2: Adventures of Martin Hewitt & The Red Triangle: Further Chronicles of Martin Hewitt by Morrison, Arthur
126. Seven Keys to Baldpate by Earl Derr Biggers
127. No Pockets in a Shroud by McCoy, Horace
128. The John Silence Collection by Blackwood, Algernon
129. Lady Molly Of Scotland Yard by Orczy, Baroness Emma
130. Skin O' My Tooth by Orczy, Baroness Emma
131. The Wrong Box by Stevenson, R. L. and Lloyd Osbourne
132. Tutt and Mr Tutt by Train, Arthur C.
133. The Clue by Wells, Carolyn
134. The Complete Trent Case Book by Bentley, E. C.
135. The Luck of the Vails by Benson, E. F.
136. The Rome Express by Griffiths, Arthur
137. The Complete Curious Mr Tarrant by C. Daly King
138. Rope and Gaslight (2-in-1 text) by Hamilton, Patrick
139. Prince Zaleski and Cumming's King Monk by Shiel, M. P.
140. The Assassination Bureau Ltd. by London, Jack
141. Introducing Clubfoot by Williams, Valentine
142. Master of Mysteries: The complete Uncle Abner collection by Post, Melville Davisson
143. The Red Redmaynes by Phillpotts, Eden
144. Thrilling Stories of the Railway by Whitechurch, Victor L.
145. The Grey Wig: Stories and Novelettes by Zangwill, Israel
146. The Lodger by Lowndes, Marie Belloc
147. The Man from Manchester by Donovan, Dick (Joyce Emerson Preston Muddock)
148. Mr. Meeson's Will by H. Rider Haggard by Haggard, H. Rider
149. Devlin the Barber by Farjeon, B. L.
150. Checkmate by Joseph Sheridan Le Fanu
151. Recollections of a Detective Police-Officer by Waters
152. The Widow Lerouge by Gaboriau, Emile
153. The Expressman and the Detective by Pinkerton, Allan
154. Zadig and Vathek by Voltaire
155. The Stillwater Tragedy by Aldrich, Thomas Bailey
156. The Memoirs of Constantine Dix by Pain, Barry
157. Ashes to Ashes by Ostrander, Isabel
158. The Jewel of Seven Stars by Stoker, Bram
159. The Thomas Love Peacock Collection by Peacock, Thomas Love

**THE COMPLETE DERLETH SOLAR PONS**

160. In Re: Sherlock Holmes - The Adventures of Solar Pons
161. The Memoirs of Solar Pons
162. The Return of Solar Pons
163. The Reminiscences of Solar Pons
164. The Casebook of Solar Pons
165. The Novels of Solar Pons: Terror over London and Mr. Fairlie's Final Journey
166. The Chronicles of Solar Pons
167. The Apocrypha of Solar Pons

168. The Triumphs of Eugene Valmont
169. The Female Detective by Forrester, Andrew
170. Cain's Jawbone by Torquemada
171. The Great Impersonation by Oppenheim, E. Phillips

**THE DASHIELL HAMMETT COLLECTION**

172. The Complete Sam Spade
173. The Complete Thin Man
174. The Complete Continental Op Vol 1
175. The Complete Continental Op Vol 2

60. Mr Bowling Buys a Newspaper by Henderson, Donald
61. A Voice Like Velvet by Henderson, Donald
62. The Deductions of Colonel Gore by Brock, Lynn
63. The Rogue's Syndicate by Froest, Frank
64. The Middle Temple Murder by Fletcher, J. S.
65. The Millionaire Mystery by Hume, Fergus
66. Below the Clock by Turner, J. V.
67. The Rouletabille Omnibus: The Mystery of the Yellow Room and The Perfume of the Lady in Black by Leroux, Gaston
68. The Complete Dupin by Poe, Edgar Allan
69. The Complete Thinking Machine Vol 1 by Futrelle, Jacques
70. The Complete Thinking Machine Vol 2 by Futrelle, Jacques
71. The Complete Thinking Machine Vol 3 by Futrelle, Jacques
72. The Complete Montague Egg by Sayers, Dorothy L.
73. The Complete J. G. Reeder by Wallace, Edgar
74. The Complete Charlie Chan Vol 1 by Biggers, Earl der
75. The Complete Charlie Chan Vol 2 by Biggers, Earl der
76. The Dr Nikola Omnibus Vol 1 by Boothby, Guy
77. The Dr Nikola Omnibus Vol 2 by Boothby, Guy
78. A Prince of Swindlers: The Simon Carne collection by Boothby, Guy
79. The Slim Callaghan Omnibus by Cheyney, Peter
80. The Fu Manchu Omnibus by Rohmer, Sax
81. The Bulldog Drummond Omnibus: The Complete Peterson Rounds by Sapper
82. The Avenging Ray by Seamark
83. The Richard Chandos Omnibus by Yates, Dornford
84. The Alan Quatermain Omnibus: King Solomon's Mines & Allan Quatermain by Haggard, H. Rider
85. The 39 steps by Buchan, John
86. At The Villa Rose by Mason, A.E.W.
87. The Eye of Osiris by Freeman, R. Austin
88. The Weapons of Mystery by Hocking, Joseph
89. The House of Dr. Edwardes by Beeding, Francis
90. The Seven Secrets by Le Queux, William
91. Call Mr Fortune by Bailey, H. C.
92. The Three Taps by Knox, Ronald
93. The Girl at Central by Bonner, Geraldine
94. The Experiences of Loveday Brooke, Lady Detective by Pirkis, Catherine Louisa
95. Mary Louise by Baum, L. Frank
96. That Affair Next Door by Green, Anna Katherine
97. Dead Letter by Regester, Seeley
98. The Tragedy of Pudd'nhead Wilson by Twain, Mark
99. The Big Clock by Fearing, Kenneth
100. The Woman in the Window by Wallis, J. H.
101. The Sexton Blake Collection Vol 1 by Hal Meredeth (or many?)
102. The Complete Simon Iff Stories by Crowley, Aleister
103. The Castle of Otranto by Walpole, Horace
104. The Adventures of the Infallible Godahl by Anderson, Frederick Irving

**THE COMPLETE SHERLOCK HOLMES**

105. A Study In Scarlet
106. The Sign Of Four
107. The Adventures Of Sherlock Holmes
108. The Memoirs Of Sherlock Holmes
109. The Hound Of The Baskervilles
110. The Return Of Sherlock Holmes
111. His Last Bow
112. The Valley Of Fear
113. The Case-Book Of Sherlock Holmes

114. Graustark: The Story of a Love Behind a Throne by George Barr McCutcheon
115. Beverly of Graustark by George Barr McCutcheon
116. Truxton King: A Story of Graustark by George Barr McCutcheon
117. The Prince of Graustark by George Barr McCutcheon
118. The Complete Zenda Omnibus by Anthony Hope
119. The Mad king by Burroughs, Edgar Rice
120. The Fantomas Omnibus by Souvestre, Pierre

## Yellowback range available...

1. The Old Man in the Corner by Orczy, Baroness Emma
2. The Complete Max Carrados Vol 1 by Bramah, Ernest
3. The Complete Max Carrados Vol 2 by Bramah, Ernest

**THE ARSÈNE LUPIN SERIES BY LEBLANC, MAURICE:**

4. Arsène Lupin 1: The Extraordinary Adventures of Arsène Lupin - Gentleman Burglar
5. Arsène Lupin 2: Arsène Lupin vs. Herlock Sholmes
6. Arsène Lupin 3. The Hollow Needle
7. Arsène Lupin 4: 813
8. Arsène Lupin 5: The Crystal Stopper
9. Arsène Lupin 6: The Confessions of Arsène Lupin
10. Arsène Lupin 7: The Teeth of the Tiger
11. Arsène Lupin 8: The Shell Shard (aka The Woman of Mystery)
12. Arsène Lupin 9: The Return of Arsène Lupin (aka The Golden Triangle)
13. Arsène Lupin 10: The secret of Sarek (aka Island of Thirty Coffins)
14. Arsène Lupin 11: The Eight Strokes of the Clock
15. Arsène Lupin 12: The Secret Tomb
16. Arsène Lupin 13: The Countess of Cagliostro (aka Memoirs of Arsène Lupin)
17. Arsène Lupin (bonus book): Arsène Lupin (novelised by Edgar Jepson from LeBlanc's original play)

18. The Complete Raffles by Hornung, E. W.
19. The Mysterious Mickey Finn by Paul, Eliott
20. You Play the Black and the Red Comes Up by Hallas, Richard
21. The Mr. Moto Omnibus Vol 1 by Marquand, John P.
22. The Mr. Moto Omnibus Vol 2 by Marquand, John P.
23. The Complete Father Brown Vol 1 (with original illustrations) by Chesterton, G. K.
24. The Complete Father Brown Vol 2 (with original illustrations) by Chesterton, G. K.
25. A Peter Wimsey omnibus: Murder Must Advertise & The Nine Tailors by Sayers, Dorothy L.
26. Was it Murder? by Hilton, James
27. The Complete Just Men Volume 1 by Wallace, Edgar
28. The Complete Just Men Volume 2 by Wallace, Edgar
29. Carnacki by Hodgson, William Hope
30. Grey Mask by Wentworth, Patricia
31. The Case With Nine Solutions by Connington, J. J.
32. Murder by Matchlight by Lorac, E. C. R.
33. The Crossword Mystery by Punshon, E. R.
34. The Cask by Crofts, Freeman Wills
35. The Bells of Old Bailey by Bowers, Dorothy
36. Crime Unlimited by Hume, David
37. The A. A. Milne Mystery Omnibus (contains: The Red house and Four days' wonder) by Milne, A. A.
38. She Faded into Air by White, Ethel Lina
39. The Wheel Spins by White, Ethel Lina
40. The Spiral Staircase by White, Ethel Lina
41. Murder of a Lady by Wynne, Anthony
42. Thirteen Guests by Farjeon, J. Jefferson
43. The Daughter of Time by Tey, Josephine
44. The Man in the Queue by Tey, Josephine
45. A Shilling for Candles by Tey, Josephine
46. The Franchise Affair by Tey, Josephine
47. Tragedy at Law by Hare, Cyril
48. The Moonstone by Collins, Wilkie
49. The Woman in White by Collins, Wilkie
50. The Circular Staircase by Rinehart, Mary Roberts
51. The Benson Murder Case by Van Dine, S. S.
52. The Philip Marlowe Omnibus by Chandler, Raymond
53. Monsieur Lecoq by Gaboriau, Emile
54. Aurora Floyd by Braddon, Mary Elizabeth
55. The Big Bow Mystery by Zangwill, Israel
56. Dossier 113 (aka The Blackmailers) by Gaboriau, Emile
57. The Mystery of a Hansom Cab by Hume, Fergus
58. The W Plan by Seton, Graham
59. Inspector French's Greatest Case by Crofts, Freeman Wills